FORGIVE ME FOR MY SINS

ANGEL ANDERS

Published by Angel Anders
Developmental Editing by Sara-Jane Higgins (Kat's Literary Services)
Editing by Kat Wyeth (Kat's Literary Services)
Proofreading by Steph White (Kat's Literary Services)
Cover Design by Maldo Designs
Interior Formatting by Maldo Designs

To the ones who told me to shoot for
the stars and found magic in my words.
Without you all, I wouldn't have gone for it.

And most importantly...
to all the good fucking girls who would get on their
knees for Father Lachlan O'Connell, this one is for you.

PLAYLIST

EVENING ON THE GROUND | IRON & WINE

MAD WOMAN | TAYLOR SWIFT

LOSING MY RELIGION | R.E.M.

BAD BELIEVER | ST. VINCENT

USE SOMEBODY | KINGS OF LEON

BEDROOM HYMNS | FLORENCE + THE MACHINE

IF I EVER FEEL BETTER | PHOENIX

TAKE ME TO CHURCH | HOZIER

TURNING PAGE | SLEEPING AT LAST

SIMPLE SONG | THE SHINS

MONEY POWER GLORY | LANA DEL RAY

LOVER (REMIX) | TAYLOR SWIFT, SHAWN MENDES

PROLOGUE

LACHLAN

I stare up to the sky, unaware and uncaring of what time of day it is. I've been sitting on these steps for what feels like a lifetime.

The rain is pelting hard against my face, now making me unsure if the water dripping down my cheeks is purely rain or a mixture of my tears as well.

My life has just been forever altered by the rejection and fate of the night. The darkness that once only flittered between my heart and soul now consumes me.

She's fucking gone.

In an instant, the perfect storm of emotions occurred. I witnessed the moment her feelings went from ones of lust to rejection before turning into an unfiltered rage and, finally, desperation. I couldn't give her what she wanted, and because of that, she's gone forever.

Hours earlier, as I laid down next to her almost silent heart, I knew there wasn't any hope that she would live. One reaction gave life to a series of unfortunate events that neither of us can ever take back.

I didn't save her in time. How can I ever live with myself knowing that I caused a death? Not just any death, *hers*.

I can feel my heart ripping from my chest as the memory of staring at her lifeless body on the asphalt repeats on a loop in my mind. Sirens and smoke all around us. Nothing but the memory of the night to devour my very existence for eternity.

I don't know what to do or say.

I shouldn't have run after speaking to the officers; I wasn't a suspect to them. If anything, I was a fucking mess the police didn't want to deal with as they took care of the dying woman on the side of the road.

But I shouldn't have disappeared, not on her. What kind of man does that make me? Fleeing as soon as possible so no one had to see me as the mess I was.

Truthfully, I didn't want to have to look *him* in the eyes at the hospital when he was told that she was gone forever. When the inevitable moment came when he asked me how and why it happened.

He'll never forgive me. If anything, I'm a man who went back on his word, and the gravest of consequences happened because of it. I'm not a good person, but I can't fucking stand the idea of what this will do to him.

A life is lost that had so much left to live. Regardless of the mess we were in, she didn't deserve to die by bleeding out in one of the worst rainstorms I've ever experienced.

What am I supposed to do now?

How am I ever going to face the others who will ask me so many questions I can't give them the answers to? This is a story that I can't share, not with anyone.

If anyone were to hear the truth of how the night unfolded, it wouldn't do any good. It would only bring her more harm, him more sadness, and fuck if I don't deserve to bear the weight of the night after what transpired.

It's my fault she's not here anymore. Her body is in a hospital room, and her loved ones are getting confirmation of what I already know to be the truth. There can be no possible argument about it—she's dead. And I'm responsible for it. I don't deserve to be face-to-face with those who care about her. I need to disappear.

The rain is still coming down hard on me. I'm sitting up high on a set of steps, resting back on my arms. Embracing the agony the rain is causing me. I need the pain to remember I'm still alive, even though she isn't.

Letting out a long sigh, I debate my next move. My white dress shirt is practically see-through at this point.

I have to go back and face them all. I can't be this coward who runs away forever, can I? Facing them is just not something I think I have in me, but what other option do I have? If only there were some way for me to repent without facing everyone.

I hang my head low before running a hand through my hair. "Fuck."

My eyes are welling up again.

"Watch that language, my child; you're in someone else's home, understood?"

I turn around quickly to face the deep, booming voice I hear behind me.

A man with balding white hair, wearing all black with a pop of white around his neck, is standing at the top of the entranceway to the building.

I just realized where I am. Of course, I came here.

"Sorry," I whisper before facing forward to return to my self-loathing. I've been on a really good roll with it, after all, no reason to stop now.

The man approaches me in the rain and sits down next to me. He doesn't seem to mind it pouring down on him, either.

We sit in silence.

Time moves on to when, eventually, the harsh rain turns light, and the sky becomes just another gloomy, cloudy Boston day.

"My child, what troubles you?"

"I can't share what happened. Not with you, not with anyone," I answer with resolve.

It's a matter of fact.

We both keep looking straight ahead, sitting on the wet stairs of this large Catholic church. I hadn't realized where I had come in my darkest hour until I faced the man earlier. If this isn't the Irish Catholic guilt in me coming to life, I don't know how else to explain it.

"I see," the man replies.

Time continues to pass. I couldn't tell you how much.

Looking around now, I notice renovations happening to the church. That must be why there aren't any other people trying to get up these steps. Or, more probable, because a strung-out twenty-something-looking man has been sitting in the rain for hours on them and is making this church unapproachable.

It's a fair assumption. I look like a mess because I am one.

"No Mass today, Father?"

"No Mass today. One of the rare days when one isn't happening at our church. But all are still welcome in the house of God. The doors are open to anyone in need."

I hum in response.

Finally, he speaks again.

"When talking about God, people often use words such as 'all-powerful' and 'merciful' or even talk about 'forgiveness.' But do you know what I think, my boy?"

I sit up a bit straighter at that sentiment.

"What's that?"

"God is all of those things, of course, but the teachings of the Lord mean nothing if you can't accept your truth."

"And what's my truth?"

Turning to face him for the first time since we've been sitting together on these steps, I don't see a weathered old man but someone kind and decent.

"That's for you to figure out. The truth of yourself is not something anyone else can tell you. But I will give you a hint. God gives you the strength you need to find it, the hope that your sins are redeemable, and most importantly, the love to keep you moving on."

The man stands up and attempts to pat dry some parts of his still-wet, black clothing. He turns away from me and begins going up the steps toward the church.

He pauses before looking back toward me.

"My boy, interested in some shepherd's pie? I'm heading toward the parish office now to join some of our staff for just the right rainy-day treat if you ask me."

For the first time in almost a day, I let the hint of a small smile show on my face.

CHAPTER 1

AVERY

PRESENT

And puts a new song in my mouth, a hymn to our God.
Many shall look on in fear and they shall trust in the Lord.
Psalms 40:4

My husband is cheating on me.

My husband is cheating on *me*.

Huh.

Honestly, I did not see this one coming. Yes, our whirlwind marriage has been crumbling since the day we said, "I do," but I just didn't think he was this stupid.

Kevin is fourteen years older than me, and when we met three years ago, I thought he was everything. My protector. My best friend. My safe haven. My dream man.

He started as all great narcissists do—charming, funny even. His energy made him someone who I wanted to be swept up into. I wanted him to think I was worthy of being part of his world.

With dark blond hair, deep brown eyes, standing at six feet tall, and a body that shows he spends hours in the gym every day, he is conventionally attractive. Anyone would think so. Even now, I can admit that.

At the time, I paid attention to all of these face-value qualities and ignored the details that were right in front of me. I was desperately in need of a connection when I met him.

I took his possessive behavior toward me as something out of a romance novel. What those spicy books don't tell you is that this quality is, in fact, a red flag, waving in front of your face in real life. It should not make your panties damp. It should not put stars in your eyes.

His possessive behavior made sense at first. As his much younger wife, I thought he was staking his claim. I was only twenty-five when we met, and thanks to my mother's genes, my body is something I don't need to work hard to keep in shape.

I thought I understood his perspective. Other men wanted me, and he wanted to make it clear to them that I was his wife.

What started out as him putting his arm tightly around my waist when we were out slowly turned into not letting me leave his side at events, telling me to cover up more, and how he thought I needed to lose ten pounds. This was all in the time we were dating.

I am five foot eight and 130 pounds on my worst day... how can I lose ten pounds?

The truth of the matter is I wanted to belong to someone. Even with all of his flaws, I loved the attention he gave me. I felt special being with him.

We met and got married within eleven months of our first date. That should have told me something too. Way too fast. Another red flag, waving in front of me.

But once again, I thought this is what love is meant to be like. Someone telling you how precious you are to them and making you feel like you mattered. I thought his words were to help me in a sadistic way.

Love moves at warp speed, and I needed to embrace it.

As soon as we got married, things began to get worse. In the past two years, his charming personality has mostly disappeared.

Our marriage has gone even more downhill recently.

His days turn into nights in the office; he's either rude or indifferent to me in private, and most weeks, I only see him at an event or in the mornings.

He's a jealous, possessive grump when I'm out with him, and at home, I'm yesterday's news.

He picks me apart whenever he sees me.

That dress is too tight, Avery. Are you trying to ask for it?

What is wrong with your makeup?

Is your credit card not working? Why don't you make a waxing appointment? You have hair on your upper lip.

I do not have hair on my upper lip, thank you very much.

His pre-marriage life of working late nights and attending functions is still his world, not me. He didn't want me; he wanted a wife. Arm candy and nothing more.

I'm not sure how he convinced me while we were dating that marriage would be different, but he did. I was such a fool. I wrongfully assumed that he would care for me until death do us part.

I'm now just another possession he has collected and is safely keeping in his historic house. Our home, I should say. But it's not a home. It's a luxurious mansion designed to make others wish for your life.

With seven bedrooms, five bathrooms, and an expansive outdoor space, it's something out of a magazine. It's in a prime location downtown, one of the wealthiest parts of Charleston,

South Carolina. A museum for others and a prison for me. Bought with a large family in mind.

A family that he has been pressuring me for the past six months to start working on. How can I agree to bear his children when I'm just another toy he brings out to play with when he's good and ready? When I am being treated so poorly?

I should have known that by not giving him what he wants when he wants it, I'd be creating the catalyst for our marriage to dissolve, not to improve.

He wants children, or rather sons. At least, that's what he talks about whenever he mentions children. What he really wants are heirs to his business and fortune. A son to take over in thirty years and continue to make him millions as he sails around the world.

Every time he talks about children, he refers to them as sons. I'm not sure if Kevin realizes that it's a toss-up that even he can't control the natural way, but it's never been worth the argument.

I stopped speaking up when we got married. I usually give him his way. Trying to avoid disagreements to keep him as indifferent toward me as possible.

Bringing a child into the world is one issue I just couldn't bend on. And now here we are. I am twenty-eight years old and just watched my husband cheat on me.

I lost myself by being lost in him. I turned myself into his shiny trophy wife. My long blonde hair is always put together. There's never a wrinkle in my clothes. I spray tan weekly. I do, in fact, get waxed everywhere. Yes, everywhere.

I became the Mrs. Matheson that everyone expected me to be, that Kevin expected of his wife. Long gone was the carefree Avery Parker, who dreamed of adventure, love, and a family to call her own.

I did this to myself. Longing to be in his orbit and now look what's happened to me. Young, miserable, childless, and a cheating husband.

All the makings of a great country song. Unfortunately, this is my life.

What I really didn't see coming was that my husband was stupid enough to cheat on me in our own home. The same home he rarely shows up to see his lawfully wedded wife in. And because he is almost never at said home anymore, he forgot to check whether the security cameras were working.

That's right—he didn't check if the cameras were on or off.

For weeks, the main back courtyard camera has been glitching, so I turned it off. As the stereotypical man of the house, he wanted to take care of the security issues instead of me delegating it to our house manager to resolve quickly. I didn't get it. Really, we have all this money, and he wanted to do it himself?

He was barely home enough to sleep; fixing cameras should not have been something on his to-do list. Once again, it wasn't worth the argument, and I said he could handle it.

I waited for him to fix it, and he kept saying he would get to it. Of course, he didn't because the house isn't a priority for him. My concerns are not a priority for him.

After two weeks of being worried for safety reasons, I went to our house manager and asked her to get it fixed. Since she's good at her job, she handled the matter.

She just so happened to do it the day before Kevin brought his new assistant to our home and had sex with her in the covered courtyard on my brand-new rug. I loved that rug, and now it's ruined.

Her fake moans were caught on the camera, as was the look of boredom. Yes, Kevin is attractive, but clearly, miss twenty-one-year-old assistant is here for the money. To try and become wife number two, perhaps.

She can have him.

I always have to get myself off with my vibrator after we finish having sex. He isn't exactly a giving lover, so I can resonate with the blank stares I was seeing on her face.

Poor girl.

But once again, I was naïve in my youth and had a terrible fantasy of living the fairytale. I accepted that sex was going to be like that, and it didn't matter, not when I'd found true love.

My parents passed away when I was eighteen, and I don't have any siblings. I've been on my own since college.

I longed for a family. A place to call home. It just never felt exactly right with him. When Kevin began asking me to start trying to conceive a child, I knew it would be the wrong decision to say yes.

Another red flag I blissfully tried to sweep under the metaphorical rug.

Thankfully, we had a pretty straightforward prenuptial agreement. What was mine before the marriage would remain that way and vice versa. I remember sitting in his lawyer's office when we were drawing up the papers, and he tried to reassure me getting a prenup was all technicalities.

"Avery, I would never cheat on you. You are the most beautiful woman in the world. This is what people like us do. I love you, sweetheart."

Maybe I'm not smart when it comes to men because growing up, I never imagined I would be planning my marriage to someone while also getting a legal document drawn up outlining the dissolution of it.

I want an everlasting love. The kind of love that rocks your entire world. Once you had it, you wouldn't take it for granted. Because it would be all-consuming and make you a better version of yourself. I wanted the fairytale, but now I'm beginning to think everyone is just living in their personal horror movie behind closed doors.

Kevin is an arrogant man who thinks real-world consequences don't apply to him. Why else would he assume he wouldn't get caught when he tossed me aside and started sleeping with his assistant?

So now, here we are. I just watched him, pants down, inside the new assistant on my new rug while our new camera captured everything.

I decided to save the video to my personal cloud storage until I figured out what to do about this new predicament I'm in.

Instead of breaking down or going into a fit of rage after seeing that footage earlier this morning, I did what any good trophy wife would do. I went to church.

I am now sitting in the early morning mass of our neighborhood Catholic church. I don't believe in Catholicism, but this is the place where our group networks. Kevin was raised Catholic, so I went along with it all. Like I always did.

I have appearances to keep up as I make my plan to leave him. I'm not going to let Kevin continue to treat me this way. Staying isn't an option for me.

Creating an exit plan is what I really should be thinking of right now instead of reliving that video. The past won't get me anywhere. I should know that better than most people. I was a foolish, naïve girl when I met Kevin, but I refuse to be that person any longer.

I'm married to a demeaning asshole who doesn't care about me. It's fine. I'm going to be fine. I just need to be smart and focus on getting out by making a game plan.

I need to become a new woman. A woman who can walk away from her cheating husband and get out unscathed.

I have to file for divorce as soon as I can. South Carolina has a law that a couple has to be legally separated for one year before divorcing. That is outside of when one person in the marriage has a video of the other inside someone else who isn't in said marriage available for viewing pleasure. I'm assuming that falls into the at-fault adultery category to please the courts.

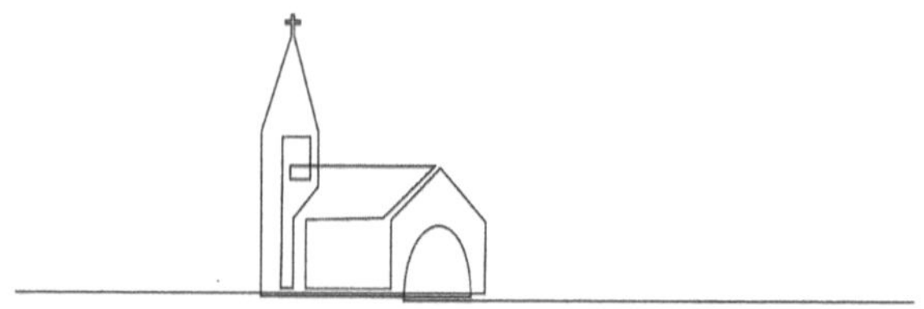

The loud banging of the hassocks, or cushioned ottoman to kneel on, being put down breaks me of my thought process. Being lost in thought, I hadn't remembered I needed to kneel when I got back to my seat after receiving communion.

For not believing in religion, I was usually the best parishioner in attendance.

After marrying Kevin, converting was a priority of his for me. I went right along with that as well, even though he knew what my feelings were about it.

Hello, next waving red flag! I see you, but I think I'll ignore you too.

I shake my head to try and focus, leaning forward now to let my hassock down. I'm sitting in a pew alone, which is a rarity.

It's almost that time of year when the church will become full again as the new school year starts back up and more parishioners are done with summer vacations.

Finally kneeling down, with my hands clasped together resting on the back of the pew in front of me, I look the part of an active churchgoer praying dutifully.

That's when a tingling feeling washes over me, starting from my neck down to my spine. I'm naturally shivering.

I can feel someone staring at me.

As I glance around the room, I can't see anyone I know or even strangers looking my way.

It's just me. It's just the day.

I try to shake this feeling off but can't.

I can't afford to be like this. I don't have time to lose my mind.

I can still feel it, though. The sensation that I'm being watched.

I look around the church once more, just to be sure I am, in fact, going crazy now on top of everything else I've had to face today.

That's when I spot him.

The most attractive man I have ever seen is staring at me from the front right corner of the church. He's leaning against a wall with his arms crossed over one another in the shadows. His eyes are looking into my being.

I shiver again as the feeling of being watched washes over me.

The mystery man is dressed in all black, which is strange for South Carolina, where bright colors and pastels are a trademark look for men and women alike.

He appears very tall and well-built from what I can make out. I can see his muscles contracting against his tightly fitted shirt, even from where I'm seated. They're mouth-watering to look at even from a distance. I long to see them up close.

How tall is this stranger? From here, it looks like he's over six feet. Tall enough that his body would intertwine nicely with my figure.

I really need to get divorced soon, so I can finally have good sex. I'm eye fucking random men in church. This cannot be good. If I believed in God, surely this would end up on the list of reasons why he wouldn't let me through the pearly gates.

My eyes drift from his drool-worthy physique to his chiseled jaw before coming back to a neck that I want to lick. The man swallows, causing his Adam's apple to bob at the motion.

My eyes snap to his, and I know I should be embarrassed. I know I should be looking away with flushed cheeks. I just can't turn away from his gaze that I can see more clearly now.

He *is* staring at me.

The light coming through the stained glass windows is casting new shadows where the man stands, allowing me a better look at him.

His eyes are piercing. I can see myself getting lost in them.

I glance up slightly to see his short, wavy, dark brown hair is nicely styled. My eyes immediately return to that penetrating stare I can still feel on me. One that's looking at me like he wants to devour me whole.

I gulp audibly.

I really need to have sex.

This can't be how he's looking at me.

We both get distracted by Father Greg's pounding footsteps walking to the podium, or as the Catholics would call it, an ambo, by the altar.

"Please take your seats, everyone," he starts.

I must have missed everyone finishing up communion because people are beginning to sit down in the surrounding pews and push up their hassocks.

I can't afford to be this distracted already.

"I have a special introduction that I'm excited to share with all of you, my brothers and sisters, sitting here today. As you know, our parish is one that highly values the community we have built."

"Yeah, right," I mutter to myself.

Of course, this church does. Everyone sitting in here easily makes seven figures. This church values our wallets, not our community spirit.

"As you know, we've been searching far and wide for a new priest to join our parish as we continue our church expansion efforts. What has started as a small parish needs more assistance to spread the word of God to our surrounding area. Our parish community deserves that; you all deserve that. I am pleased to introduce you to Father Lachlan O'Connell, who is just the man for the job. Please give him a warm welcome," Father Greg concludes before stepping back and clapping.

Some of us parishioners had been told Father Greg found the person he wanted for the role, but no one knew who it was.

As I look around the church, I find myself searching that dark corner for my stranger.

He's gone.

CHAPTER 2

AVERY

I let out a deep breath, closing my eyes momentarily. It's probably for the best. I can't be eye fucking strange men lurking in church corners. It's definitely time to reassess what I consider a red flag at this rate. I seem to ignore them all.

A deep, husky voice from the podium catches my attention.

"Thank you all for this warm welcome. I'm Father Lachlan, and I am pleased to be joining you all here at St. Peter's. I look forward to meeting each and every one of you. If you see me, please don't hesitate to introduce yourself."

My eyes snap open to find his are locked on me. The mystery man and the new priest are one and the same. This can't be true.

My body begins shivering instinctually.

His thick, gravelly voice continues introducing himself to the congregation, but I can't focus on anything but soaking it in.

I think I am getting a hint of an accent to it. Northeastern, perhaps. I can't pin it down.

What I do know is that I want to hear it every day. I want his attention on me, and I can't for the life of me figure out why.

I have got to have sex after I leave Kevin. This man is a priest; I can't be wanting anything to do with him.

What is wrong with me?

"Yes, please, Father. You can meet with me any day or night. I'll give you a *very* warm welcome," I hear being whispered through giggles behind me. I turn to glance at who it is and find it's none other than Missy Jenkins and Elaine Johnson sans husbands or children.

Turning back to face forward, I now have a slight scowl written on my face, and my arms are crossed. I was just as bad as them, but at least I kept my thoughts to myself. We are married women, after all. None of us should be looking at the new priest as if he's a piece of meat.

I roll my eyes. *Father Lachlan O'Connell*, even his name has to be hot.

Trying to focus, I look up to see *Father* Lachlan's gaze still on me as he now sits near the altar in the sanctuary. This time, his brows are furrowed together.

It quickly disappears as he needs to turn his attention to Father Greg, who's now back on the podium going over the latest expansion campaign efforts.

I'm already bored by this attempt to get more donations out of us. The collection baskets just went through these pews not twenty minutes ago, and that's on top of the online donating most of us do as well. Tithing to the church is a crucial aspect of being a member here.

Missy and Elaine are what one would consider socialites in Charleston and the biggest gossips around. They keep the rumor mill going in our circle.

Sure, I love to know things every now and then; what person doesn't get a bit nosy? I just don't like the way they speculate constantly. It really is something else entirely.

They are the standard trophy wives you would expect to find here, just like me. Missy is tall with shiny brown hair that falls down her back. She's in her mid-thirties, but with the amount of plastic surgery she's had done to her face, you'd probably guess she was younger than me.

Elaine, on the other hand, is almost the opposite. A petite woman with short blonde hair. She's also had a lot of plastic surgery done to her face that you can clearly see. Elaine obviously didn't go to Missy's plastic surgeon.

They made Jenna Hartley, three rows up from me, cry at her child's birthday party last month. Something over seeing Jenna's husband getting cozy with the newest lawyer at his law firm. What they failed to mention was that it was a group of six lawyers from the firm, and he was seated nowhere near the leggy brunette new hire.

All of this was only confirmed by Elaine's sister, Emily, who was at the same restaurant and, for some reason, spoke up against them when they told Jenna. Good for her if she wasn't timid around Missy and Elaine.

If she hadn't spoken up, I can't imagine the destruction it would have caused the Hartleys. Would Jenna have stayed or left her husband?

This was similar to the decision I was now facing, but I already knew my answer. I don't think it would have been as easy of a decision for Jenna to make with kids to take into consideration.

I'm lucky in that way. I'm only making this decision for myself. I would like to think I still would be leaving Kevin even if we did have a child together, but I honestly don't know.

I'm grateful that isn't the case. For once, staying strong against him is going to benefit me. I don't think having a child would have prevented this mess I'm in now. I know his true colors would have continued to come out eventually. It's just happening a lot quicker, given my choice not to start trying to conceive a child.

In our network, no one questions Missy and Elaine's gossip but also, they never know what to believe from their mouths. Some of what they say is unfortunately true, or somewhat true at the very least.

Rumors could easily become like wildfire. It only takes one spark, and the entire forest could be burned down. They didn't care if they burned down everyone around them. People rarely spoke up against Missy and Elaine if something was found not to be true. They simply moved on to the next piece of gossip that came up.

Missy and Elaine's whispering lasted the rest of the Mass.

I can't help but roll my eyes when I hear Missy telling Elaine she's going to greet Father Lachlan.

Father Lachlan.

I don't know how, in my shameless perusal, I didn't see his white collar stand out against all the black, especially as I was daydreaming about licking his neck. The all-black clothing now makes sense. It is standard attire for priests in the Catholic Church.

I was a bit surprised he wasn't in formal Mass attire when I saw him standing at the podium. But since he was waiting in the wings and not on the sanctuary all Mass as I would have expected, I'm assuming there was a specific reason behind that choice.

Now, Missy is about to try to sink her poisonous manicured claws into him. Just because I can't sleep with him doesn't mean I want her to either.

A pang of jealousy is ripping right through me. I need to get over whatever this attraction is. This is what happens to women who are kept in gilded cages and rarely brought out to play. That must be all this is.

He is a priest; it's not like he's going to be sleeping with anyone. Father Lachlan is God's servant, after all.

Missy lacks a moral compass. She doesn't care that her balding, overweight husband sleeps with twenty-year-old co-eds regularly. I get the impression as long as she no longer has to sleep with him, she doesn't care. I had long ago assumed that she liked to sleep with twenty-year-old co-eds too.

Her pool boy, Blake, is frequently parked in front of their house when her husband's car isn't there. I only know this because we have the same pool boy, and he comes to my house just down the street once a week.

Blake is a cute, young college guy who cleans pools for extra cash. He doesn't have many customers, mainly just ones in our neighborhood, from what he's told me. Smart move—just upcharge the wealthy residents who want to help out a struggling college student. I can't help but wonder just how Missy is tipping him in return for cleaning her pool.

Maybe that's why she gossips like she does. Be at the head of Charleston society; that way, no one can cut her by the throat like she does others. I guess the saying those who throw stones shouldn't live in glass houses doesn't apply to Missy Jenkins.

Standing up and smoothing out my light blue dress and blonde hair, I go to exit my pew.

I have to get home and start figuring out my plans, not worrying about the sexy Father Lachlan or who Missy is trying to sleep with.

Note to self: Don't call him sexy again.

It's so apparent my marriage is over. I just found the footage less than three hours ago, and this is where I am and what I'm thinking about. Already eager to spread my legs for a hot priest who was looming in a dark corner.

This is too much for one day. I need a cocktail first before heading home. Kevin won't be there, rather at the golf course, but there is something ick about that house now. Even more so than before.

A cocktail at my favorite hidden gem bar off the tourist-filled King Street will help me gather my thoughts. Or forget about them. I'm not sure which is what I need.

Day one. It's only day one. I have to remind myself of that.

The new Avery will be out of that house as soon as she can, but I need to research and plan my exit strategy. I'm not usually one to dwell or put off what I can take care of today to tomorrow.

This is different. I will give myself grace.

For fucks sake. This godforsaken religion is beginning to rub off on me.

A cocktail is definitely the right decision.

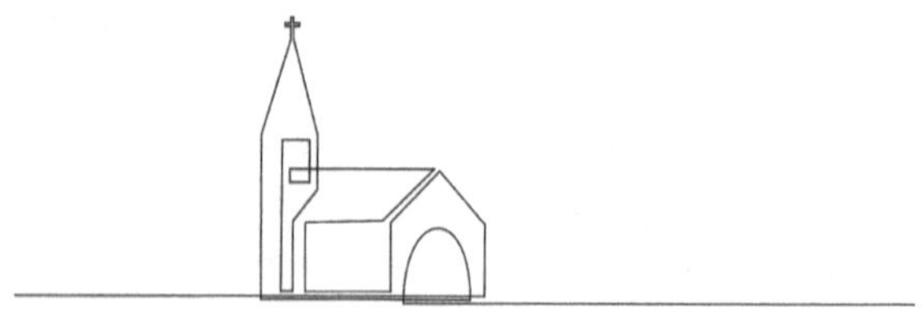

As I make my way to the sprawling doors, I am actively trying to avoid Father Lachlan and Father Greg.

Father Greg has been trying to reach me about the upcoming gala. He wants me to write another check. This whole town runs on the thirst for money. Who has more? Who doesn't have enough? Who are you going to get it from?

Society life isn't what I thought I was getting into when I married Kevin. Yes, I knew he was wealthy and successful, but I didn't realize how much he valued high-society life. Even though I was young when I first met him, I had my own money and never took to this type of lifestyle on my own.

My father had run a successful company out of Seattle, Washington, and established a trust fund for me. I had gained access to that trust fund and more when my parents passed away.

As the heir to his fortune, I was also given a majority share of my dad's company, his savings, and investments. I approved my dad's best friend, Fisher, to take over as CEO of the company. He was already a senior vice president there, and it just felt like the right move for my dad's memory to live on.

Fisher keeps in touch with me periodically, but he lives in Seattle, so it's usually only a personal phone call every now and then or when we have business to discuss.

He has his own son whom he's trying to build a relationship with and needs to focus on as well. About five years ago, Fisher found out that a former girlfriend had a baby and never told him. That baby showed up on his doorstep as a seventeen-year-old, ready to take his pent-up rage out on Fisher. Needless to say, they're still working on their relationship.

I'm grateful I still have someone who cares about the real me, even if he is thousands of miles away and dealing with so much in his own life.

Shaking out of my thoughts again, I keep walking toward the doors.

I am almost there. *Focus on that cocktail, Avery.*

A dirty martini with extra blue-cheese stuffed olives is calling my name.

"Avery!"

Oh no. It's not the dirty martini. I can hear Father Greg's voice literally saying my name, trying to catch my attention in the distance.

I wince. Shutting my eyes tightly for a moment as I hold my breath. I can't be here. I should keep going, pretending I don't hear my name being called... but I don't.

Taking a deep breath before plastering on my widest smile, I turn to where I heard his voice coming from. Yes, that's him. I see Father Greg is, in fact, flagging me down.

Father Lachlan is speaking with Missy nearby.

Slowly, I make my way there, trying to calm my inner thoughts. It doesn't help matters when I can feel Father Lachlan's eyes on me as I approach Father Greg.

It's as if he's tracking me. I'm not sure if I should like it as much as I do. But I know it's too strong of an assumption to have. I really am going crazy today.

"Mrs. Matheson!" Father Greg shouts again as he sees me coming toward him. Waving his hand frantically to signal me into his sphere.

"Hi, Father Greg. Lovely Mass today." I beam, finally reaching where he stands.

He doesn't even bother meeting me halfway. What a pompous jerk.

"Thank you, my child. It's so wonderful to have you here today. I would like to personally introduce you to Father Lachlan O'Connell," he says, pulling Father Lachlan's attention fully away from Missy to me.

Missy is talking at him without caring if he's interested or not. One of her many wonderful qualities.

He was clearly appeasing her up until that point, but I still didn't like what I saw. I did like that I could feel him side-eyeing me the entire time I was walking toward the doors and even more obviously as I strutted over to Father Greg just now.

I had tried my best during that walk not to look at him, even with the sensation of his eyes on me once again.

Every time I did steal a glance his way, I ached in need. I could try not to look at him all I wanted, but my lady parts are not getting the memo that I am still married, and he is completely off-limits.

"Father Lachlan, this is one of the most generous members of our congregation, Mrs. Avery Matheson. Her husband, Kevin, owns GT Technologies based here in Charleston. I'm sure you've heard of it before," Father Greg says dismissively, as if who isn't keeping track of the top businesses in Charleston.

Father Greg either doesn't realize or care that he just irritated Missy by stealing Father Lachlan away to talk about how prominent Kevin and I are in Charleston. I knew I donated more than Missy to the church already, but this felt like a small victory to hear I was essentially more important than she was in the eyes of Father Greg.

I don't usually care about these types of society races, but she always acts like she's above everyone else. I hate people like that, and yet, I am surrounded by them daily.

Father Lachlan's smoldering eyes are on me as a grin breaks out across his face. His eyes are an emerald-green color. They are absolutely captivating.

He is unfairly attractive. Why does he have to be so unbearably good-looking? There should be some rule that if you have eyes that can be described as smoldering and a chiseled jaw, you can't become a priest.

He extends his hand to mine in greeting. I look down to find a strong, calloused hand that causes the ache between my thighs to pulse even more.

I look back up at him to see his wide grin is still in place.

I'm now actively trying to discreetly squeeze my thighs together for some relief. *This is going well.*

He breaks eye contact with me and drinks in my movements. Father Lachlan's nostrils flare for a moment before composing himself and locking our eyes together once again.

I extend mine into his and feel a surge of energy rip through me at the connection. I think he feels it too.

I really need to get that martini immediately.

"It's a pleasure to meet you, Father Lachlan. St. Peter's is a wonderful church. My husband and I love being parishioners here," I say as I try to smile through the words.

Pretending like I still love my husband is something I'm used to, but today, I hate calling him that more than ever before.

Our hands are lingering together. His thumb skims against my skin, causing me to still. I can't pull away from his touch.

"The pleasure is mine, Mrs. Matheson."

I flinch at that name spilling from his lips.

I can feel the emphasis on my title. Little does he know Kevin was just caught having sex with his assistant on my brand-new rug.

I really need to let go of that detail, but I mean, come on, really? Kevin knew I had just bought it. When he saw it, he told me it wasn't fitting for a house like ours, like the pretentious asshole he is.

He knew how much I loved our courtyard too. In a house on the brink of shattering because of the people living in it, that courtyard was a space I found peace in. Often, it was my place of solitude to read in front of the fireplace year-round.

I peel my hand away and clasp both of them together in front of me, slowly rocking on my heels. I never usually display this kind of nervousness, but I have to get through this interaction somehow.

Lachlan is examining me as if he knows that flinch means more than I will say. He can't get this confession.

"Father Greg has told me wonderful things about our parishioners, including you and your husband. I look forward to getting to know you both more."

"Us as well. Please, if there is anything you need our support on, just let me know."

The words spill out of me before I can take them back. I don't want to support this institution any more than necessary. My soul already feels dark for doing so.

I don't think those who believe in God or a particular religion are wrong for doing so. I've just been experiencing an internal war with how I feel about it all. Faith is a journey I'm slowly understanding.

Father Greg cuts in.

"Well, Mrs. Matheson, I'm happy to hear you say that. As you know, the upcoming gala has taken a life of its own," he says before chuckling like he just said something slightly amusing.

"All in the name of gaining new support for the church. Can you and Father Lachlan get together this week to see if there are any additional sponsorship opportunities you and your husband can do? The church would greatly appreciate it. Your generosity never goes unnoticed by us," he finishes speaking with a menacing smile.

He has me cornered with this one. I know it and so does he. Father Lachlan picks up on the undertone of his statement and steps in to break the tension.

"Mrs. Matheson, please come by my office sometime this week whenever you have time. I'll be there most days and have taken over leading the gala efforts from Father Greg," he says curtly.

"I will. Thank you both. I really must be going now."

I break away from Father Lachlan's deep stare only to see Missy eyeing me suspiciously. She had stepped back but was listening to the conversation the whole time. Waiting for Father Lachlan to get free once again.

A sickening smile is on her face right now. It makes my stomach churn. I can't afford for her to stir up any trouble involving me right now. I already have too many problems I have to deal with.

Martini—I'm coming for you.

CHAPTER 3

LACHLAN

Avoid immorality. Every other sin a person commits is outside
the body, but the immoral person sins against his own body.
1 Corinthians 6:18

I come to a halt.

An adult film star is currently in my Boston church. Sitting pensively in the same pew where she was earlier that day during the Mass I performed. She's staring up at the altar, looking vulnerable yet confused.

This star is one whom I instantly recognized during Mass. Bambi is famous in the industry and known for being open to participating in all types of films. From role-playing to woman-on-woman, threesomes—I think I've even watched a foursome on an alien planet with her in it.

Of course, I'm familiar with her work. I only have my hand to use for pleasure, after all.

I've come back to the church in search of my notebook with my upcoming homilies written in it. I need to rework one almost completely for next week since the readings have changed.

Even though I really don't have time to do this, I know I need to help Bambi. It's been hours since Mass ended; there's no reason to still be here unless something's troubling her. I know the feeling of being lost all too well. Patrick helped me years ago; I can do the same for Bambi now.

Walking across the empty church, I reach where she's still sitting. She doesn't break her trance as I slide into the pew.

Some time goes by, and I know I need to be here for whenever she's ready to speak. Sometimes, having a friend to listen to you makes all the difference.

"Hello, Father," Bambi finally whispers.

She turns her body to face me, hangs one of her arms along the backside of the pew, and places the other in her lap. I mimic her positioning.

"Hello, my child. What troubles you?"

She tilts one corner of her mouth slightly in a coy smirk.

"We can drop the 'my child' bit, can't we?"

"Sure," I say before clearing my throat.

I'm not sure what she means by that exactly, but the most probable meaning is for me to try to speak to her normally and not like a priest.

"So tell me," I urge her.

I nod my head to encourage her to start.

"I need more," she states simply.

"More?"

Doesn't everyone want more? This is nothing new.

"Yes, more. I want a better quality of life than what I'm currently leading. I'm in the adult film industry, and I'm just tired," she whispers.

Suddenly, her brave face from the start of the conversation has disappeared.

"Is that what brings you here?"

"Yes, Father. I've never been religious, but I just thought..." Bambi trails off as she figures out how to explain what she's been thinking about.

"I thought I would try out being a Christian. I mean, why not, right? Nothing else is working—it's time for a change. Then earlier, when you were talking about how someone could turn their life around, it just hit me," she finishes.

"It hit you that it's possible for you to turn your life around," I say to confirm her truth.

"Exactly. I mean, I don't even know what religion this is for, but I need a change. My industry isn't forgiving. A man is always taking my body in some shape or fashion. Whether it's my movies or because they think they can get sex from me because I want to be in their movie, it doesn't even fucking matter. It's always on their terms, never on mine. I want something to be on my terms for once," she states.

"I understand, Bambi, I really do. A past is not something you can run away from, though; you need to face it head-on," I reply.

"Father, how do you know my name?"

She's looking at me with long black eyelashes framing her deep brown eyes knowingly.

"I've seen your work," I answer honestly.

It surprises her that I've told the truth.

"I see," she answers.

Bambi recomposes herself and lets out a comforting sigh.

"Maybe running away from my past isn't possible, but what do I do? I can't take a break—another version of me, only freshly eighteen, will be there to make the movies I'd be giving up," she says.

Bambi continues to share her truth with me.

She needs the money and doesn't know what else she could do at this point in her life to earn *such good money*. There are no other options for her to fall back on. With no formal education or family, she can only rely on herself.

Being at the top of her game, she knows it won't last much longer. Her days are numbered, and she wants to take as much as she can from the industry while it lasts.

And the worst part of her confliction? She likes it and doesn't know exactly what that means about herself. That's the problem. Bambi needs and wants what the industry gives her, but she's conflicted with the lifestyle that comes along with it.

As she spoke her truth, I noticed a key part of it was being hidden from me. It goes past simply wanting to be part of that world. She craves the attention, the praise, the desire from others—even if it is only fleeting.

I can tell this is where her conflict really comes from, so I decide to perform one of my priestly duties.

I explain what confession is and lead her to my confessional booth. When someone needs confession, I always try to be accommodating. We usually only take confessions on Wednesdays to standardize our schedules.

I know firsthand what that desperation to find answers feels like, which is why if someone needs me to listen to their confession, I will do my part.

Bambi goes into the confessional, and I head into my side of the booth.

Beginning to listen to her confession, I realize something. I can see myself in this tormented woman. Then, as I start to hear more about the pain she's in, I begin envisioning myself actually inside her tight body. Treating her like the other men who came before me. Only I can't act upon these dark desires.

After she finishes her full confession, she leaves her part of the confessional booth and comes to mine, slowly opening the door. The silence is deafening.

She likes being the center of attention in a slimy industry that preys on weakness. There will be no leaving the adult film industry early for someone like her who secretly relishes in it all.

Bambi's eyes gleam with hope after speaking her full truth. Hope is dangerous. It makes people feel like something better is possible. That their terrible lives can be fixed or even redeemed. Bambi's life won't turn out that way; I just know it.

Bambi looks down at me as she leans against the confessional door frame. Her big brown eyes are seeking my approval.

Slowly, she steps closer to me until I'm within her reach. I stand to stroke her cheek softly. She leans her face into the palm of my hand and closes her eyes. I use the other hand to caress her long chestnut brown hair that splays out against her shoulders.

Bambi purrs from the touch. Desperate for affection from someone honest and good like a man of the cloth should be.

She hums as I continue to stroke her hair before pausing. This act is too intimate. I'm not the man destined to offer her this type of comfort.

Little does she know I am neither honest nor good, but I know that I can't let this go any further without my demons springing back to life.

I move her hair away from her shoulder, causing a spaghetti strap to accidentally fall down the length of her arm. Immediately, I pull my hands away from her. This has crossed a line, and I can't let it go any further.

Her breath hitches, and eyes snap open wide. As Bambi stands before me with her strap hanging loosely down her arm, I take a step back to put distance between us.

The tension weighs heavily as we continue to stare at one another. This woman's despair resonated with me, and now this is where we are. As she straightens herself, I see the conviction in her eyes that she's going to continue this game.

She slowly pulls the other strap down, causing her dress to fall further on her frame. Then without breaking eye contact, Bambi pulls the dress down, and I am face to face with two plastic tits. Just like I had assumed they would be from watching her films.

Of course, this woman doesn't have a bra on in a church. She is too far gone to be redeemable. That's my final judgment against Bambi. She enjoys this too much to ever change for the better. God can make his own judgment one day. This is mine.

Bambi's lips curl into a grin. Like she knows I see her for who she truly is. A whore who lets men take what they want while she enjoys every minute of it. It has nothing to do with her profession but the burning need that courses through her to be taken advantage of in order to prove that people are exactly as she expects them to be—corrupt.

She already has come to terms with her truth. Bambi enjoys the taboo of what is happening between us far too much. The fact of the matter is she craves the power imbalance in her sexual relations. An addict for attention, she'll do anything to get that next fix. I thought she was lost, but it turns out this lamb is actually the wolf.

Her nipples harden as my gaze sweeps across her body; they are telling the only story I need to know. One that begs for my hands to massage her tits hard and rough, pinching her nipples and not letting go until the pain subsides and turns into her pleasure. She needs her story arc to continue this façade.

Bambi closes the distance between where we are both standing. My shoulders tense as I wait for her next move. That's when her hands go to my belt buckle.

She sucks in a breath of air in anticipation of what I will say to this devious act. I don't move or give any signal of what course she should be taking. My mind is confused with what I'm tempted to do and what I know is right. Bambi undoes my buckle before pushing down my pants, followed by my boxers, letting my cock free.

Bambi gasps at the size as she waits on her knees now. Taking it in, she's memorizing its girth and length in awe. She shouldn't be; I'll never be with her again after this.

The hard truth is I want to push forward. It doesn't matter who Bambi is, she's simply going to be the means of my destruction.

"I know I shouldn't want this as much as I do," she says.

Bambi takes a deep breath before licking her lips in anticipation. I can see the conviction in her eyes.

"But fuck, I want this, Father," she moans before continuing, "make me right. Make me good. Make me yours."

I reach for my cock before freezing in place as I leave the trance I've fallen under in Bambi's presence.

What am I doing?

This is not the person I am now. The person who I've worked so hard to become. Going against my natural inclinations to take what I want from this woman.

What kind of man am I willing to turn back into if I go much further with this? With my past haunting my every breath, breaking this vow that reformed me from my tragic past is surely only going to amplify that despair.

As I gaze down into her eyes, I know what I have to do. I slowly step back from the body I'm desperate to use.

Her breath hitches from the complete change of direction before waiting for my decision to put an end to this. One that I'm not even sure I'm capable of making.

Looking at her, I know that this temptation goes beyond a carnal urge. This is not who I am anymore. If I let this woman suck my cock, I really would be just as irredeemable. I can't revert back to mindlessly acting on whatever it is I desire with no repercussions.

"Put yourself back together," I whisper.

Shoving my cock back into my pants, I pull them up and tuck in my shirt before doing my belt buckle.

"What did I do?" she asks while still kneeling before me.

I stroke her cheek gently.

What did she do? It's what I was about to do. I couldn't allow it to go any further.

I was about to have this desperate woman answer my demons when what I really needed was someone to answer my prayers instead.

I almost sealed my fate. Making my years in the priesthood worth nothing if I'd acted on my urges with this woman. If I had continued, I would be confirming that I was a terrible person who didn't deserve a chance at redemption.

I made the right decision. Breaking my commitment to God after everything I had been through would only happen for my truth that I am yet to discover.

"Nothing."

It's all I could say before I turned and left the confessional booth with her still on her knees, waiting for me to change my mind.

CHAPTER 4

LACHLAN

More tortuous than all else is the human heart,
beyond remedy; who can understand it?
Jeremiah 17:9

Fuck.

What was I thinking, staring at Avery like that? Or I should say, Mrs. Matheson. *Mrs.*

I'm such a dumb fuck.

Back in my home, I stretch out on my plush bedding, closing my eyes to get my head on straight. A slow pounding is pulsing in it.

I'm slowly coming to terms with what happened in church earlier. The attraction. The spark. The energy that ripped through me. I still can't make sense of why touching her made my whole body feel like it was on fire.

"Fuck," I groan.

I run the palms of my hands down my face.

I can't be attracted to anyone here. That's precisely why I'm even in Charleston.

My new home isn't much, but it's on church grounds and is located in a great spot downtown. I was used to living much larger in my past, but I don't need that lifestyle anymore.

I had purchased a few upgraded pieces of furniture when I first moved in to help the space be more homey. It does the job. I don't feel like a peasant here anymore.

Thankfully, I was able to slip away earlier than I expected after Mass to return home. I need to change before heading out to get a drink.

I was only stopped briefly by Greg as we were both wrapping up separate conversations with other parishioners, after my encounter with Mrs. Matheson.

He told me to tread carefully with the Mathesons. They are a powerful family, and it is good they are part of our church community. He's thankful Mr. Matheson doesn't hold his wife back from donating to the church, and he himself sometimes donates to specific efforts on top of what they already donate together.

Greg told me that Mr. Matheson likes the praise for being such an upstanding member of the community. Despite this, he is a no-show almost every Sunday. I would probably only meet him at the upcoming gala I'm helping coordinate.

It was known that his wife was expected to attend Mass to represent their family unit. He would most likely be out golfing like the other men of the parish.

Fucking assholes.

I know his kind. I was too familiar with them when I lived in Boston before moving here. Wealthy pricks who treat their wives like trophies. Using and abusing them as they see fit.

Look, I'm not exactly without faults, but at least I haven't dragged someone down to the depths of hell with me.

In my past, I always made it clear who and what I was to the women I was with. I never paraded around as a good man or an upstanding member of the community.

Maybe that's why Mrs. Matheson looked at me longingly earlier. Maybe she needs an escape. Maybe that can be me.

"Fuck," I groan again.

It can't be me. I need to figure out a way to stop thinking about her like this. Seeing her once has already made me start to lose my mind, evidently. It's almost as if God placed her in front of me to claim.

Even I know that can't be true.

I'm lucky enough that this uptight parish agreed to take me so quickly. I can't afford to sleep with a parishioner here. That is one lesson I already faced in Boston.

Fuck, she is gorgeous, though. Not just gorgeous, alluring, really. Her sad, bright blue eyes and turned-down mouth had me staring at her as I was waiting for Greg to announce me to the congregation.

I had been with the church for a little over a month, but he wanted me to get acquainted with the parish operations first before throwing me to the wolves. That's not exactly how he said it, but I read between the lines. I opted out of performing the full Mass earlier today by his side, and he reluctantly agreed with me.

That fucking perfect mouth of hers is what initially drew me in. Those pouty, plump, bee-stung lips were designed by God to be consumed.

I drag my palms against my face once again in defeat. "Fuckin' hell."

I have to readjust my cock now.

I'm getting hard just thinking about seeing her during Mass when I should have been paying attention to the hundreds of new faces I will be acquainting myself with soon enough.

I just can't stop thinking about how Mrs. Matheson looked sitting alone in her pew. She didn't back down from my stare once she made eye contact with me. It's as if she needed me to be the anchor for her sadness or maybe for her hope... for whatever was tormenting her inside.

Maybe that's how she always looks, but I sure as fuck hope that isn't the case. I felt like something was off with this enigmatic creature sitting in my new church.

Nothing should ever torment my perfect, sad angel.

I saw her reaction when I was at the podium. I didn't think she saw my priest collar from the shadows and depth of where I was standing earlier, but her reaction confirmed it. She seemed shocked when I stood up at the podium and greeted everyone.

I hate wearing the collar. I hate the formal liturgical vestments I'm expected to wear when presiding over Mass. The collar, though, feels like a chain to a life I forced myself into. A life that isn't my own but one I need to fulfill.

I could tell her eyes were drinking me in. All of me. It felt like she was consuming my soul. I don't have time to get close to anyone in any capacity.

What is alarming me the most is that I am already feeling as if I would take any part of her that she would give me.

If I wasn't a priest.

The way I saw her thighs squeeze together when we were speaking earlier made my cock harden at the sight. It was a slight movement, but I watched everything she did after I first found her from the shadows.

I have got to stop thinking like this. I'm a priest, and she's married.

I can't go down a bad path again. Not here, where I'm looking to make a fresh start from my past in Boston.

Old Lachlan would have. If she were mine, I would break her just so I could be the one to put her back together. I would push Avery to her limits and then build her back up again.

I would be all she wanted. Needed. Craved. Desired.

"What the fuck," I mutter.

You're a priest. She's married. Get it together, Lachlan.

I clearly need to get it through my thick skull what a bad idea it is to try and get to know Mrs. Avery Matheson.

Several years ago, I decided to become a priest. The truth of why I did needs to stay buried. It will be going to the grave with me, and I'll be trying to repent for it for the rest of my life.

At thirty-four, I'm considered an anomaly in the priesthood. Many men aren't exactly jumping at the chance to give up sex and live a life of celibacy.

That's exactly what I did. I needed this when I signed up for the job. I fucking volunteered for this shit. I needed to be sworn not to sleep with whomever I damn well pleased whenever I fucking wanted.

It didn't stop all of the urges I have, but at least it severely curbed this immoral appetite of mine. The drive to fuck, to take, to be depraved. It's what's inside me. No matter how much I want to pretend I've turned a corner since becoming a priest, I know it's not true.

Since joining the priesthood and committing myself to the Lord, I have mostly been on a path to redemption. Except for six months ago, when I had a slip while I was a priest in Boston. My first major conflict in the years since I made the decision to join the priesthood.

I almost fucked a real-life helpless adult film star who came into my church. Another mistake to add to the list. The reason why I am now in Charleston.

The memory of my weakness that day with Bambi still haunts me.

She came back to the church only once more and looked at me with hope in her eyes that maybe we could try again. That's the moment I realized what I had done to her was worse than the others who had come before me. I had given Bambi the opportunity to hope again, but I was not the man destined for her to put her faith in.

I couldn't stay in that Boston church after seeing her again. It didn't matter that I put a stop to the madness—I couldn't face the shame I felt being there. Having to see Patrick, who helped me during my darkest hour all those years ago, on a daily basis was making me spiral.

Being in that church was a constant reminder that I almost abused my power in this role. After a few months of torture, I began my search for a new parish to call home. After I got the call from St. Peter's that they would take me, I packed up my belongings and left.

I had almost fallen back to the ways of my shameful past. I didn't deserve to be in Boston any longer with Patrick.

The worst part about that afternoon with Bambi was that I knew I was going to enjoy it. My judgment snapped with that woman, not because of who she was but what she represented.

I needed to get out of Boston altogether and start anew. That was the only way my soul could heal from my sin.

I was young and had a good reputation, so coming to St. Peter's in Charleston, where they were desperate for new life, was easy for me to do. I decided this would be my true redemption moment. I could revert to the Father Lachlan I so desperately wanted to be, even if I knew the price I was paying.

I'm not a good man, I'm not a good priest, but fuck, I deserve redemption. My soul isn't lost yet. I'm not like Bambi; I can still be saved. I could put away the dark parts of my soul and focus on being in the light. I will not let the breathtaking Mrs. Avery Matheson fuck this up for me. With her toned, tan legs and blonde hair that reached her perfect handful tits, she's my wet dream come to life; but I can't let her be anything real when it comes to my existence.

Fuck. Giving up seeing tits every day is the hardest part of this job. Tits that would bounce in my face as a wet pussy rode my cock hard and fast. I enjoyed the view no matter what size they were. Plastic or real. I am an equal opportunist when it comes to tits.

Fuck. Breasts. I need to remember I'm a priest and at least call them something more respectable than tits.

Shit.

I'm hard as a rock right now. I need to beat off before finding a glass of whiskey somewhere. A large glass of whiskey… or two.

I can't be trusted to be alone with my thoughts any longer than I already have been today.

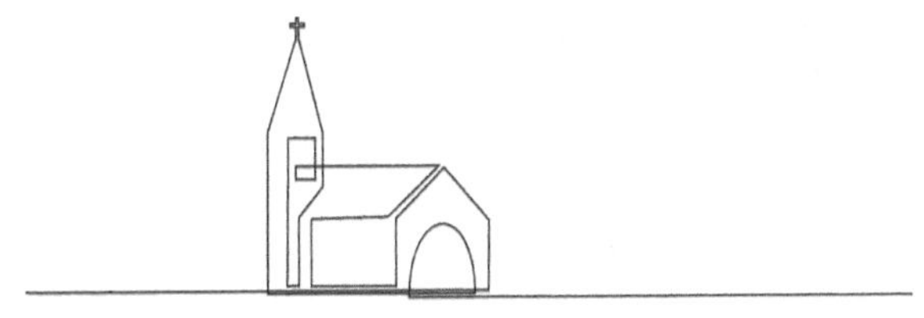

After changing into casual clothes, a dark-green Henley and straight jeans, I make my way to my new favorite bar, Jackson's. It's still in the bustle of being downtown, but few tourists know about this spot. It's a hidden patio off of a main restaurant. The restaurant doesn't advertise it, and if you didn't know any better, you would think it was a walkway to the back of the building.

My best friend, Grayson, told me about the place. He moved to Charleston years ago to play hockey. As a professional hockey player, he was talented but stayed in the league longer than usual. His coach had convinced him that he needed to stay to lead the team of new recruits when he first contemplated retirement.

When he did finally retire, he opened up a charter boat cruise service. He told me he knew it was his time to hang up his skates. Enjoying life was important to him now. I know he used his six-foot-four height and blue eyes to his advantage with women. We just didn't get into it much. It wasn't our type of friendship after all of these years.

He thought I was a fucking idiot for becoming a priest. Some days, I didn't disagree. Other days, I knew I needed this after everything that happened.

Grayson was one of the main reasons I picked Charleston to move to after the incident with Bambi. He said it reminded him of Boston. The Boston of the South was his sales pitch. Being located closer to one of the only friends I still had was reason enough for me.

I'm going down the narrow alley to get to Jackson's. As I finally reach it, I see that my usual spot at the far end of the bar is open. I have to claim it to avoid seeing any of my new members of the congregation.

Hopefully, no one will recognize me here. I do not want anyone from the church to come up and "welcome me" into the community. I need to start becoming more familiar with the parishioners so I can dodge them during times like this. When I'm just trying to be human and not a humble servant.

I hate fundraising for the church. I hate fake niceties. It's all so deceiving and pretentious, just like this entire parish is, Greg included. In fact, he may be the worst one. There's just something about him that I don't like. I haven't been at St.

Peter's long enough to figure out what it is about him that rubs me the wrong way.

The way he looked at Avery Matheson earlier today made me want to snap his neck. Greg knew what he was doing, backing her into a corner to donate more fucking money to the church.

She may not be mine to protect from assholes like him, but I can stop this particular asshole from continuing that behavior, at the very least. That would be my good fucking deed where Avery Matheson is concerned.

"What will you be having, sir?" the bartender calls from a few chairs down.

"Whiskey. Neat," I respond.

She gives me a brief nod back before beginning to pour my drink. This place has good service consistently. Sliding it across to me, she gives me a flirty wink before moving on to the next customer.

With bleach blonde hair twisted into a bun on top of her head and cleavage spilling out of her tight tank top, in the past, I would have found her attractive. I probably would have fucked her regularly. But now she does nothing for me, not when Avery Matheson has fucking taken over my headspace.

And that's a big fucking problem.

Fuck, she's married. I know I'm a priest, but that makes this whole attraction even worse. We both can't be so fucking off-limits to the other.

When I called her Mrs. Matheson, she flinched at the title. There has to be something more to that for her to have had such a visceral reaction to it.

Yes, I did it on purpose; I didn't need to say her name at all. But I sure as hell wasn't expecting that kind of response in return.

She's either not happy or feeling sheepish because of our fucking stare down earlier during Mass before she knew I was a priest, and I became even more taboo.

It's for the best. Like I said, she's married, and I'm a priest. We are both as off-limits as it comes for me to even entertain this notion at all.

I just can't believe such a gorgeous woman like her exists in this world. She takes my breath away. Her sad eyes spoke volumes as I watched her from a distance.

Taking a large swig of my whiskey helps distract me from this train of thought, at least. I love the way it burns going down my throat.

I sit my glass back down on the coaster with a light swirl.

It's a nice day outside. The temperature is starting to cool down. Looking around the patio, I begin one of my favorite hobbies, people-watching. It's not too crowded yet, but that will soon change as the evening approaches.

During my perusal of the room, I come to an immediate halt.

This is the moment I realize God sure as fuck hasn't forgiven me for my past sins. Because I'm looking right at two stunning blue eyes and a pouty mouth slightly parted, mirroring my shock to see the other.

A mouth that is demanding me to take it roughly. To be consumed.

Avery Matheson is here.

Fucking fate, right?

CHAPTER 5

AVERY

When I am afraid, in you I place my trust. I praise the word of God;
I trust in God, I do not fear. What can mere flesh do to me?
Psalm 56:4-5

Of course, I run into Father Lachlan.

One of two men I am actively trying to avoid at the moment for two very different reasons.

I down the rest of my martini in one gulp. I can't catch a break today.

As a priest, Father Lachlan is gorgeous, but now, in this Henley? I'm a puddle. What is it about men in Henleys? They instantly make any man's hot factor go up a point.

Of course, this forbidden, wildly sexy man is going to tempt me in every way possible. Including by now being at my favorite bar while I am actively trying to forget him and my marital problems.

Note to self: Try harder to stop calling Father Lachlan sexy.

After wiping the sides of my mouth with the white cocktail napkin, I plaster on my usual fake smile ready to say hello. This particular smile is like my armor. I know who I'm supposed to be with it on. The Mrs. Avery Matheson who everyone thinks they know. Meanwhile, I'm drowning on the inside.

I get up from my barstool and start to move to the other side of the bar. I can't ignore him, not when he clearly recognizes me as well. It would be rude. Yes, that's definitely the only reason I'm approaching him right now. To be polite. I do have Southern manners, after all.

As I make my way over to where he waits for me, his stare sends chills up my body. I don't know what chokehold this man has over me, but when his green eyes focus on me, I can't look away.

I want him, but it's so bad to be feeling this way. I'm on day one of finding out that my husband is officially trash, and now, this new priest has some kind of authority over my body.

As I near, he begins to shift slightly on his stool. At least I'm not the only one affected by this.

Wait? What if I make him uncomfortable? No, no... that can't be it. You don't blatantly stare at someone this many times in one day if there isn't something more there. He has to feel this palpable chemistry between us too.

This is more than staring at me like I am an annoyance or even a puzzle he's trying to solve. Every time I feel his gaze on me, it's as if he's looking at me naked. He's stripping away my fake smile and neatly pressed dress and looking at me bare.

I don't know how I feel about someone I just met having the ability to do that.

My body squirms as I continue to round the expansive rectangular bar. It's relatively empty for an early Sunday afternoon compared to other bars in the area. This spot is known as a locals-only place, and most of them are likely still at Sunday brunch. A Charleston locals' favorite activity.

As I finally reach Father Lachlan, he flashes me a full-faced smile. I can't help but turn my pretend smile into a genuine one in return.

When was the last time I really smiled? I don't think I could tell you.

"Hi," I chirp with a small wave.

Great—real smooth, Avery.

"Hello again, Mrs. Matheson," he answers in that deep, gravelly voice I'm slowly becoming addicted to.

"Please, call me Avery, Father Lachlan."

My pretend smile is making its way back after being referred to as Mrs. Matheson. Please call me literally anything other than that. I might enjoy some of the other names you could call me.

Lachlan studies me for just a moment.

"If we're forgoing formalities outside of church, we can drop the 'Father' as well," he says, grinning.

His smile is devilish. Is this an acknowledgment of the current sweeping between us?

"Lachlan, then."

Any sign of my pretend smile has vanished again. My face feels warm as his name spills from my mouth. I'm blushing like a nervous teenager just by being in his presence.

"I think I like you better this way," he muses before taking another sip of his drink.

A whiskey drinker... I like that. Another point added to his hotness scale.

"Like what?" I ask, trying to refocus.

Looking down briefly, I see an empty barstool and take a seat.

"Smiling."

"Oh," I say as my eyebrows furrow together, and that smile he likes turns down momentarily.

"Maybe I don't."

My eyes dart up to meet his. What does he mean by that? I definitely don't need to be unpacking this conversation right now.

He's looking at me with such... desire, perhaps? This is the most cryptic conversation I've had in a while.

The heat is palpable between us. I've never felt this type of intensity from someone who is basically a stranger or wanted it to continue. Today should be one of the worst days of my life, and instead, I'm smiling like a schoolgirl at the new, sexy priest.

Will I ever remember not to call him sexy?

The new, attractive priest. That's better.

What in the ever-loving God is wrong with me? This cannot be normal. I need to head home and not be sitting down with Father Lachlan, I mean Lachlan, flirting. If that's even what's really happening.

That can't be it. I'm so out of practice I've got to be mistaken. Lachlan is simply being nice to his new parishioner, and I'm overreacting to this odd form of tension.

He's a priest. I'm married... well, at least to his knowledge, I am. I am technically married but not for much longer after the christening of my new rug. I am never going to forget that part.

Why was he staring at me in the church? Why do I care? I need attention. That's all this is.

I'm attention-starved and am turning a few stares and glances into something it's not when I have way bigger problems in my life I should be dealing with. Even on my worst days, I'm usually not this frantic of a mess. Making up stories of stolen glances and longing from random men.

Lachlan lets out a small laugh before taking another sip of his whiskey.

"Sorry," I say with a light laugh.

He just caught me lost in thought. If he was actually attracted to me before, that just went out the window.

"Are you enjoying Charleston?" I ask to steer the conversation away from anything to do with Lachlan and me.

"Very much so—it's different than I expected, but I suppose I wasn't expecting much," he shares with a shrug.

"You weren't expecting much from one of the best cities in the country?" I tease playfully.

He gives me another chuckle in response before taking a sip of his whiskey.

"When you put it like that, you're right, Avery. I should have had *some* expectations."

My smile widens. Lachlan's face is stunning. His chiseled jawline creates a beautiful definition that matches well with the deep green eyes I've been swimming in.

"You're different than I expected," I blurt out.

Lachlan raises an eyebrow.

"Is that so?"

I nod my head slowly.

"You weren't expecting much from your new priest?"

My smile returns.

"When you put it like that, you're right. I should have had *some* expectations," I answer.

Lachlan grins in response.

"Well..." I stammer.

Pulling myself back to reality, I remember I have to get out of here. When I am actually single, I'll have to practice before going out to find someone to sleep with, never mind expect to date.

He eyes me, clearly wondering what I'm going to say next.

"Have a good rest of your Sunday, Father Lachlan." I half-smile as I pull out two twenty-dollar bills from my purse to pay for my two martinis.

I place them on the bar and signal to the bartender where I've left the money.

"Lachlan," he rasps.

Making eye contact once again, I wish I'd decided to stay so I could hear his voice some more. It's for the best that I leave.

"Right. Have a good rest of your Sunday... Lachlan."

I get up from the barstool slowly, unable to pull my attention away from his gaze. It's a silent war playing out between us. I so desperately want to ask him about what happened earlier in church. I don't know if I'd like the answer either way.

What I do know is I want to get to know him and that's problematic.

"Take care, Avery."

I shiver as my name leaves his lips. A smirk curls up one side of Lachlan's mouth.

Just great. He can tell what his words do to me, and he likes it. Wait, he likes it, doesn't he? Another reaction I shouldn't unpack from him.

I can't take his eyes on me anymore, so I do what I do best. Ignore whatever it is that I am feeling, leaving so much unanswered... and I walk away.

Giving him a final nod before disappearing.

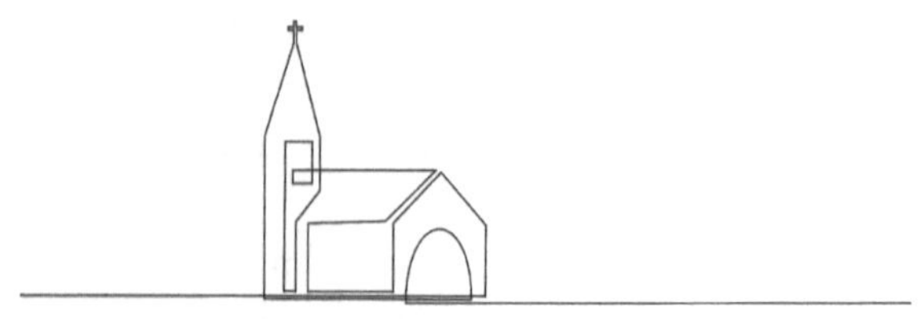

Returning home, I find Kevin in his office. He's staring at his computer screen, black thick-rimmed glasses on, and a scotch sweating onto his cherry-wood desk.

Even though I'm clearly visible in the hallway, he hasn't noticed me yet. Who is this man whom I thought I knew? Even now, as I look back on how destined our marriage was to fail, I just didn't see this happening to me.

My husband is a cheater, and I'm at peace with it. With the end of us.

I'm not sure I would have had the courage to leave him otherwise. If this hadn't happened, would I have been lonely for the rest of my life? I feel more alone than I ever have, but it's a different kind of loneliness. I'm only twenty-eight; I can start over. Maybe this is a chance to go after the life I'm meant to be living.

Walking the few paces closer to his door, I gently knock my knuckles against it to signal my presence.

"Knock, knock," I say out loud as I tap louder.

Kevin looks up, surprised to find me standing in front of him. I'm not sure why—I actually live here. If anything, his using the home office is a surprise to me.

"Avery," he responds emotionless before returning his focus back to his screen.

"Out golfing today?"

He looks up, once again surprised I'm making any conversation at all. Honestly? I'm not sure why I am either.

He leans back in his chair, gripping the armrests lightly. I adjust myself to be standing centered in his doorway. Taking off his glasses, he wipes his eyes before resting them on the desk next to his scotch.

"Yeah, went out with Frank to discuss business," he replies coolly.

"Business?"

"Nothing to worry about, sweetheart."

I wince at his tone that this topic is off-limits to him.

"How's Frank doing? I saw Missy today at church," I say to steer the conversation in a different direction.

"Good. Did she mention they want us to come by for dinner soon? I'll have my assistant arrange the details for us so it works with my schedule," he answers curtly.

Of course, his assistant will. At least I have the satisfaction of knowing she's probably fuming having to schedule it.

I plaster on my usual fake smile. One that he doesn't know isn't real.

"That's great, looking forward to it."

Even though I know I'm leaving Kevin, I can't let on to him that I am. For the time being, I need to be his trophy wife who asks, "How high?" when he says, "Jump."

Kevin eyes me suspiciously. This is probably the most we've spoken to each other in days, if not weeks. I could have just walked by his office, but I'm trying to pretend like everything is normal.

"Well, I'll see you in bed," I say to end this awkward encounter with my husband.

"Don't wait up," he replies.

"Of course."

I give a half smile and turn to leave. A few steps down the hall, I hear my name being called from Kevin's office. I let out a low sigh. Maybe I should have just walked past his door.

Making my way back, I find him standing on the opposite side of his desk with his head hanging low. Looking at him while he's pretending that he's let his guard down, I can't help but see signs of the version of him I fell in love with. It's an act he's perfected, and I've fallen for too many times before.

"Yes?" I ask.

Kevin raises his head and looks at me almost endearingly. Normally, this look would be the crumb I would hold onto for weeks to try to convince myself that I still love him.

"Your roots are starting to show," he states.

Back to reality, it is.

"I'll get my hair fixed this week," I grit through a pretend smile.

Before I have a chance to head to my room, he's facing his desk and putting on his glasses. Not concerned at all about my reaction. I turn around and disappear down the hallway to our bedroom.

Back in the darkly decorated room, I plop down onto our modern, black-framed bed. I love this bedroom. It's one room that feels like mine. Since Kevin is rarely home, he didn't mind that I redecorated this room myself instead of keeping what his interior designer—or I should say what Missy, the interior designer, created. Yes, that Missy is one and the same.

The same one I'm now going to have to sit through a dinner with soon. His assistant will surely send me a calendar invite. Kevin will expect me to clear my schedule to be there. It doesn't matter if I have any actual plans already scheduled.

This room feels like a sanctuary for me in a way. It's strange, since we do technically share it. But is it really sharing when days turn into weeks, and you aren't sure if your spouse will actually show up?

I doubt Kevin will even attempt to sleep in here tonight. The fact that he was home early was startling enough. I'm sure he'll find his way to one of the guest rooms closer to his office when he's ready to sleep.

I pull out my laptop from my bottom bedside drawer and begin researching. I need a good attorney and to check my finances. Both my individual account and our joint account.

Our joint account has money in it that Kevin knows about. He contributes to it regularly. What he doesn't know is that I have an individual account with all of my past assets from before we got married. When we got engaged, he asked me to put the money he knew about into the joint account.

For the betterment of our future together.

He wasn't fully aware of what I had been given when my dad passed away, and since we decided anything pre-marriage was ours separately, I didn't correct the assumptions he made.

That's one decision I am grateful to have made. Somewhere in the back of my mind, in the early dreamy days of dating, I knew better than to tell him the full truth.

Another red flag I blissfully danced right around.

Looking back, he believed me so easily because he never saw me as anything more than a prize. He would never assume how much money I had because all he cared about was that he had found a blue ribbon of a wife who came from any money at all.

Fisher had hidden the remainder of my money in an account for me. He told me down the road, I could tell him about it, but I needed to protect myself first. As the closest thing I had to a father figure at the time, I trusted his guidance. He didn't trust Kevin when he first met him.

That situation should have been another red flag I cared more about, but I just kept on dancing around that one too.

Sitting on my bed, I begin scrolling through the transactions in our joint checking account first. I notice something strange almost immediately. A lump sum was removed Friday. A very noticeable lump sum.

One hundred thousand dollars was withdrawn.

Even for a couple as well off financially as we are, that's not something you do every day. I can't think of anything coming up that would warrant him to remove that much.

Surely, he kept a separate account as well, so this would need to be something for us.

Maybe that's why he called me back into his office about my hair... I must be missing an upcoming event we have to attend.

I can't think of anything offhand that I would be missing. No charity event, no one's birthday is happening soon, our anniversary has just passed, and we haven't firmed up any travel plans for the winter yet. He always wanted to go to Aspen. I hate Aspen.

I've always wanted to rent a cabin in the woods and decorate it with lights, read books, drink coffee in the morning and champagne at night, then be taken to a bedroom and ravished as he told me how delicious I am.

But that wouldn't be happening. It was never going to happen. Looking back, this is yet another red flag.

How did I dance right past so many of these? You'd think I was a professional at this rate.

In reality, Kevin would never have wanted to do something like that. He would have complained about the fresh air, bugs, and lack of room service.

He also dreaded going down on me even when we were dating. This should have been the only red flag I needed to move on from him then. Any man who doesn't go down on a woman is one no woman should stay with.

CHAPTER 6

AVERY

For the love of money is the root of all evils, and some people in their desire for it have strayed from the faith and have pierced themselves with many pains.
1 Timothy 6:10

100,000 dollars...
100,000 dollars...
100,000—wait.

It was just taken out the same day he brought his assistant here. That can't be a coincidence. Something is up. There is no way it could have all been spent on his assistant. I mean, come on, there is no way her fish-like performance was worth that much money, but there has to be something that I'm missing...

Okay, fine, I won't be bitter and assume he paid her for services rendered, but it really is the most bizarre coincidence.

I have to figure out where this money went to. Did he also need to get something he kept at the house? Is that why he actually showed up here that day? And now that I think of it, what business does he have with Frank Jenkins?

I need to do some more digging. If we're about to get divorced, I have to be armed with some answers to what he's been getting himself into, at the very minimum. He already slipped up by fucking his assistant and getting caught on camera. All I have to do is wait for him to make another mistake.

I take a screenshot for the growing pile of evidence I'm beginning to gather. Now I know I need to keep a better eye on our joint account before I leave for good. Continuing to scroll, I see something else unusual.

Wait, there's a pattern here.

A pattern of withdrawals. Most aren't as large as the initial one I found, but over the course of the past few months, he's taken out several lump sums. He makes enough money to spend it however he wants to, but what is he doing with it? Nothing has changed in our house, no new cars... nothing out of the norm.

I hate to admit this, but I rarely look at our bank account. He must know that. I've had no reason to. We have a business manager who handles all the finances for us and checks in frequently. I have a few credit cards and a debit card for everyday use.

These withdrawals have taken place over the course of the past three months. It's all suspicious activity for our account.

Next on my list is finding the best attorney in Charleston. Regardless of how broken our marriage is, I doubt Kevin will back down easily when I walk away. I hope he will, but I can't assume that will be the case. I need my ducks in a row before I make my grand exit.

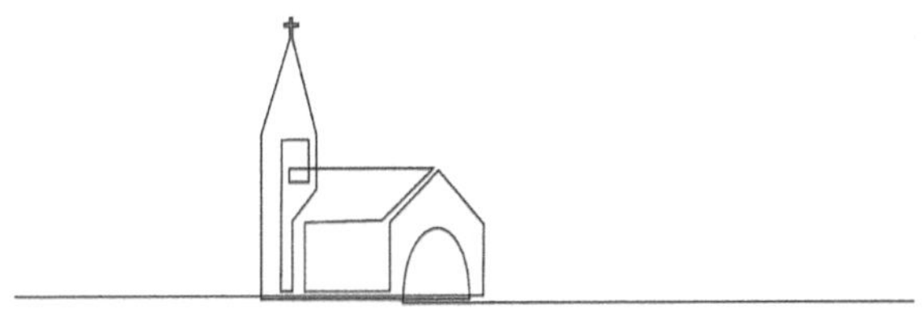

It's Wednesday morning, and I made the decision last night to go to visit Lachlan today.

Earlier, when I stepped out to get my morning coffee, Kevin had already left the house, as expected. He didn't sleep in my bedroom the past few nights he stayed at our home. I won't let his bad behavior impact me any more than it already has.

Standing in front of my full-length mirror, I'm happy with my outfit choice. I'm in a new blue, patterned dress and my favorite tan wedges. Blue is my signature color, and I try to wear it as often as possible.

It may be the end of summer in Charleston, but it is still unbearably hot. August is one of the worst months to visit the area, yet every year, thousands of tourists come in the summer months. Crossing the busy streets endlessly under the scorched sun, hoping to reach the next tourist trap.

I'm nervous about seeing Lachlan. I can admit that.

He had told me to come by his office any time this week to discuss the upcoming gala. I know it's going to be difficult to focus on anything of importance in his presence. The plus side is that I am in control. I can always make our meeting short.

If he's even there today. What do I do if he's not... leave a note? Really, his only goal will be for me to sign a check and be on my way.

I can do this.

With a final swipe of red lipstick, I feel confident. Still nervous but confident, nonetheless. I will not continue to be this desperate woman under the stare of the new, hot priest.

Two words that should never be put together. At least I didn't call him sexy this time. That's an improvement.

My skin is starting to flush just at the notion of seeing him in person.

Do I have time to masturbate?

Wait. *No getting off to Father Lachlan before going to see him, Avery.* That will surely not help me feel any less needy right now.

Although... what time crunch am I under? I glance at my bedside table. The drawer with my favorite vibrator in it is calling to me.

Pull it together, Avery. No.

I shake my head as I try to recompose myself. Less thoughts of Lachlan, more focus on getting through this meeting.

Grabbing my purse, I take the short walk to the church grounds.

Staring up at the parish office doors, I take in a final deep breath and make my way inside.

I'm spotted by Patricia, the receptionist. She's been with the parish for over ten years and is more like an office manager without the title. She's an older woman with short, white hair and silver-rimmed glasses she usually lets dangle around her neck from a dainty matching chain.

It's eerily quiet in the building.

"Good morning, Mrs. Matheson. Father Lachlan has been expecting you to stop by this week. Right this way," she says firmly.

Patricia gets out from behind the desk and immediately starts to walk toward his office before I have a chance to process that he's in right now, and we are about to be face-to-face.

"Oh, he's here?"

This woman moves fast. Even with my long strides, she's making me walk quickly to catch up.

"Of course, he is; come on now," she answers without a glance back to me.

Following her lead, we weave through the hallways toward the back of the building. I haven't seen anyone else on our walk. This place is very unnervingly quiet.

"Here you are."

She gestures with her hands at his open door. Time to fake it until I make it.

"Thank you."

Lachlan's green eyes shoot up as soon as he hears Patricia outside the door. I'm now awkwardly standing in his doorway. My nerves are getting ready to combust inside me. Red lipstick is not enough to make me feel as confidently put together as I'd hoped.

"Avery. Please close the door and take a seat," Lachlan says.

He immediately stands and gestures in front of him to the open chairs on the opposite side of his desk with a warm smile.

I do as he asks without questioning why the door needs to be closed. I'd like the privacy so no one else will witness the train wreck that I feel like I'm about to become.

Should this situation be a red flag? Putting this in my growing suitcase of scenarios I need to unpack, featuring the one and only Father Lachlan O'Connell.

"Thank you for coming in," he continues.

Lachlan retakes his seat as I sit in one of the available chairs. Fixing my dress around me first, I play nervously with a lock of my hair to keep my hands occupied.

Lachlan's eyes still on the movement. They're following the small twirls I'm making.

"It's not a problem. What can I do to help further the gala?"

Shaking his head briefly, he regains his composure. I can't say the same for myself. My fingers are intertwined with my golden blonde hair. He inspects my complete demeanor more closely now.

"Right to the point. I can appreciate that," he answers with a grin.

A full panty-melting grin I'll be using to masturbate to later tonight. What? I do have needs, you know. I hope my vibrator can make it another time. I fear I may have worn it out the past few days with fantasies of Lachlan filling my head.

Little does he know that I can't be in his presence without my nipples hardening and wetness gathering in my panties when he smiles at me. If he did, I don't think I would be getting this grin. It would be very un-priestlike to appreciate a woman being turned on because of him.

I have become a fully-fledged, needy, sex-deprived woman because of Father Lachlan. I can admit that much, at least. My body is aching for his hands to roam it. The hands of a man. Someone who works hard.

I wonder how his hands became as calloused as they are since he is a priest. I don't think priests do much manual labor, but then again, I guess I don't fully know everything that goes into it. Gala planning sure doesn't seem like it should fall under the job description, who knows what else does.

His jaw twitches and pulls me out of this haze I've fallen under. I almost forgot why I'm here.

Lachlan clears his throat and pulls at the collar around his neck. Can he sense my arousal? I certainly hope not.

I start shifting in my seat as I wonder if he can. I have to focus on the point of the meeting and not my very sinful thoughts that seem to star Lachlan.

Focus, Avery.

"If there is a particular sponsorship you would like me to do, I'd be happy to review that now. My husband and I are already a silver sponsor but could tack on something else."

I have to spit out referring to Kevin as my husband.

Lachlan's fingers are raised to his mouth, tented as he pensively takes in the mention of Kevin and my offer. He must have noticed how much I hated mentioning Kevin.

I can tell I'm starting to get flushed. This is going poorly; I have to get out of here. It's like I haven't been around a man I've wanted in ages and have no clue how to act. Dating anyone is going to go really well in the future if I keep this up.

I continue before he has the chance to say anything.

"Or if there is some other way I can be of service outside of a sponsorship, I would be open to that as well."

Oh no. That came out poorly. Shit.

What. Is. Wrong. With. Me?

And why is he not doing the courteous thing and bailing me out of this awkward and one-sided conversation?

Dear God, I'm becoming Missy.

I'm getting hotter every moment I'm under his gaze as he lets the silence drag on. My skin is definitely beginning to flush a light pink, and suddenly, I wish I wasn't wearing a bra. My breasts are feeling so restricted right now I just want to rip it all off to cool down.

Lingerie is one thing that I do for me, not for any man. It makes me feel desirable, knowing that what I'm wearing underneath my clothes would be considered shocking to someone else who saw it. No one would expect someone like me to care enough to have so many pretty, dainty lingerie sets at home.

I know there's no way Kevin will be seeing any of them ever again, at least. Especially not since the whole sleeping-with-his-assistant-on-my-brand-new-rug situation. Nope, sorry, can't let the rug part go.

I can't even remember the last time we had sex. Was it four or five months ago? Clearly, I missed another red flag of his by assuming he was just busy in the office all those late nights.

Lachlan nods his head and begins to stand up.

His towering figure has me craning my neck to maintain eye contact. His broad shoulders are mouth-watering, and I love the assertive stance he takes.

I need to stop getting so lost in my thoughts around him.

He comes to the front of his desk and leans against it. His hands grip the edge of it tightly, making his arms flex at the motion. Allowing me a close-up look of his veins pulsing on display.

Even though I'm actively trying to curb my lust-filled thoughts of him, I'm still very grateful that his sleeves are rolled up, giving me the best arm porn I could have ever imagined.

Lachlan catches me staring at them. He exhales heavily. His head is hanging down momentarily, causing some loose pieces of his hair to fall over his forehead.

My nipples are now pointy tips that I can't make go away. They're clearly showing through the thin lace bra and summer dress I'm wearing. Next time, I'll wear a sweater, even if it is a hundred degrees outside.

I know the best course of action is for me to fold my arms in front of them, but I see his eyes peeking down to my chest area. It's almost instinctual to arch my back slightly to grant him a better view.

My panties are wetter than I care to admit from being in this close proximity.

"Thank you, Avery. That's very generous of you," he finally replies.

It comes out as barely a whisper. I love the brogue in his voice when he speaks.

The energy simmering between us is palpable. It's very wrong. I am still technically married. He is a priest. This is not what should be happening, but I can't help myself trying to test the waters a bit more.

"How can I be of service, Father Lachlan?"

The innuendo is clear. I am staring up at him, waiting for him to tell me what he's going to do with me. I know I'll say yes to anything he wants. I suddenly don't feel as messy as I did at the start.

I lean forward, giving him a much clearer view of my breasts.

Lachlan's eyes are filled with lust as he tries not to stare at my cleavage. His hand reaches for my face, and he places his finger under my chin.

My breath hitches.

"Avery."

It comes out sternly, almost as a caution that this can't be happening. My mouth parts, and I can't help but lick my bottom lip before biting it as I wait for more.

His intoxicating green eyes look right at my mouth as his jaw ticks like he's battling this attraction just as much as I am.

I don't know what I want to happen. Desire is coursing through me. I have never been this aroused simply by being someone's focus.

I know I'm addicted to Father Lachlan O'Connell's attention. But it's wrong. Even though I know I'm getting separated soon, I can't keep tempting a priest like this. I have to put a stop to this unbearable game of indecision we're both playing.

He removes his finger from my chin and steps to the side of the desk. He makes the decision before I can.

Disappointment fills me almost immediately, followed by shame. I hang my head low for a few moments. It should have been me who stopped this, not the priest.

"Avery," he whispers gently this time.

My eyes shoot up to his. I really don't want to cry in his office. I'm not a crier, yet I just feel so gross and disappointed in my actions.

I should have known coming here was a bad idea. Not after days of masturbating to thoughts of him. I'm not myself yet. It's only been days since I saw that video of Kevin and realized my whole life is going to change. Days since I met Lachlan too.

"I know."

It's the truth. He doesn't even know that I'm getting separated soon. The fact of the matter is it's an irrelevant point. I am tempting a priest. Someone who made a vow to God.

Shaking out of my own self-loathing, I stand and smooth out my dress before plastering on my signature shell of a smile. Shoulders back, stomach in, empty eyes, all present and accounted for.

"Father Lachlan, I'll happily write a check to co-sponsor the entertainment for the gala. I believe that one is still pending a sponsor per the parish website. And if there is anything else I can help with as it gets closer, please contact me."

I have to get out of here.

"Thank you, Mrs. Matheson. St. Peter's appreciates your generosity."

All formalities again, as it should be.

I nod before heading for his door. As I reach for the handle, I pause. Turning back to him slightly, I can see the same pain etched on Lachlan's face as I was just experiencing.

He nods, and I slip away.

CHAPTER 7

LACHLAN

The mind of the intelligent gains knowledge,
and the ear of the wise seeks knowledge.
Proverbs 18:15

That was too close of a call to make with Avery in my office earlier this morning. I should have assumed that being around her was going to be difficult. That type of intense attraction to each other is not common, not in the least.

It doesn't matter that when I look at her, I want nothing else. She's married, and I am a fucking humble servant of God or some shit. I can't even fool myself right now that I'm meant to live the life of a priest. Not when I've been experiencing what it's like to be around a person who makes me feel so fucking alive.

The rest of the day, I try my best not to think about Avery. It's nearly impossible. Visions of her in every way imaginable consume not just my thoughts but every fiber of my being.

I can't focus on Avery right now. Not when the reality is the rest of my day, I'll be drowning in paperwork about the gala, planning upcoming Masses, and having more internal documents to review.

I have no fucking clue why Greg put this gala on my plate. I've only been with the parish for two months and have no experience in event planning. Even from my past life, pre-priesthood. He just doesn't want to deal with it anymore, and the other priest at our parish is pushing seventy; I doubt he was the better choice to lead these elitist efforts.

Greg wants the glory of a successful parish gala but doesn't actually give two fucks about it. He's no better than the men of this parish, men like Avery's husband, Kevin.

My disdain for Avery's husband comes from my gut. I don't know for sure that he's a dumb fucking prick, but Avery wouldn't be this way if he weren't. I fucking know that at the very minimum.

"Ahem," someone clears their throat from my office doorway.

Looking up, I find none other than Greg. What great fucking timing.

"Greg, what can I do for you?" I spit out.

"Lachlan, is that any way to greet me?"

I laugh casually to ease the tension.

"Of course, my apologies. I'm buried in paperwork Patricia and the team need me to review for the upcoming gala," I answer.

Not a lie, but not why I was trying to get this interaction over with as quickly as possible.

That eases the furrow between his brows.

"Right, the gala. That's why I came by," he starts.

I stand from behind my desk, crossing the room to be by his side.

"Anything in particular?" I ask.

"I saw Avery Matheson finally showed up. I was beginning to think I needed to call that husband of hers for you to get her in here," he grumbles.

"No need, sir, she's sponsoring the entertainment now as well," I answer.

Greg nods his head in approval.

"Good, that's good," he says almost to himself.

Before I get a chance to ask if that's all he wants to know, his phone buzzes in his pocket. Pulling it out, he tenses at the name he sees before sliding it back in its place.

"Everything okay?"

"Oh yes, of course, just nonsense I've been dealing with on the expansion campaign efforts. It's like herding cats, getting everyone in agreement on the next steps."

"Do you need my help there?"

Fucking please say no. Greg eyes me curiously. Almost as if he's debating my offer to assist with the campaign.

He chuckles briefly before responding to me.

"No, Lachlan, carry on with the gala. It's important that goes off without any problems. I must be going now."

"Bye, Greg," I say as he's out my door.

Greg is clearly tense as soon as he steps out of my office to head back to his. Making him the second person to flee from here today.

There are a ton of decisions to make when planning a gala. Surprisingly, we have a good team in place to get it all done.

I am becoming more familiar with the team Patricia put together. The office staff is composed of mostly older women who were previously retired assistants or homemakers and mainly part-timers. Thankfully, we're all on the same page as to what my role really is with this gala. I review their decisions to make sure they align with the community and approve the costs. Basically, the last confirmation of what they've planned.

It works for us all. They just want me to approve their ideas anyway. As long as their decisions will fit this crowd, I go along with it all. That's the main concern that I look for when they pile up the paperwork I need to review. Something to ensure the gala impresses the congregation; this community is used to the finer things in life, just like Avery is.

Her long golden hair has haunted my dreams day and night. Seeing her twirl it between her long, thin fingers was arousing. I found myself getting lost watching her sitting before me, my Goldie girl.

After wrapping up the remaining internal procedures documents I had, I begin the short walk home. Taking in the final days of summertime before false fall begins.

In Charleston, there is some version of the four seasons, but the season Grayson keeps warning me about is the impending "false fall," as he calls it. When the weather dips to a cool sixty-something degrees, and it feels like heaven outside. Then, a week later, it's ninety degrees again, and the sweltering heat is back.

I'm thankful this church did provide me with housing on the property. Some of the smaller parishes don't always have it available for their priests. It was a requirement of mine for whichever church I decided to go to when leaving Boston. Keeping it as simple as possible to move.

One of my requests for coming to this parish was being provided with an outside workspace. They gave me a small but useable shed space on what is considered my part of the property.

Thankfully, the church has enough land and common sense to build tall hedges around each property they keep for priests to live in. Nosy parishioners could be at any corner, waiting to talk your ear off or complain about the latest news in the weekly bulletin.

A passion of mine since high school has been woodworking. There is something peaceful about creating new pieces, from furniture to decorative objects; I enjoy putting in the hard work to get my desired outcome. You reap what you sow.

It's the full process for me. From the act of shaping and smoothing out the wood and how much time and patience is required to craft the perfect piece. It all calms me. It's one of the only ways I've found to clear my head without going numb.

A woodworking priest. I know. A little too on the nose with the Jesus Christ angle.

It was something I did with my da before he passed away. I grew up in a small seaside town outside Boston. There isn't much to do there when you're a teenager, and we didn't have much either. That's why making something out of myself was so important to me when I went to college.

My da had a select clientele that he would build custom pieces for to bring in money for the family. It never added up to much, but he always said we didn't need more than what we had.

I didn't fully value that time with my da until he was gone. The art he was teaching me and the time together that I didn't know was slipping away. I was in college when he passed away. I kept on woodworking as my way of staying close to him even though he was no longer with us.

As the years passed, it eventually became a way for me to still feel anything at all. When you're young and become successful too quickly, it does something to you. It sure as hell changed me for the worst. Something I am still trying to rectify.

I was the top earner at a Boston consulting firm before becoming a priest. I'd worked for this company since I graduated college and became the youngest executive they had before I packed up and left without a second thought. Making more money than you can imagine at twenty-three isn't something I would recommend to anyone.

It sounds good in theory, but at that point in my life, I was wasting money on women, drugs, alcohol, and any other way I could slowly self-destruct.

My ma didn't recognize me anymore. The shame of seeing sadness in her eyes every time I went back to my hometown was unbearable, so I stopped visiting as much. The disappointment that was written across her face was agonizing... but I couldn't stop. I wanted more of everything.

Eventually, I stopped going back to visit my ma altogether and sent her money every month instead.

I don't want to face the reality of how much I broke her heart with every check she received. She doesn't even know that I moved to Charleston. Knowing her, she'd ask all the right questions, and I can't have anyone following along with me on my trail of pain.

Almost all my friends were worried about me during those years. Concerned about the detrimental path I was on. They didn't abandon me. At least the ones who did eventually end our friendship did it because of an entirely different reason. The same reason I became a priest in the first place.

Back when I was partying too much, Grayson was in Boston for a hockey game and found me snorting blow off a stripper's tits—*I mean breasts*—in my penthouse while I was getting sucked off by another stripper. Stripper is a loose word—I paid them for their time.

These women were used to being bought by successful men for the night. Men like me. Apparently, I have a type, and that would be the self-destructive ones, like myself.

I didn't care that I wasn't special to them; they weren't special to me. I didn't have time for special in my life. I needed to keep making money. I never cared if I had more than what I needed in this lifetime; I always wanted more.

Grayson didn't get it. The golden boy of my friend group looked at me, not with disgust but sadness. Sadness for whom I was becoming and seeing the friend he knew slip away.

He's the only one who knows the truth of that fateful night that set me on the path to priesthood. He told me I needed to tell the truth to save my other friendships and relationships, but I couldn't. I would take the blame, the lie. It's what I deserved after everything else that had happened that night.

The thrill of sleeping around, alcohol, and pills all gave me the high I was chasing. I needed to feel alive one way or another. I missed feeling something, anything, after my da passed away. That's why I used and abused whatever I could back then.

Regrouping myself from memories of my past, I get to work making a new set of wooden bowls. Something easy to just be out of my house and clear my head. Trying to escape once more, only this time from thoughts of my Goldie girl.

I know we both felt the temptation in my office, but surely, she must understand I can't act on this attraction between us. It's not just because I'm a priest and really fucking shouldn't. It's for her own good more than mine.

I need to learn more about the elusive Avery Matheson. This attraction is consuming my every thought, yet I really don't know much about who she is.

That's it.

I need to look into Avery, her husband, and her actual life and see it for myself. Then I'll see the real reason why I should stay away. I can't mess up her life because of my sick desires.

Tomorrow, I'll look her up in the parish system and get her address. Maybe we'll have more details on who she is.

As her priest, it is my responsibility to put these thoughts aside and help her. Guide her. Give her what she needs and not what she wants... even if we both want each other.

I won't give into temptation.

CHAPTER 8

LACHLAN

*"Everything is lawful for me," but not everything is beneficial.
"Everything is lawful for me," but I will not let myself be dominated by
anything.*
1 Corinthians 6:12

The next day, I go into the office early. I have to give the daily Mass and need to get to work right away, finding out details on Avery before then.

After settling into my desk, with my black coffee in tow, I log into the church donor system and pull up her family file.

Avery is twenty-eight years old, and her husband, Kevin, is forty-two. That's an age gap. She and I are much closer in age than that. Six years, that's not even considered an age gap, not really, at least.

Fuck. No. Stop thinking like this.

If she were my wife, she would understand that I knew what was best for her, always. I would want my cum dripping between her thighs as a reminder of whom she belonged to each and every day and how fucking happy she was with me.

She wouldn't even be attracted to another man who found her tempting because she would know she was mine. Only mine. She would know that if she broke, I would be there to pick up the pieces and put her back together. It would all be my doing anyway. Everything would be to show her that she belongs to me.

It's becoming harder to reconcile who I am with the version of myself coming out because of Avery. This attraction feels different than just desiring someone. It's a dangerous feeling of hoping for something more.

I check the internet next. There has to be a lot on here about the Mathesons. More than what our donor system stores.

That's it—here we go—dozens of webpages are listed for me to look through.

Kevin's company is based out of Charleston as Greg mentioned, but several employees work remotely from other parts of the country.

From the way she looked at me, I can tell Kevin takes her for granted. If she were happy at home, she wouldn't be looking at me with lust and longing in her eyes. He's an asshole for treating her this way. Who wouldn't want someone as beautiful as my Goldie girl every day forever?

A fucking pussy, that's who. Actually, I take that back.

A pussy can take a pounding.

He's a fucking pair of balls. Can't take shit.

That's the picture I have of him now. I'm never going to change my mind about him, even if I read that he saves orphans or the whales.

The rest of what I find online is all superficial. Nothing out of the ordinary for what you would expect to find on a prominent local couple. My beautiful girl leads a meaningless society life.

Every time Avery looked at me, she had these big doe eyes that begged for something different.

She needs more but is trapped in a life of despair. I have to learn more about her marriage to Kevin and confirm my suspicions.

It is the priestly thing to do, after all.

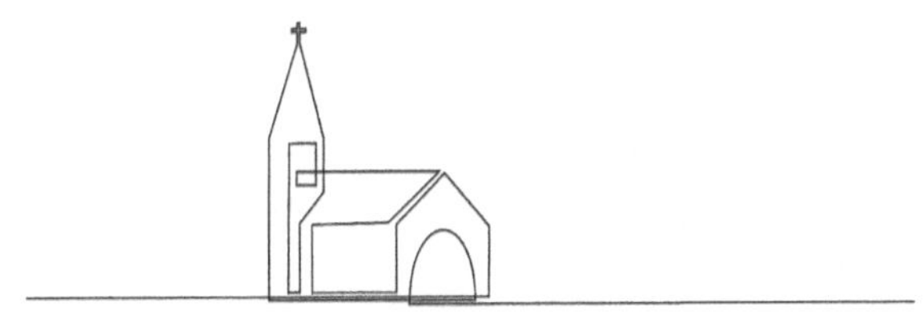

After the morning Mass, I return to the parish office for a few hours to wrap up the Mass schedule I have to plan out. I'll be leading several in the coming week.

As I finish up the plan, I hear whispers from down the hall. Usually, it's quiet where my office is located in the building. People rarely come to see me outside of the office staff needing my help, and that's usually just about the gala.

The whispers are growing louder the more frustrated the two parties get.

"What do you mean you can't do more?"

A man's voice is speaking.

"Just that, what do you want from me? I'm doing what I can."

Another man's voice.

"Don't fuck with me, this isn't how much you promised," the first man repeats.

"Fuckin' Christ, fine. I'll see what I can do," the second man responds.

A buzzing sound breaks up their argument.

"Watch your tongue," the first man chastises.

The second man shuffles in his clothes from what I can make out. I'm assuming he's pulling out his phone.

"I've got to go," the second man says.

"Fine," the first man huffs.

Footsteps begin walking hurriedly down the corridor until I no longer hear any sign of the second man at all. The break room door down the hall opens and swings shut behind the first man.

After a few minutes go by, I decide I can finally pack up and prepare to leave the parish. I couldn't quite make out who either man was. Most likely, two people visited to make donations to the church and then stopped, looking for a restroom. The first man probably got lost and went into the break room by accident. But why didn't I hear him coming back out?

It doesn't matter. Not my problem to deal with.

With my bag by my side, I walk slowly down the hallway, looking for a clue of who either person was. No one is around.

Coming to St. Peter's is proving to be the fucking weirdest experience of my life, and that's saying something.

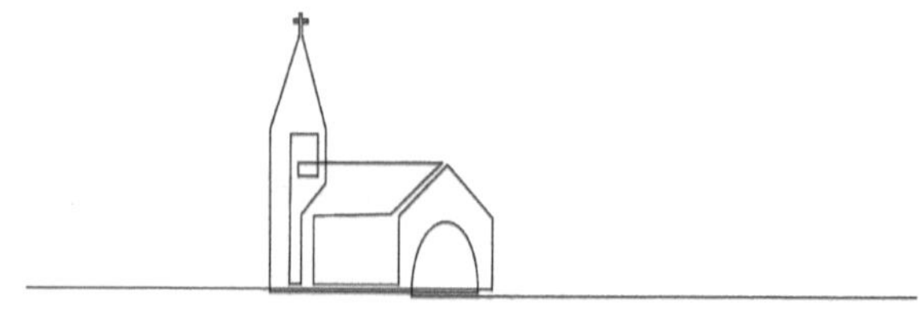

Back home, I change into running gear to finally see where Avery lives. I have this inexplicable urge to see it first-hand. I lace up my running shoes and begin a slow jog toward the waterway that skims her neighborhood.

I'm jogging at a steady pace as I dash in and out of the streets now. My headphones are in my ears, blasting hard rock. I love the rush of running. Not everyone who exercises likes running. The pounding of the pavement does take its toll on my shins, but I love every second of it.

Once I became a priest, I started to make running part of my new religion. A new high to take in, if you will. I couldn't only have my woodworking. Not when I had relied so heavily on drugs and copious amounts of alcohol in the past.

Circling back toward Avery's neighborhood, I find her street. I don't want to make myself too obvious right away if she's outside.

I fully understand this is borderline stalker behavior, but I just have to see her life with my own two eyes. Have my theories be proven wrong about her sadness and marriage to Kevin.

I could always reach out to Cara, one of the few people from my past, who would still answer my calls, to give me the rundown. Cara owns a technology security company out in California and used to be one of my best friends until I shut her out too. I just don't want to do it that way with Avery. This is one time I don't want to have the upper hand when getting to know someone.

Fuck, this is bad. I can't be getting to know Avery like this.

I stop jogging and put my hands on my hips as I look down to the ground and contemplate what in the actual fuck I'm doing right now.

Maybe some people would assume I have an addictive personality. I don't fucking care what labels people want to give me. Wanting to speak with Avery, to see her in person—it's not exactly *Fatherly,* and I am all too fucking aware of it.

This is old Lachlan behavior. Not Father Lachlan behavior. That's it. I shouldn't be doing this. I need to go back home. I can't be fucking going any further than what I have already done. Running to the home she shares with her husband is bad fucking news.

I've got to get out of here right now. I have to put distance between us, not be stalking the woman. I can't get to know her. I'll only fuck her life up... and mine. Pursuing her any further than this will ruin everything I have worked so hard to achieve.

Just look at me now, a thirty-four-year-old priest obsessed with the first woman to ever capture my attention truly, and she's off-limits.

She can't get close to me ever because of my past. She wouldn't want me once she found out what happened and what type of person I was before I ran into the arms of God. Hell, I'm clearly hanging on by a thread and can barely handle the truth myself.

Beginning to leave her street, an instinct takes over. I know she's there.

Looking back to the front of her house, I see Avery outside on her lawn, kneeling before a dozen rose bushes. I must have run past her house on the street while spiraling deeper into my madness.

She's wearing a tight, white tank top with a white lace bra peeking out from the edges. From where I'm standing, I can see right down her shirt. Right at her beautiful set of tits.

I wince. *Breasts.*

You know what? Fuck it, this is one part of me I can't change.

So what if I'm allowing myself to drink in her perfect tits that are on display for me. Ones that I want to swallow whole. Nip and scrape as she moans in pleasure. I want to fuck them with my cock before shoving it down her throat. Avery's mouth full of my cock and her perfect tits out on display just for me is the prettiest sight I can imagine.

Hanging my head momentarily, I can't seem to shake these intrusive thoughts.

Fuck it. I'm in too deep as it is. I've got to talk to her now that I know she's outside. I can't let this go—her go... not yet, at least.

I take a few strides to be right at her fence.

She sits straight up as I make my final approach. Her back is currently facing me. I hear the sound of falling gardening tools as I track her wiping beads of sweat from her forehead with the back of her hand.

I brace myself on a fence post. Her face lights up as she turns around and sees it's me. I would kill to be the reason more smiles appear on her face every day.

She gives me a small wave. I can't help but give her a smile and a wave back.

"Hi, Avery," I grin before giving her a playful wink.

"Hi," she chirps as she stands.

She nervously plays with the end of her ponytail, and I wish it were me fisting her hair instead.

"How are you?" I ask, trying to keep it simple.

"Good. Great. Yes, doing well."

I like that I make her flustered. Her chest is rising and falling in anticipation repeatedly. I love the way it makes her tits swell together.

Those fucking tits.

I can't help myself. I revert to a version of my prior self when I'm around Avery. I am only a man, after all.

"How are you, Lachlan? Out for a run today?"

Avery drinks in my body. I know I'm sweating; I couldn't help but run a little further than I intended to make this a real workout.

Her eyes land on where my hands are resting on her fence post, and I see her lick her lips as I flex my arm muscles subtly.

"Yeah, I've been trying to find my new running loops, figured I would try this area for a change of pace. I usually go a little closer to Tradd or Queen Streets. So not too far," I answer.

She continues breathing at a very noticeable, uneven pace even as she returns her gaze to mine.

I like that I have this effect on her; it's one of the reasons I can't resist tempting myself. Maybe she really is slowly becoming my new addiction. In the long term, I need to try to avoid her becoming my *anything*. In the meantime, I'll go ahead and enjoy these encounters more than any man of faith should.

"Those are both such great streets. I totally get why."

"They are. These are great rose bushes." I gesture that way.

"I'm surprised you don't have a gardener tending to them," I finish.

She frowns.

"Some things I prefer to do myself. Gardening is something for me. Not because of how it makes this museum look to outsiders," she answers with her hand on her jutted-out hip as she waves her other hand at her house.

I like this side of her with attitude. Fuck, I think I like every side of Avery.

"I meant no disrespect," I say as I raise my hands in the air to show I come in peace.

"If I ever mean to disrespect you, you'll know it," I wink at her once more with a grin.

Shit, I shouldn't have said that. It's too easy to be like this around Avery.

She blushes. Thank God.

She's trying to contain her smile by biting on her bottom lip. A lip I want to take between my teeth right now. I need to try and steer the conversation away from fake pleasantries.

"While I have you here," I say, trying to formulate a reason to see her again.

"Interested in a walk to chat? I'm just going to do a cool down if you're good with that."

She's trying to hold back her smile again but can't resist flashing me her pearly whites. I love it when she smiles almost as much as the sadistic part of me that lives for the desperation I find in her sad eyes.

"I'd... really love that."

Looks like she can't resist these moments with me either.

She makes her way through her yard and catches up to be beside me on the other side of the fence.

I sure as fuck notice that she is shamelessly taking me in from top to bottom and back again. Fuck, her wanting me is the best goddamn feeling in the world. It's a whole new kind of high I want to be chasing.

I've been hit on at church more times than I can count, but no one else has ever sparked this much attraction in me.

Her whole body lets out a shiver at our closeness. I know what she's feeling; I'm experiencing it too. Now, it's me who can't contain my grin.

"The gala is coming up soon, and as you know, it's a big deal in our community," I begin as we walk slowly together.

She nods in response.

"For some reason." I laugh, and she smiles up at me.

"Father Greg has put me in charge of it, but I'm getting to a point where I want to make sure the decisions I'm making are the right call. I trust the office staff, but they aren't part of the society scene," I share as we reach the end of her street.

We continue walking as she keeps bobbing her head along in agreement. I need to get her to do this with me.

"I would really appreciate your insights, Avery. If you'd be willing to help me for the next several weeks."

"I would love to help you."

"That's my girl."

I hear an intake of air from her and realize that wasn't a private thought.

"Good," I say more firmly.

No point in pretending I didn't say it now. I just can't let that slip define us.

CHAPTER 9

LACHLAN

I am steadfast in my resolve. I will be able to handle this newfound... friendship? Yes, friendship with Avery. I can separate enjoying her presence from the notion of wanting to consume her body.

That's why when I see Avery today in Mass, I won't stare at her beautiful face, round blue sparkling eyes, or daydream about fucking her six ways from Sunday.

I put on my vestments in the sacristy, the room at the back of the church where we prepare for Mass. Taking a look at myself in the mirror, I hate who I see looking back at me.

I'm not this man of faith, but the more I pretend I am, hopefully, it will rub off on me. It has been years, but maybe that could change. Maybe I can still change. Be a better person.

A better priest. There are so many ways I wish I could just be better.

Growing up Irish Catholic outside of Boston, this religion was indoctrinated in me. I knew the ins and outs of it before I even entertained the notion of becoming a priest. It was rooted in my childhood and seeped throughout my blood.

Just because I know it better than I know myself doesn't mean that I believe in what I'm saying at Mass. It's fucked up, I know. My feelings toward the religion are complicated. Do I really think I'm turning cheap wine into Christ's blood? Of course not. It's the symbolism that I can understand and get behind.

This faith was what I subconsciously leaped to whenever I felt so strongly that my life was over. Maybe becoming a priest was extreme, but extreme was what I needed at that time.

After what happened, I had sat hungover on the steps of a Boston Catholic church, feeling drained, beaten, and unsure of what to do. How to move forward. Who to tell.

My now mentor, Patrick, eventually saw and sat beside me silently. I needed him that day. Soon enough, the days faded into weeks and months following that fateful night. The night I would never forgive myself for.

Patrick reminded me a lot of my da.

He believed that God was guiding me on the path I needed to experience. That I could be forgiven but I just had to forgive myself first.

That was something I knew I could never do.

Instead of working on forgiving myself, I poured myself into the Catholic faith and began helping Patrick at his church. I went through the daunting process of becoming a priest to show how much I could change my ways. Years later, I was finally ordained.

For a moment in time, I believed I was a new person, but it was fleeting.

I never once slipped into the temptations of drugs or women in those beginning years. I still allow myself to have a few drinks. I didn't have the same desires I did at twenty-three, but drugs and women were clearly off the table.

A whiskey neat periodically is still acceptable though. It wasn't until the day the busty adult film star came into my church that I faltered and almost gave into temptation.

Since then, I've been less confident in my role and the purpose of this path I'm on. The actions of a twenty-three-year-old man were not those of a thirty-four-year-old one. Not in my case, anyway.

I continued as a priest, albeit questioning it.

It all came to a tipping point the moment I laid eyes on Avery only a week ago. The moment that my fate changed.

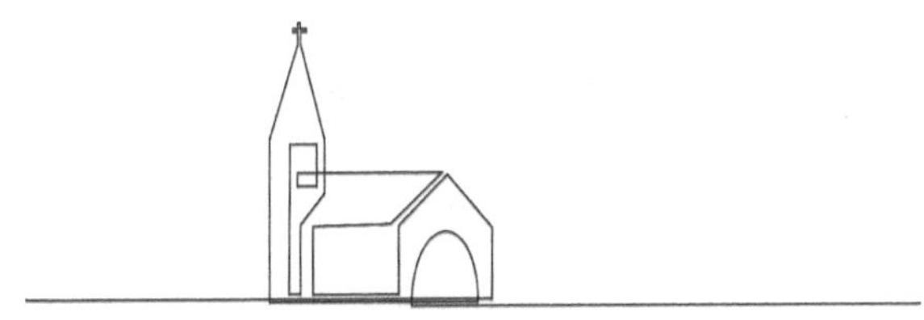

After Mass ends, I take my place on the outside steps to greet the parishioners. It's a beautiful day with birds chirping and all, but I can't really appreciate any of it. Not when a temptress in a pale pink dress is walking up to me with a wide smile, looking like a doll.

She wore this dress to test me. I know it. She can clearly tell I love the dresses she's been wearing.

Instead of sitting toward the back near one of the pillars, this week, she sat in the third row, right in front of the altar.

Her dress dips low, but not too low. It curves around her delicate collarbone. At the altar, I was wishing to lick that collarbone right there in front of the congregation. She brought these wicked desires to the forefront of my mind every time.

She leaned forward more times than was necessary during Mass. Either to pull something out of her purse on the floor or to pick up the Mass pamphlet she kept tucked in the seat in front of her. Avery knew what she was doing to me. I shouldn't have fucking cared, but the depraved part of me loved every second of it.

Tits are one thousand percent my weakness. I don't care what kind of cliché that makes me. Seeing hers made me wish I could make them my new religion.

I would worship at the altar of her tits, giving them every bit of the attention they deserve. Thank fuck, this robe can't show what is my very apparent bulge.

"Good morning, Mrs. Matheson," I say in greeting.

She flinches again at the name. I can't call her Avery here, not with so many eyes watching both of us, including Missy Jenkins. Calling Avery by her first name is too personal for how little everyone would assume we know of each other. No one knows this isn't the second time we've met.

"Father Lachlan, wonderful Mass today."

"Thank you. It's a pleasure to have you here this morning. I was hoping to see you."

She lets a small smile reappear.

"Do you have time today to work with me on a few gala details? I'm afraid my talents do not lie with design, and it can't wait until tomorrow. Patricia and the team won't be happy to know I didn't finish them over the weekend," I say while laughing at the notion.

They are actually really fucking scary when I miss a deadline. I swear Patricia must have been an army general before coming to St. Peter's.

I have to keep Avery here with me. It's been days since I went to her house.

"Of course, not a problem. I'll wait outside the parish office?"

Avery gestures to where the office building is, and I nod in agreement.

"I'll be there soon."

Avery walks away, and I can't help but watch her go. The way her body sways draws me in. She turns back slightly and catches me staring at her; who fucking cares at this point. We both know we have a slight problem.

As I watch Avery disappear, Missy Jenkins comes up to me.

I fucking hate dealing with these women. Women like Missy never have been my type, even when I was fucking almost anything with tits and a pussy.

"Father Lachlan, I couldn't help but overhear. If you need help with the gala, you should have asked me," she purrs before continuing.

She's eye fucking me without shame or a care in the world in front of the few remaining parishioners who are talking nearby.

"I own an interior design firm that handles so many of our congregation members' office and home designs, including Avery's own house. Her husband hasn't trusted her with a redesign because of how beautiful my work is," she muses.

Missy's trying to put Avery down. I don't like this one fucking bit. Who cares if any of that is true? I won't let her talk about Avery like this. Not to me.

"Thank you, Mrs. Jenkins, for your concern. I fully trust Avery's taste and decision-making capabilities. I put my full faith in her regardless of that of her husband's."

Missy's mouth drops open as she gapes at my words. She wasn't expecting me to be so sure of Avery and, most likely, wasn't expecting for me to say what I did about her husband.

Fuck that prick. For fucking sure, he's a pair of balls.

"Well…" she stammers, unsure of what to say.

"Good day, Father Lachlan," she finishes snippily.

She flees faster than I thought she would. Off to talk to Elaine Johnson, her sidekick, I'm sure.

I watch her walk down the church steps and… yep, right to Elaine. Missy is something else. They're whispering to each other right now about what I said and no doubt about me staring at Avery as she walked away. Making it as apparent as can be by peeking out from behind their hand-blocked faces in my direction.

I need to shake that off and make my way to the office where Avery's waiting.

"Whoa there," I say to someone who almost runs right into me.

I brace the person's shoulders gently so they really don't knock into me. That's when I realize it's Avery. She's staring up at me with those same doe eyes I've seen before. Only this time, she's looking at me like I'm her savior.

I like this look more than I should be admitting. I want her like this all the time. Looking at me like I'm the only person who she needs.

"Avery," I say softly.

She shivers at my voice. Her body is so responsive to me.

"No one has stood up for me in a very long time," she whispers.

"I'll never let anyone do anything to hurt you."

She closes her eyes, and when they open again, I see that they're glistening on the verge of tears and burning with pure hunger.

In barely a whisper, she says, "If only that could be true."

Fuck me running. What's going on in the life of Avery Matheson?

"We should head this way," I respond.

"Yes, Father Lachlan," she answers in a breathy moan that goes right to my cock.

Maybe there is an exception for when I want her to call me Father Lachlan after all.

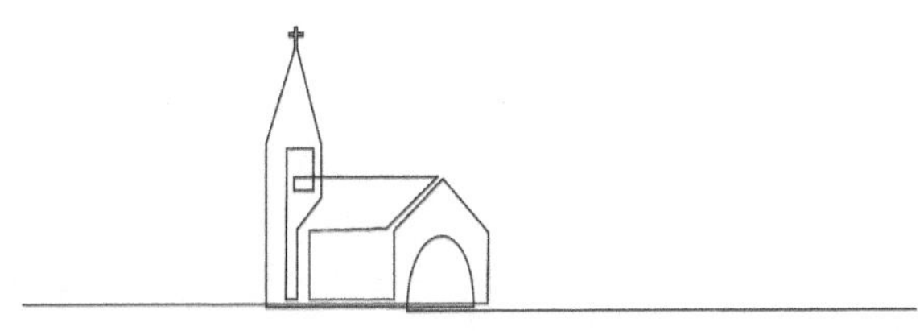

After a successful Sunday afternoon reviewing the gala, Avery came to my office the following Tuesday. I was looking forward to seeing her, and it had only been two days. Something small had shifted between us after I stopped Missy from speaking ill of her.

Wearing another blue dress as she saunters in, she kills me in these.

She starts by reviewing the next set of items we have to make decisions on for the gala. I can't keep my eyes off her. Every time I look at Avery, she's eyeing the paper in front of her with such intensity.

I love the way she looks when she concentrates.

Avery looks up from her paper and blushes before focusing again on the paperwork.

Ever since I was caught in the act of staring at her, she, every so often, tries to steal glances my way too. Avery has no idea I can tell each time she does, and I fucking love it. I'll take them all, really anything she'll give me that I can have without either of us breaking the vows we took.

We're wrapping up for the day, and I'm already dreading going home alone.

I'm watching her now as she organizes the paperwork to put it in the designated binder we're keeping gala-related information in. It is one hundred fucking percent old school.

This church's office technology is not modern at all. Not outside of the donor system we've invested in because that's clearly a fucking priority to Greg. I've been trying to scan and save documents on my laptop, but we don't have that kind of time to waste.

Our eyes connect, and once again, I'm caught stealing glances at my beautiful Goldie girl.

All of a sudden, the folder falls to the ground.

"Oh no!" Avery squeals.

It takes me a moment to realize that the papers and binder are sprawled out everywhere. She was about to put the papers inside the binder when our eyes connected.

We're both now trying to scramble to pick them all up off the floor.

Our hands graze each other as we reach for the same piece of paper. She stills at my touch, and I can't help but do the same.

Fuck.

With my hand on hers, slowly, I stroke the back of her hand gently with the edges of my fingertips. Avery closes her eyes and hums momentarily. She opens them and looks at me purposefully before pulling away.

After finishing gathering the papers, she places them in the binder and sets it on my desk.

I shouldn't have done that. *Fuck me.* I was too tempted by our closeness. I had been wishing to touch her all fucking day.

"Father, a confession in here still counts as something just between you and me, right?"

I nod in response.

I hope she isn't about to break down what little walls we have between the two of us. We both know there's an attraction here, but I can't show her who I truly am. Someone like Avery deserves more than my fucked-up self in any capacity.

"Father Lachlan, I've done what has been expected of me my entire life. I married a man I thought was different from who he truly is. A man who is evil and deceitful. A man who has forgotten me. A man who has been sleeping with his assistant, like a stereotype, while I take care of myself in the shower daily with a vibrator, sometimes twice, if I'm being honest. A man who I should be sad to have come to these realizations about after only two years of marriage, but I am not."

I'm in pain right now listening to this confession. I nod for her to continue as I cross my arms and lean against my desk. Her eyes track my movements.

"This is my confession. I am not a good girl, and I don't care if I'm about to get divorced. About to have a red stain from this society on me. I'm taking control of my life. I won't act on whatever this is between us. We both know that we're feeling some... way... about the other. I've never experienced this before," she pauses before continuing.

"I won't do that to you," Avery finishes with conviction.

She doesn't give me a chance to reply. Before I can say anything, she's walking out of my office. Leaving me speechless as I watch her go.

I hadn't heard anything about the Mathesons getting divorced around the parish to date. I doubt it's making the rounds of her society friends yet since there weren't even whispers about it this past Sunday. A priest always hears the whispers of his congregation.

Avery's confession was the confirmation I needed to hear. I was right about her life. My Goldie girl is lost.

Fuck, she had to add in that part about her under the spray of a shower, naked and touching herself with a vibrator. Why am I so perverted when it comes to all things Avery?

I am taken aback by her confession. People rarely surprise me. Clearly, we both know there's an intense pull between us that we can't act on.

What she doesn't understand, though, is that her words only caused my cock to harden even more than it already was from being in her presence.

Hearing her refer to herself as a good girl and a bad one, too, was the dichotomy of the ideal woman for me. A concept that I can't afford to let be true.

I can't hurt anyone else.

Not someone who actually has a pure soul like Avery.

Her staring up at me with those bright, sad eyes almost caused me to snap and forget all about my rules and history. I wanted to make her mascara run down her face, smear her red lipstick, and have her begging me to punish her for her confession.

I need to seek counsel from my mentor, Patrick, soon before I act on these urges. I just have no fucking clue how I'll explain this one.

I'm glad to hear that she's decided not to stay with that bastard of a husband. Who the fuck cheats on a woman like Avery? Someone out of their damn mind, that's who.

In my short time here, I already know that most of the other women in my parish would stay. Stay for the money, the security, the life.

Not my Avery. She's much braver than she thinks she is.

Fuck.

Coming to St. Peter's is going to prove to be the test of my life.

CHAPTER 10

LACHLAN

I wasn't expecting Avery to return the very next day. She came into my office and pretended like she didn't just twist my heart from her confession.

Avery smiled at me when she walked in, but it didn't reach her eyes.

"Where can I start?"

I know what she's doing. Trying to move past what's happening between us. I have to let this run its course. Surely, after some time, we could get past our attraction to one another.

"Here," I start, handing her a folder of décor problems we're facing. I don't think they're problems, but Patricia and the others on the team do.

"Thanks," she responds.

Flipping through the folder, she nods her head in recognition of the issues. I'm glad she understands what's wrong.

"I see," Avery hums.

"Think you can help?"

"Of course, that's why I'm here," she says with a smile.

Only I know that this isn't Avery's true smile. It's the one I see on Sundays when she's speaking to a number of parishioners. Not the one I've come to pray to witness.

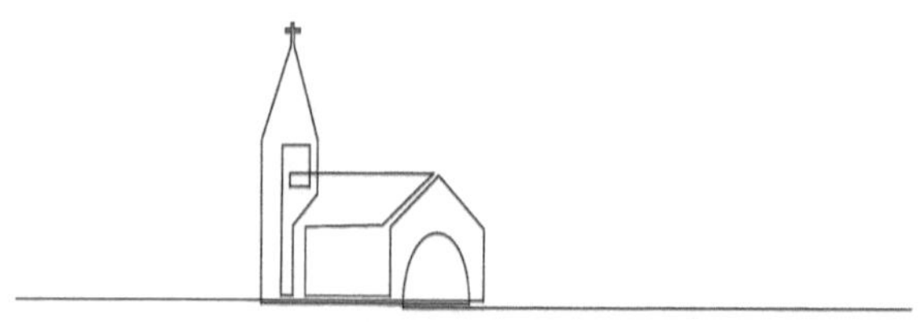

The following week, Avery and I found ourselves in a familiar place. We were finally beginning to get into a steady rhythm. Avery showed up three days last week and stayed after church on Sunday. An unspoken agreement took place between us after her confession.

Now on this Tuesday afternoon, I find myself once again seated across from Avery, working on the usual list from Patricia. The list has grown longer in the short time that Avery has been helping me. I didn't initially really need her help with this gala. However, after some of the decisions she landed on, I was grateful I'd used this as a way to be around her. Even if I can't take Avery like I want to.

Avery really has a great eye for picking out everything we need, and it is all coming together. The team has even started going right to her when she's in my office to approve plans and give additional options.

They never thought to give me any options when this first started; I was basically just given a singular choice and a place to sign. Clearly, I didn't know what I was doing with event planning.

Being in Avery's presence is as hard as I imagined it would be.

Watching Avery across my desk as she stares at the food menu we're trying to finalize now, I notice she pulls her eyebrows together and bites down gently on one end of the pen she's holding when she gets deep in thought.

Avery glances up from the menu options and catches me in the act. She blushes before returning her gaze to the menu once more.

I smirk from being caught. I can't help it, really. I try not to steal glances at her, but when an angel sits before you, you take notice.

Avery starts bobbing her head as if she's finally reached her decision.

"What are you thinking?" I ask.

"I think I've finally got it," she says while continuing to bob her head in excitement.

She removes the pen from her mouth, and how I wish I were that pen. It's fucking pathetic, I am well aware.

"This should be it," she continues as she circles dozens of options on the three pages.

Finally done with her decisions, she places the paperwork on my desk and spins it around to face me before getting up to stand beside me.

Leaning over next to me, she bends down to show me her menu planning. Like I fucking care when I am inches away from the set of tits I wish I could suffocate in.

"Okay, so for the appetizers, the budget should allow us to have the mushrooms, the bruschetta, the escargot, a caviar bar, the oyster station, and a giant charcuterie table—what do you think so far?"

The end of her pen is back in her mouth as she stares at the paperwork, waiting for my answer. Her tits squeeze together as she leans forward slightly.

Avery looks down, and suddenly, awareness strikes. The pen comes out of her mouth slowly before she places her other hand down on my desk.

Our proximity is far too close and way too comfortable. She's inches from my face at this angle. I can't help but take a glance down at her tits again as they press inward together. Avery's dresses give me the perfect opening to test my commitment to the Lord. I fail every time.

She watches on. When I look back up at her beautiful blue eyes, I see yearning replace the determination that was just there.

"Lachlan?"

Her voice comes out as a hint of a whisper.

I swallow thickly, causing Avery to look down at my neck. Clearing my throat, I break us both from this intoxicating trance.

Avery straightens and takes a few steps back.

"They're great, Avery, thank you. Once again, no changes. I'm sure the rest of the menu is the same," I say as I gather the papers to give them back.

She takes them with a smile and nods before returning to the other side of the desk.

My office desk has been acting as a literal and figurative barrier for the past week between us. One that we both rarely cross and never linger on the other's side.

"Great, I'll take these up to Patricia then and be on my way," Avery answers.

I know Patricia is happy to have someone like Avery on the team who's putting her all into this gala. More than she ever needed to.

I know she wants to be around me just as much as I want to be near her, but Avery's talent is really starting to shine brightly.

She packs her bag and takes the menu options as she leaves.

Another day God is testing me—another day I almost fail.

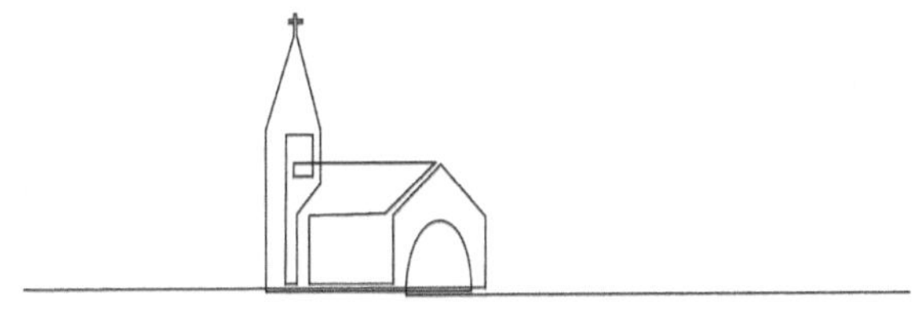

A few weeks go by, and Avery and I haven't put each other in that position again. As much as I think my Goldie girl is beautiful, I've come to realize how smart and capable she is as well. A total package that, in a different life, I would be wondering how I could get a woman like her to fall in love with me.

Avery and I have fallen into a pattern. She visits the same days each week, and now we order lunch or dinner together, usually a take-out place she recommends that I have to try because it's a local favorite, or we order from *our place*, a nearby deli called Papa's Deli that makes the most fucking delicious ordinary sandwich combinations.

"What do you want to do for lunch?" Avery asks as she stretches out against my back wall, scrolling on her phone for a place. On days we know Patricia has extra-long lists coming our way, she's taken to wearing athleisure wear so she can stretch out.

Dressed-up Avery is fucking gorgeous, but dressed-down Avery makes me want to feast on her all day and night.

She looks up at me and smiles. One of her breathtaking smiles I lock away as a core memory when she gives them to me.

Getting up from where she's sitting, Avery rounds my desk approaching me with what I know will be Papa's Deli.

I laugh lightly when I see it on her phone.

"Do you mind ordering today? Here's my card. I'll do the turkey sub," I grin up at her before giving her a wink.

I slide the card in front of where she stands. Avery laughs and swats my shoulder playfully before taking the credit card.

"Big surprise, Lachlan," she responds with her sweet laugh continuing to float around us.

"What can I say? I know what I like, and I stick with it," I say.

Avery's laugh turns into a knowing smile.

"I can appreciate that."

The unspoken lingers between us. Avery laughs again before placing our order.

After a full afternoon, the sun is about to set, and we find ourselves being one of the last people in the parish office, outside of Patricia and Greg.

Being a fucking glutton for punishment, I decide to test taking the next step in our friendship. A friendship is all this will ever be, so I figure let's embrace it. I'm all fucking in on this friendship situation.

"I think I may head to Jackson's, interested in a drink?"

The place we locked eyes after Mass that first day, what I'm assuming to be a favorite bar that Avery goes to.

Trying to play this as nonchalantly as fucking possible, I pick up papers that I don't need and place them in my bag. Like a coward, not wanting to play my cards.

"Now?"

Finally needing to make this a real conversation, I look up to find Avery looking at me with big wide eyes shocked at my request. I can't place whether she thinks this is a terrible or great idea.

"Yeah, I mean, no pressure, it's just been a long day," I come back with.

I'd really kill to be twenty-three-year-old Lachlan right now; he was ten times smoother than this pathetic version I'm portraying.

Avery smiles, and I can't help but mimic it. Thank fucking God. This girl makes me fucking weak for her because of a simple gesture.

"I'd really love that," she answers with a confirming nod.

Avery tucks a piece of her hair behind her ear, and I wish it were me doing it.

"Great, do you want to get us two seats at the bar? I'm going to pop by Father Greg's office on my way out."

"Yeah, that works; see you there," she replies.

Avery gathers up her belongings and leaves me alone in my office.

I let out a long sigh of relief.

"Fuck," I mutter.

Thank fucking God she said yes. To this friend... hang out session? I don't even fucking know what people call it anymore, but I can get excited a friend said yes to a drink. This is what people who are friends do.

Picking up my bag, I discard a water bottle in my recycle bin and lock up before making my way to Greg's office.

Earlier this afternoon I found a note he must have left me the day before. Something about needing to take off Sunday altogether and basically demanding that I perform the first Mass on Sunday in addition to the later one.

Getting closer, I realize his door is closed.

"He's been in there for over an hour with someone not on his calendar," Patricia scoffs from her desk without facing me.

"Really? You don't know who it is?"

That's surprising. Nothing happens in this parish without Patricia knowing about it.

She snorts.

"I've been waiting for him to wrap up so I can leave. He needs some documents mailed," she says, still without turning to face me.

Patricia clicks away on her computer.

If she has been waiting this long, I can't wait around for him to come out. I just sent Avery to save us seats; I don't want to worry her that I won't show up.

"Right, well, I'll just catch him in the morning. If you do speak to him, can you let him know I'll do both Masses this Sunday? He left me a note, and I just found it."

"Sure thing," Patricia replies, still clicking away on her computer.

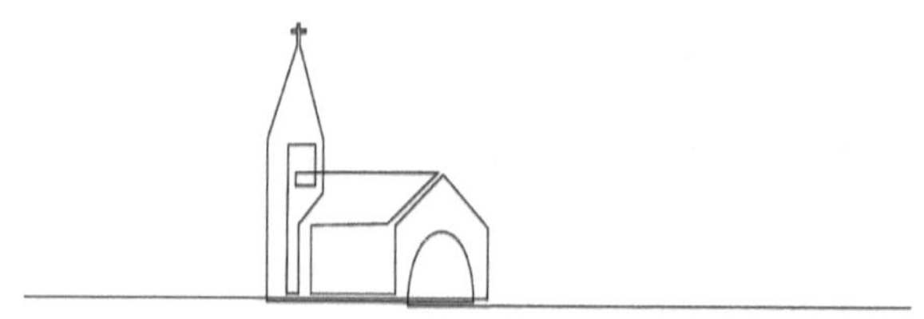

A short walk later, I find myself at Jackson's, staring at Avery with a glass of champagne and a whiskey, sitting in front of the open barstool by her side.

"I see those wheels churning," I say to Avery as I come up to claim my rightful seat.

She's deep in thought. I know something is going on by the way her brows furrow together as she stares at her drink.

"Oh yeah, sorry about that. I've just been in another world lately with everything going on. You must be tired of me always in my head," she quickly shares with a half laugh.

"I could never be tired of you."

Her breath hitches in surprise.

"Oh."

"Yeah. *Oh*." I grin at her before sipping my whiskey.

It's perfect timing as the bartender comes by at that moment, interrupting our stare-down. Avery asks for another glass of champagne before turning her full attention back to me.

"Everything okay when you left?" Avery asks, attempting to change the subject.

"Great. I didn't get to meet with Father Greg, but Patricia made it clear she wasn't going to stop her day to speak with me much," I respond with a laugh.

Avery giggles in response before finishing her first drink.

"She's just so funny," she says.

"If I didn't know that she worked for a church, I swear I would assume she was going to murder me some days," I tease.

"Patricia definitely has a cool past I would love for her to finally tell us," Avery confirms.

We let a comfortable silence take over for a few moments.

The bartender slides Avery's new drink over toward us. Avery takes a small sip of it.

"How long have you been a priest?"

Okay, I can get behind this. We are about to attempt small talk without the gala as our buffer.

"About seven years. I joined the priesthood in my late twenties," I answer.

"That's not long. What made you want to devote your life in this way?" she asks before sipping her drink.

I debate the answer to share with her, knowing I need to tread lightly. It's the most complicated question I could be asked.

"Life sometimes has an interesting way of refocusing you. I needed a new path, and this is the one God gave me."

She looks at me like that answer isn't enough. I knew it wouldn't be, but she won't press the issue. As much time as we spend together, we've been in our own bubble without the distraction of our real personal lives.

"That's really great. And what brought you to Charleston?"

I can't help but smile at her attempting more small talk, but I'll take it. On my walk over here, I was nervous I had done the wrong thing by inviting her out for a drink.

"Another new path from God," I respond as I swirl my whiskey around.

"God... right," she says with a nod before giving me a shy smile.

"You don't believe in God giving you a new path when you need it?"

I can't help but ask as I tilt my head to the side, genuinely intrigued.

This is interesting. I wouldn't have expected her to have doubts like I do, but I guarantee it would catch her more off guard if she learned the truth about me.

I run my hand through my hair. She follows it automatically.

With everything going on in her life, I would have assumed that's what she would be thinking about her situation.

"I shouldn't be discussing this with you," she answers with a light laugh.

"Avery, out of everyone, you should be discussing this with me. Not because I'm a priest but because I can relate to needing guidance."

My sad, broken angel is back in place of the bright light I have come to savor in my presence. I'll take either version, but I hate it when I can't help her find the light.

I can tell the second she decides not to give me her truth on this. I won't press her like she didn't do to me earlier.

"Why were you staring at me in church that first day?" she blurts out.

I can't help but grin, not expecting such an abrupt topic change. One that there is no way she meant to say out loud. Isn't it obvious after all this time together? Avery needs me to give her this small confession.

"I may be devoted to God, but I'm still a man."

A light, rosy blush takes over her face.

"Oh."

"Yeah. *Oh.*"

Avery refocuses herself and begins asking me more questions about my past. Mostly easy ones about my childhood, family, and safe topics that still say so much about who I am. I couldn't help but do the same, wanting to find out as much as I could about the real Avery.

"Thank you, by the way," she finally says after a few thoughtful moments of silence have gone by.

"For what?"

"Offering to be there for me," Avery says.

Fucking Christ.

Offering to be her sounding board, to give her guidance, like anyone close to her should, is causing Avery to break.

She drains the rest of her second drink.

Before we can go too much farther into this, she begins to pull out money from her purse. Two drinks are her limit I've noticed. Avoiding being vulnerable is another.

"I've got it," I say as I gently place my hand on hers.

A surge of electricity goes through me. She tries to pull back slightly, but I can't let go. I rub small circles with my thumb again against her hand blatantly. I find myself staring at the connection while she's staring at me.

"Thank you," she whispers.

"Any time, Avery. I mean it. If you ever need someone to talk to, please confide in me. I'm here for you."

I look up and meet her gaze.

"I'll see you tomorrow, Lachlan."

"It's a date."

I lift her hand up and kiss it. A soft peck to get my fix of my Goldie girl. I instantly hate the loss of connection as I drop her hand to let her walk away.

Slowly, right before the exit, she turns to look at me. I smile widely because Avery just caught me staring at her perfect backside.

She blushes hard in realization.

I wink at her before turning back to the bar to finish my whiskey.

Fucking caught again. As I signal to the bartender that I'll take one more drink and the check, I've come to my own realization about Avery and me.

There is one truth that both of us won't be able to deny.

Today is the day Avery and I will both forever remember as the one when everything changed between us.

I don't think having Avery be just my friend is an option anymore. I think I'd like to keep her for myself.

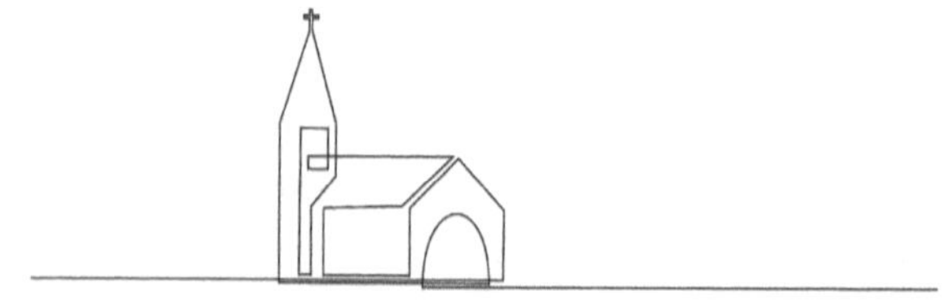

The next day, dressed-up Avery returns to my office. She's holding a box in her arms.

"What's that?" I can't help but ask.

"Samples from Patricia," she says with a small giggle.

Avery plops the box onto the ground. She kneels next to it and starts pulling out the samples of invitations, menus, place cards, and what looks to be any fucking paper item we want to order.

Rolling up my button-down dress shirt sleeves, I find a place to get to work with Avery.

Her breath hitches, and now it's my turn to grin because I just caught Avery staring at my arms once again. Biting her bottom lip, she gently shakes her head to get out of whatever it was she was just thinking about. I have an idea of what that was. I get a sick pleasure out of having her stare at me. Desperate times call for desperate measures.

She sets up the different samples and gets comfortable nearby. I follow her naturally.

I can't help but look back on our transformation. What started as her sitting in the chair across from my desk during that first week has turned into her and me leaning against my office walls on the ground with our samples strewn everywhere.

We are currently sitting shoulder-to-shoulder, and I hate to admit how comforting it is.

Every time my arm brushes against hers, she takes a deep inhale like it's almost too much. I know the feeling all too fucking well. These stolen touches are beginning to not be enough anymore.

I'm craving to deepen the intimacy we've created. I want more, and I'm beginning to think I need more. I don't know what it will mean for either of us if I decide to take the next step.

Avery has made me start to feel again.

Getting to know her during this time together has been different from any relationship I've ever had with a woman before. I dated in college, but nothing serious. Then, in my twenties, I was just about getting laid.

I know she feels the energy that sizzles between us every day we're together. It's getting harder to ignore the small moments that add up to everything. The collection of the everyday life that we've begun to build together.

The way she laughs at my jokes, hums in approval when she likes some things I've picked for the gala, and shows she cares when she listens intently whenever I tell her a story.

I'm beginning to be a fucking sap.

Fuck. She's doing something powerful to me.

"What are you staring at?" she says, looking up at me with a grin.

Avery bumps her shoulder into mine playfully.

"You."

She blushes in response.

"I think we are finally almost there," she continues under my gaze.

"Sunday will probably be the last time I need to come here for gala planning. Everything else after that, Patricia will be able to handle," she finishes.

We both understand what Avery is implying right now. Our time is almost up.

"Sunday. We have Sunday," I say, almost trying to reassure us both that we have time to still make our decision. A decision that neither of us should even be entertaining.

"Yes."

Gazing at each other longingly isn't helping either of us right now. We don't want whatever this is to end, but without the gala, we have no reason to see each other this frequently. I have to come up with something, anything, to keep seeing her like this.

I crave her laughs and smiles; they feel like they are mine to have and mine alone.

In our time together, I haven't wanted to ask her about her marriage. It's felt like an invisible line we both weren't going to cross. I know she's figuring out her plans to leave him, but that's it. I'm not going to make her an adulterer, not when that scum already is one.

Her mouth is parted just slightly, and I want to consume it to make her mine. My cock is stirring to life at the sight of those pouty lips begging to be used.

"Thank you for all the help you've given me. I couldn't have done this without you," I start.

"You know that, right?"

The question I ask hangs heavily in the air.

One thing that has stuck with me since the altercation with Missy several weeks ago is how beaten down it came across that Avery has been treated.

Maybe I'm reading too much into it all, but I want to make sure she knows how wonderful of a person she is. A perfect creature who deserves the world.

She deserves better than Kevin. Better than me, if I'm being honest. I know that, yet here I am, pining to be in her presence every chance I get.

"Thank you, Lachlan. You've given me more than you know by letting me help," she whispers.

She's staring at my mouth as she speaks.

"Fuck," I breathe out as I lean my head back against the wall and close my eyes.

She adjusts her body and puts her head on my shoulder.

I can feel her body moving at an even rhythm. She doesn't want to break contact. I don't want to either. For her, I will, though. I'll show strength that even I don't think I have at this rate. I will not give in.

What Avery needs during this trying time in her life is a friend, not someone chasing her for something more to give. Especially not when that person has nothing to give her in return. But fuck if I don't want her more than anything.

I want to free Avery from this life she doesn't belong in.

Just maybe, I can fix myself with Avery by my side.

CHAPTER 11

AVERY

Resting my head on Lachlan's shoulder just feels right despite the looming tension as we continue to walk this tightrope.

Getting to know Lachlan has felt like a dream.

After the first few times I came by his office to help out with the gala, it became as if I'd always known him. We just clicked.

Yesterday, when he invited me to Jackson's, I was hesitant but excited he finally broached the topic of us seeing each other outside of the parish office and church.

When we were at Jackson's, I wasn't sure how it was going to go. I was surprised that he answered my questions about who he is outside of being a priest.

Lachlan told me about where he grew up and about his parents. His mom sounds like someone out of an idyllic movie you would watch and wish it were your own life. She baked cookies with him every Sunday after they ate family supper around a candle-lit table.

I couldn't help but notice he didn't share much about his relationship with her in recent years. Everything was about the past. He said he funneled all his time into being a priest and prioritized it more than he probably should have in retrospect.

Lachlan told me about his career before becoming a priest and how he loved the challenges he was faced with every day.

I wanted to know why he made such a big switch. I didn't pry further into asking what the real reason was he became a priest. When I initially asked, he avoided the question, and I got the hint that it was a sensitive topic.

Giving your life over to the church is no easy decision to make.

Behind the broody and intense walls he has built up around his heart is someone funny and generous. Someone I like who I get to have any type of relationship with.

As I rest my head on his shoulder, in the here and now, I know that I want him. Father Lachlan O'Connell is my forbidden fruit, ripe for the taking. I know I shouldn't, *I really know I shouldn't*, but that doesn't stop me from deciding to make my move.

I'm no longer the awkward Avery Matheson who can't handle being in his presence. I'm Avery Parker, and I'm taking back my identity starting with claiming the man I want.

I know Lachlan as more than the off-limits, sexy priest, and I like what I've learned. At least this way, if I try to go for it and he rejects me, I'll know that I tried. I can handle the rejection... I think. I hope at the very least.

Lachlan is everything I want in a partner, in a man. If I don't try, then I'll never know what could have been.

I don't care that it looks like I'm jumping from one man to the next. This feeling isn't something someone walks away from and doesn't regret they never tried. It's not just lust—it has the potential to be something bigger, something scarier for my heart if he accepts my offer and we finally face our truth.

In all our time together, we haven't spoken in detail about my crumbling marriage. The only mention was my confession. I know it's part of the line he's drawing in the sand to keep me at arm's length.

He's trying to be there for me, as my friend. Lachlan recognizes that I need a true friend. The only problem is, how can two people with this much chemistry ever just be friends?

The last string tying me to the idea that I shouldn't go for it is I don't want to make him regret me or our time. I know in my heart I am right about how he feels about me, but it's frightening.

Finding your person is scary because you both have to take the final leap together.

Our days have been some of my happiest in a long time.

To everyone else, he is the new guarded priest who is devoted to God. Someone approachable but standoffish. To me, he is a man who has so much love and kindness to give. Standing up for me when he barely knew who I was, not assuming I was just as bad as Missy and Elaine, and the way he interacts with Patricia and the rest of the office staff, he's good on the inside.

I know he doesn't see himself this way; he's tormented by something in his past. Lachlan is troubled. There is a reason he has yet to share with me what has made him this way.

Originally, I was going to wait to make a move on Lachlan until I had final news from my attorney on the divorce plan I had built out. A plan that, any day now, I will finally be putting into motion.

I have learned a lot about Kevin in the past few weeks. Turns out, I was in the dark about quite a few things.

The day he pulled out one hundred thousand dollars, it was to put it toward an apartment on the main downtown strip, King Street. He's been spotted there with his assistant. Apparently, an apartment is better than fucking on my courtyard rug, in his office, or her dingy apartment twenty minutes away from downtown.

I would love to say that's it, but outside of the new apartment and lavish gifts, Kevin is up to something suspicious. My attorney's team is still unraveling it all. What we do know is that some of his financial activity isn't adding up.

On Friday, I am planning to go through his downtown office while he's at a doctor's appointment I had scheduled for him months ago.

There is no way he isn't doing something shifty with this money, and I need to see if I can figure it out. It can't be good, not with the pattern and sums of the withdrawals.

I can't think about any of that with what I have to do now. Not when time with Lachlan is so precious and about to expire. I don't want to waste any moments that I could be soaking in.

Our moments together as just a man and a woman are fleeting. But they are what I hold onto as a reminder of what my life could be after I am no longer Mrs. Matheson.

I love it when Lachlan rolls up his sleeves. He caught me staring earlier, but I couldn't help it. His muscles are a work of art that belongs in a museum. One where I am the only person who holds a ticket.

With a deep breath, I turn and face him. I can cut the last string that binds us to our roles as priest and parishioner.

He's looking at me intently as I gaze up at him.

"Father Lachlan, I think I need to make another confession."

He closes his eyes before exhaling. The torture he knows that I'm about to inflict.

Please don't resist me. Give in. Give in to me.

"What is it, Goldie?" His voice is low and husky, dripping with honey and sin.

I don't know if he realizes he just called me Goldie. It's the first time I've heard him refer to me as that nickname.

I smile. A name he has given me making me more his than not.

"Forgive me, Father, for I have sinned. It has been weeks since my last confession," I begin.

"Go on, Avery," he whispers.

I could bask in his glow and have him whisper sweet nothings to me forever.

I take in a deep breath before continuing.

"I have been having impure thoughts about the new priest at my church," I confess.

Another confession is now out in the open.

With our closeness, I can sense his arousal as he slightly writhes next to me.

Lachlan's eyes open, looking hungrily at me. I move closer to him than should be possible. He nods for me to continue with a newfound intensity burning in his eyes.

"I have fantasized about him for the past few weeks. I have masturbated to the thought of him punishing me for it. Spreading me wide and pounding his cock into me repeatedly as my penance."

His nostrils flare as a small groan escapes.

One of his hands finds its way to my thigh and squeezes it hard. I try to stifle a whimper. His grip tightens, and his fingers dig into me further. I want to be marked up by him. A new-found fixation to see his touch for days to come.

"I have dreamt of getting down on my knees for him," I say, beginning to rise from where we are.

I slowly fall to my knees in between his legs. He spreads them apart to make room for my frame.

"Of putting his full length in my mouth and taking him deeply. Having him fuck my mouth until I am forgiven for my sins."

My hands go to his knees to spread them wider. Leaning forward, I reach for his belt buckle, pausing to allow time for him to stop me.

He doesn't, so I carefully unbuckle his belt.

Slowly, Lachlan gathers my hands in his. Having us stand upright before releasing them. Giving me a better opportunity to move forward with my plan.

I unfasten the belt holding up his black pants before pulling them to the ground, followed by his boxers and then me.

I'm on my knees before him as his cock springs free. I gasp at the sight. I'm greeted by a thick, long cock that makes me nervous and excited all at once.

My confidence is running dry now that I see what I'm working with. I see the pre-cum on the tip and can't help but lick my lips instinctually. I want him badly.

I look up at him, waiting for his direction. I'm no fool. I've been playing at being confident, but I know he's in control.

"Father, am I forgiven for my sins?"

Lachlan remains stoic yet domineering in his stance.

His right hand goes behind my head and grips my hair hard. Pulling me back roughly as he takes control. I gasp at the slight pain but love it all the same.

He strokes my face gently with his other hand. The mix of pleasure and pain from both acts is coursing through me. This is the side of him I was coaxing to come out to play. Praying to experience firsthand.

His stare is powerful as he looks down on me.

He crouches down to meet me at eye level. His eyes darken as they still on mine for only a moment.

Lachlan gazes down at my mouth as he leans closer. I can feel the warmth of his breath dancing on my lips.

This is his decision to make.

Please take the chance, Lachlan.

"Fuck it," he growls loudly right before he crashes his mouth to mine.

Kissing Lachlan is the high I never knew I needed. I love his strength and the force of his hand behind my head as he deepens our kiss.

He breaks away suddenly. I'm left panting heavily as I wait for his next move.

Lachlan stands up tall. I wait patiently in anticipation. That's when I look at his cock right in front of me. He begins taking purposeful strokes along his shaft, causing more pre-cum to gather at the tip.

"Please," I almost beg.

He gives me one of his half smirks before pausing.

"Pretty, greedy girls don't need to beg," he says with a wink.

My mouth opens wide.

"A wanton little thing, aren't you?"

Lachlan grips his cock harder and slams it in between my open lips.

I squeeze his ass with both hands to demonstrate my eagerness as I swallow his cock as deep as I can. I need him to take me as he wants. I want to be his in every sense of the word.

Pulling him in and out of my mouth, I suck his cock deeply. Breaking away to lick up along his length before returning to sucking him in fully again.

His hands go to the back of my head once again as he tightly grips my hair to steady our pace.

"You are beautiful on your knees for me, Goldie."

I hum at the nickname. One given to me, no doubt, because of my blonde hair.

Digging my nails into his tight, muscular ass, I continue to swallow his length. Working it with one of my hands as I bob my head back and forth.

"Taking my cock like the good fucking girl you are," Lachlan says.

His praise only makes me want to work harder to receive it.

I lick, suck, and scrape my teeth along his shaft, repeatedly finding a good rhythm. His hands roam my hair as he takes over, leading the motion of my head bobbing on his cock.

Lachlan's cock hits the back of my throat, and I hear a groan rip through him.

My red lipstick is smearing all over his cock. Staining it as he continues to fuck my face at a punishing pace. My eyes are stinging as mascara runs down my cheeks. I won't give in or ask for mercy.

I look up to find him staring down at me in a way I haven't experienced before.

Lachlan had been holding back in the moments we shared. I know that now. He wants me more than I dared to hope.

"That's it, take every last inch of me," he rasps close to the edge of coming.

I can tell he's about to come as he continues to drive his cock in and out of my mouth.

"I'm going to paint your mouth with my cum," he groans.

I moan loudly against his cock in anticipation. My panties are drenched from giving him head.

"You'd like that, wouldn't you?"

Attempting to nod, Lachlan lets out a satisfied moan in response. His movement is demanding even more so now as he realizes how much I want his cum to fill me up.

I move one of my hands down between my thighs. My sex is aching in need, dying for relief.

Lachlan pulls my hair back hard, causing me to lose contact. My eyes go straight up to his. My spit is hanging off his cock and my mouth. He's made me into his mess, and instead of wiping it away, I want to go back to being his rag doll, sucking him for his pleasure.

"Don't play with what's no longer yours, Goldie girl," he smirks before continuing, "this is my pussy now, and I plan to take care of it."

"Yes," I whimper before my mouth is back on his cock, resuming the fast pace from moments ago.

"I can't wait to see you swallow every last drop."

Lachlan goes harder and faster; his hands frame the sides of my head. He's using me like his fucktoy, and I'm enjoying every second of it.

He stills right before his cum fills my mouth.

I lap it up willingly.

Finally done, I lean back on my hands as I wait for his next move.

I'm on my knees for him. Waiting. Praying. Hoping that this really isn't over yet.

I'm going straight to hell.

He kneels down to meet me. Taking his thumb, he gently wipes my mouth. I suck on his thumb at the right moment causing him to groan.

I'm aching in need of his touch.

His hands grip my thighs and pull my legs forward, causing me to brace myself before I'm forced to lie down completely. The burn of the carpet on my ass stings from my dress flipping up.

He adjusts my legs, extending them and putting me on display for him. Lachlan looks at them both from my thighs to my toes before spreading me wide.

I have never been this exposed before in front of someone. I'm on display for his pleasure.

"Off, Goldie," he demands.

It takes me a minute to realize he means my dress. I quickly pull it over my head, leaving me in my light-blue lace bra and panty set.

He fingers the edge of my panties, teasing me slowly.

"The bra too," he grins.

I'm getting even wetter from just this faint touch. My hips naturally begin bucking forward.

His eyes meet mine.

Reaching back, I snap my bra and toss it to the side.

"You are so goddamn gorgeous; I'm not worthy to see you like this," he begins.

I gasp at his confession. Before I can say anything, he continues. "But I'm not a good man, Avery. I don't care if I'm not worthy of you. I'm taking you as mine now."

"Yes," I murmur.

"You don't want a good man, though," he rasps as he starts to palm my clit with his large, rough hand.

I need more. My body is feeling achy everywhere in need.

"You and your big, beautiful eyes want to be punished for your sins."

Before I realize what's happening, Lachlan rips my panties right off me.

And I'm dead.

Fuck. That's hot.

On any average day, Lachlan makes me feel so many things under his intense stare and proximity, but this unhinged version of him is going to make me come on the spot. I'm surprised I haven't already.

"You aren't forgiven for your sins, Avery," Lachlan starts before continuing. "You're my greedy girl in here. Pushing your perfect tits out for your new priest to pray he gets to worship at their altar."

I can't hold back my breathy moans as he continues to palm my clit, rubbing in circles across the sensitive area with one of his fingers. The motion causes me to wince from pleasure.

"Making me want to beg God that one day I get to feel these long, gorgeous legs wrap around me and this perfect pussy ride my face all the way to heaven," he continues.

Lachlan brings my panties to his face with his other hand and inhales deeply.

"Heaven or maybe I'm destined for hell," he groans right before he leans his body forward and licks up from under my breast to my collarbone.

Brain overload right now. He puts my panties in his pocket before ramming one and then two of his fingers inside me.

I gasp at the intrusion but love it all the same. It's painful and pleasurable all at once. I rock my hips against him, needing more friction.

I know what Lachlan means—this feels like my own personal version of heaven and hell combined.

"You like that, my Goldie girl?"

"God, yes," I moan.

Lachlan laughs darkly as he continues bringing me closer to the edge.

"God's not here, Avery. Only me. Make sure you remember to scream *my* name when I make you come."

I nod frantically, practically begging for him to take me to the place I've been chasing.

"Lachlan, I'm going to come. Please, I need more from you."

"You need exactly what I say. Trust me to give you exactly what you need."

His one hand is still working my clit, and he moves the other to my hair. Gripping a fistful of it in one hand to pull my head back. He leans down and takes an all-consuming long lick of my neck, causing me to moan louder than I should.

Lachlan knows me too well already. He dives in and gives me a punishing kiss to stop the moan from escaping even more.

Lachlan breaks his mouth away first before moving one of his hands to squeeze both of my breasts together, strumming his thumb across my hard nipples.

I can't contain the way my body is vibrating to life from his touch and tongue.

I let out another whimper. Rolling my hips against his hand, I'm almost there.

"Fuck, Lachlan. I'm about to come," I sob as I arch my back.

I'm shamelessly riding his fingers right now. Panting heavily as my hips thrust harder against him.

I'm about to come when he stops playing with my breasts, pulls my ripped panties out of his pocket, and shoves them into my mouth right as I detonate.

"Lachlan," comes out muffled, but I give thanks to my God.

I come hard as the effects ripple through my body. I'm still slowly rocking against his fingers. He doesn't let up as the feeling consumes my body and soul.

After what feels like an eternity, I finally still and come down from the high. Lachlan removes the panties from my mouth and puts them back in his pocket.

I fall further into the floor, feeling limbless. I don't know what I was expecting, but that was the most intense orgasm I've ever had.

Of course, it feels like this with him. We have essentially been having two months of foreplay getting to know one another.

Lachlan brings us both to our feet. He has to keep his hands on my hips to steady me with how sex-drunk I feel right now.

He drinks in my naked body.

"Goldie, I'm not done with you yet."

"You're not?"

"Not even close." He smiles at me like he knows the code to make me burst open all over again. I've never had more than one orgasm at a time.

He picks me up like I'm weightless. That's how I feel right now as I wrap my legs around his waist.

"Heaven or hell?" I grin, delivering his own words back to him.

"Fuckin' heaven on earth, baby." He grins back.

I can feel his hard erection against my folds, and I feel exactly like a greedy girl, wanting to grind against him so soon already.

I whimper when his fingers grip my ass harder as he carries me toward his desk. I can't wait to be decorated from his touch tomorrow.

I know I took my chances begging for him earlier. The sexual tension between us has been unbearable.

I just came harder than I ever have in my life, and I want—no need—more.

His hands move to the outside of my thighs to keep me in place. My wetness is getting on his cock, and if anything, he seems to be getting harder from the sensation.

We're already in sync with our desires. Weaving a perfect web of our limbs.

Lachlan lowers his head to my neck and begins taking small nips before replacing them with his tongue to ease the light stings.

His breath is coming out rigidly as I start to slowly roll my hips onto his erection. With nothing between us, I love the feeling of his shaft teasing my entrance.

My folds start to naturally spread around his cock, causing me to be wetter than before. I don't even know how this is possible.

Not even the crucifix I see centered on the back wall can make me feel like what we're doing is wrong.

"That's it, Avery. Smother my cock with that pretty pussy," he whispers in my ear.

I pick up speed, riding against his length. His cock is getting soaked from me. My head naturally falls back, and I feel my hair sway against my skin.

"Lachlan," I breathily manage to moan.

Lachlan wraps his arms tightly around me as I continue my pace.

Staring back at the cross, I say a silent prayer that Lachlan won't feel ashamed when we're done. That somehow, this is our saving grace.

What we're doing should feel wrong, but I just can't let it when I know in my heart how right it feels. The budding connection we have been building on is coming to fruition.

I return to face him directly.

He is my salvation, and I am his undoing.

I only hope that I'm right and not going to hell for seducing him.

"Goldie, get out of that head of yours and be in the moment with me. I need you to come at least one more time for your penance."

I love his sinful words spoken to me. I never knew I was into this type of role-play.

Lachlan readjusts how I'm positioned so he can palm one of my breasts. His hands are now my new kryptonite. For someone who hasn't been with a woman in years, he certainly knows how to play my body like I'm his instrument.

He's teasing me now by moving his hand slowly over my hard nipples.

"Lachlan, I can't take much more," I pant.

Lachlan's eyes darken at my words.

"You can and you will," he demands.

He keeps going back and forth between grazing my nipples and taking rough squeezes of my breasts.

"I'm going in for a taste of these perfect tits."

"Fuck." I can't handle his mouth on my breast as he sucks hard.

He laughs darkly for a moment and continues to repeat the motion. Letting his mouth come off with a pop just briefly each time before diving back in and onto the other.

We're both whimpering as I grind my hips harder against him, covering his cock even more with my wetness. He moves his hips right back into me, almost in tandem. It feels like he's fucking the life out of me, and he's not even inside.

"That's it, use me. Use me, baby. Take what you need. Fucking destroy my cock with your cum."

My breath is ragged, and I can barely take much more of this. His hand goes from my breast to thread through my hair and pulls me back roughly. Right then, his cock hits just the right spot against my clit, and I feel the rush of finally reaching my release.

Before I have a chance to scream, he crashes his mouth to mine. He's consuming my cries with his mouth. I feel the vibrations pulsing through me.

I was so lost in my own need that I didn't realize he was close as well. I feel spurts of hot, wet cum dripping on my sex and down my legs.

I stop rocking along his cock, breathing heavily.

Our foreheads are a sweaty mess as we lean forward to have them touching.

"You are something else," he whispers.

"I hope that's a good thing," I laugh.

I'm still smiling through hitched breaths as I try to come back to life. I can feel his smile, too, against my lips.

"Goldie girl, that's the best thing."

He gently sits me on his desk, where I finally get a good look at him post-sexual high. Lachlan looks genuinely happy. For the first time since I've known him, he doesn't look tortured or unsettled; he's almost at peace, really.

"I'll be right back," Lachlan says.

That's when I realize that the door has thankfully been closed. Panic starts to set in as I realize we didn't lock it.

Not only did I just seduce my priest, but I could have given the parish office staff quite the show if someone had come in. Thankfully, I don't think many people, if any, are still here.

Lachlan must have just been thinking the same thing because, on his way back to me, he looks at the unlocked door and smirks at me. Flipping the lock so no one can come in.

"Better late than never while we're still naked," he says with a wink.

Lachlan goes to start cleaning me up. I'm feeling vulnerable now, sitting here naked with cum and sweat all over me. I love it, but it still feels like maybe too much for the first time we've done anything sexually.

"I can do it," I whisper while I watch him take the folded paper towel and begin wiping away his cum from my body.

"No, let me. I want to take care of you," he whispers back.

Lachlan must have cleaned himself up a bit when he was getting me paper towels, he's not nearly as much of a mess as I am.

We're both silent as he wipes the red lipstick stains and cum off my body.

"Thank you," I say, finally breaking the silence.

I still see desire swirling in his emerald-green eyes. He kisses the top of my forehead in return.

I can't help but let a small smile replace any concern.

CHAPTER 12

LACHLAN

Be sober and vigilant. Your opponent the
devil is prowling around like a roaring
lion looking for someone to devour.
1 Peter 5:8

I stare at Avery as she puts herself back together. She's breathtaking to watch. Her blonde hair cascades down her back as she faces the small mirror in my office bathroom, examining her splotchy makeup. She's the most beautiful woman I have ever seen.

I may feel guilty about what just happened, but we both felt the intense attraction between us building for weeks. Our connection kept getting deeper as we spent more time together. This was inevitable.

Hearing her confession was the most aroused I've felt in years, maybe ever.

The metaphorical collar around my neck does feel tighter. Something I'm not about to dive into with my Goldie girl still standing before me.

After seeing Avery on her knees, I knew I'd say yes to anything she wanted. Priest or not, no man would be able to say no to a woman as magnificent as she is with those big, beautiful, blue eyes staring up at me with hope.

Hope that I wouldn't say no to her. Hope that I'm not a good priest. Hope that this attraction is as strong for me as it is for her.

It's not that I didn't want to use her like I had done to everyone who came before her. Having Avery suck my cock is a memory that will stay with me forever, regardless of our future. An interesting development is how I want to piece her back together afterward. It's a new feeling I'm experiencing.

Spending so much time with Avery is changing me. I don't want to leave her broken from being with me. My natural inclinations come to a halt when we're together.

Avery reapplies her red lipstick in the small bathroom mirror. The same red that was all over my cock earlier. I have to readjust myself already. It's only been minutes since she was riding the outside of it, and I'm already hard again.

She closes her eyes, and I know she's bracing herself for the impact of our actions. Waiting for me to say something, anything to let her know what direction this is going in.

I may feel guilty, but that doesn't mean I don't want more. "Avery."

Her eyes snap open and over to mine. I see that same mix of emotions I've become more familiar with when our gazes land on one another. I love it all—the lust, the sadness, the fierceness that is in one perfect package, Avery.

I see she's noticing me while I adjust myself again. It's clear as day that I have a bulge in my pants. I'm straining against them, and I just fucking came twice.

Her eyes snap back up to mine, lips slightly parted, unsure of what to say in response.

"Avery."

"I'm sorry."

Avery's expression is one of longing and confusion.

"There is nothing to be sorry for. We were doing what we've been wanting to do. Consider it your penance," I almost plea.

I can't let Avery think any of this is her fault.

She opens her mouth and snaps it closed quickly. I know I'm confusing her more by not saying that this was very wrong of us. That what happened shouldn't happen again. All I know is that I want more, and I can tell she does too. I'm not going to deny either of us that.

"This isn't over, Goldie."

"It's not?" she whispers back to me.

She looks down toward the ground between us. I can't let my Goldie girl think that this is her fault.

I gently place my thumb and finger under her chin, pushing slightly to have her return my eye contact.

"It's not. You can trust me to always give you what you need."

Her breath hitches, remembering the same words that were spoken between us earlier.

"And what do I need, Lachlan?"

Her eyes are trying to look into the depths of mine to find the answers she needs to hear. Answers I know only I can give her after what happened. None of this is going according to my plan, but I've already broken my vow. I can get one more fix of her before I have to end us for good.

"Me."

She gasps and quickly tries to contain her smile by biting her plump lower lip. It's clearly been fucked recently, and a surge of pride courses through me.

Avery speaks before I have a chance to.

I already fucked up by letting this happen. Seeing her like this one more time won't change that fact.

"I'm on birth control, and I'm clean. I checked after I found out about Kevin."

"I'm clean as well."

She blushes, probably assuming I am because I'm a priest.

"I want to see you again. Not like this," I say.

She smiles in return while nodding her head.

"I want that too. How?"

"Come by my house Saturday night. Late. Let's say after nine. I'll leave the back door unlocked."

She stands on her tiptoes and gently presses her lips to my cheek, giving me a light kiss. Warmth spreads throughout my chest. I don't think anyone has ever treated me this gently before.

"Saturday."

I pull my phone out of my pocket and gesture for her to take it.

"Put your number in here."

She quickly does.

I can't help but take a loose lock of her hair and twirl it next to one of her shoulders. She's fucking gorgeous, and I'm the lucky bastard that gets her... for now.

I slowly let go of her hair and trace along her collarbone, then down over the upper part of her cleavage. I try to keep my fingertips as light as possible on her skin.

She lets out a breathy moan in response.

I pull away before we take it any further again. We're most likely alone in the building, but we've taken too many chances already.

I can see myself being all kinds of reckless with Avery.

"Goldie, I'll see you Saturday."

She smiles before heading to the door. I catch her hand before she opens it.

She looks at me with a simmering heat. I know we both feel this magnetism. She makes me want to act out every wicked desire I can think of with her body.

I lower my face to her ear and let out a few breaths before speaking.

"Be my good fucking girl now and make yourself come tonight with the thought of you rubbing that tight little clit all over me. I'll be using your panties to do the same," I say through gritted teeth.

I trace my tongue along her ear, gently nipping at the side. Avery whimpers as her sprawling curls fall back. I lick along the column of her neck up to her cheek.

"Lachlan," she cries out my name in a breathy prayer.

I'm pretty fucked. It's so easy to get lost in Avery.

We both come back to a reality we don't want to face. Avery turns and opens my door. As she walks down the parish corridor away from my office, I can't help but take her in. Her perfect apple-shaped ass is swaying, and I know I'm a tits guy, but fuck if I can't imagine pulling her cheeks apart and licking up her crease.

Almost as if she knows I'm still watching her, she turns back for a second and beams that perfect smile at me before giving me a small wave and disappearing.

It was beyond careless what we just did in my office. Door unlocked, my cock in her mouth, her pussy sliding against my length.

I'm meant to be a man of God, not trying to fuck a married parishioner. I don't want to lessen what's happening between us, but it's the truth. The hard truth we'll both have to face sooner rather than later. I may feel turmoil over accepting my fate as a priest, but that doesn't make me any less of one.

There is just something about her that draws me in. A soul like mine perhaps, or maybe the opposite. Or just maybe my pure girl is the other half of my soul. Heartbreak for one of us is inevitable if we continue on this path.

What was she thinking, sinking to her knees for me in my office? I know the answer. *She wasn't.*

What I didn't want to tell her earlier is that I am, in fact, conflicted about what just happened. I want her, fuck I want her so badly, but I just broke my vows to God. Vows that do mean something to me. I'm just not sure how much or what exactly.

Knowing she broke vows as well doesn't help the situation either. Even with her being just days or weeks away from leaving her husband. We shouldn't have done what we did.

I was meant to be reformed. Changed. Repented.

Instead, I let Avery in. The worst part about it is I fucking know my thirst for her won't be quenched just by seeing her like that one more time. I'm eternally fucked, now that I know what it's like to have a small part of Avery in my life.

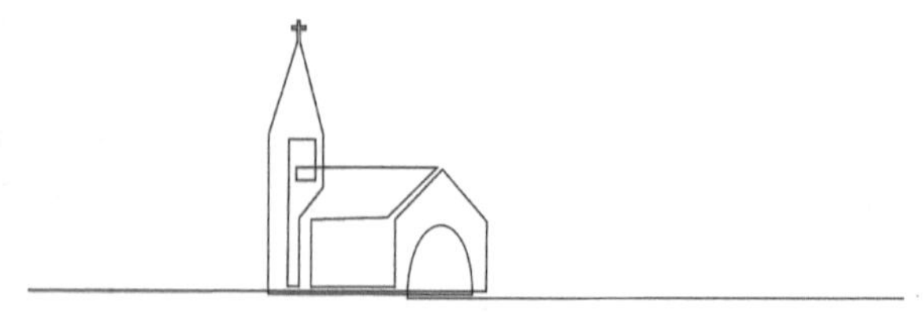

Back at home, I'm lounging in my grey sweatpants and white shirt, looking anything but priestly.

Fuck, I'm already addicted to this woman. I'm trying to distract myself with any fucking show on my television, but it's not working. I can't get enough of Avery. My mind is consumed with thoughts of long, blonde hair, pouty lips, and sad, blue eyes that come to life when she sees me.

What is she wearing right now? Can I reach out to her or is her soon-to-be ex-husband at home too?

I sure as hell fucking hope they don't still fuck. I'm not sure how this all works, but if she goes anywhere near his dick again, I'm going to kill him. I need to find out what's going on with them before I fall over into the deep end. I'm just going to pretend like I'm already not.

All I want to do is text her and see if she's doing what I asked of her earlier today. Is she fucking herself to thoughts of me? Do her perky tits have hard tips as she fantasizes about riding the outside of my cock like it's her gateway to heaven?

I have to know. Regardless of the fact I really fucking shouldn't.

What I should be focusing on are the vows I made to fucking God instead of trying to fall further into Mrs. Avery Matheson. My new addiction after only one taste.

Tonight, I will not be a man with vows to God but rather just a red-blooded one who had a golden-haired beauty riding his cock earlier that day.

How do I approach this with her husband possibly there... It's not too late, so this should be fine if he does ask who she's texting with.

Me:

Avery, it's Father Lachlan. Thank you for the help today.

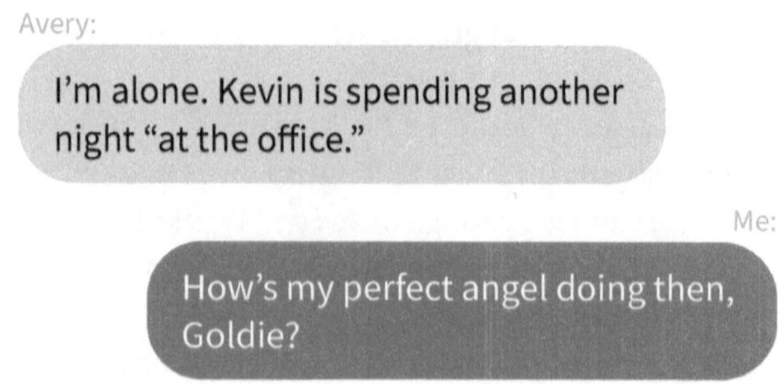

It's way too easy to slip into this new version of me. Fuck it. I'm in this now.

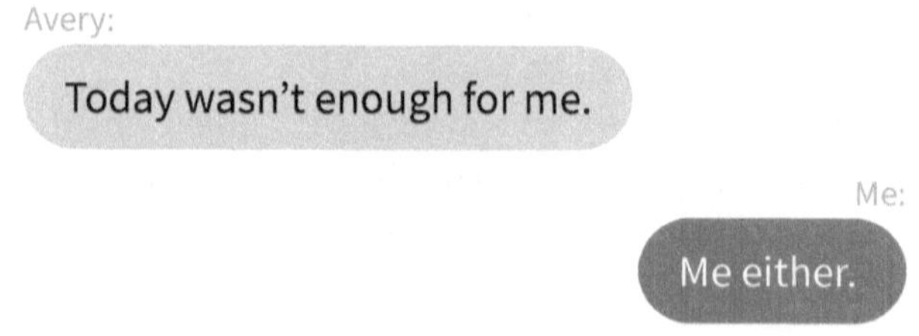

Text bubbles appear and disappear. I wonder what she's debating sending me. This whole situation isn't normal. I get it. I just don't want her to stop right now.

Are you in bed?

… Yes. I was about to do what you asked me to.

I groan and nearly toss my phone out of my hand. She is going to kill me slowly.

Want to watch, Father Lachlan?

Fuck, she really is going to kill me. I know she gets just as turned on by our role-playing.

I always want to watch you.

A few moments go by, and it's my Goldie girl video calling me. I answer immediately because I'm fucking hers already.

"Goldie, are you about to make that sweet, perfect pussy come?"

She hides her face into her side before whispering, "Yes."

Her golden locks are covering part of her face as she turns further into the pillow, blushing.

"Show me, baby. Let me see how wet that greedy pussy is because of me."

Avery's breath hitches before she smiles shyly. She returns to face the camera directly so I can see her on my screen.

"Yes, Father," she moans.

I can't breathe as she moves the phone down, slowly showing me her whole body. She's not wearing a bra because my girl already knows I fucking love those tits, and she's wearing a pair of black lace panties.

"Avery, baby, your body is absolute perfection."

"Thank you," she murmurs.

"Push your pussy lips apart for me—let me see all of you," I groan as I watch her immediately do as I ask.

With the hand not on the phone she shows me how glistening it is already. I ball my hand up and bring it to my mouth because, goddamn, I can't get enough of this.

"Take your finger and massage your clit. Let me see how desperate you are for it, for me."

"Okay, Lachlan, anything for you," she answers, as she begins doing as she's told.

She's rubbing her clit as if she has no control over her speed. Lost in the moment. I understand—watching her right now is the most intoxicating view.

Hearing her breathy moans will forever be my favorite sound. Her skin is starting to gleam as she roughly rubs herself.

"It feels so good; I wish it were you," she cries out loudly.

So close, yet not there. I need to give her more guidance.

"Me too, baby, me too. Put one finger inside."

"Oh, yes," she purrs.

"Harder. Let me see more of you."

She picks up her speed and presses hard on her clit, causing another loud moan to spill from her lips. I wish I could capture these moans with my mouth.

If there is a God, he is shining brightly on me right now. Watching Avery start to break apart from phone sex with me is everything.

I'm fucking hard watching. I pull out my cock and give it rough, long tugs. I need to come after witnessing this magic tonight. That's right, fucking magic. I'm seeing all of heaven tonight.

I'm not about to actually waste the pair of Avery's panties I took earlier. I need to keep the scent of her pussy on them until I can get more. I don't fucking care how wrong or right any of this is.

"Baby, you are the most gorgeous sin I'll ever see. Pull out that vibrator you told me about. Let me see what you do when you're alone."

She reaches beside her and puts the vibrator against her clit.

"I love that you're watching me like this," Avery moans.

"Avery, I would watch you every goddamn night like this if I could. I can't wait to be inside you."

It's true. I'll watch her break apart for as long as she'll let me at this point.

"Come for me, I'm right behind you," I rasp.

"You are?" She pants while continuing to teeter close to the edge.

"Yeah, baby, watching you play with yourself like a perfect dirty angel is all I'll ever need."

My words finally push her over the edge. My Goldie girl likes to be praised; she loves being my fixation.

I follow her moments later after seeing her finally break free. I come on my stomach harder than I have alone in a while. I'm going to let this cum seep into me, it's because of Avery.

She brings the phone back to her face, and I see she's exhausted. Hair all sweaty with pieces sticking to her face, but she is still the most beautiful creature I have ever seen.

"That was something else," she murmurs while trying to find a blanket to cover herself up.

"Don't hide from me. You're always beautiful."

"I've never done anything like that before."

I smile.

"I love that you did that with me."

She smiles widely, and it feels like my heart is slowly opening up even more.

Avery puts on a tank top and the tiniest sleep shorts. They shape nicely around her firm ass. I'll definitely get inside of it, too, eventually. It's begging for my attention.

Who was I kidding that I thought I'd be okay with just one more night with Avery?

After some minutes pass by, I see her get serious by sitting up tall in her bed and looking contemplative at me through the phone. I love her like this too. I can't help but let a small smile reappear.

"Lachlan, what is this that we're doing? I don't want to be the reason you feel guilty about anything that's happening."

"Let's talk about it Saturday night. But you have nothing to feel guilty about, Avery. This is on me. If anything, I should be the one feeling guilty."

"No, there's nothing with him anymore. As of this weekend, I'll be on my own."

"Then Saturday," I finish.

My smile gets bigger at that.

She smiles, too, and now I can't help but let my wide smile take over my face completely.

I sleep peacefully for the first time tonight in ages.

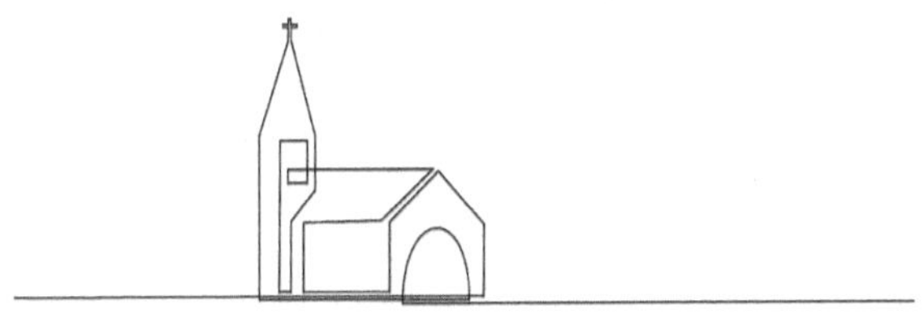

The next day, I come into the parish office to find everyone frantically moving about. It is way too fucking early for this kind of commotion.

"What happened?" I ask Patricia as I sip my coffee.

"It's Greg," she sighs loudly.

Great, let's see what this is about.

"Missy is working with him on the expansion campaign efforts, and she's given even more last-minute revisions. Nothing for you to be worried about with the gala coming up."

I roll my eyes.

"Of course, she isn't happy. What's he doing about it?"

"He's in his office now reworking to accommodate her complaints. He actually asked for me to send you to him as soon as you arrived this morning to get an update on the gala."

She's shuffling papers quickly around her, clearly looking for something.

I head for my office. I need to finish this coffee before I talk to anyone else.

A little later, I finally make my way to Greg's office. I have no idea what is happening with the expansion campaign since my focus has been on the gala taking place soon.

His door is open, so I lean against the frame and give a slight knock to let him know I'm there.

"Greg. I heard you wanted to see me?"

He looks up, relieved that I'm here.

"Lachlan, yes. One second," he answers before pushing his glasses further up his nose as he examines a paper. After making a note he turns his attention to me fully.

"Please have a seat," he says curtly.

"Sure."

I have a feeling I'm not going to like this.

Honestly, if he has complaints about the gala, he can go fuck right off. With all the money we have at the church—coming in outside of any new expansion campaign plans—we should have hired event planners. It's bullshit giving the responsibility to the new priest.

This is the Catholic way, though, not loosening our purse strings any more than necessary.

I take a seat in one of the chairs facing opposite him.

"I've heard from Patricia and some of the other staff that the gala plans have been finalized with the exception of a few minor details. Are you pleased with where it's at?"

"Yes, we are in an excellent spot for it coming up in the next couple of weeks. Mrs. Matheson has been an integral part of the planning process."

He examines me for a few moments. Indecision is on his face.

This should be interesting.

"Lachlan, I trust you. You've only been here for a few months, but I know with your past experience, you can understand what I'm about to explain to you about the Mathesons."

I already don't like where this is headed.

"Of course."

I can't let him see my reaction. I've got to make sure my poker face is firmly in place. I lean back further in my chair, in a relaxed position, with my leg kicked up over my other knee.

Greg breathes a sigh of relief.

"The Mathesons are very special to this parish. As you know, Mrs. Matheson is very generous with her donations."

I nod, urging him to continue.

"Mr. Matheson has been a… silent partner in the expansion efforts campaign."

I nod again.

My plan is to keep quiet and let him do the talking. Something is weighing on him about Mr. Matheson that I don't understand yet.

"Mr. Matheson has asked us to keep this separate from Mrs. Matheson's activities here at the church. I'm letting you know because I need you to not let her know about his visits to my office."

That's the ringer right there. I didn't know it was him, but someone has been coming here at odd hours who wasn't office staff. Parishioners don't usually frequent our offices, but I hadn't given it too much thought.

Yes, it was odd someone was coming in to meet with Greg under the radar, but at the same time, I've been so wrapped up in my time with Avery I didn't fucking care about what anyone else was doing.

Greg must be under the impression I'm suspicious about this behavior; otherwise, I have no fucking clue why he would be bringing it up with me.

"I'm only telling you because of how close his wife has become to the gala. You can't let her know about his time with me."

What the fuck is Kevin doing with the church? This is not normal. I have to tell Avery soon about this conversation. It just doesn't add up any way you slice it.

Maybe it'll be easy enough for her to walk away from whatever it is. Either way, she has to know before she's blindsided by Kevin somehow about this situation.

"Understood."

Look, I'd like to get Avery and me as far away from whatever is happening between Kevin and Greg as possible. I could press for more, but I don't want Avery in this mess any more than she already is.

"Your discretion will be rewarded."

I can't take this conversation. What a fucked-up thing to say to another priest. He knows nothing about the conflictions I already face. What's going on with Avery and me is new, yes, but I feel like my instincts are kicking in when it comes to needing to provide her with protection.

I need to guard her from whatever the fuck is going on between Kevin and Greg.

CHAPTER 13

AVERY

Today is the day I am finally leaving Kevin. The weight of what I'm doing is heavy on me, but I know I'm finally about to break free. No longer will I be the weak Mrs. Matheson; I'm reclaiming my identity. Avery Parker is coming back to life.

Since I found out about Kevin's affair, I've been arming myself for the potential battle to come.

My attorney, Noah, has been my lifeline to a brighter future. Even though I've only recently met Noah, the way he's been not only by my side but my fierce supporter has meant the world to me. I know I can trust him. He's proven that with as much as he and his team have helped me navigate this trying time.

Kevin won't like the embarrassment our divorce will cause in our social circle. Sure, divorces happen; they just don't usually happen without a disastrous reason.

In our way of life, typically, problems are swept under the rug. Either mutually beneficial agreements or empty promises are the answer.

You can fuck whoever you want, but so can I, or the latter, *here is a brand-new Porsche; please forgive me... I promise I'll change.*

Looking back, I don't know how I got to this place.

I hate who I've turned into because of my marriage to Kevin. Now, with a new sense of clarity and my plan in place, I will hit him right where it hurts.

His perfect life of mirrors will be shattered to all of his friends and colleagues. They'll know he can no longer contain his golden trophy locked up alone, bringing it out when he sees fit.

Getting to know Lachlan has shown me what it can be like with a partner—someone who wants you with such ferocity.

I know what Lachlan and I did may seem like the same as Kevin. I get it, really, I do.

I know getting involved with him right now is not the best idea I've ever had. Truthfully? I want to see what will become of us. I just hope he wants to explore whatever this is with me as well, and I'm not some newfound kink he's discovered.

I hope tomorrow, I'll get my answers when I go to his home. Another scandalous act in the hopes of sleeping with the new priest.

Lachlan texted me earlier this morning telling me not to drive my car to his place. I should be hidden if I walk along the main street by his house before walking behind his tall hedge-covered lawn.

Truly the definition of being irresponsible, but I'm discovering I'll do anything for a moment alone with this man. Part of me loves that Lachlan is willing to forgo his duties as a priest for me. The other part wonders if we've gone too far already and should stop acting on our cravings for one another.

Planning the gala with Lachlan has provided some of my favorite memories. I took a risk sharing my confession, and now I'll be taking another to see him once more.

Maybe this path was given to us by God. Maybe it was the Devil himself. I know I shouldn't let this continue, but every touch, moment, and glance breaks me down. I have another confession for him tomorrow night too. If I'm brave enough to share it.

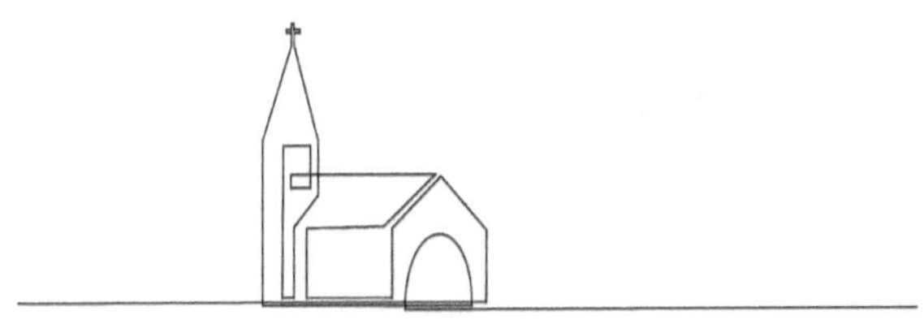

Arriving at Kevin's office, I hope my plan to do one final round of snooping for evidence will pay off. He has a doctor's appointment that I know he won't miss. He had me schedule it for him months ago, and this was the first available opening.

All I have to do is get through potentially seeing his "pick me" assistant and get into his office. Oh, you know the women with the "pick me" vibes. The ones who will do anything for a man's attention. Only men like Kevin actually liked being around them.

I am banking on her going with him to his appointment. He hadn't asked me to go, and somebody would most likely need to drive him back to the office. Who better than the assistant he's fucking to play the role of his wife? Apparently a more apt choice than the one he is already married to.

I just really need her to be gone to prevent being caught. I've already come to terms with the end of my marriage and the possibility of what more will become of Kevin and his assistant.

Pulling open one of the double glass doors, I'm greeted by the office receptionist. Not the personal assistant in question.

I'm confident, knowing what I'm about to do is putting a final nail in the coffin of my marriage. Dressed in my signature color, a navy-blue dress that comes to my knees, and matching navy lingerie set underneath, *just for me*, I look the part of a dedicated trophy wife.

I've got a big plan for today. Whether it's in my best interest or not, today is it. I am bringing Kevin lunch as a surprise to get access to his office. I need an excuse for why I'm here and to get into his personal office without anyone being suspicious.

Since Kevin and my marriage is clearly non-existent, I rarely show up to his office building. Which is why I don't even know the name of the new tart of an assistant he's sleeping with.

The receptionist recognizes me at once. I take a deep breath and plaster on my signature fake smile no one else in Charleston, but Lachlan, knows isn't real.

"Mrs. Matheson," she chirps, startled that I'm here.

What is her name again... Rachel? Rebecca? Rose? It definitely starts with the letter R.

"Hi, yes, is my husband available?"

Keep that smile in place. No one here knows the difference.

"I'm sorry, ma'am, but he's at an appointment right now. Would you like me to contact him?"

"Oh, silly me, I forgot that was today. What a shame. I brought him lunch," I say as I pretend to pout.

I hold up the takeout bag to show that my story could be real.

"He still has the mini fridge in his office, right? I'll just leave it there," I say, pretending as though the idea has just come to me.

"Yes, of course," she answers.

The receptionist gets up from her chair and fiddles with a ring of keys nervously.

"His assistant, Lemon, is out with him, so here is a key to his office to get in. Unless you have one already?"

"Thank you," I reply.

Having my smile firmly in place, I don't answer her question as I take the key and head to his office without another word.

Well, this is a new one. Who knew they named whores after fruits these days? You learn something new every day.

Making my way down the hallway, I unlock his office and quickly shut the door behind me. Finally able to unscrew the smile locked in place.

I have to put this food away to at least make it seem like I was telling the truth. I wonder what Kevin will think when he finds out I came by. I hope Lemon is with him when he finds it.

His office is mostly as I remember, although because of how long it's been, I don't fully recall what it looked like back then.

I do notice he got himself a new couch. It's one of those that can fold out easily. He's clearly slept here. Perhaps before he bought himself that new apartment.

Looking even further around the room, I spot a cabinet nearby with something peeking out. That has to be where he keeps the bedding.

Sure enough, as I pull the cabinet out, there is a pillow and a pile of blankets. Maybe it's leftover from before he purchased his apartment, or maybe he still actually sleeps here some nights. At least this part of his story is somewhat true.

I sit down on the couch and slump forward. I knew by coming here I would find something that would confirm the truth of our relationship. It doesn't matter that I was prepared to see something like this. It's still hard to wrap my head around actually seeing he's this set up.

I don't want to be with him anymore. I know that with every fiber of my being. It's just hard to process seeing the destruction laid out in front of me.

Shaking my head out of my thoughts, I stand up from the couch.

I have to pull it together to get out of here quickly before someone comes to check on me. I need to look everywhere while I have one last opportunity before I'm cut out of his life. I don't want to leave any stone unturned when a battle is surely coming my way.

I'm hoping this office visit will shed some light on what he was doing with the unaccounted-for money or anything about his relationship with his assistant, Lemon, that I don't already know.

Lemon.

When did twenty-eight become so old? Or at least feel old.

Oh, that's right. When your husband starts fucking a new graduate who is barely twenty-one.

This society is terrible. I'm nowhere near the age to even joke about trading me in for a younger model. Yet here I am, being traded in for someone seven years younger because I refused to give him children when our marriage was already in the process of dissolving.

I head to his desk next. His computer or drawers have to give me something more useful than what I've found so far.

Sitting down in his office chair, I'm shocked at what I'm looking at.

It's a photo from our wedding day. My smile doesn't reach my eyes as I look at a memory of our past. That day was a bad omen unto itself. It rained. My dress ripped before walking down the aisle. I got a zit. Okay, but really, I never get zits.

I was so isolated that I didn't have friends to stand up at the altar with me as my bridesmaids. It was a simple affair with only one hundred of Kevin's closest friends and family, plus Fisher, in attendance. I was lucky to have him there. He's still young, only in his late thirties, yet he walked me down the aisle like I was *his* daughter.

I shuffle around the papers on Kevin's desk trying my hardest not to move them too out of place. I'm coming up short looking at this paperwork.

I've got to look at his file folders next.

Nothing of interest here either. Which does make sense since it's the modern age, and most people under the age of sixty probably don't even own a printer.

I hope I can log into his computer. I figured out Kevin's password from his laptop at home by accident. He didn't give it to me, but one day, I saw him typing it in, and I locked that knowledge away for a rainy day.

Today is that rainy day.

Typing in what I pray is his password on this computer too.

LocalsOnly843!

Yes, locals only; tourists get out of our fine city that brings year-round revenue. What a mindset.

Bingo! I'm in.

I'll start with what he's saved locally on his computer and not just on the cloud. I'm seeing way too many files. There's so much here that I don't really know where I should be looking.

As I click around, nothing seems unusual; most file names ring a bell from past discussions about his work. As his wife, I had to have some understanding of what he did at the functions I was expected to attend by his side.

There is one that I don't recognize. I open up a folder called "True Innings Corporation."

Holy fuck. *What the fuck is this?*

It's me. A headshot of mine is staring right back at me. One that he easily could have downloaded from one of the handful of charities' websites that I'm a member of the board.

Why am I in this folder?

I click on another file, followed by several more, until I stop in my tracks. All of the blood has to be draining from my face because I cannot believe what I'm looking at.

I, Avery Matheson, am the alleged CEO of this company. My signature is right there.

But I don't remember signing this... oh no. My face pales even more as I realize what has happened.

Several months ago, Kevin told me he was setting up new investments for us and just needed a "quick sign" on a few pieces of paperwork. It had to have been then.

Traditionally our business manager would be the one requesting anything new for us that required my signature. Although I was unhappy at the time, I didn't realize we were here. In this dark place of no return. It's almost enough to question if I'm also to blame for how we got here. But fortunately, I know the truth.

Kevin is good at pretending in order to get his way. That includes placating his naïve wife, showing off family memories to clients who come into his office, and planting false truths wherever he goes.

True love doesn't fuck someone else on your rug. It doesn't steal money from your bank account. Being in love with someone means you do not convince them to sign paperwork to help you with your schemes.

He got me to be the CEO of this company. I don't know why he did this. What I do know is he doesn't care if I'm collateral damage left in his wake.

I can't let him ruin the rest of my life.

Quickly, I print out everything in this computer file as evidence to take to my attorney. I put my findings in my purse with shaky hands and take a final look around his office.

A truth of mine has finally been set free.

Fuck Kevin Matheson. Avery Parker is back.

CHAPTER 14

AVERY

Blessed is the man who perseveres in temptation,
for when he has been proved he will receive
the crown of life that he promised those who love him.
James 1:12

Back in the house I share with Kevin, I know I have to make a choice. Do I still leave like I planned, or should I stick around and buy more time to look into all of his activities without suspicion? Doing the latter is potentially the smarter option, but I just can't take one more night in my prison. The chance that Kevin could come home any night and get in bed with me makes my stomach churn.

Pretending as if we aren't living a lie.

The information I've been gathering is enough. I can take it all confidently to my attorney and have him look into it. If I use this new fake company as an excuse, I fear I might keep finding reasons to stay trapped in my loveless marriage.

I, Avery Parker, am no longer afraid of this truth.

It's time to face it. I have to leave Kevin so I don't lose myself any more than I already have.

I paid movers to pack up only what was mine in the bedroom; clothes, shoes, purses, even some of my favorite jewelry, and move it to the new apartment I'm now renting.

Knowing I would be doing this, I gave my house manager a paid day off.

I picked a trendy, secure building downtown that had a quick move-in date available. It's young, fresh, and exactly what I want for this next chapter in my life.

Mrs. Kevin Matheson is dead with this last stake in the ground.

With a final check around this house, I am ready to close this chapter.

My phone buzzes in my purse. Pulling it out slowly, I see it's Kevin calling me. I'm surprised he is, but I'm resolved in our ending. I click the side button on my phone to send it to voicemail.

A few moments go by, and I see I have a voicemail now.

Nervously, I click on it and listen.

"Mrs. Matheson, this is Lemon Carter, your husband's assistant. He wanted me to call and thank you for the lunch you left behind. Unfortunately, we had already stopped to eat lunch after I handled his doctor's appointment. His intern said the lunch you brought was delicious. Also, dinner with Frank and Missy Jenkins has been scheduled for next Saturday evening. Your attendance is required."

Click.

That's rich. I don't care if Kevin was the one to ask her or if she felt the need all on her own to piss on her territory to try and show dominance. Kevin is exactly who I think he is.

And I certainly will not be attending dinner next Saturday at the Jenkins residence. He can explain to them why he needs to cancel.

After that message, I decide to leave Kevin a note along with my rings and the most important item... a copy of the courtyard fucking on a USB drive. I had several copies made. I'm not about to let him screw me over with this, at least.

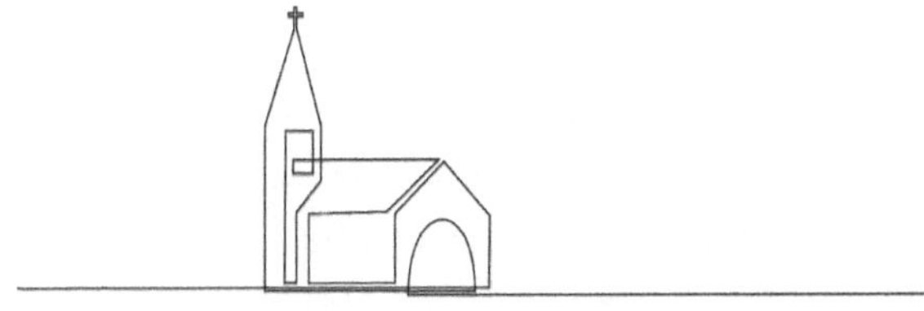

I fold it up and place a singular kiss at the center of the paper so my red lips leave a mark. The last kiss he'll get from me.

This new version of me is one for dramatics it seems.

I'm feeling invigorated as I arrive at my new apartment. This is it. I'm finally moving on from Kevin after months of sneaking around and meticulous planning.

A man with white hair and a round belly greets me at the front of the building. My new doorman. He tips his hat to me as he lets me in. A security guard stands near the reception desk. I smile at them both as I head up to my new apartment.

Stepping inside my tenth-floor apartment feels like a transformation. I finally did this. After all this time, I am on my own.

I put my bag down and take it all in. This is where my new life begins.

A feeling of peace washes over me.

I haven't had enough time to decorate the new space. The walls are empty, and the cabinets are filled with plastic cutlery and paper plates instead of real dishes, but it's mine to do with as I please. I want to take my time and do it right, exactly how I want it to be.

I'll get to it eventually. For tonight, I'm happy to have a new, blue velvet couch set up in front of a gas fireplace and a television show on in the background.

Moving on from Kevin is the right decision. Even if he didn't cheat on me, I'd been living a miserable existence.

I don't have the luxury to relax right now—I need to dig into the revelations I found at Kevin's office.

I begin a simple search online for "True Innings Corporation" and come up with basically nothing. A terrible website with no information and a few public domain documents. No additional noteworthy records or any real sign that it's real. This company is a ghost. It's a shell of a company.

I've got to grab the files I gathered from his computer.

The rest of the night, I read everything I could get printed on time and continue my online search. I have a bad feeling I'm going to come up empty-handed.

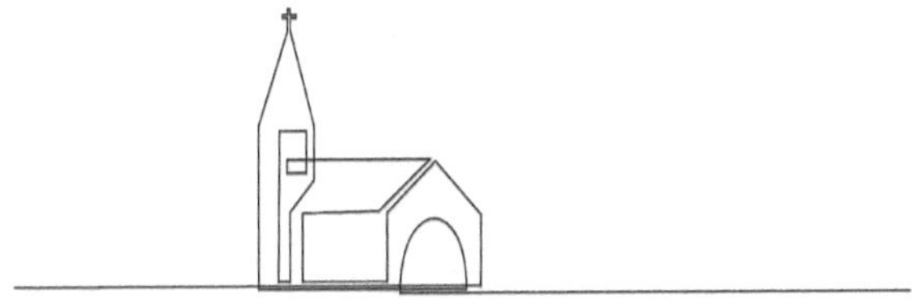

The next day, I'm anxious for Kevin to contact me. I know he's not going to be happy when he figures out that I left.

I wait all day at my apartment to avoid having him scream at me in a public place or have to send a dozen calls to voicemail, but nothing comes. No call, text, or email from Kevin or anyone who would speak on his behalf. It's unexpected.

I don't want to enter into this false sense of security that Kevin won't be reaching out to me. I wish I could assume he won't, but this isn't the Kevin I've come to know after the past few years.

He may not want me anymore, but that doesn't mean he will let his toys out to play without his approval.

Admittedly, I may not understand what game he's playing, but I do know trouble is around the corner for me where he's concerned. The new Avery isn't going to let her soon-to-be ex-husband control her anymore. I will not be anxious that Kevin will be coming for me somehow.

Tonight is about Lachlan and me.

As I begin getting ready, I focus on making sure every inch of me is smooth and moisturized for our night together.

I'm going to put on the new sultry lingerie set I picked up the other day at a boutique off King Street. It's a black lace bra and has matching panties that connect with thigh highs. I'll top it with my new fitted black dress, where I know my cleavage will spill over, and my favorite black high heels with red soles.

If I'm going to hell for wanting to be with a priest, I may as well do it in style.

Lachlan doesn't officially know that I left Kevin. I'm planning on sharing the news tonight in person.

I'll be fine on my own, but my feelings toward Lachlan are growing stronger with each passing day. My confession was the final piece of the puzzle to make us break down our barriers. What we have is unexpected, but it's real.

I just hope tonight he lets that version of himself out. I know Lachlan said he didn't feel guilty for what was happening between us, but I'm worried he could think of it all as a giant mistake we shouldn't be repeating.

The truth of the matter is that I simply want him and hope he feels the same way. I don't know how I'll react if he wants to return to being only friends. I'll probably be devastated if I'm being honest with myself.

I know I don't have a right to be. Lachlan isn't mine; he belongs to God. It shouldn't matter that he sends me to a euphoric state of mind whenever he touches me. The problem is, I wouldn't be able to stop wanting him even if I tried.

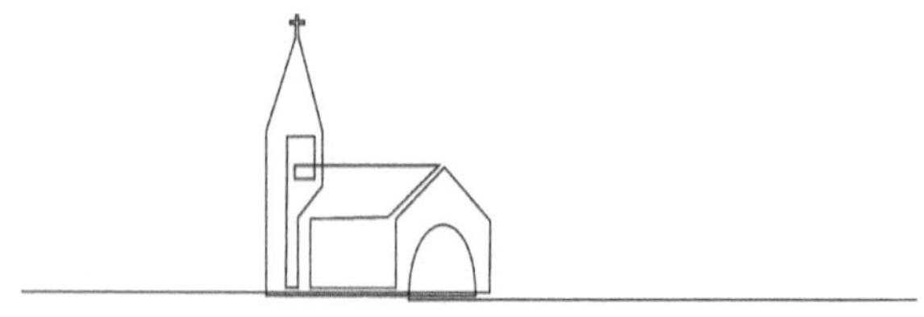

I put a thin black scarf around my head and black sunglasses on. I feel like a sexy cat burglar as I slink around his tall hedges and onto his front porch. I go around the side to the back door he told me I could use.

My new apartment is still an easy walk to his home, even in heels.

This is it, Avery. I take a final breath and try to exude the confidence I want to be real on the inside.

I slowly open the door only to be greeted by dozens of lit candles around his fireplace in the distance. The warm ambiance instantly settles me. *He's trying.*

That's when I begin to drink in the attractive man standing in front of me. Lachlan is dressed casually in dark-washed jeans and a black Henley. I hope he has a drawer of those.

"Hi," I say as I continue to rake up and down his body.

A beaming smile breaks out on his face.

Lachlan is unfairly attractive. I don't think I'll ever get over seeing him like this. He looks like every woman's fantasy, and his smile is directed at me.

"Hi there, Goldie."

Now it's his turn to take all of me in. He looks me up and down repeatedly. His gaze lingers on my chest for a moment before his green eyes find mine. He shakes his head with a smirk before bringing me into an embrace.

"Thanks for having me over," I murmur, feeling content already in his arms.

All of my worries about us are starting to slip away.

"I'm glad you were able to come. I know what the implications are for you. How big of a deal this really is."

He breaks contact with me for a moment to grab two glasses that are on the counter nearby. A glass of champagne in one hand and a whiskey in the other.

"It is, but having you is worth the risk."

I feel electric underneath his gaze.

His eyes can't help but roam the top of my breasts again. I knew this dress was the right choice for tonight. When we were intimate, I noticed he paid special attention to my chest and that's on top of the one too many stolen glances he took when we were planning the gala.

"Is that for me?" I ask as I nod toward the champagne glass.

"Yes, Goldie," he replies, handing me the glass as a tendril of his brown hair falls across his forehead.

Before I take the glass, I remove my scarf and glasses and set them on his countertop. He takes a step back and looks me up and down before smiling again.

"You look absolutely sinful tonight. You already know that, though, don't you?"

His head is cocked to the side, and that grin's in place, waiting for me to reply. If he can dish it, he can take it.

"I don't have any idea what you're referring to, Father Lachlan," I tease.

He does a full-body laugh that I can't help but respond to with a smile of my own. His head tilts to the ceiling, and I feel his warmth radiating off him from his laugh.

"Come on, Avery. Let me do this right."

He takes my hand and leads me to the living room, where I spotted the candles moments ago.

There are more lit candles on the coffee table. He has a charcuterie board, a bottle of champagne sitting in an ice bucket, and an extra champagne glass on the table as well.

I'm surprised he has all of this prepared for our first night together. He's a romantic at heart, it seems. My doubts are continuing to be erased the longer the night goes on and it's just getting started.

"This is beautiful."

"As are you, my Goldie girl."

Hand-in-hand, he lowers us both onto his deep-brown leather couch. This place looks nicer than what I was expecting a priest to be given or to be able to afford.

"I see those wheels turning again," he says as he takes a sip of his drink.

"I just wasn't expecting this, that's all."

He scratches the back of his neck. For once he looks nervous about us together. Almost a sign that he is, in fact, human.

"I've been out of practice for a long time, Avery. I've never done anything like this for a woman before."

Seeing a bashful Lachlan is new.

"It's perfect."

Lachlan pulls me closer to him so I'm practically in his lap. His fingers graze the top of one of my shoulders. Such an intimate gesture between two lovers.

"Forget about everything we have to deal with out there. You are mine tonight," he whispers.

His eyes are focused on the spot he's tracing so delicately. A slight gasp comes out of me before I can take it back.

"For tonight?" I can't help but ask.

There is so much I could interpret from that.

"Avery, I'll take you for forever, but I don't think you're ready for that yet. Let's take this one day at a time. Can you do that for me, baby? Take it day by day and see those days turn into something bigger?"

Lachlan is so confident as he says this for someone who is wed to God. He scoops my hands in his and is looking at me so deeply.

"I don't deserve someone like you. I'm trying to be honest with you. We have a lot to work through. I told you, I'm not a good man. There is a lot I want to share with you in time. But I'm not going to pretend that this isn't happening. Do you know what I want?"

"What?" I whisper.

Silently praying the answer is as obvious as it seems but needing the reassurance, nonetheless.

"You."

I can't help but gasp. It's a confession in his own right.

"I want this. I want you, too, Lachlan."

He brings our hands to his mouth and gives mine a gentle kiss.

"Good, the rest we'll figure out together. Day by day."

We spend the next couple of hours talking with each other about our lives, drinking champagne and whiskey, and taking a few bites of the charcuterie board spread.

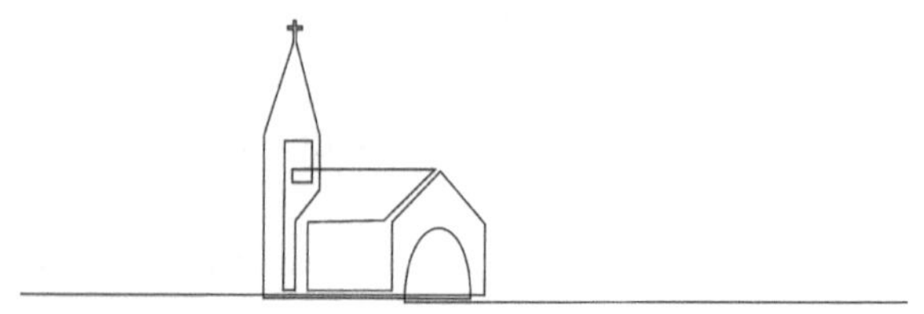

"Okay, next question," I say with a laugh.

Lachlan and I are leaning against the foot of the couch now.

"Oh no, Avery, there is no way I'm letting you just slip past this one," Lachlan teases.

"There is no slipping past anything; I simply said what I said, and now we can move on," I giggle.

Leaning forward I pull a grape from the bunch resting on the board.

"Is that so?" he asks with an eyebrow raised and a smirk in place.

"Yes, it's just a matter of fact," I retort before popping the grape in my mouth to try to conceal my laughter.

"So what you are trying to say is that it is perfectly acceptable to have never tried eating apples in your entire..." he trails off, teasing me.

"Twenty-eight years of existence? And no allergy. You do realize that the apple is speculated to be the forbidden fruit in the Garden of Eden. I can't let you not try one now that we have this happening," he laughs while gesturing back and forth between us.

"Are you implying you're the forbidden fruit, Father Lachlan? Should I just take a bite out of you?" I manage to say through a fit of giggles.

"Don't tempt your priest any more than you already have," he says with a wink.

Lachlan dashes into the kitchen.

"I know what you're up to in there. Not trying it!" I shout out loudly.

I hear shuffling in the direction he headed. Slowly, I turn my body around to face that area.

"Just one bite, Goldie girl." He laughs from the kitchen.

My body shakes from laughter.

The more we share the more I know what he said is right. No matter how wrong or forbidden this is—Lachlan feels like coming home.

I'm *in like* with my priest. The priest of a religion I don't belong to. One that I don't agree with. The truth of the matter is that I can't look at Lachlan like he's just my priest any longer. He is the man who is slowly sinking into every part of me.

"Okay, fine," I relent with a roll of my eyes while trying to hide my smile.

Lachlan appears from the kitchen area with two different kinds of apples. I couldn't tell you what kind they are.

"I'll go with the green one," I say as I reach my hand out for it.

Lachlan stalks closer to where I'm sitting and tosses it in the air before catching it.

Finally, back to where I'm sitting on the floor, Lachlan takes a seat next to me. Turning to face where he is now, I pull my hand back to me, waiting for what he's about to do.

He smirks before taking a bite of the green apple.

"Delicious," he says with a grin.

Am I getting jealous of a fruit right now? I want to be the only thing Lachlan thinks is delicious.

"I'll try some," I respond coyly.

"Here," Lachlan replies as he hands me the apple.

I take a bite of the tart, green apple right where Lachlan had previously bitten into it.

"Delicious," I mimic with a smile.

Lachlan laughs before going to pour himself another whiskey and me a champagne. I set down the apple on the coffee table before taking the champagne glass from his outstretched hand.

"Thank you," I whisper before taking a sip.

Lachlan stares at me as I drink.

"So how did you like it? Missing out, right?"

Lachlan is full-on grinning at me now.

"Best thing I've ever had." I grin back.

I don't think we're talking about just the apple anymore.

Lachlan picks up his glass of whiskey and goes to take a sip. Before he does, I interrupt him.

"You know, there's something else I haven't had in a while. I might not remember the taste of it either," I say while feigning innocence.

Lachlan pauses with the whiskey glass almost pressed to his lips and moves it aside. I lean back to be resting more comfortably against the corner nook of the couch.

"Oh yeah, and what's that, Goldie girl?"

Lachlan eyes me carefully as he tilts his head to the side and wears a devilish grin.

"Whiskey—maybe I'd like a glass of that instead?"

"I see…"

Lachlan inches closer to me—our knees are touching now. I'm the prey, waiting for its captor to pounce.

Getting on his knees, he spreads my legs apart and gets between them. My dress hikes further up my thighs as my sex gets wet from his closeness.

I immediately forget my whole act.

Lachlan turns around and lifts his whiskey off the coffee table. I bite my lip in anticipation, feeling myself soak for what's to come.

"Head back, open that pretty little mouth for me," Lachlan rasps.

It's instinctual for me to do as he asks. Without trying to look, I can hear Lachlan taking a gulp of the whiskey glass and setting it down.

Leaning over me, I see his face hovering over mine. Slowly, Lachlan lets a small amount of whiskey out of his mouth and into mine. The burn of the whiskey goes down my throat. I make a point to suck it down and lick my lips after.

He finishes the whiskey in his mouth as his eyes devour my every move.

"Thank you, Father Lachlan," I moan.

"You're welcome, baby."

Before I have a moment to adjust myself, Lachlan crashes his mouth to mine and consumes my lips. I bring my hand to the back of his head and grip hard at his wavy short hair to give as much as Lachlan is. He breaks away first and brings us both to sitting upright.

Leaning forward, he grabs his whiskey glass and takes another sip right as he winks.

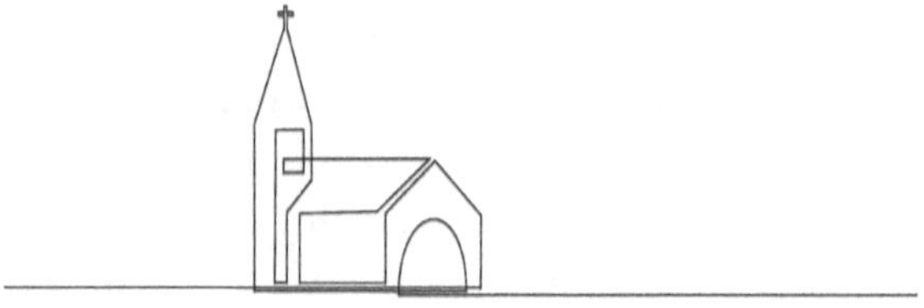

Later in the night, I know I have to give Lachlan another confession.

"I have something important to tell you. I don't want it to ruin the night," I say, getting more serious than before.

I know I have to talk to him about what I did yesterday. Lachlan looks at me with nothing but tenderness in his expression. His body is still relaxed, like anything I bring up can't possibly be a problem.

"Nothing you could say could ruin the night," he replies.

Lachlan laughs lightly before continuing, "Well, almost nothing I should say."

"In that case, this does not fall into that category. The opposite, actually."

I'm absolutely nervous to be sharing this with him. But I feel like talking about my separation will give us more permission to explore what's happening between us.

Deep breaths, Avery.

"I did it. I left him. Yesterday."

I stare up into two twinkling green eyes, crinkling at the sides. His mouth is turning up slightly before he can't hold back his mega-watt smile from taking over.

His smiles are contagious. One takes over my face as well in response.

"Goldie, that right there is about the best news you could share with me."

"Really?"

"Yes, really."

I can't stop smiling at him.

"I know this is new, but I know I've never felt like this before. I want to explore what you and I could become."

He pauses, and I see his forehead crease slightly.

"You didn't leave him for me, right?"

My heart pounds harder than I can imagine right before the feeling of my stomach dropping takes over.

"No, no, of course not. I told you weeks ago about how we were broken," I say almost defensively.

A terrible thought is pulsing through me. I force myself to take my hands away from him and sit up straighter to process what I'm thinking.

"Would it have been such a bad thing if I did?"

He shakes his head, letting those locks fall even more out of place before swooping his hand through them.

"Fuck no, Goldie. I didn't mean it like that at all. I wanted to make sure you did it for you, not for some bastard like me who would take you however you would give yourself to him."

I let out a heavy, thankful sigh.

There is one more unspoken notion we have to address.

"What about you, Lachlan?"

His smile is fainter now, and he stiffens slightly at my question.

Lachlan knows what's coming next.

I'm not the only one with a past I need to work out. It's time Lachlan answers the question that I need to know the truth to.

"I know you said you want to try and explore what this is, and we should take this day by day... but are you really willing to just walk away from the life you built as a priest?"

Lachlan pauses thoughtfully at my question, so I continue.

"Are you ready to test your faith for me?"

CHAPTER 15

LACHLAN

Avery's looking at me with hope in her eyes. Praying that I'm not about to let her down. I can see it written all over her tense frame and worried face.

Her pouty lips are turned down now, taking the place of where her sunshine smile was just moments ago. Those sad, bright-blue eyes are staring straight through my being.

Those eyes. I've come to adore every feeling they express so vividly. Right now, they're saying everything I need to know about how Avery is feeling about her unanswered question.

Leaving the church is a decision I haven't fully come to terms with. It's something that I know I have to do. It's just frankly more complicated than simply deciding to move on.

The church saved me. Patrick saved me. How can I let him down? How can I come to terms with being laicized when I know how much he believed this was the right path for me?

Truthfully, I don't want to lose him, and I fear that leaving the priesthood behind will have repercussions on his and my relationship. He's the father figure I needed when I was lost.

What I do know is that these past months with Avery have been unlike any other relationship I've experienced and the absolute fucking opposite of my time being committed to God as a priest.

I can see myself falling for her, and that's the only real thing I know right now. What I have to base my answer on is that truth.

Growing up, I didn't expect my life to turn out this way. When my da passed away, I took it hard. Anyone would, but I became a fragment of the person I was.

I took my sadness and fueled it into working harder than any of my colleagues were. With the money I was making, I didn't have to live in the sadness; I could do countless drugs and take too many women to forget the truth.

That's my past. It's dark and gritty, and there is nothing holy about it. How will Avery look at me when she hears all of those details? Will she leave me when she finds out about the accident that ripped me open?

My heart isn't ready for that kind of pain again. But one thing I know is that I'm obsessed with my Goldie girl, and for that, I'll give her what I can of me until she pulls away. No matter how much heartache I'll experience when Avery ultimately leaves me when she uncovers my darkest secret.

I'll at least have had my time with the remarkable Avery Parker.

With all of the complexities that are my truth, I decide to go with the simplest answer.

"Yes."

True, no matter how conflicted I am about it. The confliction and guilt I feel about what we've done, and are continuing to do, is my cross to bear and mine alone.

I'll unravel my life here if it means I get a chance with Avery.

Her shoulders relax, and a small smile appears. Clearly relieved by my response. She'll take the simplicity of it, for tonight at least.

"I told you. I want this, and I want you. I'll handle the rest. My faith is separate from the commitment I made by becoming a priest. I can separate the two," I share.

She lets out a long sigh and leans her head on my shoulder.

"Please be honest with me, that's all I'll ask of you on this. I know how much this will weigh on you. If you ever need to stop or change your mind, honesty is all I ask. I want you, but I don't want to hurt you in order for you to be mine," Avery whispers.

Hearing those words spill from her lips makes me know my decision is the right one. She's somehow chiseling away the walls I've put up around my heart. I won't let them get erected again, not when Avery is begging me for the same chance I want.

All night, my plan was to do it right with her after our incident at my office.

It's been harder than I imagined not to consume her entire body right away.

Avery deserves to have someone try and show her what it's like to be cherished and even fucking courted. Her dickhead husband hasn't treated her right in ages.

One of my hands can't help but go to her golden hair and stroke it slowly, twirling the ends and repeating the playful pattern.

Her breath hitches, and I see goosebumps cover her skin. Avery's eyes are shut peacefully, and I see her nipples start to peak through the outline of her dress.

She is so damn responsive to my touch. She longs for me the same way I do for her.

"Avery, you're gorgeous, you know that?"

"I love that you think that."

"I know it."

I gently skim her cheeks and bring my fingers lower to sweep along her neck and collarbone. Avery's skin is so smooth, I'm addicted to the feel of it.

She shivers in response again.

"You deserve to be cherished by any man who dreams of even touching you, but I think I've been patient enough for tonight. Wouldn't you agree?"

Her head lifts, and her eyes open wide. I can see she wants this too.

"Lachlan?"

"Yes, baby?"

"Fuck me."

I pull her closer to me, and she takes the opportunity to climb fully onto my lap. She's straddling me, and I can already feel the dampness from her wet panties on the outside of my jeans.

"Fuck, Avery," I groan.

Her dress hitches up higher in this position, exposing the part of her long tan legs that I've been dreaming about being wrapped around me once more.

I rub my hands along her mostly exposed thighs before sinking them into her tight ass. She squeals as I dig my nails into her flesh.

I pull her dress up over her body and toss it aside onto the ground next to us.

I'm trying to stay in control here, but it's not fucking easy when I get a good look at Avery. Straddling me in her matching lingerie set, only this time with thin black stockings going up to her lower thighs. I'm beginning to realize how much she loves lingerie, and I sure as fuck will not be complaining anytime soon about it either.

Her nipples are pointy, pink peaks exposing themselves through the lace bra. Tiny rosy buds, begging for my touch and mouth. She's gripping my shoulders tightly as she begins making small thrusts.

I take the opportunity I've been dreaming of experiencing again since that day in my office.

Bringing my face to her right tit, I graze my teeth along her nipple slowly. Alternating between licking and sucking for comfort before going in again, grazing my teeth.

I switch to the left tit and back again.

Avery begins rocking harder against my already fully erect cock. I grip her ass tighter, encouraging her to keep going as I focus my attention and mouth on both of her gorgeous tits.

She's letting out soft moans as she continues her even pace.

I know what will get her going even more. Removing one hand from her ass, I move it to the front and begin stroking her clit through her panties.

"Fucking soaked for me already, Goldie?"

"Yes," she moans loudly as she now slides harder into my hand.

Her hands are gripping my shoulders punishingly, and I'll take every last bit of pain that she offers me. She's chasing her pleasure, and it's a fan-fuckin-tastic sight to witness.

"My greedy girl is here to play, isn't she?"

"Yes, Father," she breathily replies.

"Take it, baby. Take whatever you need from me. Make me jealous of my own fucking pants getting your pleasure all over them," I growl in her ear.

Her head falls back, making her tousled, blonde waves sway along her back, skimming my legs. Avery's tits are on display.

"Come for me. Let me see my new fucking heaven, Goldie."

She's close—I can feel her pace increasing even more. Her skin is glistening as she grinds harder against me.

I go back to sucking on each of her beautiful tits through her bra while Avery continues to ride my hand with vigor.

"That's it, baby. Come all over my hand like the greedy girl you are."

She starts to come on top of me, still rocking along my length.

"I'm coming," she cries out loudly.

As she finishes, she slowly brings her head down to my shoulder, where she places a light kiss. Slightly out of breath. It's what I want to witness every single day.

"Fucking perfect," I groan.

I give her a light kiss on the side of her head before moving us both to stand up.

Slowly, I sink to my knees before her. Removing one of her high heels, followed by a thigh-high stocking, before doing the same to her other leg. Leaning forward, I give her pussy a light kiss when I'm finished.

Avery moans as she grips my hair tightly.

Standing up again, I lift her in my arms. She automatically wraps her legs around my waist and lets out a carefree laugh. I move us toward my bedroom and toss her gently on the bed. She lets out the cutest yelp in surprise.

"You can't just toss me around," she says with a giggle.

I smirk.

"Is that so?"

She blushes before nodding as she bites down on her lower lip in anticipation.

"Does my Goldie girl not like being tossed around? I think you like being who I want to worship in this bed." I grin.

I start stalking toward her as she pushes her way back to rest her head on my pillows.

This fucking shirt and my jeans have got to go. She's already ready for more as she watches me undress, studying my body like I'm her answered prayer.

"I think my perfect girl likes being the center of my attention. Are you ready to show Father Lachlan how well you can take what I give you?"

"Yes," she responds eagerly, nodding her head.

I climb onto the end of the bed. In anticipation of my next move, Avery arches her back as I keep coming closer.

"Come on, baby, show me that your perfect pink tits are ready to be played with again."

She giggles as she unclasps her bra before tossing it to the ground. Fuck, she has the best tits I've ever seen. Big and full, the perfect handful. I gently begin to massage both of them. Slowly, I apply pressure to her hard nipples with my thumbs.

We are going to get along just fine if these are the tits I get to worship on my altar forever.

I start kneading them harder. Avery moans as she gets lost in the ecstasy of my touch.

"Such a responsive little thing, aren't you?"

"I love the way you touch me," she manages to respond.

I can't fucking resist these fucking tits.

"You like me playing with these perfect tits, baby?"

She bites her lower lip, trying to contain her louder moan as she nods wildly.

"My baby's perfect tits want my tongue?"

"Oh God, yes, Lachlan."

"No point praying to God, we're in my house tonight."

I dive in headfirst. Bringing my mouth to one of her tits, I suck it hard before going to the next. Back and forth, I'll go all fucking night and let it turn into the day. I can't possibly be expected to pick a favorite to give my attention to.

I remove one of my hands from my favorite playground and start stroking her pussy through the outside of her panties. Adjusting my body to lay next to her as she writhes in pleasure.

"Fuck, Lachlan," Avery whimpers.

"That's it, my greedy girl is back so soon, isn't she? Begging for another release for that aching pussy."

"Yes, Lachlan, yes!" she yells, arching her pussy into my hand.

She's loving every second of this. Her fingers are gripping my pillows tightly as she rides my palm.

"I'm going to get *my* pussy nice and ready to take me after this. You want my cock, baby?"

"I want your cock. I *need* it."

"What do you say?"

"Please, Father Lachlan, I want your cock in my pussy. My mouth. Anywhere you'll give it to me, I'll take it."

Fuck. Now it's my turn to try not to groan as loudly as her. For fucks sake. I'll be taking every hole in her body eventually.

Pausing for a brief second, I pull on the side of her panties and rip them off her tight body. Avery screams in surprise. Bringing them to my face, I inhale my favorite scent before tossing them to the ground.

She moans as she watches me.

Moving back to her pussy, I stroke her clit harder. I desperately want to watch her explode by my hands again before I get inside her warmth. She rocks back against my hand as I insert one finger first, followed by a second.

I use my thumb to continue to rub her clit hard.

"That's it, Avery. Give me another."

I lean down to scrape her nipple with my teeth before sucking as much of her tit as I can into my mouth.

"Fuck, Lachlan. I'm coming, I'm coming!"

Her body stills as the orgasm ripples through her body and all over my hand. She's breathless as she lays on my bed. I pull my fingers out of her and suck the cum from them one by one.

"Fucking delicious, baby."

"God, why is that so hot?" she asks.

I can't help but smile as I stand up to remove my boxers. With my cock out, I give it firm strokes. Avery licks her lips at the sight before biting down on her lower lip once more.

"Are you okay, my Goldie girl?"

She nods before nervously asking me, "Do you think it'll fit?"

"Your pussy was made for me, Avery."

She falls back onto my pillows to recompose herself before leaning slightly upright on her elbows so she doesn't miss me entering her body.

As she leans up on her arms more, I kneel on the bed in front of her—spreading her thighs wide to gain better access.

"Does my greedy girl still want this cock?"

"Yes, yes, I need it in me."

I begin to tease her entrance with the tip.

"Is this where you want me?"

"Yes, Lachlan," she pants, shaking her head up and down repeatedly.

"I'm taking my pussy bare."

"Fuck," she moans loudly.

"I have to warn you, it's been a while, but I imagine I can handle the challenge," I say with a smirk.

She laughs lightly at that. Avery grips my shoulders as I line up my cock against her entrance. I tease her by rubbing the tip along it back and forth.

"Stop teasing me, Lachlan. Put your cock inside me."

"What my greedy girl wants, she gets."

I position myself better at her entrance and push myself inside.

Fuck, I'd forgotten what being inside a pussy is like. Being inside hers is better than anything I've had before. I don't care if I'm going to hell because of it.

Avery winces as I thrust further into her slowly.

"Breathe, baby. Relax. You don't even have all of me in you yet."

"I'm trying—you're just so big. I don't know if I can handle it."

"It'll fit. I promise."

Finally, Avery relaxes after a few more moments, and I push the final few inches inside her.

"So fucking wet and tight. My perfect angel has the tightest pussy I could dream of being inside."

"Lachlan," she whimpers as I thrust in and out.

"That's it, that's my girl taking me so well."

CHAPTER 16

LACHLAN

After giving her another orgasm, Avery is now resting in the crook of my arm. I wasn't ever one for cuddling, but this just feels right with her here.

"I have to leave."

I know she's right; church is tomorrow, and we're on church grounds. Anyone going to Mass could see her if she waited until the morning.

I sigh before leaning into her golden locks and kiss the top of her head.

"I know, Goldie girl. Doesn't mean I have to like it."

"If you didn't live right next to the church, I would chance it, but tomorrow's Sunday. There will be too many people."

"Let's get you cleaned up then. Will you be there tomorrow?"

One of her breathtaking smiles appears as she looks up at me.

"Of course I will. I'll be in the front row with another one of your favorite low-cut dresses on."

"I knew you did that on purpose," I say through laughter.

I head for my bathroom to get a towel to help clean her up. Normally I would be pulling her into the shower with me, but it's already so late. We're taking too many chances as it is.

I come back out of the bathroom to see my Goldie girl looking like a real-life angel on my bed.

Sex with Avery was better than I could have ever imagined it would be. Her tight, wet pussy is my dream come true, but seeing her relaxed waiting for me? Even better than any dream I could have imagined.

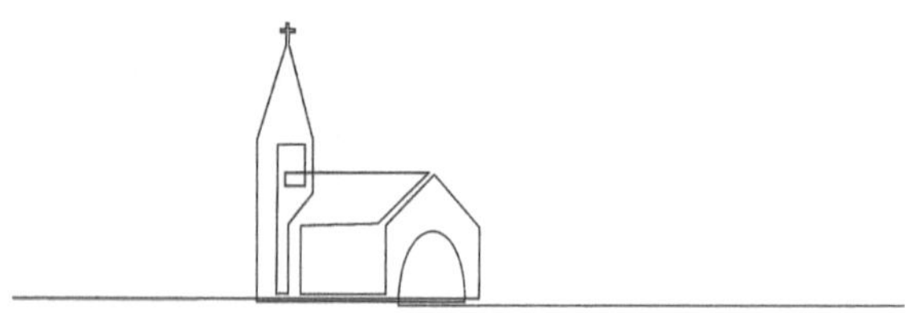

The next day at morning Mass, Avery did as she said she would and wore a low-cut, pale-blue dress to church. I love her in these dresses.

"Good morning, Father Lachlan," Avery greets me.

The priest performing the Mass usually greets parishioners as we wait with the altar servers for Mass to begin.

"Good morning, Avery. I hope you're doing well."

"Yes, Father, I'm feeling very refreshed these days. Very relaxed. It's a wonderful day," she beams.

"Relaxed is good; what kind of de-stressors have you been using? I may have to try them out," I tease.

She blushes.

"Lots of yoga. I find bending to be very helpful in relieving stress. Getting to the right spot just makes a world of difference."

"Thank you for the tip," I wink at her.

"See you after Mass," she giggles.

Avery saunters down the aisle to the front near where I'll be seated. I watch her as she finds her now usual spot. I'm beginning to recognize most of the regulars who attend.

This part of performing Mass isn't something I'm going to miss. One of the negatives to being a priest is needing to greet people even when you aren't in the right mindset.

What I will have to figure out is how to still help people in need when I leave the priesthood. It's what I enjoy most about being a priest. It's one of the ways I repent for my past sins.

What I don't enjoy are the people who come in here just to be seen. Do they even have a relationship with God? I'm already just like them by starting down this path with Avery. I'm no better, even as I parade around as a priest this morning.

After Avery left me last night, I began to question everything. Being with Avery is wrong. Wanting her is wrong.

The guilt I'm facing is for me and me alone. Why does being a priest feel like the absolute wrong decision for the first time since I sat on those church steps in Boston?

Avery did nothing wrong. I should have stopped her in my office that day. I shouldn't have turned my home into a fucking setup that could rival anyone's Valentine's Day plans.

I want Avery, and what I told her last night is the truth. Knowing that just doesn't subside the internal guilt I'm coming to terms with. Catholic guilt is real.

I'll have to figure out a way to move forward because I'm not going to stop what's happening between us. I won't pretend like that's an option anymore.

As I greet Elaine Johnson, sans Missy Jenkins, I notice a flash go before my eyes right down the center aisle. The man is walking quickly, not caring about who's in his way.

It's such a bizarre act to see in a church. Usually, people are on their best behavior.

"That's Mr. Matheson," Elaine whispers to me.

"Mr. Matheson?" I ask her perplexed.

"Yes, Avery's husband. He's never here. I wonder what's going on," Elaine speculates.

Realization dawns on me. Fuck. This is not good for Avery.

I hadn't met him in person yet, so I had no clue he was the person barreling down my aisle until Elaine said something.

I don't know if they've talked or not yet. Avery didn't want to go too far into it with me last night. I understood her reasoning. We have a lot to discuss, but she wanted last night to be about us, not them.

It's so fucked up, but I get it.

This shit is not going to be okay though. Kevin Matheson cannot be flying down my fucking aisle to harass his soon-to-be ex-wife.

"Thank you. We're going to begin."

Elaine's eyes widen before she glances down at her designer watch on her wrist.

"There's still five minutes until eleven?"

"We're starting early."

Because I fucking say so.

He won't pull her out if we are rolling on with this show. I signal to everyone to begin. No one else thinks to question my course of action.

Mass begins, and I walk down the center aisle quicker than usual.

I finally get to the sanctuary and can see Avery. Her slimy husband is sitting in the same pew as her, only at the end.

Someone offered to move their family down so he could sit with her, but Avery shook her head politely.

I hate that fake smile she has to plaster on here. It's a mask. A part of her knows she shouldn't make a scene here for her sake, but she's also trying not to bow down to his demands.

I love the fire in Avery. She's beautiful, brave, and hopefully, soon to be all mine.

Getting through Mass is painful. I try not to steal glances at her now that Kevin is in my church. The urge to protect her from him is overwhelming.

I will have to intervene if he starts causing her problems after Mass.

It's not a good sign of how her divorce is going to go if he's showing up at Mass to confront her after months of me never seeing his face.

After Mass, I begin saying goodbye to the parishioners as they trickle out of the church. Clearly, I'm not the best conversationalist at the moment since I'm trying to spot Avery in the crowd. I'm getting anxious to have her within eyesight.

That's when I find her.

And then him.

His face is filled with rage as she looks up at him stoically. She may have been trying not to cause a scene all Mass, but he clearly gives two fucks with the way he's talking to her in front of everyone.

Avery saunters down an aisle, causing Kevin to now be speaking to her back. He's following closely behind as she walks toward me.

I look to the side to see Missy and Elaine, who are already watching the spectacle unfold. Of course, Elaine found Missy after witnessing Kevin's grand entrance earlier.

They know something bad is happening. Fuck, who wouldn't with the way he's acting? I should have told Avery not to come here today. If only we had talked about what comes next in more detail last night.

Avery finally reaches me, and I can't contain my low sigh of relief. She's here.

"Good Morning, Father Lachlan. Beautiful Mass today." Avery smiles up at me.

Kevin finally catches up to where we are and grabs her by the elbow. Fucking not on my watch. I have to de-escalate the situation.

"Mr. Matheson, it's a pleasure to meet you. I haven't seen you here since I started," I greet him.

Kevin looks disheveled as he processes that I'm speaking to him now.

"Oh right, yes. Pleasure to meet you, as well. My wife and I must be on our way now. We have a very important lunch to attend," he sneers through a fake smile before glaring at Avery.

Not a fucking chance in hell, buddy boy.

I turn to Avery.

"Mrs. Matheson, today is the final day we have to work on the gala details. It's really crucial to have you join me. It's for the church, after all."

She smiles brightly at me. "Yes, that's right. Of course, I wouldn't do that to the church."

She turns to face Kevin head-on.

"If you have anything to say to me, please speak to my attorney. You'll be getting his contact information tomorrow after he files."

She turns back to me, "Father, can we go, please?"

Kevin's mouth is hanging open. He pulls himself back together quickly.

"This isn't over, Avery, sweetheart," he says before spinning on his heels and walking down the steps to finally disappear.

Avery and I lock eyes right as we both hear a gasp.

Turning to see Missy and Elaine. Standing so close to what just happened, enough to hear what Avery just said.

"Mrs. Matheson, let's go to my office," I say with a tilt of my head in the direction of it.

We walk away knowing that this is just the beginning of our problems with Kevin. In order to help her, I need to know the details. I can't remain in the dark any longer.

Our days are just beginning together, but we need to start dusting off the cobwebs from Avery's former life with Kevin.

CHAPTER 17

AVERY

For God did not give us spirit of cowardice bet
rather of power and love and self-control.
2 Timothy 1:7

I knew that Lachlan would eventually want to know more about my impending divorce from Kevin. I just wanted to have a chance to enjoy our time together, even if it was only for one night, without this negativity entering our space.

Truth is, I shouldn't have gone to church today. It was a mistake I should have anticipated since Kevin hadn't reached out to me. It was two days since I left my note.

I wonder about the fury that went through him as he came to terms with the fact that I knew the truth and left.

His precious toy walked away.

The past seventy-two hours have gone by in a blur. I wanted it to slow down, but I couldn't be naïve.

My attorney would be filing the paperwork tomorrow morning, and then Kevin would be getting served. It was all in motion.

Part of me had hoped that Kevin would scoff at my note and not care. He has his shiny, new fucktoy to play with; he doesn't need the tarnished one he's kept locked away in a gilded cage.

It was a blow to his ego, and for that alone, I shouldn't have been so hopeful this would be easy.

Pausing outside of the parish doors, I wait for Lachlan to enter the building first. Formalities and all, with the watchful eyes of my so-called friends staring at us in the distance.

This is going to be everywhere now.

Avery Matheson filing for divorce from her dear husband, the great Kevin Matheson.

The red mark is going to be attached to me forever now in Charleston society. I will wear it with pride. I didn't fall down to him. I stood up bravely and took back my life. They can go to hell for judging me.

Lost in my thoughts, I follow Lachlan into his office. It's time to talk to him about my life with Kevin.

"Avery," Lachlan says gently while shutting and locking his office door. He comes up to comfort me. His warmth seeps into my body as I wrap my arms around his waist tightly, and he returns the embrace.

Being in his arms feels like my sanctuary. With him by my side, I can get through this. The whole situation is just all so much, and I don't want to bring him down with me.

I put my head on his shoulder and take a deep breath. A tear starts to trickle down my face. I don't want to cry about this any more than I already have. Before I can wipe my cheek, Lachlan swoops in and gently brushes it with his thumb.

"Avery, baby. I know this is hard, but I have to know. Why did he show up like this today? What's been happening? Let me in."

Taking another deep breath, I tell myself I can do this.

"I'll tell you everything."

So, I do.

I tell Lachlan all about the past several weeks and my plans. I share details about the video and how I left him by leaving a note. I explain how he's been silent the past couple of days, how I felt embarrassed, and that I didn't think he would come to find me in a public place.

Lachlan just holds me in his arms, wiping away tears as they trickle down my cheeks.

"Avery, I'm so sorry that you've been dealing with this alone."

"Thank you, Lachlan. Thank you for being here for me."

"Always."

I pull my head away from his chest and look up at him.

"You mean that, don't you?"

Lachlan seems to have no reservations about being with me. The truth of it all is that I need to take some time from this, from us.

Time to think and time to breathe.

A warm smile plays on his mouth, and fine lines appear around his eyes. Knowing that I get his true smiles almost makes me want to change my mind about what I know I need to do right now.

"Of course I do. Whatever you need from me, I'm here," he answers matter-of-factly.

Being with Lachlan is a relationship I want to last. I need to come to terms with everything on my own. That I seduced my priest unapologetically. That I left my husband. That now, everyone I know will be spun a story from Kevin, and I have no control over that narrative.

Without breaking eye contact, I say what I need to.

"I think I'm going to take tonight to myself. It's been a rollercoaster of a day. A week. Weeks. Months, really," I stammer.

"I understand. Just because we both feel what we do doesn't mean we can't pause what's happening. No matter what, I'm here for you. I care about you. You know that, right?"

Lachlan's smile doesn't fade after the blow I just landed.

I know the words he's saying are true. He's looking at me as I gaze at him, soaking in his words. I can't help but sigh.

"I don't need a pause on us. That's not what I mean. You've done more for me than you could ever know. I feel like I've known you for a lifetime. I just need time to think. I want you, but this is all so hectic. I have to figure out some things in my head."

"I understand, and I'm here. Always. I'm here for you, Avery. Just remember that."

"I will."

Kevin showing up at church has taken a toll on me emotionally and physically. I'm just drained. As much as I would like to say I've held it together, I think seeing him today just made me realize how much I've been dealing with and how much more is to come.

Life with Kevin was not right for me, regardless of the cheating. I need more out of a partner, and I've found that in Lachlan. I want to be seen, heard, and wanted, and Lachlan gives me all of that and more. It's just bad timing. The worst if I'm being honest.

I'm a terrible person for putting Lachlan in a position to break his vows. I know he said that he wants me, but how can I let him do this?

Everything between us is moving too fast. Love may move at warp speed, but I can't make another big mistake when it comes to my life. I have to figure out a balance between wanting him and facing the truth.

Lachlan is a priest.

When we're together, it's hard to remember that fact. We might both enjoy the kinkiness of it when we're together sexually, but it's not really role-play when that's what his job is. He really is forbidden and off-limits.

But when I'm with him, all I care about are his emerald-green eyes being focused on me and his caring words penetrating my soul.

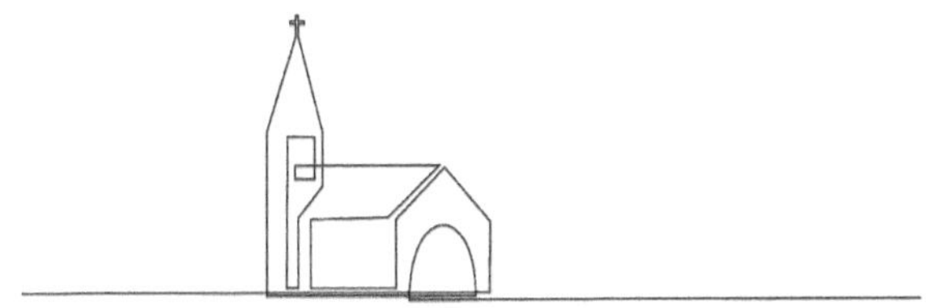

"Avery, I have good news. You have officially filed for divorce from Kevin," my attorney, Noah, tells me on the phone.

"That's great. I'm really surprised he didn't manage to file this morning before we did."

"He didn't make it on time. I was surprised as well not to have more of a situation on our hands," he shares.

"Do you think I'll have to wait a full year before I'm officially divorced?"

Settling on my living room couch, I turn on the gas fireplace as I wait for his response.

"No, despite the rules of South Carolina law, I think we should be in a good place to have this expedited. That's on me to handle."

"I have more to share," I say with a sigh.

"What happened?"

"Yesterday, Kevin came to the church I go to and tried to talk to me; he knew I'd be there. It wasn't necessarily a scene, but he'd been quiet up until then, so I thought maybe he just wouldn't care enough."

"You need to get a restraining order against him to protect yourself. He's radio silent and then shows up where he knows you'll be and can't make a scene? It's already feeling unsafe to me."

"Why? He's not really dangerous per se..." I trail off.

"Avery, I understand, but right now, he's taunting you. I know you may not see it that way, but it could be a good option in your case."

I never thought I'd be in this position. Twenty-eight years old and getting divorced.

A restraining order would just make things messier between us. I still have hope that after the rage settles, he will let me move on. At the very least not harass me again. I'm not asking for any money, the house, or anything at all.

"Let's hold off for now. I promise I'll let you know if anything else happens. I don't think we're there yet."

He doesn't seem happy with this, but I am the client.

"Okay, but please let us know if anything does happen, and remember you have to stay vigilant. This may seem like a small incident, but usually, these types of men escalate their activities to get the reactions they're looking for."

"I will, but... there's more."

I share with him the company paperwork I found in Kevin's office. Noah is alarmed, to say the least. He promises me he'll put a member of his team on it.

I'm grateful I found someone this renowned in the community before Kevin had a chance to ruin my chances of working with Noah. I am paying him a hefty fee to take care of all this. I trust he can figure it out before something happens to me. I want a clean break. Thankfully, I am in a financial position to do that.

I haven't heard from Kevin or Lachlan since yesterday. Last night Lachlan gave me the space I asked for. I want him, and he wants me, but this isn't as simple as we're making it out to be.

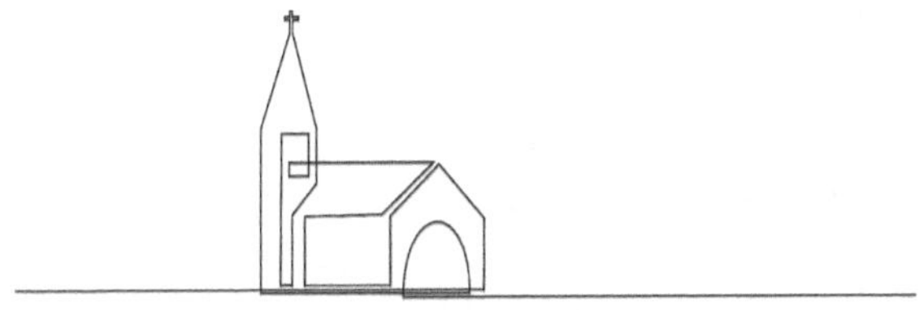

Over the next few days, I focus on fixing up my new place. It's spacious for an apartment. I ordered the rest of the furniture, picking pieces that would get here this week versus anything backed up due to supply chain issues.

Picking out décor that fits my style was refreshing. I mainly stuck to shades of blues that tied together with my new rug. A rug I wouldn't have to worry about anyone but me having sex on.

It's pink and blue with swirls of teal. I love it. It's the opposite of the old-fashioned style of my house with Kevin.

Lachlan hasn't reached out to me yet. I want to be happy about that, but I'm not. I miss him deeply. He clearly thinks I need more time, which I do... I think. Yes, I do. A heavy weight is on my shoulders because of the guilt I feel for seducing Lachlan.

I just hope he's not having second thoughts about me and him. I'm putting myself back together and need to feel better before our relationship goes any further.

Next on my list is figuring out what I want to do with my life. Since I'm no longer a trophy in Kevin's home, I need to remember who I was to form who I will be. I need something more. I'm going to slowly try and figure that part out.

I make a list of my favorite activities. Before meeting Kevin, I was a manager at a small boutique downtown. It wasn't much, but it made me happy to help people.

I also love to read. Reading is my favorite pastime. I read my spicy books with no shame.

Unexpectedly, I loved planning the gala. Not just because of all of the time I spent with Lachlan but I enjoyed the process we went through. Picking out the menu, lighting, invitations—it was a huge undertaking that didn't feel like one to me. I can't wait to see it all come to life soon.

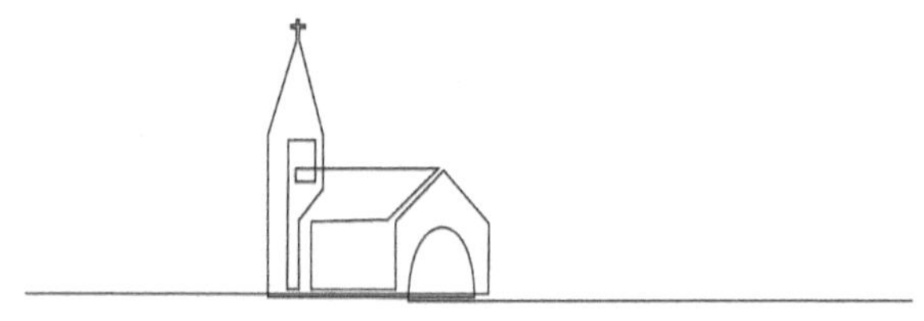

By the time Saturday comes around I'm feeling better about my direction.

I can do this. I can stand on my own. I will apply Lachlan's words of wisdom to my life. Take it one day at a time. If only I could come to terms with that regarding Lachlan.

I decide to spend my Saturday roaming the shops on King Street. It's filled with designer stores, small boutiques, restaurants, and other goods like any bustling downtown is.

Right as I'm leaving my favorite bookstore, I look up to lock eyes with one person I do not want to see this week, Missy

Jenkins. I can't avoid her. If I turn the other way, she'll think I'm embarrassed by what happened on Sunday when I am not.

If I hadn't left Kevin, I'd be eating dinner at her house this evening.

I straighten my shoulders and give her a curt wave as I walk toward her.

"Hi, Missy; how are you doing today?"

"Wonderful. I actually just left a meeting with Father Greg, Frank, and your husband."

She gives me a sly smile that makes me want to shrivel up.

"Or I guess I should say your soon-to-be ex-husband?"

Missy slowly drags out the last part of her question. She knows I know she heard our spat last Sunday. I hate her games.

"That's right. It's unfortunate, but Kevin and I have simply gone our separate ways."

I'm going to just keep this short and try to get out of here fast. I don't want to give her any new ammunition to spread.

"Interesting."

She's baiting me. I have to take it.

"What's so interesting about that?"

I cock my hip out, placing my hand on it.

"That's not what poor Kevin has to say."

It's like pulling teeth with her, and she knows I can't resist this. Not when the gossip is focused on me.

"And what did *poor* Kevin have to say?"

"You left him by a note. He's devastated and doesn't know what he did wrong to lose you. He loves you, he said. Poor, dear Kevin. I hope you know what you're doing is destroying him."

I'm stunned.

He's going to play the victim?

After he fucked his assistant on my new fucking rug, this is how he is going to play it?

The nerve. I won't give Missy what she wants.

"There are always two sides to every story, Missy. You should know that. I have an appointment and must be on my way now. Have a good evening."

I give her my fakest smile and storm through a couple walking past us. My mind is racing, and my heart is pounding. I know I should have expected this. I just keep underestimating how Kevin is taking me leaving him. He's not reaching out to me by phone but instead is showing up where he knows I'll be and spreading lies to our community.

I can't help but laugh maniacally. Anyone passing me must think I'm going crazy. Right when I thought I had a handle on how to deal with this whole situation, something new had to pop up.

Needing to clear my head, I keep walking farther away.

I still haven't heard from Lachlan.

This is not a break—or a pause, I should say—but just some time for me to get a handle on everything happening.

Lachlan deserves someone who he can lean on if he really does uproot his life for me. I know he understands my silence, but it's still hard not being in contact with him for this long. I'm conflicted about how to come to terms with my feelings for Lachlan and the mess that is my life.

In all of the rush and excitement of finding my person, I lost sight that I was hurting him by deciding to share that confession. Knowing that, and our feelings, is difficult to wrap my head around.

I don't believe in Catholicism, but maybe spending time praying to God to see what I should do will help. I'll take anything at this point. Maybe God *can* guide someone like me.

The day turns to night as I keep wandering the streets of downtown Charleston. I find myself now in front of St. Peter's. The lights surrounding it are casting the most beautiful dim glow.

I walk up the steps and open the door.

The church is lit inside, thankfully. Coming to life by the lights framing it. Maybe I should be feeling nervous being alone in a church at this late hour, but I don't. I feel at peace being here.

Slowly, I make my way to the first pew and sit. I stare up at the crucifix and pray. I pray for guidance and grace. I want to move past this stage of my life without looking back with guilt.

I know I should feel worse than I do about seducing Lachlan. The guilt I've been facing all week is really because I don't want to hurt him. He doesn't deserve to have had a temptress with blonde hair in a blue dress saunter into his church and make him hers.

What I feel more than anything is that I know I'm going to be with him if he still wants me. I need to let go of this once and for all.

I, Avery Parker, have fallen for my priest, Father Lachlan O'Connell. Somehow, I found my soulmate while I was in the process of divorcing my cheating husband.

I can't lose Lachlan now.

Finally finding my resolve, I'm ready to face him and promise that I won't do this again. That I'm in this for the long run if he'll still have me.

A loud slam of a set of church doors startles me.

I don't have to turn toward the sound to know who it is.

He's here.

He found me.

He's come to forgive me for my sins.

CHAPTER 18

LACHLAN

I had been sitting on my porch in the dark, getting only the casted glimmer from the sidewalk streetlamps. It was a peaceful and cool night, one of the first since I moved to Charleston.

I'd just taken a sip of my whiskey when I saw my Goldie girl walk past my house. She looked like a beautiful, lost angel. My perfect angel.

After we last spoke, I knew that she had a lot to come to terms with. There's nothing conventional about either of us or our newly founded relationship.

Kevin spooked her that day. It was clear that's what happened.

The past several weeks have been a whirlwind of good and bad for Avery. It had been for me as well. There was nothing easy about our time together. We were both two lost souls in desperate need of salvation.

When I saw her dart past me, I knew what I had to do. It was almost a week since I last saw Avery.

It was time. Time for me to start peeling away my layers. Time to start showing Avery who I can be. I can be her savior and reason to sin. We can be that for each other.

She just has to see the truth—our truth.

I quickly followed Avery to find her entering the church.

The perfect place to meet her savior. Meet me for who I am, who I was, and who I will be.

I gave her some time inside by herself. Waiting patiently for my tortured angel in the shadows outside of an entrance. After some time, I approached the doors cautiously so that I didn't frighten her. I opened them to see she was praying.

Instantly, her body stiffened. She somehow knew it was me after the door slammed closed. My depraved side loved that she could sense it was me. How severely her body reacted to my presence.

While Avery was taking time this week, I was becoming even more steadfast in my resolve that this was my new path.

I knew that becoming a priest was something I never fully fit the mold for. It was a means to an end. One that I don't regret doing. How could I? It led me to Avery.

After Avery left me that Sunday, I realized that I could give being the man my da always thought I could be a chance. It wouldn't be easy for me, but I had followed such wildly different paths my entire adult life; why not try this one? Nothing in my life since my da passed away has been easy.

Maybe being with an angel like Avery is my actual chance at redemption that I have been seeking this whole time.

I requested three days off from Greg, telling him I had a family emergency at home.

Family was one area that Greg did respect as a man of God. He granted it and shifted around the mass schedule. I needed to perform Mass on Thursday and most of the services over the weekend that followed.

In order to be with Avery, I needed to speak to the two people in my life who meant the most to me. If I am going to truly leave the church, and all I had worked toward, I wanted their blessing and understanding.

When I landed in Boston, I went to visit my old church for the first time since I left for Charleston.

It was an odd feeling being back inside the place that both built up and ripped down my priestly walls. My armor from my past life of sin.

I had told Patrick I would be visiting and needed his guidance.

I couldn't explain over the phone because I needed to look him in the eyes to see how he truly felt about it. He's important to me, and for fucks sake, I still just want him to be proud of me. To make sure he knows I understand what I am giving up, but the reason is for a life I haven't ever dreamt was possible.

Sitting in the empty church, I breathe it in. My past, my present, my future.

It's all coming to a head at this moment. I will be telling Patrick that I broke my vow to God, and I am leaving the priesthood.

It's time to make one of my many confessions.

I knock on Patrick's door lightly.

"Lachlan, my boy, it's really you."

His joyful smile almost breaks my heart. He's truly happy to see me after all these months.

"Couldn't leave you around here alone all the time, old man."

He chuckles heartily.

"I'm glad you stopped by. I couldn't believe my ears when you said you were coming back and visiting your ma. She's going to love seeing you, son."

I take a seat in one of his big leather chairs. He sits across from me in the matching one. Patrick does have a desk for meetings, but he always prefers the warmer nature of being in this less formal sitting area.

"I hope so..."

I clear my throat.

"It's been a while," I continue.

"Nonsense, Janet is going to be thrilled."

I nod in reply. Fuck, I'm nervous to be here.

"Tell me now, what troubles you? I know this isn't just a pleasant visit," he replies after a few moments of silence.

Patrick was always good at knowing when a silent pause was needed for me to collect my thoughts.

I laugh at that as I lean back further into the chair.

"No, I'm sorry about that. Really, I am."

"Oh, hush now, I know you, Lachlan. I can see something is really bothering you now. Share it with me."

He gets up as I ponder how to start. Even with an entire plane ride to think this through, it's still harder sitting here face to face with the man who saved me. He pours us two scotches and places mine on the coffee table in between us before taking his seat again.

"There is no way to say this other than to just say it. But I do want you to know that this isn't easy. Not still. It won't be for a while."

"Go on."

He sips his drink, eyeing me carefully.

"That day you found me on those steps, you saved me. You showed me a life full of goodness and hope. Hope is the most dangerous word I can think of still—yet that is what you provided me."

I have to keep my confession going.

"You took the time to work with me and allow me to serve the Lord here while I was attending seminary school. You were patient with my schedule and still gave me a place of refuge. I will never forget that."

His eyes still as he hears the undertones of my words; growing even more serious now as he takes them in. Sipping his drink once more, I still haven't touched mine yet.

"Lachlan, my boy, I did that because everyone is worth saving. Even someone who doesn't see it. Only God should cast judgment. That day was one of the best days in my life because it brought me the son I never had. Don't forget that love knows no bounds."

His words are what I need to hear but make me feel worse all the same.

"Patrick, you know I see you as a father figure, which makes what I have to tell you that much harder."

I clear my throat again before continuing.

"I met someone."

He doesn't look surprised as he slowly nods in understanding. He takes another meaningful sip of his scotch before placing it on a coaster.

"I know."

"What do you mean you know?"

I'm sputtering up at this. How the fuck can he know?

"There was only ever going to be one reason you would leave the church. That reason is love. It's a funny thing, love. You can have all kinds. Love toward me, your ma, this faith, and the communities you serve, but there is a rarer kind of love that most people falsely think they have found time and time again. I knew that if you found true love, you would hold onto it because that is what you have always needed the most."

"True love is what I've needed the most?" I ask bewildered.

Patrick has a small smile, allowing the wrinkles around his face to show his happiness. Shaking his head, he continues.

"Yes and no, my boy. What you've needed is a partner who believes in you enough for both of you. So much that you start to believe in yourself too."

That's it, isn't it? Yes, I am attracted to Avery beyond belief, but her warmth and tender heart are what have me changing my entire life.

"So, when I called you, you assumed I was coming up here to tell you I was laicizing?"

"Lachlan, you so rarely call. Something big had to be the reason why you would be coming up to Boston and finally deciding to see your ma again after all these years."

It's true, and I know it, but that doesn't make me feel any less shameful.

"I'm sorry," I answer, hanging my head slightly.

"God and I both forgive you for your sin," he chuckles.

I return my gaze to his attention, running my hand through my hair.

"Now go. See that ma of yours and do a better job of staying in touch with this old man," he finishes.

I finally reach for my scotch and gulp it down. We both stand at the same time before embracing in a hug.

"Thank you."

I break away first and begin to head out the door.

"Lachlan."

I turn around to face him.

"Some words of advice before you go. Just because you will no longer be a priest does not mean you cannot continue to have God in your life."

I understand what he means. I can still try to be a good man, but this time it will be for Avery and myself, for our future, not because of the guilt that haunts me.

"There is a reason why most weddings share the reading from the book of the Corinthians. 1 Corinthians 13 specifically. Love is patient, and it is kind. It does not envy, it does not boast, it is not proud. It does not dishonor others, it is not self-seeking, it is not easily angered, and it keeps no record of wrongs. Keep that in mind as you move forward. You deserve happiness, Lachlan. You always have."

My eyes are beginning to well with tears. Fuck. I haven't cried since that day on the steps of the church. Now, these tears are for an entirely different reason.

I am going to give happiness a chance.

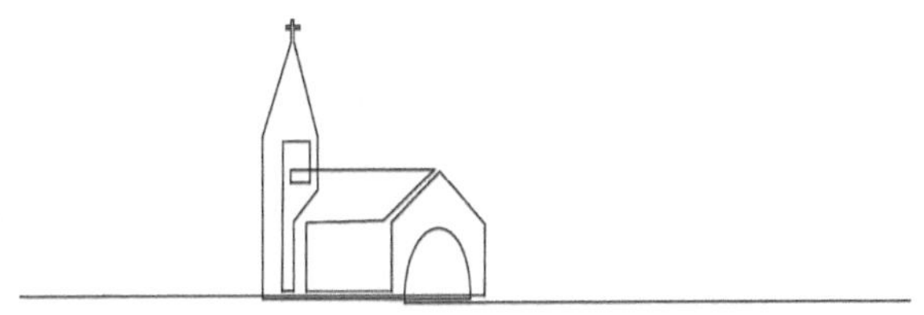

The drive out to my ma's house is about an hour outside of Boston. It's a small seaside town on the coast of Massachusetts.

She stayed in my childhood home long after I left and stopped visiting. It's her personal sanctuary. A place to be reminded of the good memories we shared as a family.

I've been a selfish bastard wasting these years without her. What would my da say if he knew I had all but abandoned her? She needed love just as much as I did. Instead, I left her to fend for herself.

I won't do that to her anymore.

Pulling up to my ma's home is bringing back more memories than I can probably handle.

The first time my da taught me to carve a small wooden cup, and Christmases where my ma went over the top even though it was just the three of us. Even the memory of breaking my arm, trying to climb the largest tree in my front yard.

How long has it been since I came back here, really? Too long.

I knock on her front door. It doesn't feel right to just let myself in after all this time. She isn't expecting me. I thought to call, but I didn't know what to say, and I still don't. I am coming to make amends with her; how do you say that on the phone?

The door opens, and her eyes go wide as she stares at me.

"Hi, Ma."

She pulls me into a hug and squeezes me tightly.

"Lachlan, is it really you?"

She asks as she lets go of me and puts my face between her hands.

"Ey."

"Come in, come in."

The living room still looks the same. Nothing has been updated since I last came home. We both take a seat on the oversized couch, facing each other.

"I'm surprised to see you here. Is everything okay? Tell me everything. It's been months since we last caught up over the phone. What's wrong?"

I take a deep breath and release my next confession.

"That's part of the reason why I'm here, Ma," I say before pausing to look her in the eyes.

"I'm sorry. Nothing is wrong with me health-wise or anything like that. I'm sorry for abandoning you when you needed me the most. I'm sorry for breaking down after Da's death. I'm sorry for not coming to see you sooner. I'm sorry for it all."

My ma's eyes fill with tears.

"Lachlan, I love you no matter what. Always."

We embrace again.

We spend the next few hours catching up on what's been going on in each other's lives. I tell her about how I moved to Charleston and what my life is like. I decide to leave out the parts about Avery for now.

She takes me back to my da's woodworking shed, leaving me alone to spend some time in my former happy place. It is more cathartic than I imagined it would be. I haven't stepped foot in here since he passed away. I just couldn't.

Looking around, I find some of his favorite pieces that he saved and didn't sell. One commonality is that they're all ones we created together and hadn't given to Ma to put somewhere in the house.

After feeling at peace with being back in my childhood home and reconnecting with my ma, I realize it's time to tell her the full truth. It's time for me to tell her about Avery and leaving the priesthood. It's the last confession she needs to hear from me today.

Becoming a priest was something she never expected, but she still supported me. Whatever I needed to do to survive the terrible tragedies I had been dealt. My ma's love is one that I will never take for granted again in this lifetime.

Stepping outside of my da's woodworking shed, I take in the fall scenery. Being back in New England in October is one of the most beautiful times of the year. The leaves are changing color, the temperature is dropping, and there is a peacefulness that swirls in the atmosphere.

My ma has two coffees sitting on the kitchen island when I come back in. She made mine exactly how I like it—black and two sugars. Of course, she remembers.

"Ma, there's something else I need to share with you."

She looks up at me with a small smile.

"Yes, dear?"

"I met someone. It's new, but it's real. Real enough that I've decided to leave the priesthood."

I swallow hard, waiting for her reaction.

"Wow."

My ma's eyes widen momentarily before letting understanding wash over her.

"I know."

"Lachlan, are you sure this is the right decision for you? What if it doesn't work out with this girl?"

"It's not about her in that way. Yes, I think she is the one, but it's more than that. She's shown me that it's okay to grieve, embrace the good and the bad... to find happiness," I start to ramble before pausing.

Ma's eyes glisten with tears again.

"That's all I've ever wanted for you. Happiness. It's a big decision, but you've always had your wits about you. I hope the next time you come to visit me, you'll bring the girl with you."

"I'm hoping that as well."

She smiles happily.

"Alright, now don't you think you're getting away with not telling me all about this lovely young lady who stole my boy's heart," she teases.

"Of course not," I laugh.

"Alright now, go on, tell me everything."

"Where do I even start? She's an angel sent to me from God," I say.

I stayed the next two nights with her in my childhood home. Telling her about my life, Avery, everything. She listens and shares stories of her time as well. I'm beginning to feel free with every step I take on this newly forged path.

My time away made me realize my truth. Not everything is good or evil, right or wrong, black or white. Sometimes, the best decisions are the ones that start in the shadows.

I'm getting my girl.

I was planning on giving her until Sunday when I knew I would see her again. Here she is, though, my sad angel with broken wings. I'm ready to teach her who she belongs to.

I am in love with Avery Parker.

She isn't allowed to run or be scared by our truth.

My Goldie girl is going to see the right path for her is to take the final leap with me.

CHAPTER 19

AVERY

He's here.

My savior has come to claim me. I don't know how he found me, but I'm glad he did.

I am going to be with Lachlan no matter what, as long as he'll still have me. No matter how right or wrong it is that I fell in love with him, my priest. That's what it comes down to, doesn't it?

I am in love with Lachlan O'Connell.

I shouldn't have been as distant as I was this week. He was doing the right thing by not reaching out to me. Still, I should have at least given him the reassurance that we were okay and that I simply needed more time. He somehow knew what I needed even when I didn't.

I now know another one of my truths. I will not feel shame or guilt for the feelings I have for Lachlan. What we have is real.

It is not, in fact, bad timing with the right person. We can work through this as long as we're together. I have a lot to repent for with him.

Lachlan slides in beside me.

I can't face him yet. Not with this range of emotions taking over me. Happiness for what's possible, sadness for time lost, and relief that he's really here.

"Hi, my Goldie girl."

He faces straight ahead staring up at the crucifix, like I was before he walked in.

"Hi, Lachlan."

We don't say anything for what feels like forever. It could be seconds or minutes.

"Avery, I have my own confession to make to you tonight."

I take a deep breath in. We both turn to look at each other. How I missed those deep-green eyes focused on me.

"Avery, you scared the shit out of me this week. I tried like hell not to come after you right away, but I missed you like crazy."

"Lachlan, I've been wrestling with the guilt that I knowingly seduced you. A priest. Someone who should have been so clearly off-limits to me. I mean, look at where we are even now?" I scoff, raising my arms to the altar momentarily before folding them in my lap and continuing.

"I loved your attention and praise. I wanted more of you. I wanted everything. The past couple of months have been better than I ever could have imagined. But you are a priest, and I was trying to leave my husband."

I pause, staring into his eyes.

"I couldn't come to terms with how messy my life was with the need I felt for you. Thank you for the past week. It was terrible for me too. If you'll still have me, I want you, Lachlan; I want you for myself."

"Goldie girl, you're what I want. This is it. Can you be with me?"

"Yes, I can move forward if you still can."

"Thank fucking God," Lachlan says relieved, momentarily looking up at the church ceiling before returning his eyes to me.

Placing his hand behind my head, Lachlan crushes his lips to mine. This isn't a kiss between lovers or partners, this is a soul-consuming claim on my heart.

I missed the taste of his lips on mine.

He breaks the contact before I'm ready for it to be over. My lips burn from the sting remaining.

Lachlan takes my hands in his. We look at each other with love and lust, a new sight I hope to see forever in his eyes.

"Avery, now it's time for my next confession. Another of many to come as we move forward together."

I squeeze his hands slightly in reassurance.

"I'm ready. Whatever you have to say, I'm ready for you."

Lachlan lets out a low sigh at my response. It's true—I'm ready for whatever Lachlan needs to say. I'll accept his next truth, no matter what.

He stares at me deeply before continuing.

"I've told you time and time again that I have a past I need to share with you. I'm broken and bound to a time in my life that has caused me and the people I love an immeasurable amount of pain. I'll share it all with you, I promise. But you have to realize that going into this with me."

"I'll take you as you are, Lachlan. There's no reason to be afraid."

Lachlan's eyes darken as desire takes over. I'm ready for this side of him to come out and play.

"Goldie girl, tonight, you're going to be given a lesson in sin. It took all my patience to know you weren't trying to end what we have. That you just needed space to work everything out in your head."

I suck in another deep breath. I want whatever he needs to give me.

I squeeze our hands together once more.

"Father Lachlan, please forgive me for my sins."

His eyes dilate, and I can feel the heat begin radiating off him. He keeps our hands together as he pulls both of us to a standing position.

He lets go of one of my hands but thankfully holds on tight to the other. Our hands are intertwined, and I love the sensation of being touched by him again.

He leads me up the steps to the sanctuary. Hand-in-hand.

Lachlan gently positions me to face out toward the rows of pews with my back against his front. We are behind the altar, a sacred place I should not be standing at.

Looking out at the pews, I can't help but feel the power from being behind here. The dimly lit rows all seem alive. They are the same pews I sit in every Sunday. Yet right now, being up here with Lachlan, I feel more alive than ever before.

Lachlan lightly grips my shoulders from behind. He's standing so close to me that I can feel the sexual heat rippling between us.

I bite my lower lip in anticipation. I can't possibly moan already. This is more sensual than I was expecting after our time apart.

He gently caresses my shoulders and arms with his fingertips. My body shivers from the touch.

"Avery, you have to repent for your sins. Do you willingly accept your penance?"

"I do," I whisper.

This sensation is everything. My whole body feels like it's burning with longing, excited that this man who is all heat and desire is about to take his wicked way with me.

"My precious angel…"

His fingers now skim the length of my back, picking up and twirling my hair at its ends.

He comes close to my ear and whispers, "Mercy, that's your safe word, baby. It's my turn to show you who I am and how I like to play with filthy temptresses."

Lachlan nips at my ear roughly, causing me to whimper in return.

My whole body shivers again. My panties are already soaked, and we haven't even gotten started yet. It's been too many days since we were last together. I'm craving every part of him.

He drops down low and traces my body with his fingertips. Starting at my legs, he makes his way up along my sides. He gets to my breasts and traces small circles around my nipples.

I arch my back slightly, letting my head fall onto one of his shoulders.

I need more. He isn't going to just give me what I want. He's going to slowly kill me like this. I am paying for the time apart. Giving him the release we both need for trying to act like what we have is anything but love.

The words that we haven't dared to say out loud to each other.

When I saw that Lachlan found me in the church earlier tonight, I knew this is what we have between us.

Love.

Love is the rarest gift anyone could receive, and I found it by tasting the forbidden fruit. Tonight, I am his temptress who has come to seduce him, and I will embrace that title fully.

I move my head off his shoulder and straighten myself. I turn my face up to look at those piercing eyes that I love.

"Father Lachlan, make me pay for my sins. I'm yours to do with what you please. Give me my penance. Give me what I deserve. Give me what you need."

A low groan comes out of Lachlan before he pulls my body even closer to him—wrapping his arm around my waist.

"Fuck baby, I don't know where I'm going to start first. Maybe I'll start by eating that sweet pussy I've been craving or bend you over and make you take your punishment first."

"Yes," I whimper.

I'll take anything and everything.

Lachlan slowly begins pulling down the straps of my dress, letting it finally pool on the floor.

I suck in a deep breath. I'm standing here in a matching white lingerie set feeling so exposed in this empty church. He leans down and presses a kiss to each of my back shoulder blades. I face forward completely to get back into my role.

"You're fucking perfect," he murmurs.

Lachlan slowly removes my panties first. He takes his time removing them, slowly inching them down my legs. The act is so erotic I can feel that I'm getting wetter by the second.

He goes to unclasp my bra next. Before he does, I feel him putting a line of slow and deliberate kisses along the center of my back before finally undoing the clasp. It falls down with the rest of my clothes.

I'm a needy, wet mess waiting in anticipation for him to pounce on his prey.

"Hands on the altar, baby."

I arch my back and push my ass out like the needy slut I most definitely am for Lachlan right now.

I can't help but let out a loud moan as he spreads himself against my back and reaches for my chest. He takes one breast in each hand and rubs them roughly together and apart.

I feel his hard length against my ass, and I need it anywhere inside me.

Pushing my breasts together, rubbing them inward, he presses his thumbs hard against my pebbled nipples. I'm panting now. I could come right now from this alone.

He lowers his mouth to my back and nips my skin gently as he continues to caress my breasts.

"You know what, Goldie?"

He nips my skin some more as I feel his hard erection begin to rock in between my ass cheeks.

"I'm going to love stretching this pussy wide. Showing in front of God who it belongs to."

I pant heavier.

"Yes, Father Lachlan."

Holy statues of saints are surrounding us. Jesus Christ is watching me be defiled from behind.

My only prayer right now is that Lachlan knows something I don't about anyone from the parish walking in. I am putting my full trust in him. If this doesn't show that, I don't know what will.

One of his hands leaves my breasts, and I immediately hate the feeling of the cool air touching my skin instead of his rough hand. Slowly, he moves his hand further down my stomach, never leaving contact with my body.

Finally, he reaches his goal, and he starts firmly massaging my sex instead. He easily finds my clit.

"Fuck, Father," I whimper.

Lachlan groans as he continues the act.

"That's it. You want to break apart for me, don't you? Show me who this pussy belongs to," he whispers into my ear before nipping at it again.

"It belongs to you, Father Lachlan," I barely get out as a moan.

He dips one finger in and out of me before applying a second finger. The sting of the intrusion is one I have missed. Spreading my lips apart. I love the feel of his weight against my back. His hard cock is firmly in between my ass cheeks now.

He knows exactly what he's doing as his fingers find the right motion, and I cry out in pleasure. Slowly, he pulls his fingers from me.

I whimper at the loss. Lachlan laughs darkly before turning me around slowly to face him. I can see my wetness on his fingers as a wicked grin spreads across his face. He brings one finger to his mouth, followed by the other, and licks them clean.

"Fuckin' delicious, like always," he grins.

I suck in a breath and lick my lips. I have no idea what else is in store for me tonight.

"I can't wait until I finally devour your cunt. I fucking love the way you taste."

I am deceased.

This is not Father Lachlan or the sweet Lachlan I've come to love. I know I won't be able to get enough of this version of him, either. There is nothing sacred or holy about him; only his carnal urges are coming to life.

"You know what, baby, I'm starving. I'm ready to eat, and I happen to be craving more sweet cherries from my Goldie girl."

His hands go down to hoist me up onto the altar. I sit where the most sacred sacraments are usually presented to the congregation.

I spread my legs as wide as I can and rest on my elbows, waiting for his instruction.

"Does my needy girl want me to eat her pussy? Don't make me wait any longer," he says with a smirk.

Lachlan doesn't wait for my answer. His hands grip my thighs as he spreads them even further than I ever thought possible. I have no choice but to lean back fully on the altar at his mercy.

Lachlan dives into my wet sex, and instantly, I feel like I won't be able to take much more. My hands go to his hair as I ride his face while he licks, sucks, and consumes me.

I'm squirming as I try to find the right friction against his tongue. It all feels like too much sensation at once. I'm so close to combusting.

He lifts his head slightly between my thighs.

"Lachlan," I breathe out.

"Goldie girl, let me enjoy this. I want to eat you every goddamn day."

He goes back down between my thighs, and the achy feeling that's been there since I first saw him today is finally going to get relief.

Lachlan is eating me like a man starved. I naturally rock my hips harder against his face, seeking that final hit of relief.

"My greedy girl is back. Do you need Father Lachlan to take care of you?"

Lachlan's fingers are playing with my clit as he speaks to me.

"Yes," I breathe out in more of a moan.

"Does my greedy girl deserve to come?"

He's bringing me to the edge.

"Yes, Father Lachlan, I deserve to come. Please. I'll beg. Please make me come."

He laughs darkly.

"Pretty, greedy girls don't need to beg. You just have to make me a promise."

"Anything."

I need this release; I'll say yes to anything he wants.

"I am your salvation now. Do not run from me, baby."

"Never again."

He brings his head back to my wet sex and finishes me off harder than the last time. It feels impossible, but I don't hate this new goal of his. Lachlan makes me come harder than ever before.

I see heaven right here on the altar. I lie back on it lifelessly. Lachlan ate me out like he was born to do it. *Holy fuck.*

"You think that's all you're going to get, Avery?"

His husky voice brings me back to life.

"Never," I smile through an almost drunken haze.

"Good."

Lachlan pulls on the outside of my thighs and slides my body forward so my sex is resting on his stomach.

"My greedy girl, we're going to have so much fun together."

He flashes me my favorite smile of his, the wicked one. The one that says it's playtime between Father Lachlan and his temptress.

He grabs me by the hips and slowly rocks me into his stomach. For a moment, I lose the feeling of his touch as he begins removing his clothes. When he comes back to me, I see he has something in his hand.

"You still need to be punished for running away from me. Don't you?"

"Yes, Father."

He grunts as I call him his holy name again.

Lachlan takes the item he has in his hand and lightly grazes it across my stomach and the top of my sex. He teases my sensitive clit, and I am already wanting more from him. I moan in anticipation. I need his cock in me now.

I look down to see what he's using to tease me when I realize what it is. Lachlan shoots me that same wicked grin as he inches it lower until it's now right at my entrance.

"Remember, if you want me to stop, just say mercy," he says with a wink.

He inserts a fucking cross into me.

Repeatedly, he pulls it in and out. It's almost too painful to take, but I don't want to use the safe word. I want to take everything he needs to give me tonight.

Lachlan leans against me as he continues to fuck me with it. He starts roughly massaging one of my breasts with his other hand.

This type of edging is unbearable to take. I need to come again.

"Lachlan, please," I manage to get out.

He stands up straight and removes the cross slowly. Then, he picks me up off the altar and sets me on my feet. My limbs feel lifeless as I stumble into him.

"You know what to do," he whispers into my ear.

I turn around and put my hands on the altar, arch my back, and push my ass out. Anything to come again.

His touch is intoxicating. Lachlan skims the spine of my back with the same cross he just used to fuck me. I cry out. I can never be anything but his after this. He now owns me body and soul. My body became his long before my soul completely followed.

With my hands gripping the altar, I know I'm ready for what will come next.

"Sweet girl," he whispers in my ear.

"Yes, Father?"

His hand teases my backside before he grips my ass with one of his hands.

"Count them."

What did he just say? I'm not sure what I'm meant to be counting. His hands are off me.

"What?" I stammer as I start to glance back at him behind me. As I do that, a loud smack lands on one of my ass cheeks.

"Fuck," I whimper.

My eyes begin to well up.

He immediately goes to rub the same cheek gently—taking away the sting.

"One. Nine to go."

I can do this. Lachlan switches cheeks as he repeats the action nine more times. Each time, he gently gives me the care I need afterward to make the pain go away.

With each smack I take, the wetter I get. I love the power he holds over me. I will forever crave this immoral side of him. Maybe I enjoy being punished after all.

I count each one out until we finally get to ten. Spreading my legs further apart after the final smack on my ass.

I put my elbows on the altar and turn back slightly, panting, "What else do I deserve?"

His eyes darken as he continues to caress my flesh from the stings. Unexpectedly, after the tenth smack to my ass, he picks me up and sets me back on the altar facing him. My ass is sore from the sudden pressure from sitting on the altar. He's treating me like a rag doll, and I couldn't possibly ever be more turned on than this.

"Give me another one, please, Father Lachlan."

"My greedy, greedy girl." He laughs knowingly.

He pumps his cock a few times. His muscles flex as he repeats the motion.

"Ready for me, baby? Ready for my cock to be inside that soaked pussy?"

I moan loudly, "Yes."

I can't contain them in this deviant series of acts.

Lachlan lines up his cock at my entrance and thrusts hard into me. He repeats the purposeful, hard thrusts with such intensity. I know I'm not going to last much longer. I lean on my elbows, giving Lachlan a perfect view of my breasts.

He holds my legs apart as he continues pounding into me. Harder and harder each time. I am going to be sore tomorrow, but I love it right now. It has been too long. I am breathless at this point. Any second now, I'm going to come again.

"I want to hear you say it."

He continues to thrust hard into me, gripping my hips.

"Anything," I reply.

"Tell me you're mine, Goldie girl."

He isn't letting up as he demands I tell him the final words he needs to hear from me today.

"Tell me you're not going to do this to us again," he continues as he thrusts harder. Feeling his fingers digging into my sides, I'll be bruised tomorrow from the pain I love to receive.

"I'm yours, Lachlan," I breathily reply.

"That's right, Avery. You're mine."

Lachlan fills me up as I come on his cock.

We're both breathing heavily, leaning our foreheads together as he stays inside me. Sweat is dripping down my body, and his cum is spilling down my leg.

"Mine," he whispers.

The rightness of us together outweighs any thought that it's wrong. I don't care if I'm going to hell for seducing my priest. I found my salvation, my heaven, my soul mate with the man in the shadows. I can live in the gray if it means a lifetime with Lachlan.

This is what all of the heartache and pain of my life has been leading up to: finding Lachlan O'Connell.

He breaks the contact first with our foreheads and then by sliding out of me.

"Avery, I mean it. I'm all in. Can you finally say the same?"

"I'm all in, Lachlan."

CHAPTER 20

AVERY

"Come back to my new place with me," I hesitantly ask.

I'm nervous to know whether Lachlan will or not. Tomorrow is Sunday. The holy day that Lachlan presides over Mass to a thousand or more people.

"Goldie girl, do you think I'm done with you tonight?" he answers with a smirk as he continues to clean up the altar space.

I blush in return.

"I hope not," I reply honestly.

After we're both dressed and the church is pristine once again, Lachlan takes me out a side entrance, and we make our way to his car.

His car is a black, sleek-looking luxury sedan. Thinking back on it, his home is nicer inside than I expected. I'm not with

Lachlan for money; I have plenty of my own. But how does a priest afford this? There is so much I still don't know about him.

"Just take King Street straight, and I'll tell you where to turn," I say.

"Got it, Goldie."

He winks at me and takes my hand across the console. We're together. I give his hand a squeeze. Lachlan releases it before settling his hand on my thigh. I could get used to this.

Arriving at my apartment, Lachlan opens my door for me and takes my hand. It's a small gesture that makes my heart flutter. I take it, linking us together as we walk inside. It's so easy to get lost in the small moments with him.

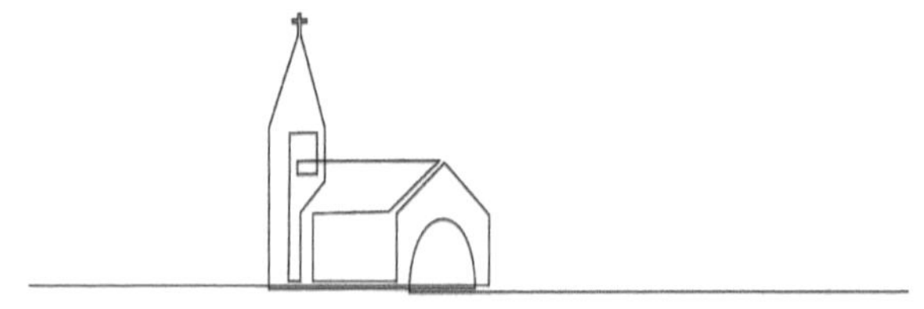

I turn on the lights once we get inside my apartment. Now that Lachlan is here, I assess what it must be like from his viewpoint. I'm proud of what I've done to the place.

"This is it," I announce.

Lachlan wraps his arms around my waist and leans his head down to my right shoulder.

"I'm so proud of you, baby. This place is great. It reminds me of you," he says before gently placing a kiss to my cheek.

My heart swells. I have poured my personality into making this space my own.

"Thank you," I reply coyly.

"Now, why don't you lead us to your shower? I know you have lots of fun in it," he teases.

"I should have never told you about me using my vibrator in there." I giggle as I lead the way.

"I beg to differ. That was my favorite part of that confession," he says with a wink.

Inside the bathroom, the heat from the shower spray starts to create a fog quickly. I go to strip out of my clothes when Lachlan stops me.

"Let me take care of you."

We smile at each other.

"Arms up."

I do as I'm told. He gently brings my dress over my head first, then removes my bra and panties.

"Avery, have I told you how beautiful you are? I'm a fucking fool if I haven't tonight."

I laugh at him and playfully swat his shoulder.

"You tell me all the time."

He begins stripping out of his clothes. I'm caught staring at his muscular thighs as he pulls his pants away first.

"Let me tell you one more time then, you're fucking stunning, baby. I'm the luckiest man on this planet to get to be with you."

I know the feeling because now Lachlan's taking off his shirt, and I'm staring right at a Greek god. Lachlan is pure, hard muscle everywhere.

I can't help but lick my lips as I stare at his thick, strong thighs once again before my gaze rises toward his chiseled chest and sharp jawline. I am never going to get over seeing him naked.

He smirks knowing he caught me shamelessly roaming my eyes all over his body.

I shrug when he catches me and laugh. Lachlan gives me one of my favorite smiles, the ones just reserved for me.

"Like what you see?"

"As you would say, I fucking love what I see, baby." I grin.

He shakes his head with laughter as he reaches for my hand. I can't help but join in.

"Come on, Goldie girl, let's get you cleaned up."

Lachlan pulls me under the spray and starts massaging the water into my hair. He lathers it up next with shampoo.

"So this is why you smell sweet like flowers every time I see you."

Is it possible to blush in a shower? My cheeks warm at his compliment. After he finishes washing my hair for me, he goes to start on his own.

"No way, mister, I get to do you next. Only I'm not going to use restraint like you clearly did," I say with another laugh before continuing.

"You totally missed the opportunity to lather my breasts up. Aren't those you're favorite part of me?"

Lachlan lets out a booming laugh.

"I was trying to be a gentleman. I would love nothing more than to massage body wash into your tits, baby."

"Nope, sorry, it's my turn now," I sing-song.

Taking the body wash from him, I pour some onto one of my hands. He takes it back from me and puts it up in its place.

I start to lather up his broad shoulders first and make my way down his muscular arms, which I love so much. I continue to his chest next. Lachlan lets out a deep sigh as I massage his pecs and abs.

I sink to my knees. Lachlan stares at me intensely. I can't help but smile, knowing what I'm about to do to him.

"Look at you, Goldie," he says in his husky voice.

I look up at him as I open my mouth. His eyes roam every inch of my body and land on my breasts before making his way back to where I'm now gripping his cock.

"Down on your knees for me already. You like getting dirty for me, don't you, baby?"

My thighs squeeze together as I let out a small moan and nod my head. I start to lick the tip, putting his pre-cum on my lips before licking it up with my tongue.

"You like teasing me, Goldie girl. Don't worry, I've got all the time in the world to have that perfect, pouty mouth wrap around my cock."

Fuck. Lachlan and I are always on the same page sexually. This time, I'm not going to be quick about what I'm about to do.

I put my mouth around his cock and take it deep to the back of my throat. I'm not going to gag on it. I want him to know I can always take what he's willing to give me. I'm so turned on by sucking him deep like this.

There's a quick inhale of breath before I hear a *fuck* being whispered.

Lachlan braces himself against one of the glass shower walls, towering over me now.

"You like working my cock like a greedy little slut? Keep showing me how much you like sucking me off," he says in his gravelly voice.

I hum in response.

"That's right, just like that," Lachlan encourages.

I continue to lick and suck, using my hands to help me take him in even further. His hips gently rock forward as we both pick up the pace. I can feel him pulse in the back of my throat.

"I'm about to come, baby, be my angel and swallow it all. Can my perfect girl do that?"

I moan at the command and do just as he asked. Lachlan is pushing his cock harder into my mouth until finally, he thrusts forward a few final times. His cum fills my mouth as our eyes hold on one another.

"Swallow it," he demands.

He's looking at me with pure lust in his eyes as I do. I lick my lips to wipe up the final bit of his cum remaining.

"Fuck, Avery. I sure as fuck hope I get to keep you."

I stand up to meet him closer to eye level.

"I'm yours, Lachlan," I answer as I wrap my arms around his neck.

He crushes his mouth to mine and consumes me. His tongue works mine like it's his dying wish. This kiss speaks volumes about us and our direction. It's powerful and makes me think I'll die a happy woman if I get to kiss Lachlan like this for the rest of my life.

After we dry off from the shower, I go to put on a pajama set when Lachlan stops me.

He doesn't have a change of clothes with him. He'll have to start leaving some of his stuff here at my place, if not everything, if I'm being honest.

"Baby, do you think I'm going to leave my needy girl without relief?"

"What do you mean?"

"I saw you, Goldie. Thighs clenched, eyes looking up at me dying to be fucked ragged."

Lachlan pulls me with him as we sink onto the bed. My thighs are straddling his sides as I sit on top of his hips and waist.

"I'm going to love stretching this pussy apart again."

I'm naked on top of his rock-hard body, still wet from going down on him in the shower. I didn't expect anything in return, not after the multiple orgasms I received in the church.

Lachlan grips my hips tightly as he raises my body slightly. I instantly feel the start of the sudden intrusion in me as he brings my body down onto his.

I let out breathy moans as I sink further onto his shaft.

"Ride me, baby. Make yourself come all over my cock."

I sit up as straight as I can, resting my hands on his chest, and begin moving up and down slowly. I'm trying to take as much of his length as I can without it being painful.

"Lachlan, I don't know if I can take it right now," I whimper.

Slowly leaning closer to his body instead of being upright.

"You can and you will, baby."

He leans forward and starts sucking my breasts, lapping them up in long strokes with his tongue.

"Perfect, pretty tits," he murmurs.

Lachlan grips my hips harder and starts moving me faster on his cock. I am drenched, making it too easy to ride his long, thick cock now.

Lachlan must notice that I'm lost in him and picks up the pace. He lets go of my hips and lies all the way down on my bed, folding his arms behind his head.

"What a fucking view I get right now. These perfect tits bouncing in front of me while you ride my cock. You're my fucking wet dream personified."

"Fuck, Lachlan, yes."

I ride him faster, trying to reach that spot I know I'm so close to.

Lachlan moves to start palming my clit. The instant touch makes me break, and I come, just as requested.

Lachlan pumps a few more times into me before coming again. He goes to my bathroom for a washcloth and cleans us both up before pulling me onto his chest.

I lie on top of him, breathless, feeling like every bone in my body is limp. Laying on top of a naked Lachlan is everything and more. His arms feel like all the comfort I've needed this week. He is sex on a stick and all mine.

I start to think about my future with him. Something I hadn't allowed myself to fully do before. Where would he go after he left the church? When is he planning on doing that? These were the answers I needed.

"I can feel those wheels turning again," he whispers.

I'm cuddled up at his side, strumming my fingers against his chest.

"We have to have some big conversations."

"Let's pick one for tonight."

"That sounds good."

I pause. What do I go with first? I know we'll talk about it all eventually. I don't want to break down tonight. Not when I'm finally cozied up in his arms.

"Avery? Your choice."

"Let's go with timing."

He chuckles, "Timing of...?"

I sigh. I know it's a hard one.

"When do you think you'll leave the church, Lachlan? I know it's a tough decision you've come to."

Lachlan slowly caresses my arm and side, tracing small circles on my skin.

"I've given this a lot of thought. With the gala being next weekend, I'm going to give my notice to Greg early next week. Finish up my duties with the gala and then wrap up a few loose ends the following week. I don't want to put anyone in a bad position if I leave before then."

In two short weeks, Lachlan will no longer be a priest at St. Peter's.

"While we're at it, I have to tell you what I've been doing this week while we had some distance."

He shares how good he feels about his decision. How right it feels to be with me. The pain he has from his dad passing away.

That to do it all right with me, he needed to speak with the two people who matter to him the most. I was so grateful to hear how happy Father Patrick and Janet were for us. I can't wait to meet them one day.

We slowly drift to sleep. I feel at home in the nook of his arm.

I hope that the peace we are both beginning to feel can last.

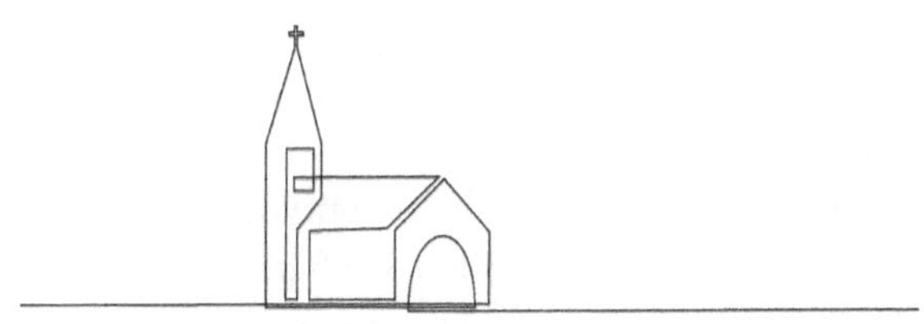

The next day at church, I sit in the front row. I'm nervous Kevin is going to show up again, but I haven't had any contact with him since last Sunday, minus my run-in with Missy.

I really don't get what game he's playing. Maybe he's expecting me to beg for him to take me back after spending some time apart.

As I wait for church to begin, I stare up at the altar. The same altar that Lachlan delivered my penance to me on the night before. He worshiped my body. He made me come alive.

And honestly, how can I not be thinking about how I was just fucked with a cross up there last night? I'm surprised the church didn't go up in flames when I walked in here today.

This Mass is a somber one for both Lachlan and me. We both knew this was going to be the last Sunday homily he would ever give. Once Father Greg receives his notice next week, there is no way he will be allowed to preside over a Sunday Mass.

Lachlan grips the sides of the podium before walking out from behind it.

We lock eyes for a moment before he starts his last reflection on the readings. I see resolve when I look at him. I have never been more sure about our decision to be together.

"Today's readings focused on one central theme. Do you know what that theme is?"

He looks around the room before continuing.

"Hope. I've always said that hope is the most dangerous and powerful feeling someone can have. Even more powerful than love itself. Hope gives one the ability to move forward when life seems out of bounds, when you feel despair, and when you want to give up. That's when hope steps in and gives you something to get up for the next day, to stand up tall and push ahead. Hope brings you a level of resolve that the choices you are making are the right path for you."

My tears are glistening with pride as he continues.

"Even as a man of God, standing before you here today, I've scarcely allowed myself to hope for more. Hope should not be confused with want or need. Hope goes beyond that. Remember that even in your darkest days, God is here to guide you to the path you need. To give you hope that it'll get better. I hope you all remember that as you live your lives."

Lachlan has given me just that—hope. I won't take it for granted. Not today, not ever.

After Mass ends, I gather up my belongings and make my way outside the church and onto the steps.

That's when I spot him.

Standing on the bottom step, eyes fiercely looking right at me and anger exuding from his body. Kevin has shown up again. He's talking to Missy and her husband, Frank. I didn't see him in Mass.

He must have met them here. Why is he using the church as the place to mentally torment me?

Missy slyly grins at me before giving me a faint wave. That fucking bitch.

She walks toward me. Of course, she does.

"Good morning, Avery. How are you doing today?"

"Just fine, Missy. I see you're here with Kevin, so I think it'd be for the best if we don't speak with one another right now."

"Oh nonsense, poor Kevin is so down about you leaving him. Rumor has it for a much younger man. Are you playing cougar now, Avery?"

One of Missy's eyebrows raises slightly as she tries to goad me.

What is she talking about? Trying to get me to say something about what I've been up to.

She's digging for Kevin.

I didn't realize they were so close. What was that meeting she attended with him the other day? Kevin was never involved in anything church related without me. I know nothing about whatever business it is they are tending to for the church.

"No, Missy, as I'm sure you know, I found Kevin, pants down inside his assistant," I say with my perfect smile in place. I said it loud enough for him and everyone around me to hear. I could have sworn I just saw him mutter to Frank, *fucking bitch*.

It's his fault he's having Missy bait me like this. What does he expect?

"Oh my. My poor dear, bless your heart," she says, pretending to have sympathy.

"I must be going now," I interrupt.

I turn on my heels and backtrack to leave down a set of side steps. Lachlan is looking at me in the distance with a worried expression on his face. I text him to meet me at Jackson's.

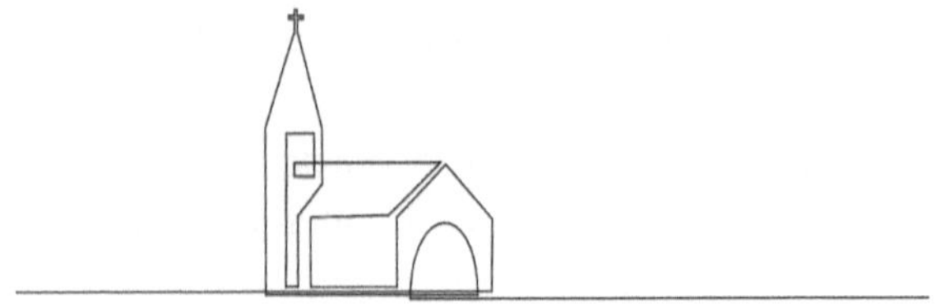

When Lachlan arrives at Jackson's, he takes a sip of the whiskey I ordered him ahead of his arrival.

"What happened with Missy today? Looked like another confrontation."

I take a sip of my glass of champagne, letting out a long sigh.

I explain that Kevin was there and that getting Missy on his side is clearly a tactical move. I go into how I saw Missy earlier in the week and couldn't figure out their connection outside of me and some meeting they were having.

"Fuck. I think I have an idea what that's about."

"What do you mean?" How could he have any inclination about what's going on between them?

"I meant to tell you this sooner, but it's been so chaotic lately. Father Greg brought me into his office the other week. He told me Kevin is somehow involved in the expansion campaign. Apparently, Kevin has been coming by the parish office too."

He takes a sip of his whiskey before continuing.

"He told me specifically not to tell you. I thought it was odd at that time since you were his wife. He said no one could know about his association with the church expansion effort."

"Do you remember why?"

Lachlan takes a moment to ponder what it was.

"I didn't ask further; it felt very off, and I didn't want this to be something that could be used against you."

"I wonder if..." I trail off.

"Wonder what?"

"I found documentation that Kevin started up a company and named me the CEO of it. He had me sign paperwork a while back, but at the time, I didn't think anything of it. My attorney's looking into it for me. I wonder if it has anything to do with that. I could be reaching, but it all tracks."

"Fuck."

Fuck, indeed.

Lachlan starts to stroke my back to calm me.

"What do you think Missy knows?" I ask out loud.

"It could be as little as just him helping with the church's expansion campaign, or she could be more involved... if there is more. Who knows? Either way, she wouldn't question Kevin regardless."

That's true. Missy would play her hand to her advantage.

"I have to tell my attorney. It's definitely related to what I've already been discovering."

"Baby, I'll be here every step of the way. I promise."

"Thank you, Lachlan. Your support means everything to me."

Lachlan kisses me. His soft lips press against mine, and my body melts at the touch. Softly, he pulls back. His eyes are a deep emerald green that are sparkling in the light.

Those three words are at the tip of my tongue.

CHAPTER 21

LACHLAN

Apply your heart to instruction,
and your ears to words of knowledge.
Proverbs 23:12

The next day, I have plans to meet with Grayson. Since meeting Avery, I haven't been catching up with him as frequently as we both hoped when I moved to Charleston. We made time to see each other periodically, but most of our plans fell through because of how busy we both were. I need to let him know what's happening. How I'm leaving the church.

I know when I talk with Grayson, he's going to ask me the most important question: the elephant in the room. He's the only one who knows about it because he's my best friend. The issue that irrevocably broke most of my other friendships. The reason, no matter how much I want to believe that being with someone as good as Avery will help my soul, I'm still damned to hell.

Not the Catholic Church, not Avery, no one can save me. I just fucking hope that Avery still wants me when I tell her the truth about the night that set me on this path.

It's funny, really. I preach about hope being the most powerful weapon out there, and here I am, full of hope for a future that, for years, I couldn't fathom would be bestowed on me.

Avery has changed me. I know I won't be willing to take no as an answer from her, and where will that leave us? She's fallen for a broken man who is praying to God that she's the one to piece him back together. Her care and spirit are already helping me do just that.

Grayson and I decide to meet at Jackson's. He was the one to tell me about it when I first moved to Charleston. Now, this bar has become Avery and my secret spot in the open but away from our worlds.

I'm sitting in my favorite spot when I see Grayson walking toward me. His optimism always radiates from him, and I can finally see myself having his outlook. A world where not everything is bleak and full of despair.

"Hey, man," Grayson says as he slides onto the barstool next to me.

"Hey." We go in for a handshake hug.

Grayson's one person I know I can count on. I need to talk to him about what's been happening.

"How's the boat business going?" I ask as I sip my whiskey.

Grayson shrugs noncommittally before placing his order. I never know what beer he'll want to order ahead.

"A shrug, really, man?"

Grayson laughs at my skeptical gaze.

"It's good, it's good, no complaints. Just living the dream, one bachelorette party at a time," he says with a smile.

The bartender slides his drink in front of him as Grayson pulls out his credit card to start a tab.

That's right. I forgot his primary clientele is all bachelorette parties.

"I think Charleston is the number one destination this year, beating out Nashville. It's crazy but good. I'm buying another boat or two and hiring more crew members."

He takes a sip of his craft beer. Grabbing the saltshaker in front of him, he puts some on the coaster so the glass doesn't stick to the cardboard before setting it back down.

"I'm hoping these new boats will be different styles than the others. Have to experiment to keep the parties coming."

Grayson glances down at the napkin the bartender gave him. He picks it up and twists it toward me, showing she left her number on it.

"What do you know?"

I laugh, shaking my head.

"Fucking of course, the great hockey player is here," I say jokingly.

Grayson pockets the number and grins.

"You never know," he says with a tilt of his head before sipping his beer again.

Grayson is a smart businessman. During his time as a professional hockey player, he didn't waste the money he was earning at his peak. He turned his money into investments and then, after retirement, wanted something as stress-free as possible. But that didn't last long. One boat has now turned into more with no stopping in sight.

"Really proud of you, though. What you've been able to do since your retirement is just awesome."

"Thanks, man. It hasn't always been easy for me to look at retiring as a good decision, but ultimately, it was. Now look at me," he says as he spreads his arms wide and lets his larger-than-life smile take over.

I laugh at his over-the-top gesture.

"Alright, man, I get it."

"So, what's going on with you these days? I don't hear from you in weeks, and now you look..." Grayson trails off as he studies me.

"Happy?"

It's almost like he hasn't thought to associate me with that word. I wouldn't have either three months ago.

"Yeah, you look fucking happy as shit, man. What's going on?"

He's getting serious now, and I know I have to tell him.

"Some big changes. Fuck this is hard. But some big fucking changes."

Grayson waits for me to continue. Even though I've already had this conversation with Ma and Patrick, having it with Grayson is still tough as shit.

"I met someone."

Grayson's eyes go wide before catching his reaction. Fuck, I get it, I do.

"Yeah, exactly," I comment before gulping down the rest of my whiskey.

I flag down the bartender to get another. Grayson studies me again, but this time more intensely. We wait a few beats. He finishes his beer and signals for another one.

His body's completely turned toward me now.

"Care to elaborate?"

Grayson is now full-fledged fucking grinning at me. I can't help but let out a laugh in relief.

"Yeah, man. Her name is Avery. I think..." I trail off. I've wanted to tell her I love her, but it hasn't felt like the right moment with the hurdles we've had to face in these few short months.

"I know, I fucking love her. She's the one."

"Love looks good on you, man."

"I'm resigning. Tomorrow."

"It's about fucking time."

Over the next hour, I tell Grayson about Avery and our time together. I don't dive into our sexual history. I may have been a manwhore in my younger years, but I don't fucking kiss and tell. Grayson isn't the type to care about details anyway. Although, I bet hearing about how I bent her over my altar and fucked her pussy with a cross would catch his attention.

"Wow, this is good news, man. Really, I'm happy for you. But I have to ask. Does she know?"

"No."

Grayson nods his head in understanding.

"I'm telling her. I plan to tell her and fucking hope to God that she doesn't leave me."

"Lachlan..."

"Don't, Grayson. I don't want to hear it."

"Well, too fucking bad. I'm not going to let you fuck all of this up. You deserve peace, Lachlan, and Avery gives you that. Before you tell her your fucked up version of events, you have got to come to terms with the lie. The lie that is eating you fucking up inside and that you've somehow twisted into the truth," he breathes out.

He's not going to stop.

"What happened that night was fucked up and tragic. Fucking tragic as hell. But you took the rap to protect them both. You can't own her lies and your truth anymore. I think there's someone else you need to tell the truth to eventually too. But please, for fucks sake, stop killing yourself slowly. You know the truth. It's time to believe the version of events that actually happened."

I hang my head low before scrubbing a hand down my face.

"Fuck," I groan.

"The most important person you have to forgive about this whole fucking fucked up situation is you. You've got to forgive yourself for that night, but you have to stop trying to protect everyone else at the cost of your fucking sanity, my man."

"I know. You're right. I'll work on it before talking with Avery."

I start to pull out cash before heading out. As I get up and go to say goodbye to Grayson, he catches my arm.

"Lachlan, I love you, brother, but don't take too long before telling her. She deserves to know the truth of your past and present."

I nod.

It's not fucking good that I haven't told Avery yet, I know that.

That night still haunts me, but she deserves to know my truth. What happened the night that set me off on the path of becoming a priest.

Fucking hell.

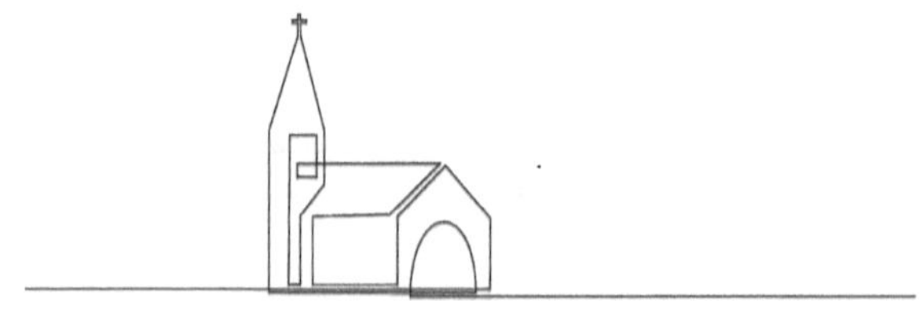

It's Tuesday morning, and I'm the first person in the parish office today. It's earlier than usual for me. I tossed and turned all night thinking about Grayson and my conversation. I can't fuck this up with Avery. How can I just get over the past when it's brought me down this path toward redemption?

I spoke with Avery briefly last night. She was meeting with her attorney today to go over new updates on her divorce from Kevin. That prick, I can only imagine what kind of news she'll find out. I can't worry about that right now as I type up my official resignation letter to give to Greg. I don't think he cares about me any more than a traditional colleague would, but I know my resignation is going to come as a major shock.

I really found my place at St. Peter's. It's only been a few months, but the church staff and parishioners have come to accept me and my duties here. Now that we're all finally in a good place, I'm about to rip the rug right out from under everyone.

I would wait, but I'm not one to fucking linger. I don't want what's happening between Avery and me to become a scandal. Right now, we've been lucky that no one has caught us. It's a small town for the locals, so luck has definitely been on our side.

Early in the morning, I print out my resignation letter and head to Greg's office.

I lean against his open doorframe and give the door a few gentle knocks so I don't startle the old man this early. His head perks up, and his shoulders clearly relax when he realizes it's me and not someone else.

Now that I know something bigger is happening behind the scenes with Kevin, I can't help but wonder if that was in reaction to it not being him or Missy or someone else close to whatever disaster is really happening.

The expansion campaign seemed like a simple enough concept, especially with a title like that, but that's it. It's too fucking straightforward to be causing this much ruckus and getting this much attention—it has to be a ruse of some kind.

"Lachlan, come in, to what do I owe this pleasure?"

Greg's closing up file folders on his desk. I come up and take a seat in front of him.

"Well, Greg, there is no easy way to say this without being as blunt as possible. I've enjoyed every minute of my time here at St. Peter's, but I'm resigning."

I slide my resignation letter in front of him. So much for not startling the old man this early; he is stunned.

"I know this is a big surprise, and I've only been here for a few months. I fully intend to finish my remaining duties here at the parish—priestly and regarding the gala this weekend."

"Lachlan, why?"

He's too alarmed to say anything more complex. I was expecting this, but it doesn't make it any easier to explain, even to someone I barely tolerate.

I have two options here. I can go with the semi-truth, or I can lie. I plan to stay in Charleston with Avery, so eventually, that cat will be out of the bag, but Greg isn't worthy of any of the confessions I've been passing out like candy these days.

"Truthfully, I've been doing a lot of soul-searching. My final days at my parish in Boston and since coming here. I love my relationship with God, but with much reflection and conferring with my mentor in Boston, I've decided to end my service as a priest and worship God as a regular member of society."

"You're leaving the Church?"

"Just as a priest."

He doesn't understand. Most priests wouldn't leave unless there were a scandal. I don't technically have one of those, but that's what I'm trying to prevent. Not for myself but for Avery. I know she'll already have a lot to deal with from her peers as she continues to navigate this life without being on Kevin's arm.

"I understand this is a shock but when it's this severe of a change, I felt in my heart I had to tell you immediately. I'm sorry."

Was I sorry? I suppose, on one hand, I really didn't enjoy leaving the parish to be one priest down again, but for the first time in my life, I'm chasing happiness. A fucking phrase I never expected to be thinking.

"This is a lot to take in. I'll have to schedule some follow-up time with you. When is your last day?"

Greg starts scanning my resignation letter.

"Two weeks from today."

He leans back in his deep chair and gives me a firm nod, accepting my decision.

"You'll still manage this gala through to the end?"

"Of course. I know it's a tough spot I'm putting you in, but I plan to fulfill these final duties. It just wouldn't have been fair to the parish to have come to this decision and stayed on."

I head back to my office feeling like one of the last weights on my shoulders has been lifted off. There's still much to go through, but this is one giant step forward to a life with Avery Parker by my side.

CHAPTER 22

AVERY

After leaving Lachlan on Sunday, I knew I had to reach out to Noah right away. I'm still waiting for my divorce from Kevin to be finalized. Kevin isn't making it easy on me, even though it should be the clearest-cut divorce case to ever take place in South Carolina.

In this state, traditionally, you have to be separated for one year before filing for divorce. My situation is grounds to skip that rule all because I have video evidence of Kevin sleeping with his assistant on my beautiful rug. Cheating is a clause that means I can speed up the process.

I let my attorney know more of the pieces that Lachlan and I discussed. He asked me to meet him in his office on Tuesday to go over the next steps. I just want this to be done with.

I never wanted this long, drawn-out process to take place. I want to move on with my life and forget that the past three years even happened. I want to remove the image of Kevin fucking his assistant, Lemon, on my rug from my mind. But he's just not letting me.

I have a feeling if Kevin catches wind of me knowing about this new company that he won't be happy about it. For some reason, he has gotten me involved in something he shouldn't have. But that's it—he just never saw me leaving him.

I open the light-blue front door to Noah's office and immediately find a friendly, petite, blonde woman ready to greet me. A shiny gold sign on the wall above her head reads, "The Law Offices of Reynolds and Mullhound."

"Hi, I'm here to see Mr. Reynolds. I'm Avery Matheson."

I hate still having to say his last name. I can't wait until I'm legally divorced and able to return to being Avery Parker officially.

"Of course, right through this door," she says while gesturing to the open door to her right for me to go through.

"Thank you."

I make my way down the short hallway to his office. I've been here a handful of times now, but I'm surprised I remember where to go. We usually communicate by phone to keep it all as easy as possible. I like that he isn't a bullshitter. Not trying to extend conversations or meetings just to bill more hours for my case.

Noah's office door is open, and he's leaning against it, waiting for me.

"Noah, it's nice to see you," I greet him while sticking out my hand to shake his.

"I'm not sure how nice it is to see your attorney, but the pleasure is mine," he laughs.

I laugh as he goes in to shake my hand.

"You're right, Noah."

We both go to take our seats.

"Well, Avery, I'll cut right to the chase. I don't have good news."

I exhale an audible breath. This is exactly what I was dreading coming here.

"How bad?"

"Honestly? Bad. Kevin is up to no good across it all. This company you had me look into is a shell corporation. Without a forensic finance team looking into it further, I only have assumptions. We can go down this path, but that's what I need your permission for today. And that's just us getting started. Nothing adds up with anything we've looked into."

"What's he doing? Why is my name on those records?"

"A shell corporation is essentially a cover for him doing crooked business. There's a lot to it, but that's the bottom line. He planned to use you as the scapegoat if anything were to be found out or someone had to get caught."

"Fuck," I whisper out, leaning back into my chair.

"Indeed. But the good news is that we have an advantage here. We can stop him."

"What about the Church? How is the Church involved?"

"My guess?"

"Yeah," I reply.

"Right now, it looks like one of two options. Either someone found out and is blackmailing him, or he's using the Church as part of his defrauding scheme. Either option means jail time for Kevin and probably other parties involved. This Father Greg character you've shared details on is most likely the connection to the Church. I don't know that for sure, but that's what it's all looking like to me at this point."

I let this news soak in for a few minutes.

Kevin used me. He knowingly used me as a pawn in his scheme to steal money. I don't need to know the ins and outs of it. Fuck him for doing this to me. I hope karma comes back around.

"Noah, do whatever you have to do to find out what's going on and get my involvement wiped clear. I don't want to go to jail for whatever he's up to."

"Avery, you aren't going to jail. That's why you have me and my team. I need you to continue to trust me."

"Just get it done and let me know anything important."

Noah nods in response, looking thoughtfully at me.

"Thank you," I say before turning to leave his office.

"Avery?"

I spin back around to Noah.

"Yes?"

He takes a moment before speaking again.

"Don't let this change you. We're going to get him for this. He's just a bad seed; there is nothing you could have done to stop this from happening. You simply trusted your spouse."

"You're right, but look where that's gotten me."

I weakly smile before leaving Noah's office.

I know what he means, but it still stings a little to realize that I really held such little value to Kevin. Every day, I discover a new reason why leaving him is the best thing I'll ever do for myself. It's just a lesson I wish I learned sooner than I did.

On the walk back to my apartment, I decide that I'm going to explore more career options when I get home, now that I'm focused on the future. I can't let my ongoing battle with Kevin interfere with me making any more plans. Ones that will only help me grow into the new woman I want to be.

Since living in my new apartment, I've realized that I still love residing downtown. It's a trendier area that's filled with a mix of ages and demographics in the buildings nearby, but it's more me.

After Lachlan leaves the Church, I'll stop attending St. Peter's, and that part of my life will practically be over. In Charleston, where you live really determines who your friends are. It's difficult to maintain friendships with people who live in different areas or have different lifestyles. It's especially hard when you try to maintain friendships with those across one of the bridges. Each section of Charleston feels like its own world, and it's difficult to leave.

The area that my apartment is in is considered upper King Street. More of a partying area, but my luxury building is tucked away on a side street. Most of the residents are successful professionals, young and old. I don't know if I want children or not, but if the time ever comes, I'll decide if moving is the right decision. For now, I'll enjoy every minute of being where I am.

Lachlan and I will have to discuss his future living arrangements too. I want him to move in with me regardless of the optics. Once he's no longer a priest, I could care less about what people say about us being together. Even though I know how he feels about me, we haven't had many conversations about our future together.

That's my fault. After the guilt nearly tore me apart, Lachlan decided to treat me with kid gloves when discussing what we are. I understand—I probably needed it. But now that we are it for each other I don't know if I want to take it day-by-day. I want to know that Lachlan is committed. And more importantly, I want him to know that I am as well.

We have plans to see each other later tonight at my place. Both of us have news to share with each other.

I know Lachlan is confident in his decision, but I can't help but wonder how Father Greg took his resignation. Lachlan's only remaining duties to the Church will be to wrap up outstanding religious components that I really know nothing about, the gala, and to move out of his home.

Tonight, we need to focus on our future, on us. Since reuniting... if that's even the right word for our week apart, I've wanted to tell him I love him. These past few months with Lachlan have been the best of my life since my parents passed away.

When I'm with him, I feel it every way and everywhere. Lachlan has seeped his way into every part of my being, and I don't plan to ever let him go.

I love the fall season in Charleston. It's not like up in the northern part of the United States where it's completely different colored leaves and chilly temperatures, but it's a feeling of calmness everywhere.

The tourists have mostly gone, and its locals bustling about in their days. The weather fluctuates between a crisp morning to a cool sunny afternoon, and the leaves are slowly changing and falling from the trees. It's the best time of year to visit the area.

In a navy-blue cashmere sweater and fitted jeans, it feels like I'm in my own movie where the days are perfectly strung together. This new version of life isn't going to be one I take for granted.

On my walk, I spot that one of my favorite boutiques has changed its window display. Now featuring fall trends, I can't help but admire the plaid skirts I'm seeing the mannequins in. I have time before Lachlan comes over, what's the harm in popping in? When I return home, I'll just be doing more planning of my career. I can take a few easy moments for me.

Going to open the boutique door, I'm almost trampled by two people coming out of the doors side by side. I'm stunned as I look up to find the one person I never want to run into.

Kevin.

At least his expression shows that he's not stalking or harassing me—he's equally as shocked to see me.

Someone says "ahem" in the middle of our stare-down. I turn to see my new favorite tart, Lemon.

"Kevin," I say curtly.

I gesture to the door frame to imply I need to get through. Anything to keep this from happening.

"Lemon, I'll see you back at the office," he replies, not taking his eyes away from me.

"But Kev—," she starts.

Clearly flustered, she pulls herself together before continuing.

"Mr. Matheson, we really both should be going for your two-o'clock call."

"I'll see you there, Lemon. Go."

Lemon takes off in a huff down the street. Kevin stalks a few steps toward me, bringing me slightly away from the entrance door and more onto the sidewalk.

I let out a loud sigh in frustration.

"Kevin, I think we both know it's not a good idea for us to be speaking to each other without our attorneys present. And to be frank, I have nothing to say to you, or Lemon for that matter. You should have gone with her."

I'm not giving in here. Not now, not ever, with him.

I knew one day I would face him alone outside of a courtroom or with someone like Missy, and we would either cause a scene or he would try to dive into our divorce. We haven't ever really addressed his cheating and my leaving.

What would be the point?

I wasn't forgiving him, and now too much time has passed. I'm no longer angry, but I'm done. I don't want to drag this around any longer. I don't even care about his clearly illegal businesses. *I know, I know.* I should care, but I just can't. My only concern is that my name is not linked to anything, and I don't get in trouble with the law.

Actually, fuck him for that. Maybe I am still pissed off for that part. I've let the rug fucking go.

"Avery, you never gave me a chance to explain," Kevin starts.

I know what he's doing. This tone and gesture are year-one Kevin. The one filled with charisma that lets his sex appeal shine through. I will not be falling for it.

"Explain what exactly? How I saw you fucking Lemon in our courtyard? How are you going to explain that one away?"

I cross my arms over my chest and don't return any sign of humor or smile.

"Avery, don't do this to us."

"Us? You haven't even tried to reach out to me in what, a month? Months? You are here buying Lemon clothes, don't pretend to give a rat's ass about me now that I'm in front of you."

"I have tried to call you multiple times. Did you block my numbers? Lemon isn't you. After you left that note and the way I handled seeing you that day in church, I just couldn't bring myself to face you again so soon. And Missy. Fuck that day with Missy, it went all wrong. I miss you, Avery. I'm sorry about Lemon."

"No, you aren't," I laugh.

"I don't believe that you've tried to reach out. I mean, come on, you're with Lemon right now," I finish.

Kevin takes a frustrated breath before recomposing himself.

"Avery, sweetheart, let's talk. You and me. I can book that little candlelit table in our favorite Italian restaurant. Please give me a chance to talk with you."

I can't let him get the better of me.

"Kevin, I'm only going to say this once. Don't call me as you claim you have. Don't try to have friends reach me. I won't be forgiving you. We are getting divorced. You cannot have your cake and eat it too. Go be with Lemon or whoever the fuck else. I don't care. Leave me alone, or else I'll tell my lawyer to file a restraining order."

I turn on my heels and start to dart away, but I can still hear him yell in the distance, "This isn't over, Avery. You're my wife."

I scoff at that. Not much longer, Kevin. Not much longer.

"No, I am not," I shout back.

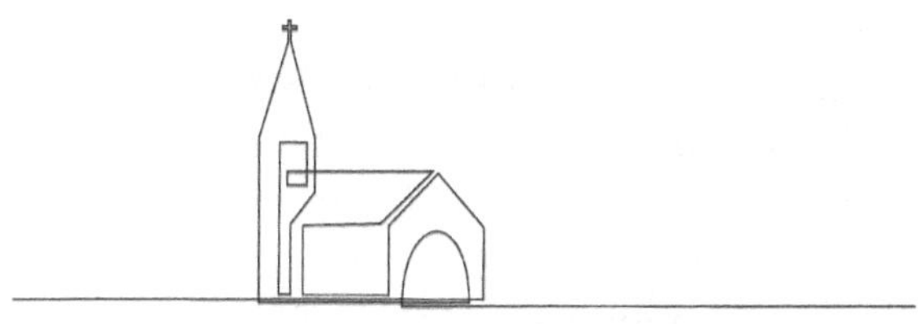

Returning home to my apartment, I fall right back onto the couch. Looking further into my career plans will have to wait after that incident.

I turn on the gas fireplace before heading to my bedroom to change into a cute but casual lounge set. Lachlan will be here in a few hours, but seeing Kevin in person unexpectedly just drained my whole being.

Maybe this town isn't big enough for the both of us after all.

No, I can't think like that. God, I just wish Lachlan was here already.

After changing, I head to the kitchen and open up one of my favorite bottles of pinot noir. I give myself a heavy pour before heading back to settle onto the couch. A reality show and shutting off my brain for an hour or two will do me good.

"Avery, sweetheart, it's me," I hear being whispered.

I slowly sit up and adjust my eyes before coming face to face with my favorite person, Lachlan. I can't help but smile.

"How are you doing, baby?" he asks as he settles in beside me on the couch. I gave him a key last time he was here for emergencies. I'm glad I did. Hopefully, after tonight, it will be his permanently.

"Good now that you're here. Sorry, I must have fallen asleep out here when I got home. What time is it?"

"It's only five-thirty. I came over right away." He gestures to the priest attire he's wearing.

I giggle.

"We've got to get your clothes over here."

I pat his chest playfully, and he catches it. Lachlan pulls me so I'm resting on his chest. He rubs my back slowly.

"I like that idea."

He continues rubbing as I sink further into him. I could get used to days like this.

"I was going to have takeout ready when you got here," I sigh.

"Goldie girl, coming home to find you is all I'll ever need. We can order takeout in just a few minutes. We've got the time," he breathes.

Recently I've discovered I love the quiet.

It's the silent moments with someone else that you can find your truth in. With Lachlan, his love shines through in the quiet and in the noise. I know with him I can be myself. I have someone in my corner.

I don't know the last time I felt like I had someone on my side like this. Not even with how amazing Fisher has been over the past decade.

"Lachlan, you'll never know how much I appreciate you."

"I appreciate you, Avery," he answers while continuing to stroke my back.

I brace myself on his chest to look him in his emerald-green eyes. He's looking at me lovingly.

I want to say it. I need to get it out.

His smile fades away and is replaced with a pensive stare out the patio sliding glass doors.

"What is it, Lachlan? Did everything go okay today?"

CHAPTER 23

LACHLAN

No one has greater love than this,
to lay down one's life for one's friends.
John 15:13

I can tell what Avery is feeling at this moment; fuck, I feel it too.

Avery, my perfect Goldie girl, the dream I never would have asked for, is in love with me. I can tell she wants to say those three words to me. Right now is the perfect moment to.

Avery doesn't know that I have one last confession to make. The most important one for her to understand who she's fallen in love with. The confession that could easily tear us apart.

I haven't told anyone, other than Grayson, the truth of the night that haunts me. He believes that I should never have lied to everyone about how the events of that night unfolded. That I didn't need to bear the weight of everyone else's actions on top of mine.

What I did that night wasn't good, but Grayson doesn't think I deserve to have lost people I love because of it. I never thought I could forgive myself for what happened.

The one night that changed my path forever has now brought me to Avery. Wouldn't that make it the path I was always meant to be on?

I've come to terms with my truth from that night. I was just a young adult, doing what I thought was best to protect my friends.

"Avery," I say solemnly.

She instantly sits upright at my tone.

"What is it, Lachlan?"

I take a deep breath and prepare for my final confession before we can decide to be together for the rest of our lives. If she'll still want me after she hears this truth.

"I've mentioned to you that I'm not a good man, Avery. Fuck, I want to be. In the past, before I became a priest, I was reckless. Beyond reckless. I was a fucking joke, if I'm being honest with you."

She gathers my hands in hers and places them in her lap. Avery's now seated with her legs crossed over one another as she waits for me to continue.

"Right around the time I graduated college, I was a mess. My dad had died, and I was angry. Really fucking angry," I start before taking a pause.

I need to try to compose myself as much as I can for Avery's sake.

"I channeled all my time and energy into my job. I thought if I made something of myself I would feel proud, happy even. That wasn't the fucking case. The more I climbed the corporate ladder, the more insane my life became. I fucked countless women, did every drug I could get my hands on, and drank until I blacked out daily—I was a fucking terrible human being. Everyone was worried about me and who I was turning into."

Avery squeezes my hands showing she's here for me. I know this must be painful for her to listen to, and I haven't even gotten started yet.

"Avery, promise me. If this gets to be too much, you'll tell me? I don't want you to hate me."

Avery releases one of our intertwined hands and cups the side of my face.

"Lachlan, I could never hate you. Never. Don't be afraid to tell me. Please tell me as much as you're willing to."

I take her hand back into mine before she pulls them into her lap.

"You know my friend, Grayson?"

She nods.

"Well, Grayson wasn't always my only friend. Fuck, that's pathetic to say out loud." I sigh before shaking my head in disgust.

"Lachlan, basically all I have are fake friends; you don't need to be ashamed."

I squeeze her hands this time. I hate the thought of my Goldie girl being lonely before she met me.

"We used to be part of a group of friends who all grew up together. We went our separate ways because of college, but our group was strong. We knew we could always rely on each other."

It was the truth. Grayson, Liam, Cara, and I were best friends growing up. I wanted nothing more than to stay friends with our group, but I ruined it.

Looking back, I'm not sure if what I did was right or wrong, but fuck, she was dead goddamn it. I couldn't tell the truth about a dead girl who was also my friend in a way.

"I love that you had that."

"Had is the key word."

Avery winces.

"Sorry." I give her a half smile as I shrug a shoulder.

"It's fine, please go on."

"There were four of us in the group. Liam was one of my best friends. He moved to Boston after college for medical school. Cara went off to California to join this special program. And you know Grayson was recruited to be a professional hockey player."

Avery gives me a nod as she rubs her thumbs against the outside of my hands.

"Liam was dating this girl, Jenny. They met when he moved to Boston. They'd only been dating for maybe a year or so. Liam thought she was the one. He even showed me the engagement ring he was going to give her at Christmas, her favorite holiday. It was practically half a year away, but he had the whole thing mapped out."

I can tell Avery is bracing for it. Fuck, this is hard to get out after all this time.

"Liam didn't have a lot of time to spend with her because he was prepping for some exams he needed to pass to keep going in school."

"So tough to go through that, I'm sure."

"Yeah, Liam is fucking smart as hell. I'm sure he's made a great doctor."

Avery flinches.

"Yeah, well. Liam and I don't talk anymore. Or Cara, really, for that matter."

"What happened, Lachlan?"

"Jenny also liked to do drugs. Since she was my best friend's girl, I invited her out from time to time. Liam didn't care about the drugs since it wasn't a serious problem of hers, and he knew she was with me. He thought I would take care of her."

I let go of Avery's hands and get up from the couch. I begin pacing around her living room. Time is slowing down. I know I just need to say it. Speak the words and be done with my confession.

Avery is twisted around on the couch watching me loop around her nearby dining room table now.

I pause before bracing to tell her this truth.

"Sorry, this is only the second time I've ever told this to anyone."

"Grayson knows?"

"Yeah... he thinks I need to tell everyone the truth."

I lean down against the back of the couch and take her hands in mine once more.

"That night, Jenny and I were at some colleague of mine's party. He threw these massive parties all the time. It was getting really fucking late, and I had to be up early for a client meeting. I was fucked up, though, so I went into a room to lie down. I knew I had to get home so I could sober up before that meeting, but I just needed a few minutes to pull myself together. The cocaine that night must have been laced with something because I hadn't taken as much as I normally would have because of that client call."

I stand upright again, dropping Avery's hands.

"Jenny came into the room and seemed wildly out of control. She laid down next to me on the bed and started rubbing my leg before stroking the outside of my cock through my pants. I let it happen for maybe a minute or two, fuck, maybe longer, before realizing it wasn't fucking right. Even fucked up, I knew it wasn't right."

I take a deep breath before continuing, needing to finish.

"I pulled Jenny's hand away, and she lunged for me. I was so startled by what she was doing, I froze. That's when I realized she was straddling me. I was about to push her off when she pinned my arms down and rammed her tongue in my mouth."

"Fuck," I hear Avery whisper.

"I pushed her off and told her she was fucked up. She began crying uncontrollably. I told her it was going to be okay. This was just a mistake; she must have been more fucked up than usual because of whatever drugs she took at the party. I told her I wouldn't even tell Liam. Anything to get her under control and to stop sobbing. I offered to call her a ride and get her home. She refused."

Avery's silent as I keep sharing my story.

"She ran out the front door and fucking sprinted down the building stairs. Flights of fucking stairs, it was insanity. I followed behind her, trying to keep up. I found her sitting in her car with the doors locked and the engine on."

"Lachlan..." Avery chokes back a whimper.

"I begged her not to drive. I fucking begged her, Avery."

"I believe you."

Fuck, now it's me trying to hold back tears from this memory.

"And you know what she did?"

"What?" Avery whispers.

"She started to run me down," I say in disbelief.

I pause before continuing.

"I was in front of her car, and she nearly ran me over. I had to jump to the side. When I did, I tried to cling to the open window and begged for her to just stop. That's when she gunned it out of there, and I fell to the ground. I had a few banged-up parts, but I was fine overall."

"Oh my God, Lachlan," Avery barely gets out.

"Not knowing what to do, I started to chase after her on foot. I didn't have to run far when I saw her car. It was fucking smashed into someone else's. It looked so fucking crushed."

I feel the tears streaming down my cheeks. The same feeling of despair that I felt sitting on those church steps all those years ago is haunting me now.

"Lachlan, you can stop if you need to," Avery whispers.

I wipe my tears before leaning forward to run a finger across one of Avery's.

"I made it to her right before the ambulance and police arrived. I didn't fucking wait. I pulled her body out of the car before it went up in flames."

I hang my head low in shame before standing up straight again. I circle the couch that Avery's sitting on and come to sit by her side.

"I lay down next to her and just fucking sobbed. Smoke was everywhere. And that's when the medics and police came. The police took my statement, and I just fucking ran after that. I had no phone, no control, no fucking idea what just happened."

"Father Patrick," Avery whimpers out between tears.

"That's right. I ran right onto the steps of Patrick's church, where I spent the next several hours just crying, confused out of my mind."

I collapse further onto the couch, lying down completely. Moments or minutes go by before I feel Avery lie beside me. We're both staring at the ceiling. Unsure what to say next.

It was cathartic to get that out. I do feel lighter, in a way. But on the other hand, I'm nervous about what Avery thinks of me now. Am I a terrible person who doesn't deserve happiness? It feels like it no matter what anyone has to say.

"Lachlan," Avery whispers as she holds one of my hands against my chest.

"Lachlan," she repeats after I stay still.

I keep my hand in hers but begin to move into a seated position. Avery follows. If the love of my life is about to break my heart for good, I'd like to not be lying down like a mess for it.

Avery is looking at me with such emotion swirling in her eyes.

"Lachlan, thank you for sharing that with me."

I scoff before shaking my head. Avery takes both of my hands in hers and squeezes tightly.

"Sometimes sharing your truth sets you free. Do you feel free?"

"Not yet."

"What will it take?"

"You."

"Let me be here for you, Lachlan."

Avery gets up off the couch before coming back to straddle me. I have to readjust myself with her on me like this.

I slowly stroke her outer thighs before moving her in closer. Avery pulls my head to her chest and hugs me. She shows me her strength and devotion in the simplest of acts.

I stroke the ends of her hair before running my hands down the length of her back.

"Avery," I whisper.

She breaks contact slightly and leans back to face me directly.

Avery puts my head in her hands and gives me a small smile.

"Lachlan," she replies.

I need to know if this is pity or if Avery has accepted my confession. If she can forgive me for *my* sins.

"Do you still want to be with me?"

I need to hear it from her.

"Lachlan, love is not fleeting. It does not falter at the first sign of weakness. I could never not want to be with you as long as you continue to love me only the way you know how to."

My perfect Goldie girl is giving me grace. Allowing me the chance to forgive myself.

"Avery, baby," I say before pulling her into a tight squeeze.

Avery's hands drop from my face as she returns the embrace. "Fuck, my heart is pounding."

"Mine is too, Lachlan. But I need you to know this," she starts before pulling back again.

"I love you, Lachlan. Every part of you. I'll take your past as you've taken mine. I want you forever and not a day less. Can you do that for me? Can you return my love every day?"

"Avery, I love every part of you with my whole being. I love your warm heart and pure soul. I love you. Thank you for showing me that there are still parts of me worth loving."

I tilt my head up slightly before grabbing the back of her head and crashing my lips onto hers. This kiss is different from the others. It's the first one made of true love with all our truths out in the open.

She breaks away, panting.

"Before this continues. Please, Lachlan, let me hear you say it. Not for me, but for yourself."

"Say what?" I reply slightly incredulously.

"Tell me you forgive yourself."

CHAPTER 24

AVERY

*Let love be sincere; hate what is evil,
hold on to what is good; love one another with
mutual affection; anticipate one another in showing honor.*
Romans 12:9-10

Lachlan stares at me like I'm the one who's saving him, not the other way around. Hearing his story about the night that changed his life was devasting. I could feel the ghosts of his past consuming his soul.

I know there is even more to it than we discussed—I'm sure of that. But what I'm even more sure of is my love for Lachlan.

He's brave for telling me his darkest secret. A young adult who was lost and confused turned to one person who gave him a helping hand when he needed it most.

I couldn't wait to meet Father Patrick. That man saved the love of my life. Lachlan needed a fatherly figure to guide him to the right place. I'm just thankful that led him to me.

"I promise you, Avery, with my last breath, I will try to fully come to terms with the fact that I am not at fault for that night. It's hard for me to know that I couldn't save her. That I let Liam down as well. I promise you I will try every day to get there with you by my side."

I close my eyes tightly and smile.

Opening them, my smile takes over.

"Thank you for trusting me. I'll always be here for you. When you are in the dark, let me be your light."

I slowly bring my head back down to his face before leaning in to give him a gentle kiss. Lachlan slowly gives me small kisses back. First on my lips, then he moves down my neck to my collarbone and back up again. My head falls back to give him more space as I grip his broad shoulders tightly.

"Fuck, I need you, Avery. Can I take you as mine?"

My head snaps forward as my eyes find his.

"Right now?" I ask, a little shocked.

Yes, our sexual connection is a big part of our relationship, but I don't want to use it in place of what Lachlan might emotionally need from me right now.

"Yeah, baby. I need you."

I hesitate before nodding.

"Yes, Lachlan. Take what you need from me."

I stand up to pull my shirt over my head, leaving me in my white lace bra. Then wiggle my shorts down, leaving me in my matching panties.

"Fuck," he says as he drinks in my body.

"Are you sure about this?"

I can't help but ask him again.

"Avery, thank you. Thank you for being worried about me, but I just need to feel the connection between us," Lachlan answers with fire in his eyes.

I move from where I'm standing to straddle his body once more.

He instantly resumes peppering my neck and then upper body with the same gentle kisses, alternating them with deep breaths in against my skin like he can't believe this moment is real.

I can't help it as my hips slowly roll against his, rocking into his hardening cock underneath.

"Avery," Lachlan whispers against my skin.

It comes out with such hope that this moment is real. That he's shared his truth, and I've accepted it. Being lost for so long, it's a reality he didn't dream was truly possible in his heart.

My hips grind against him a little harder as his hands travel the length of my back. He sucks deeply on the skin against my neck. I let out a low moan from the sensation.

Something about this feels different with Lachlan. There is no guilt or silent prayer that the other will stay. Only Lachlan and I, pledging to each other that this is it. We are each other's person.

The promise that we have a chance of a happy ending if we both continue to trust the other person. The messes we still need to wade through will be easier with him by my side.

Lachlan's confession is the last step, bringing us to this place. His truth has opened the last door of possibility between us. He is finally able to accept that the person he is today deserves to be happily in love.

"Avery," he groans like he's finally reaching heaven.

"This is us, Lachlan," I whimper.

Suddenly, Lachlan begins to stand, taking me with him. He grips the outside of my ass with his hands, and I wrap my legs around his waist. Lachlan brings his mouth to mine before consuming me.

This is what love is. I feel it now.

Lachlan isn't breaking away from my lips as he carries me to the bedroom. He gently lays me down on the edge of the bed. I prop myself up on my elbows and whimper at the loss of our closeness.

Lachlan stands tall, gazing lovingly at me. I feel so exposed from the red, blotchy kisses along my body and the dampness visibly gathering in my panties.

I'm breathing out heavily. Ready and waiting for his next move.

"Avery, you're fucking exquisite."

I tilt my head to the side as I blush.

"Thank you, hunny," I reply.

"Hunny, huh?"

Amusement fills his facial expression.

"Well, let's see, you have baby, Goldie, Goldie girl…" I can't finish before Lachlan pushes me back gently, and a giggle escapes me.

"I love every fucking nickname I've given you, Avery. You know why?"

Lachlan is so close to my face that I want to lean up and give him another kiss. I instinctually grind my hips against his. A groan escapes him. I giggle again, playing innocently.

"Why is that, *hunny*?"

"Playing dirty, Goldie girl?"

"I have no idea what you're talking about," I feign innocence.

"Hmm…"

Lachlan peppers tiny kisses against my lips, cheeks, and ears. He takes a tiny nibble of one of my ears, and I let out a little laugh from the nip.

"You want to know why I'm allowed to give you whatever nickname I want, Goldie girl?"

"Yes, Lachlan, why is that?"

"Because you're mine."

He leans in for a gentle kiss on my lips.

"Mine to love." Another kiss.

"Mine to cherish." And another kiss.

"Mine to fuck." This time, a deeper kiss.

"Mine to keep safe." A longer, more consuming kiss this time.

"Goldie girl, you're just fucking *mine*."

It's me this time who leans forward to devour Lachlan's lips. I wrap my arms around his neck to bring him as close to me as possible.

"I love you, Lachlan."

I let these three words spill from my lips once again. It feels so natural as if we've been saying it for years.

"And I love you, Avery. With my whole being. I promise you, that's my only truth, the only one that really matters anymore."

Lachlan dives in to devour my mouth.

His left arm braces above me, bringing our bodies skin-to-skin, and his right hand goes to my breasts. Lachlan's touch is rough as he alternates between the two. I love it when I get this version of him. The one who doesn't know what to do with me. I feel as though my whole body is on fire, waiting to ignite.

Lachlan spreads my legs further apart and begins thrusting his pelvis into my soaked panties. He pulls my bra down to expose my pebbled nipples and then my entire breasts. Sucking hard at first on one before blowing slowly against my nipple. Lachlan repeats the action on the other one before switching back and forth.

"Stop teasing me," I whine.

I need more from him, so much more.

"Does my greedy girl need to come already?"

"Yes," I manage to say.

Lachlan's mouth leaves my breasts, then he drags his body down the length of mine. I love the weight of his body on me. Before I can catch up, he grips my panties and rips them off my body.

"Hey!" I fake complain.

"Adding them to my collection." He grins.

Lachlan kneels before me.

"Fucking can't wait to taste you, baby."

Lachlan spreads my legs wide apart.

"Avery, can you do something for me?"

I'm so lost in lust that I don't even realize he's asking me a question. Lachlan starts tracing circles around my folds, and I moan in response.

"Avery, baby."

"Sorry, what is that?"

Lachlan palms my clit with his hand first before putting a finger inside.

"Do me a favor, will you?"

Lachlan grins as I look at him in confusion.

"Sure, what's that?"

I'm a needy mess right now, not understanding why he's trying to have a conversation with me.

"Wrap those legs around my head and suffocate me with your thighs," he says with a wink.

Before I have a chance to keep up with what he just said, Lachlan's finger is replaced with his tongue inside me. Licking and sucking me like it's his dying wish.

I scream in pleasure as I grip the bed sheets. Thrusting my hips on his face, I finally remember what he wanted from me.

I wrap my legs around his head, and I hear his smothered grunt of approval. Back and forth, his rhythm is almost there as I continue to rock in response. I'm so close I can tell he's edging me toward the perfect spot.

"That's it, ride my fucking face, baby," he says, muffled between my legs.

Lachlan unwraps my legs from around his head and looks up at me. I whine from the loss. I was so close to coming.

"I want to hear you say it again, Goldie," he says before going back to licking me. I can't focus on what he even means.

"Tell me again."

"What's that?"

My fingers are twisting on the sides of my pillow.

"Tell me what I need to hear," he continues.

Lachlan goes back to repeatedly sucking me. One of his hands starts pressing on my clit when the realization hits me.

"I love you, Lachlan!" I scream as I come on his tongue.

My body is limbless as I lie on my back against the bed. Lachlan slowly rises and lies down next to me on his side.

"My perfect girl and her perfect pussy," he whispers to me.

With my eyes closed, I slowly feel his fingers tracing patterns against my flat stomach. This feeling of peace slowly steadies my breathing from deep to shallower breaths.

"Avery, I love you," he says almost breathless.

I turn onto my side to face him. I'm propped up on my hand, staring at my favorite color, emerald green.

"You own my heart, Lachlan," I say with a smile.

"And you own mine, Goldie girl," he grins back.

"Thank you for tonight," I say.

He smirks.

I slap his shoulder.

"I should clarify—thank you for sharing your story with me." I lightly laugh.

"Goldie, you don't think we're done yet, do you?"

I can't help but laugh. When does Lachlan ever leave me with just one orgasm?

"No, Lachlan, I think you're training my body to demand multiple orgasms forever. I hope you can keep up when you become an old man," I tease.

"Old man? Never. Now get on all fours, Goldie—I need to sink my cock in this pretty pussy of yours," he playfully demands.

There is no denying it—I crave being his love as much as his plaything. I quickly position myself onto all fours on my bed and arch my back.

I can feel Lachlan behind me. He gently caresses one of my ass cheeks before squeezing it. He repeats the motion with the other.

"Want to play dirty, Goldie?"

"Yes," I practically beg.

I don't care if we love each other. I need this form of intimacy as much as he does. Lachlan squeezes my ass cheek harder before caressing it again. I push my ass out farther. He takes his palm and swats one of my ass cheeks before rubbing it gently.

"Fuck," I moan.

"Does my needy girl like it when she's been bad?"

"Yes, Father Lachlan," I whimper.

"My temptress is here to play, I see."

Lachlan smacks the other ass cheek, then once again, he rubs it to ease the sting. It's our favorite role-play at this point. One he and I both fall into seamlessly. It's all for the next orgasm we're chasing, after all.

The next moment his hand comes down on my other ass cheek. A loud smack makes me gasp. Lachlan repeats the motion of spanking me and soothing the sting a few more times.

With each one, I become wetter.

"Is this tight little pussy ready for me?"

"I think so..."

"You think so? Don't worry, baby, you'll fit my cock like a glove."

He lines up his cock and begins slowly entering me.

I wince at the connection. Lachlan's cock is bigger than any I've ever taken before. Every time, I have to brace myself for his size.

"That's my girl," he continues.

I whimper at the praise. Lachlan grips the side of my hips as he slowly finishes getting fully inside me. It takes a few moments to adjust.

"Fuck," I whimper.

"That's it, baby," he says as he removes one of his hands from my hip to my front. He starts gently rubbing my clit, and it helps ease the intrusion.

"I feel so full," I moan, slowly rocking my ass back against his cock inside me.

"This perfect fucking pussy, every time. Feel how deep I'm buried inside you," Lachlan says with another hard thrust.

He grips the side of my hips again, picking up his pace as he thrusts harder into me. My fingers are gripping the sheets tightly in front of me. I love feeling his stomach against my ass as he thrusts harder.

Lachlan moves one of his hands from my hip again to find my clit. Slow strokes pick up as he pinches hard.

"I'm about to come," I moan loudly.

"I know, baby, make a mess on my cock for me."

I let out a loud scream as I come harder than I did earlier. Moments later, I feel Lachlan's cum slowly seep into me. Filling me up.

After a few moments, Lachlan pulls out of me and sinks to my bed, taking me with him in his arms.

"Fuck, Avery, you are utter perfection," he croons as he places small kisses along my shoulder.

I hum in return, smiling.

"Lachlan, let's be this happy forever."

"Every day, Avery, every fucking day."

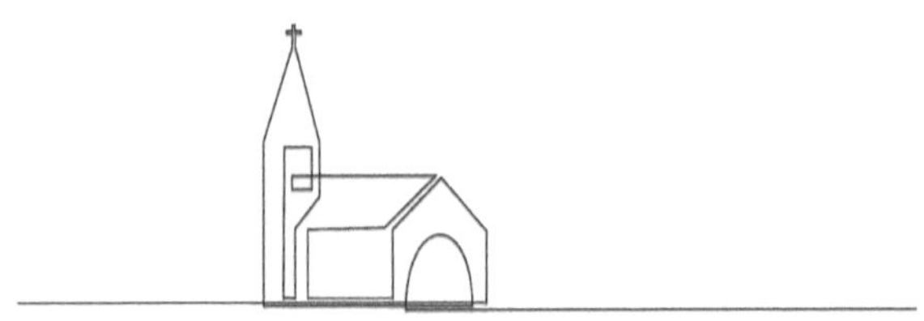

I'm almost fast asleep when Lachlan gently stirs me awake. "Goldie girl, let's get you cleaned up."

Lachlan slowly peels me away from the bed and leads me into the bathroom. I see a few candles lit and hear low music playing in the background. My whirlpool bathtub is filled with bubbles on top.

"I don't know when I'll stop being surprised by how romantic you are," I say.

I lean the side of my body against his, and he curls his arm around me.

"Baby, I hope you always expect this amount of love and more from me. Taking care of you after sex is the bare minimum."

Lachlan guides me to the tub. I step in slowly, sinking into the bubbles. The warm water is easing the tension that's been building all day. Somehow, my orgasms haven't completely relaxed me.

Looking up, I see Lachlan standing before me and sliding into the other side of the tub. He positions my legs on top of his and grips them.

"Thank you," I hum out in pure bliss.

"Don't get my cock hard again, I'm trying to be a gentleman here." He laughs.

"Maybe I need to keep going then," I tease back.

Lachlan lets out one of his full-body laughs that I adore.

"I want to live here forever," I say.

"Baby, you do," he jokes.

"You know what I mean." I giggle.

After some time, Lachlan steps out first to dry off. He leaves the bathroom and comes back in, wearing a different pair of boxers and holding a towel for me. He dries me off and brings me to my bedroom, where a tiny blue pajama set and no underwear awaits.

"No panties?" I ask, arching an eyebrow playfully.

"What's the point? I like to tear them off your body anyway." He shrugs.

I swat his shoulder before putting them on.

Lachlan and I get under the covers of my bed, and all I feel is peace.

"You're so beautiful," he whispers.

I don't even know if he meant for me to hear his words.

I smile into his chest.

"Should we talk?" I ask.

I hate ruining these moments but so much happened to us today.

"Yeah, baby, what about?"

"I know there's so much to say, but, Lachlan, I have a question for you."

"Uh-oh, popping the question already, Goldie girl?" he smirks.

"I guess I am," I tease back.

"What is it?"

He's playing with the ends of my hair that have fallen forward. I love the comfort and ease between us.

"Well, I know you have to move somewhere since you can't stay where you are..." I stammer.

This is harder than I thought it would be, somehow.

"What if you move in here with me?"

"I'd fucking love that," he replies with a wide smile.

Lachlan pulls me in closer to him, placing one of his fingers under my chin and pushing up gently. I'm looking up at him when he crashes his lips to mine. I lift my leg over his hip to bring him closer to my body.

He breaks away first.

"Are you sure, Avery?"

"Definitely. I've never been more sure of anything in my life than I am of you, Lachlan."

I know we still have a few more roads to cross, especially with Kevin, but I want him. In my bed. In my apartment. I want it all to be ours.

Lachlan is mine. My person. My soulmate. My forever.

"Then it's settled."

I smile up at him and soak in the moment.

"We probably have some other things to go over, too... like our days." I laugh.

"Oh right, the hurdles of our lives." He laughs.

"But we'll get through it all," I remind him.

"That's right, fucking everything together. We're a team now, baby." He grins.

"I wouldn't have it any other way."

And for that, I get one of my favorite blinding smiles from Lachlan.

"Well, I guess to jump right into it..."

I brace myself for his reaction to me seeing Kevin today. Not because he'll be mad but because I know he worries about me.

I finally have someone in my corner. And it's the person I want to stay there forever.

CHAPTER 25

LACHLAN

Avery recounted seeing Kevin earlier today. I was fuming when she told me. Kevin is a piece of work for trying to corner her once again in public, even if it was an accidental run-in.

Kevin and his pitiful attempt to try to win her back. And, of fucking course, he's with the assistant.

To be honest, I was surprised by his random contact with Avery. I haven't been able to figure out what his end game with her is. Furious with her one moment and silent the next. Apparently, he's been trying to reach out, but that isn't believable either. I have no fucking clue what this guy's deal is.

He's an enigma. From the business dealings to the random money being pulled out of their account to fucking his assistant. And here I am, thinking I have problems. Kevin is single-handedly destroying his life and doesn't seem to realize it.

Lies and deceit always catch up to you. I sure as fuck know that's the truth.

After Avery told me about Kevin, I caught her up on me resigning to Greg. She wasn't all that surprised that he was shocked and wanted me to stay.

As we lie here in our bed together, I know that all the pieces are falling into place for us to be together. We just need to be able to make it through her divorce and the next couple of weeks that I'm still a priest at St. Peter's.

Avery's nestled tightly against my chest as I stroke her back and play with the ends of her long, blonde hair. I place a small kiss at the top of her head.

I love this woman so fucking much. I can't wait to make her mine forever.

"Lachlan…" she whispers to me.

"Yeah, baby?"

"I love you."

I can feel her smile against my chest, and I can't help but smile too.

"And I love you, Avery."

More than she'll ever understand. Avery was an unexpected gift from God to a broken man. I don't deserve her, but I will try to be the man she needs every day for the rest of my life.

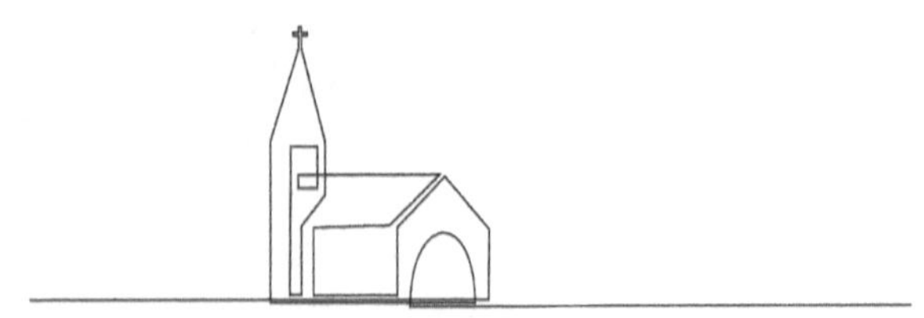

The next day, I return to the Parish office early. Everyone who's already there is eyeing me suspiciously.

I'm sure news has already spread that I'm resigning. It's not common for a priest to resign without there being a major scandal pushing them out.

We've all seen the news when a priest is caught doing something fucked up, and the Catholic Church isn't able to hide it from the public. Since no one knows about Avery, everyone is confused about why I'm leaving. As I begin settling in to take a final look at the gala details, I hear a curt clear of a throat.

I look up to find Patricia.

"Good morning; how can I help you?" I casually ask.

"Leaving already?"

I pull at my collar around my neck. Every day I still have to wear it makes me feel like a fraud.

"I have my reasons."

Simple, I won't give anyone any reason to be suspicious.

"I'm sure you do."

I trust Patricia to an extent, but not enough to think we're anything close to being friends.

She walks toward me and pulls out a chair on the opposite side of my desk before beginning. I notice the gala binder that's usually on my desk is in her hands.

"I took the liberty of going over this already, and here are the remaining approvals I need. Just finishing up the paperwork with vendors," she states.

I take the papers from her hands and begin reviewing them before signing each one.

"Thank you, Patricia. For everything. You've been a big help to me here, and I wish you the best after I leave. This place couldn't run without you."

Patricia eyes me with suspicion.

"Father Lachlan, go find a pretty girl to make babies with. Getting out of this stuffy place is the best thing a young man like you could do."

To say I'm stunned would be an understatement.

"I'll take the lead on Saturday—you enjoy yourself. I'll let you know if I need anything."

And with that, Patricia gets up and leaves my office. I shouldn't have expected anything more sentimental. I think that probably would be considered loving for her.

Some time passes at the office when I hear whispers right outside my door. These whispers catch my attention after everything that's been going on around here. I slowly get up and make my way to the wall near my open door.

It's Greg talking to someone. I usually keep my office light off throughout the day unless I have a visitor. Yes, I treat my office like a cave most days. I can concentrate better like this.

Greg must not know I'm here. Fuck, I can't get away from this mess.

Wait... these are the same voices I heard last time, aren't they? Trying to be as quiet as possible, I listen for more.

"What do you mean leaving?" I could make out being mumbled.

"Leaving as in resigning, he gave me his notice. We can't try to use him any longer," Greg replies.

"Fuck," I hear muttered from the unknown source.

I look down at my watch and see it's a little after noon. Greg probably assumes I'm at lunch. Patricia is stationed near his office and always takes a late lunch since most parishioners stop by around this time if they need anything.

"Don't blame me; you're the one who lost your pawn early on," Greg scoffs in return.

"Watch your step," the other man replies defensively.

A silent war is happening on the other side of my door. I can almost recognize the other man's voice. I haven't heard it much, but I know I have before.

For a fact, I know Greg is referring to me. What was he going to use me for?

"It doesn't matter. The deal will still take place at the gala on Saturday. Then we'll be free and clear of this mess."

"Kevin, don't you forget who helped you with that money problem you were having. If it weren't for this church, you'd be in jail already."

Kevin? Fucking hell. Avery's Kevin. Of fucking course. Another secret meeting. Only this time, I'm listening in.

Kevin's secret meetings with Greg, the large lumps of money he's been donating to the church, the withdrawals from his personal account, the shell company, all of it is connected.

I have to tell Avery. From the sounds of it, I was a planned fall guy for a piece of it. More importantly, this has to do with the company she's listed as the CEO of, I'm fucking sure of it.

This whole situation is more complicated than either of us really know. It's time we involve the police officially. Avery and I need to get to the bottom of this today.

"Get out of here, I'll see you Saturday."

I can hear Kevin's hurried footsteps leaving, and the front parish door slams closed. Greg hasn't made any movements.

I can't move until he leaves, so he doesn't question me. At this point, if he does see me, it'll be pretty fucking clear that I've been in here listening.

Finally, Greg's heavy footsteps walk right past my office and down the hallway. A door slams shut in the distance.

"That was close," I mutter.

Backing away from the door area, I slink back to my desk to pack up and leave for the day. If Greg needs to see me, he can call. At this rate, I don't have many fucks left to give.

After tossing my bag into the passenger side door of my car, I fumble with my phone before sending Avery a text. Thankfully, she instantly replies that she's home.

Home.

Soon to be our place. After the gala, my primary focus will be packing up my small home, selling the furniture that's mine, and moving in with Avery.

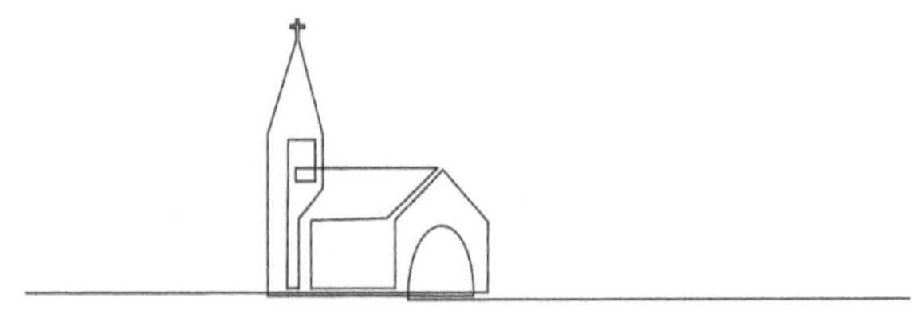

The elevator ride up to the apartment is surprisingly quick for this historic building. Before I can even insert my key into the door, Avery opens it and is a sight to behold. She's flashing me a bright smile that makes all of my worries melt away.

"Hey, gorgeous." I lean in to give her a small kiss.

Her arms go around my neck, and I scoop her into me. Instantly, her legs wrap around my waist.

"Hey there, handsome." She smiles against my lips.

Carrying her to the kitchen counter, I finally set her down.

"God, I missed you."

Avery giggles.

"Hunny, it's been like..." she looks down at the dainty watch on her wrist.

"Four hours," Avery finishes.

"Four hours too long if you ask me."

Leaning in, I give her a kiss on her plump lips. My tongue begs to be let into her warm mouth, which she instantly agrees to. Gripping her sides roughly, I know I'm getting hard already.

Avery breaks away first.

"Rough day?"

"One of these days, we won't have dire news to share, and I can't fucking wait for that day, Goldie girl."

She frowns before asking, "What happened now?"

I explain to her the conversation I overheard, and that something has been planned for me to be a scapegoat for Kevin's deal he's planning on conducting there. The gala is only two days away. I can't wait for my involvement in the Church to finally be over.

Avery lets out a loud sigh. Slowly closing her eyes, she takes steady breaths to regain her composure.

"That day is right around the corner, Lachlan. I'll let Noah know this news and see if he wants me to bring in the police directly. For now, I've decided I'd like to plan my future with my boyfriend."

"That sounds like a cocktease of a statement, Avery."

"Which part is that?"

"Calling me your boyfriend is the second-best thing I think I've ever heard, right after the fact that you love me," I smirk.

"I've told you I love you already, and you're getting hard from me calling you my boyfriend?"

Avery lets out a light laugh.

"Damn straight I am."

"Someone is going all caveman on me, I see, but you know what?"

A full smile can't be contained as she attempts to bite down on her lip bashfully.

"I think I like you the best all territorial like this."

"Avery, you're mine, baby, all fucking mine."

Bringing my lips back down to hers, I can't help but take them roughly in my mouth. Consuming her fully like it's my last opportunity to do this. I don't think I'll ever stop craving her. Wanting her everywhere, all the time.

Avery wraps her legs around my waist again. My cock is already fully hard and painfully straining against my pants.

Her blonde locks are flowing around her back, and I gather a fistful in my hands. Pulling her hair back harshly, I draw away from her lips to lick the length of her neck.

"I need to fuck you immediately."

"Take me to our bedroom," she pants.

"Fuck, don't go making me any harder than you already have."

She laughs wildly as she clings to me. Making my way the few paces to our bedroom, I toss her onto the made bed.

"Take it all off, now."

She pulls her yoga pants off, followed by her sports bra—putting her luscious tits on full display.

"Panties, too, or else you know how I'll take them off." I grin.

Avery's eyes widen before she pulls them down and tosses them aside quickly. I had a feeling that's what she would do. Regardless of how wet she gets when I rip them off, I know my girl loves her lingerie.

"Turn around, ass up," I command as I undress myself.

Avery can't help but take me all in.

This woman is quickly turning me into an ass man too.

"Now, baby. Unless you think it's time for me to take this pretty little hole?"A loud moan ripples through her before she turns around. Bracing herself on the edge of the bed this time, she plants her hands on the edge. Legs are spread wide, and her perfect ass is on full display.

I stalk forward. Finally there, I press my body weight against her back and grope her tits roughly.

"Is my pretty girl wet for me?"

"Yes," she pants.

"Let's find out, shall we?"

I remove one of my hands from her tits and slowly massage the length of her stomach. Dipping one finger inside her first, I find she's soaked already.

"Your pretty little cunt is dripping wet for me," I whisper against her ear.

I insert another digit inside and begin rubbing her clit with my thumb.

Pulling both fingers out abruptly, Avery whines.

"Baby, do you want me to take this pretty pink hole back here?"

Avery moans and nods slightly.

"I'm nervous. I feel like we should prepare for this or something," she pants as I continue to finger her pussy.

"No reason to be nervous, baby, I've got you."

I nip at her ear as I remove my hand from her tit and start making circles around her asshole.

"Do you have any lube?"

Avery shakes her head no as she bites her lower lip to hold back her moans, causing her back to arch further into the back of my hand.

One of my fingers teases her asshole.

"What a shame. Soon, baby, soon."

I kiss the center of her back and move my hand back to one of her tits. With the other, I continue to plunge one finger in and out of her pussy.

"My greedy girl is ready for this cock, aren't you?"

"Yes, please," she pants.

I pump a few strokes along the length of my cock before lining it up to her entrance and use my other hand to grasp the back of one of her shoulders.

I thrust inside her fully, causing her to wince.

"Easy, baby."

"Fuck," she replies on a breath.

"This is your cock, isn't it?"

"Yes, it's my cock."

"What do you want to do with your cock, Avery?"

I continue to thrust into her pussy. Moving my hands from her hips to grope her tits swinging wildly.

Avery pushes back against me every time I thrust forward.

"Harder it is." I laugh.

"Fuck, Lachlan, I'm so close already. Make me come. Make me come."

"Anything my baby wants, she gets."

I move one of my hands down to her clit again.

Working Avery's body is an art I have down to a science. I know instantly what to do to make her come all over my cock.

"Fuck," she moans loudly.

A few more hard thrusts inside her, and I come too.

We're both out of breath, panting from the frenzy that took over us. I slowly pull out of her. Avery stretches before turning around and wrapping her arms around my neck.

"You're my everything, Avery. I'm so fucking lucky I get to call you mine."

"I love you."

She rises onto her tiptoes to give me a tender kiss.

"Now…"

Avery is motioning toward her sides and looking down at her legs. Looking at the same area, I notice what she's implying.

"Right, let's get you cleaned up. Although, I have to admit, I do love seeing my cum drip out of you." I hold back a grin.

Avery laughs before pulling me toward the bathroom.

"Definitely turning into a caveman."

CHAPTER 26

AVERY

With one day to go until the gala, I have been becoming more at ease with my future. I have been looking into possibilities for what to do with my life for some time now. This new future is laden with possibilities. A chance to finally create the life I want.

I have a past now filled with more hurt than someone should experience in a lifetime, but I've proven to myself time and time again that I can conquer what's in front of me.

I decided to change up my routine from my days as Kevin's trophy wife. I've been switching up my exercise routine and trying new workout classes that don't focus solely on my appearance but also on how I feel inside.

The gala showed me that I love being creative and that my main passion is helping people. I should have realized this before, but I never really understood what kept drawing me back to the Church outside of my role as Kevin's wife.

I'm now on the path to starting up my own company. One where I'll find a cause that I want to support and pour my energy into it. It's the best of all worlds for me. Helping people, finding new ways to get new donors, creating events to support it, and everything else that will go into it.

First and foremost, I need to find the right cause to support. Then get Fisher to help me start it up. I know he'll be happy that I've found my voice and passion. He's stoic but always supportive when he needs to be.

"Lachlan, what do you think about me starting a charity organization? One that wouldn't keep anything for itself other than to operate and could really help people. I have the money, and I think that's what I want to do with my life."

Lachlan and I are sitting on my—our—balcony watching the sunrise. It's a crisp day, and I'm cuddled into the nook of his arms. My warm coffee is steaming on the table in front of me.

I never knew happiness could look like this—cold sunny mornings, fluffy socks, and an easy conversation with the love of my life.

Lachlan places a gentle kiss on the top of my head. I cuddle even closer into him.

"I think that's perfect for you, Avery."

I smile.

"Really?"

"Yeah, really. You're an angel. I think you'll find fulfillment in it. Your next step should be something that brings you joy and peace. And helping people is my passion too; I can be involved if you like."

"I would like, very much so," I smile against him.

Wait...

"Joy and peace? Is Christmas your favorite holiday?" I tease him.

He laughs lightly.

"You know, I haven't been a fan of holidays, but I think this year I'm going to say yeah, fucking Christmas is my favorite holiday, so watch out, baby." He chuckles.

"You're going to go all out, aren't you?"

"You better believe it, Goldie girl," he teases.

I reach forward to grab my coffee and bring it close to his mug.

"Good, I like the idea of starting new traditions with you." I clink my mug to his before taking a sip.

Gently, I place it back down on the coffee table.

"Me too." He gives me another kiss on my head.

I've come to cherish these small kisses. A little reminder that he's mine.

"But yeah, Avery, I think you just need the right cause to support. You already have all of the connections you need here. It's a great idea."

"Thank you." Another smile takes over.

I used to never smile this much, but around Lachlan, I just can't help it.

"And I'll be your first donor, whatever you pick."

That reminds me...

"Lachlan, I don't mean to be so nouveau riche, but how do you have money? I've seen your car, and that is not a priest's car." I laugh.

Lachlan joins in, amused by my question.

"It's from my time at the consulting company before I became a priest. Too much money too young, but I did one thing right and that was invest some of it."

"Oh, so you won't need to work?"

"No, baby, I won't need to work. But will I? Yes. I can't sit around for the rest of my life, either. Like I said, I'd be happy to help you with your new company; otherwise, I'll be finding something else."

"To new beginnings together then," I say.

"Together is all I care about," he remarks.

Titling my head up slightly, I give him a peck on his cheek.

"Alright, Father Lachlan, you have got to get ready for the day. Almost done," I sing-song as I pull him up with me.

"Thank fuck," he mutters.

I swat his shoulder playfully at that.

"Come on, my angel, want to get dirty with me in the shower?" he smirks.

"You know I always want to."

Lachlan guides me into the shower and really shows me that he meant every word about how if we were together, he would guarantee orgasms every morning.

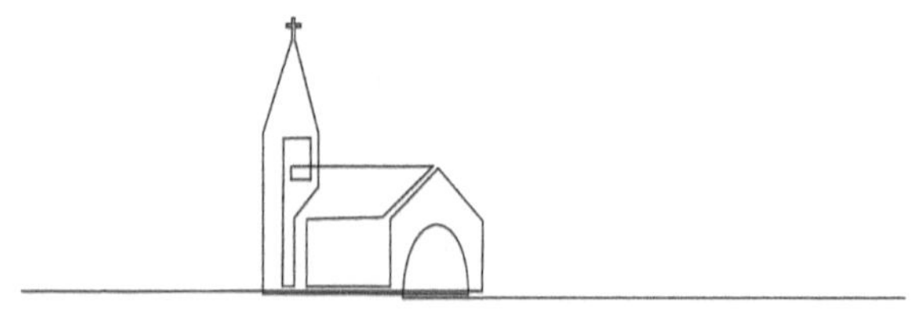

I went out with Lachlan hoping to reach my attorney, Noah, before his day started. It's before nine a.m., but I expect he's always at the office early. I frequently received emails before eight a.m. from him with updates.

Giving Lachlan a small wave goodbye, I cross the street to Noah's office.

I open the front door to his building and greet his receptionist. She calls Noah to confirm I can head back. He says yes, of course.

I fill him in on the latest that Lachlan overheard and ask where we're at with everything. Getting divorced is never easy, but I've been praying to make this go away. Make my Kevin problem disappear for good.

Noah sinks further into his chair and looks at me pensively. Taking in everything I shared before responding to my questions.

"I think it's time to go big, Avery. I know you didn't want to fight hard, but it's time. I've been working on it behind the scenes since we last spoke, but my question is, do you trust me?"

I don't even have to think about it. Noah is one of the few people in Charleston I do trust.

"Yes," I reply.

"Good, don't go anywhere you think Kevin might be in case of retaliation. We're going after him now."

"I won't, thank you."

I prepare to leave when I remember the gala.

"Wait, when are you doing this? I have a gala I've been planning tomorrow. The same one he's going to be attending."

"Avery, you can't go to it. We need to do this today. I'll make it my office's top priority, but we have to get you out of this situation," he begins.

"By the time I do this, chances are he'll know today. Go home and stay home. He doesn't know where you live, right?"

"No, he doesn't. I don't see how he would," I answer.

"Good. It's for the best. You have nothing to be worried about if you listen to me. It's almost over," Noah replies.

He's so sure in himself and his team, I have to be as well.

I nod in reply before heading out. I know he's right, but I can't help but feel disappointed in this. Planning the gala is one of the first real activities I've done in a while that I'm proud of. I'll also have to miss out on a night with Lachlan dressed in a tuxedo.

I take the long way back to my apartment building. There is something so peaceful about these almost secret downtown neighborhood streets.

"Well, don't be late tomorrow night; it's important that our entire family is there to represent us. I don't care if you find this boring, you'll show up," I hear being whined in the distance.

I strolled a little too far off the path to my building, lost in thought about missing the gala.

I look up to see I'm right next to Elaine berating her sister, Emily, outside of what I gather is Emily's home. Emily and I aren't even casual acquaintances. She doesn't like society life and avoids it as much as she can. Because of her family, she doesn't have much of a choice in some cases.

Elaine was never like this before she became Missy's sidekick. I wonder what Emily thinks of her now.

"Elaine, get off of my porch. I'll be there, but don't you dare speak to me like this again."

Emily turns on her heels and slams her door on a fuming Elaine.

Elaine hasn't realized that I'm here as she curses under her breath and descends the steps.

She whips out her phone, and the person on the other end answers immediately. I duck behind a tree, hoping not to be caught. I hate snooping like this, but I'm in it now. I need to know what just happened and avoid the awkwardness of facing Elaine.

"No, she didn't take it well. Just as I expected."

I wish I could hear the other line.

"Missy, she said she'll be there, and that's what you wanted."

Oh no. Elaine's probably involved in this mess too.

I shouldn't be this surprised, but I am. It hadn't occurred to me that Elaine could be corrupt as well.

I peek my head around the tree and see Elaine walking toward King Street and out of my path home.

I let out a heavy sigh of relief.

Getting out from behind the tree, I finish my walk to my building and promptly lock myself in my apartment. I don't know what to expect for the rest of the day, but I know I trust Noah's guidance.

He's gotten me this far. If he says to stay put, then that's exactly what I'll do.

Inside, I send Lachlan a quick text update.

Me:

Some news to share later, nothing to worry about. Noah recommends I stay home. See you here later. Love you xx.

He almost immediately replies.

Lachlan:

Hm… doesn't seem like "nothing to worry about."

Lachlan:

Why is he recommending you stay home? For how long?

I was hoping to not tell him this by text, but I should have known better. He's going to be worried about me.

I fluff my hair and remove my sweater, leaving me in the revealing tank top I had on underneath. Turning my phone around, I take a selfie, showing that I'm wrapped in the blanket I have on. I hit send and wait for his response.

I laugh at his response.

Lachlan:

See you soon, Goldie.

Of course, that would be how Lachlan took it.

I toss my phone to the side and turn on my favorite reality TV show. I must be a glutton for punishment, living a life that could easily be replicated on this show of women stabbing each other in the back for our viewing pleasure.

Only one episode in, I hear movement on the other side of my front door.

I smirk.

I knew he'd leave early, but this is quicker than I expected. I know he resigned, but Lachlan still has duties to fulfill.

Getting up from the couch to greet him at the door, I see an envelope being pushed through the bottom crack of it. Quickly, I go to my door peephole to see who it is.

We have mailboxes on the first floor and a building board where news and invites can be shared. I'm not friends with anyone in my building yet.

When I look through the peephole no one is there.

I keep both latches of my door firmly locked and pick the envelope off the ground.

I open up the manilla envelope. It's thin but larger and bigger than letter-size. This is peculiar.

I shake the envelope to have the contents spill into my hands to pull it out. When instead of a letter or a party invite, dozens of pictures fall to the ground. I lean down to gather them up.

I gasp in shock and my hands fly to my mouth, goosebumps appearing on my skin because of what I'm looking at. Dozens of photos of Lachlan and me are now scattered on my floor.

I scan the outside of the envelope. No sender information.

I look inside to see if anything else is in there, but of course, there isn't.

Someone is trying to send me a clear message. And the frightening part about it is, I know who this has to be. Kevin, or someone involved in this mess, is threatening me.

None of these pictures are scandalous, but it's the threat that these pictures don't look good if they were to get out. People will question why we've been spending so much time together.

I try to think this through before letting my imagination get the best of me.

Priests have friends; yes, of course they do. It makes sense I could be his friend. We did plan the gala together. This means nothing.

I bend down to gather all the photos up and place them on my counter. Something catches my eye on one of them. Slowly, I turn the photo around to find the real message that was meant for me.

"SLUT" is written in red lipstick at the very top. Similar to how I left my message to Kevin when leaving.

Below it, written in pen in block lettering, it says, "Your secret isn't safe with me."

I need to tell Lachlan.

CHAPTER 27

LACHLAN

Sitting in my office as the morning light spills in gives me the opportunity to reflect. The peace that can be brought only by the silence of not being tormented by your mind is unmatched.

I'm no longer torn about my direction in life. The guilt of that fateful night no longer weighs so heavily on my shoulders, and the hope of what the future may bring energizes me.

I am not the man I was nor the man I thought I would be.

Today, I'm submitting my request to speak with the bishop regarding the laicization process to no longer be a priest. I'll always in some way be a priest since I was ordained, but I need to take this extra step to be officially removed from the clergy.

It doesn't sit right with me to just leave and pretend I wasn't a priest for almost a decade of my life. There will be no convincing me to stay. My resignation from this church will help drive home that message.

I don't want to leave by simply marrying Avery and changing who I'm committed to. Marrying Avery has been at the top of my mind recently. I can't wait to make her my wife one day.

I move to my computer screen and begin drafting my request to the bishop. Another bullet item is checked off the list.

Soon, this will just be another chapter of my life. In retrospect, each version of me seems like a separate chapter. Not the same person going through the past fifteen years of life.

I'm ready for the version of myself I am with Avery to be my final chapter.

After sending off the email, I pull together my notes on the gala. I know Patricia said she has it covered, but I want to be prepared for the high donors. That's a part of my role that I still plan to do tomorrow night, even with the mess going on with Greg and Kevin. News of my departure hasn't fully made its way to our congregation, and I don't want any uninvited attention to be on me.

I open up our donor list and study the notes I have for each person.

The morning begins to drift away from me when I see I have a text message from Avery. She instantly makes my day better.

What she has to say is alarming. Her attorney is recommending she stay home?

In no circumstance can that ever be fucking good news. She's insisting that I don't head home straight away, but after that picture, how the fuck does she think I can stay away?

The swell of tits and tiny nipples poking out against her scrap of a tank top. She knew what she was sending, and I love the way she still teases me.

I can do this research from home anyway. I have access to this database for anything last minute I want to add to my notes.

Packing up the few papers, I put them in my briefcase. That's when I see something strange on my desk.

A manilla envelope addressed to Father Lachlan. It must have been lost in the shuffle of the remaining paperwork I was sorting through. Patricia must have placed it on here before I got in this morning.

It was easy for me to get wrapped up in my day. When I do anything, I do it correctly. I don't waste time scrolling on my cell phone or reading the news when I know I have a job to do.

I smirk.

Well, that's almost always the truth, except when Miss Avery Parker distracts me. It's happened more than a time or two in this very office. A distraction I'm itching to get home to right now.

I pull the envelope out of the mess and open it. Reaching in, I feel a stack of something.

Pictures?

I discard the envelope and start flipping through them slowly. Someone has been taking pictures of Avery and me.

These are all of our times out in public settings. A few from our favorite bar, another set on a walk; there's maybe less than fifteen photos here, but enough.

The hair on the back of my neck pricks up. Who sent this to me?

I notice markings on one of the photos and flip it over.

"Ready to repent, Father?" is written on the back of it.

Fuck.

Quickly, I put the photos back into the discarded envelope and tuck it into my briefcase.

I head to Patricia's station in the front.

"Patricia, how are you?"

"A little late in the morning to be asking, but fine. Business as usual here."

She doesn't even ask what I want.

"Someone left me a package, well a manilla envelope, on my desk this morning. Was it you?"

She finally turns to acknowledge me and eyes me cautiously.

"No, that wasn't me."

"But then how could someone get into my office before you arrived?"

She takes a moment to consider my question.

"I was the first person in today."

Clearly annoyed that someone dared complete a task she needed to have oversight on. In this case, I wish she had.

Finally, she snaps her fingers together.

"The office cleaning company. They were here last night; they might have been handed your package after we all left for the day."

"Thank you."

Not helpful but at least a plausible answer. Whoever gave me these pictures doesn't want me to know who they are.

Turning back down the hallway, I go to grab my briefcase. Pulling it up on my shoulder, I take a final look around to see if there are any other mystery gifts waiting for me.

A slight tapping at my door makes me turn around. Greg is standing in my doorway and makes his way in.

"Greg, to what do I owe this pleasure?"

"Just checking in..."

He's lying. I know he wants to use me for whatever he's up to with Kevin. I won't be his pawn, but since Avery's attorney is handling it, I have to pretend like everything is okay.

"All still good here—just doing last-minute preparations for tomorrow night," I reply.

"Good... that's good. The gala tomorrow is sure to be a hit. After that, we can part ways."

I eye him suspiciously. This is just strange behavior, even given what I know.

"If that's all, I'll be working remotely for the rest of the day to concentrate better."

Not a lie, exactly. Being cozied up on the couch with Avery doing this definitely sounds a hell of a lot better than in this office.

"Is there something else?" I can't help but ask.

At this rate, only God knows what the fuck else is happening. I wouldn't be surprised if a literal bomb dropped on the parish.

After the Church and Kevin are behind us, I'm going to enjoy living a peaceful life with Avery. I think we've gone through enough to last us a lifetime.

Greg clears his throat.

Wait, was it Greg who sent these photos to me? Or is he the one who delivered the package?

"Nothing I can do to get you to change your mind and be a bigger part of the team? There are some..." Greg pauses to collect his thoughts.

"New opportunities on the horizon I could get you involved with. Big opportunities for people like us."

I fold my arms against my chest as I take him in. This man is nervous around me. He doesn't know that I'm aware he's up to something, so I wonder why he's acting so off. It can't just be because he intended to use me somehow, could it? Nothing about him is adding up.

"As much as I appreciate it, I know it's the right path for me to move forward. Thank you for your understanding. It's been a pleasure being here."

He clears his throat again.

"Right, well, had to try one last time. I'll see you tomorrow evening."

"See you tomorrow."

Before he leaves, he adds, "And Lachlan, there have been some... whispers about where you lay your head at night. Just something to consider before your time ends officially."

I don't freeze or react at all. He's threatening me.

First the envelope of photos and now this message. It might not be him who helped deliver the photos to me, but it's all connected.

The problem is, he doesn't know I'm a loose cannon. I could give two shits if this town knows that I'm with someone. I only care if there is suspicion that it's Avery until she's officially divorced. For her sake, not mine. She's been through enough to have to deal with another scandal.

Sure, when she and I do go public, it will be the talk of the community for a while, but not nearly as much if she's still married and I'm an active priest.

Greg disappears down the hallway, leaving me feeling disgusted at his measly attempt to blackmail me.

I pick up my briefcase and head out to return home to Avery.

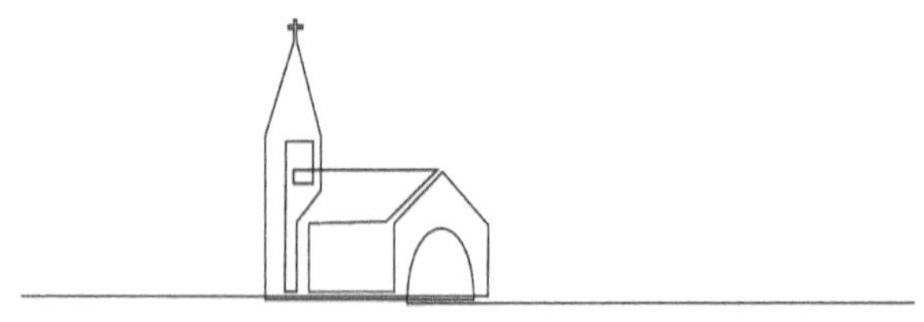

Getting home much earlier than Avery expected, I try to open the door, but the chain is on from the inside. Strange. She usually doesn't do this during the day.

With the door slightly ajar, I call out.

"Avery, it's me. Are you okay?"

"Lachlan!" she squeals in response.

Running to the door, she lets me in. I shut the door behind me and lock it again.

Avery's arms swing around my neck, pulling me into an embrace. I wrap my arms around her too. I slowly run one of my hands down her back to try to soothe her panic.

"What happened?"

She breaks away first, and tears start to trickle down her cheeks.

"Ugh, sorry, I'm not actually sad about this, but I'm so happy you're home," she says as she wipes the tears away.

Avery disappears into the bedroom before returning with a similar manilla envelope.

She hands it to me.

I open it up knowing exactly what I'll find but needing the confirmation.

As I'm doing that, she continues, "Someone knows about us. Or is suspicious, at least."

I quickly flip through them. It's the same set of photos. Someone is trying to scare us. I set the photos and envelope down on a nearby table.

Taking Avery's hand, I lead her to the couch before pulling her on top of me. She's straddling me, waiting for my response.

I don't want to spook her, but after everything, we both deserve the truth no matter the circumstances.

"I got the same set today. Right before I went to leave, I found the package on my desk. Then Greg implied there have been whispers about how I haven't been staying at my house lately."

"I need to call Noah and see what's happening. This has Kevin, Greg, and whoever else is involved with this written all over it. You agree, right?"

"I do; let's give him a call and see what he says."

"God, when will this nightmare just be over."

"Don't worry, we're in this together."

"I know," she sounds relieved but still nervous.

"Avery, those photos are innocent. Meant to scare us. If they had something more intimate, then we would have gotten those. Right now, all this shows is that we see each other outside of the church grounds, and there is nothing wrong with that."

"I know, you're right," she whispers.

"And if anything, who better to be spending your time with than your priest while going through a divorce?"

She leans down and gives me a soft kiss on the lips.

CHAPTER 28

AVERY

Better a poor man who walks in his integrity
than he who is crooked in his ways and rich.
Proverbs 28:6

I waited until Saturday morning to call Noah. I needed time to process everything, and I didn't want to further distract him from his plan on my case. He explained everything to me, so much that it's almost a blur.

He's worried about these packages that Lachlan and I received.

Explaining to him that I'm in a relationship with my priest was a strange experience. It was the first real acknowledgment that I'm in a relationship with Lachlan.

I don't have many friends anymore, especially not in Charleston, and I don't have any family that I am still in touch with. I haven't mentioned it to Fisher yet, but we haven't spoken in a while.

Noah told me it wasn't a problem I needed to worry about, but I should try to keep it under wraps until my papers are signed.

Noah had filed complaint after complaint against Kevin, and I even have a restraining order against him now. My divorce will most likely be finalized in the coming weeks instead of months. And now we have legally stated that I am not, nor have I ever been, the CEO of this shell company. Honestly, I don't even fully grasp how much Noah is handling for me with all of this.

He is the best possible attorney I could have selected, and I'm glad he's taking all of these twists and turns in stride. I'm grateful for him and his team of attorneys.

Lachlan comes up behind me and rubs my shoulders. Naturally, my head falls back to rest on him.

"That feels nice," I whisper.

He places a kiss on the back of my head.

"Feel better?"

Turning around, I look at the man who has turned my world upside down for the better.

"Yes, but I can't believe how much he's been doing. I know he didn't do all of that in a day, but the fact that he had that much foresight to begin preparing all of the necessary documentation is so relieving."

"I'm sure he's had plans for that restraining order since you first met with him."

"You're right, and you know his practice is more expensive than some of the other attorney offices here." I laugh before continuing.

"But I get it. What a team to get all of this done. Well worth the cost."

If I can't find amusement in the little things, I think I'd go crazy.

"So tonight, you aren't going to go?" Lachlan asks.

Taking his hand in mine, I lead us to the couch.

"No, chances are he's still going to be there, and he is probably furious with me."

"Don't you think he knows you'll be there, and he can't show up now there's the restraining order in place?"

"I just can't chance it."

"Don't worry, Goldie girl, I understand. I think it's for the best. I'm just sad for you that you won't be able to see all of your hard work pay off. The gala is going to look amazing, thanks to you."

"Not just because of me," I start.

"Definitely because of you, baby," he repeats.

"Well, thank you, but take lots of pictures for me and then return home as fast as you can." I smile at him.

"Home, I fucking love that." He returns my smile.

"I just can't let him win. I wanted a clean break, and he's made it all so chaotic."

"I know it's hard, Avery. I can't even imagine what it's like for you, but Kevin is clearly corrupt. We know that. Let's just get you out of it all, and he won't win. You've got a team with you, you aren't alone anymore," Lachlan gets out.

"I do, don't I? So are you part of this team?" I tease.

"I'm the fucking number one fan at the very least," he laughs out.

I lean in and give Lachlan a kiss. My hands thread through the back of his hair to deepen our connection.

"Fuck, don't start something we can't finish," he groans against my lips.

"I think we can be quick," I smirk.

Lachlan lets out a louder groan as he stands before scooping me up into his arms.

I yelp in surprise as I wrap my legs around his waist.

"Let's go." He smiles with a shake of his head.

Before I know it, I'm being tossed onto our bed. I can't help but let out a laugh. Life with Lachlan is just fun—the way life is supposed to be. I finally get what people mean about being happy. Time well spent with someone who truly is your partner makes all the difference.

Standing next to me, Lachlan reaches down and pulls my shirt over my head.

"Those tits look fucking delicious; I don't think I've gotten a taste in ages," he says as he admires my bare chest.

Being held under his gaze doesn't make me nervous or self-conscious, I just feel the heat of his want.

"It's been hours, Lachlan." I giggle.

"Too fucking long," he smirks.

Lachlan begins undressing, tossing his workout shirt and shorts on the nearby dresser, followed by his boxers.

Settled back on the bed, Lachlan hovers over me. I arch my breasts closer to his body.

"Are you ready for me, Goldie girl?"

"Yes," I breathily reply.

Lachlan slowly pulls down my sleep shorts first, followed by my thong.

"Surprise, surprise, you don't have to rip them all the time," I tease.

"I hate to disappoint you..." he trails off, eyeing my thong in his hands.

"Don't you dare, Lachlan!"

I laugh as Lachlan leans back on his heels and holds his body weight off mine. He playfully swings them around one of his fingers.

He grins before tossing them onto the same dresser and giving me a quick wink.

"Lachlan," I say through a smile and rolling my eyes.

"Avery, baby," Lachlan's tone has changed as his eyes roam my naked form.

"Fucking gorgeous, body of a sinner," he says almost to himself.

My breasts ache for his touch as my nipples harden from his gaze.

Lachlan leans his body forward more so he's closer to me again. Slowly, he moves so his legs are in between mine. Naturally, I spread my legs further apart.

"Look at you, glistening pussy out on display for me," he says as he takes me in.

Lachlan grips my thighs to spread me further.

"My perfect angel, ready and waiting for my cock. Do you need it, baby?"

"I need it, Lachlan. Please," I start to beg.

Letting go of my thighs, he goes down to rest one arm on the bed and squeezes one of my breasts before popping it into his mouth. Sucking hard, he takes the same hand and starts to play with my clit. He knows the exact spot I need it right now.

"Going to come already, Avery? Fuckin' perfection in front of me every single time," he says before licking and sucking my other breast.

Both of these sensations at once are my kryptonite. I can't help but love that he knows my body so well. I could be his muse any time of the day if I get treated like this.

"Now be my good fucking girl and come for me, so I can fuck you senseless."

He presses down hard on my sex and uses his fingers to strum against my clit.

I moan loudly as I begin to let my orgasm take over my body.

Repositioning himself over me, Lachlan lines his cock up against my entrance, and I wiggle around, trying to get his cock inside me.

"Already want another one? My greedy girl." He shakes his head, teasing me.

"You know I love your cock inside me the most," I manage to get out.

"And my cock loves being inside you," he replies before pushing into me.

No matter how many times I have sex with Lachlan, the feeling of fullness always overwhelms me at the start.

"Relax, baby, you'll adjust for me—you always do," he rasps.

"I know," I breathily answer.

I take a few steadying breaths, and slowly, it begins to feel normal. He must sense that I'm ready because he slowly starts thrusting inside me.

"I'm the luckiest man on the planet," he groans.

This is not the quickie I'd anticipated. Lachlan is looking down on me with nothing but affection, nothing but love.

"I love you," I reply.

Lachlan continues his gentle thrusts.

"And I love you, Avery."

He pulls out of me momentarily before adjusting our positions.

I instantly move as he requests.

He's lying against my back and slowly re-enters me from behind. One hand instantly goes to my breasts as he massages them slowly but roughly. Plucking and teasing my nipples, the sensation is overwhelming.

I begin panting, needing to find relief from the stimulation.

Lachlan slides his other hand to my clit and starts rubbing slow circles.

"My perfect angel today, but tonight I'm going to fuck you like the filthy temptress you are. I think I'll finally take this ass," he growls.

I moan loudly in reply.

"You'd like that, wouldn't you? My cock throbbing inside of your tight virgin hole. Ready to be used for my pleasure," he says, his thrusts getting harder.

"Yes, Father," I whimper as his cock thrusts in me.

"My girl loves to be fucked by her priest," he grunts.

Lachlan starts thrusting harder into me. Picking up speed with his hand on my clit.

"I need to come," I whimper.

"Come, Goldie. Break apart for me."

And I do.

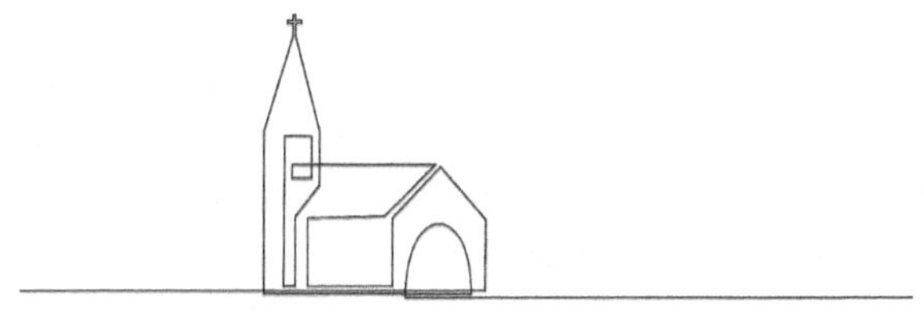

Lying in bed, I watch Lachlan come out of the shower wrapped in a towel. His lean muscles are on display for me.

"You're so hot," I accidentally say out loud.

He looks at me and grins.

"Right back at you, baby," he says, still grinning.

Now that he knows he has a dedicated audience, he whips the towel off from around his waist and tosses it in the hamper.

Swoon. We love a clean man.

I notice that the clothes we discarded earlier are also already in said hamper.

He turns to his now specific drawer and pulls out a pair of his boxers. His ass flexes, and I'm ready for another round of worshiping his body.

Almost as if he can feel my eyes raking his, he turns slightly to look at me and smirks.

"Oh stop." I laugh as I toss a pillow at him.

"If I had more time, I'd give you a punishment for that," he says with his grin in place.

I'm getting wet from the idea. He knows his punishments are the rough play I enjoy.

Lachlan grins even wider.

"Oh stop," I say again.

Going to the closet, he pulls out his tuxedo and puts it on. It's the early afternoon, but Lachlan has to get to the gala early in case any issues arise.

It starts at seven p.m., and there are only a few hours to go.

"I'm going to miss you." I sigh as I watch him tie his bowtie.

Not being able to go to the gala is disappointing, but if Kevin shows up, it'll only create a scene.

"Don't worry, it's only today. Tomorrow will be you and me."

"That sounds nice."

Lachlan finishes getting dressed and looks dashing in his tuxedo. Seeing him put on his cufflinks I notice how his muscles flex as he does. Watching him like this could be a televised sport on its own. I'll never get over that this man is mine.

I walk him to the front door, not wanting him to leave. Stretching up onto my tiptoes, I give him a soft kiss on his lips.

"Keep me posted later."

"Always."

His arm engulfs me, and he kisses me once more.

"You promise you'll stay here? I don't like the idea of you being out and Kevin following you or worse."

"Promise."

I have no intention of leaving this building with a wild card like Kevin out there upset with me.

I do have some self-preservation instincts.

Lachlan heads out the door, and I lock up behind him immediately. I have every intention of staying inside my apartment, but I can't focus on anything of importance to distract me while Lachlan is gone.

I'm too anxious to continue working on the next steps for my non-profit organization or anything of real importance.

This feels like Kevin is still controlling my life. But that's not completely true. I am getting free from his constraints because Noah is working on it. He's working on this for me so I can be free to live my life without Kevin.

With everything intense already happening, we had to get those photos yesterday. Someone knows where I live and what Lachlan does.

As much as I believe it's Kevin, I don't know for a fact who it is or what their intentions are. Is it just to scare me? It's working if it is.

Maybe getting a hotel room would be a smarter idea than staying in my apartment after receiving such an ominous message, but I don't want to run. This is my home, and I won't let someone make me feel unsafe in it.

I need to speak with the building security guard on duty. Someone let the mystery person up to my apartment to slide the photos under my door. Either the person lives here or someone was given access. I need to rule out the possibilities.

I quickly change into athletic gear and lock up behind me.

Making my way quickly downstairs, I see Bart, one of the security guards, behind the front desk.

"Hi, Ms. Parker, how can I help you?"

"Hi, Bart. I was hoping you could help me figure out who left a package at my door."

His eyebrows bunch together, and he has a quizzical expression on his face.

"Excuse me, miss? A package?"

"That's right. It was really one of those manilla envelopes. It didn't have anyone's contact information on it, and it's a super generic item. I am trying to figure out who it was," I say.

I don't want to share that I'm worried about what I received with him just yet.

"Sorry, ma'am, but no one would be allowed to do that. It would have to be a resident. I can take a look at the footage. Do you know anyone in this building?"

I shake my head no.

"Very strange. My best bet is that someone handed it to a resident to take to your unit. I can check security footage and get back to you this evening."

"Thank you, that would be great."

I already have my answer, though. I know it was Kevin or someone who works with him on his corrupt business dealings. Bart and I review a few details to help him narrow down when it would have happened.

Back out front of my apartment, I look around at the other units on my floor. I really should get to know my neighbors.

After unlocking the door, I step inside and nearly slide across the room. I bring my hand to my heart to steady myself.

"Fuck," I mumble.

What was that?

I look around on the ground to find another envelope. Just like the one I was inquiring about downstairs.

Goosebumps take over my body.

Quickly surveying the room, I dash to the kitchen and grab a knife. I check my apartment room by room and find it's empty.

Reaching into my pocket, I find my cell phone and call Lachlan. It goes to voicemail. I shoot him a quick text to call me back.

At least I'm not going to be attacked in here... right?

I bend down to where the envelope is on the ground and pick it up. Reaching inside, I pull out another stack of photos. More of Lachlan and me. Slowly, I flip through each one.

The first is of us at Jackson's.

The second is us outside the parish office, and my hand is placed on his shoulder.

The third is of us, shoulder to shoulder, walking along the street one evening.

The fourth is me in his car.

And the fifth is what gets me.

Kevin knows.

Lachlan and I are walking hand in hand to the elevator inside the apartment building lobby. It was so natural we must have felt safe in our space and didn't realize we were still technically in a public place.

I have to let Lachlan know. Kevin will show up tonight. He's not going to stop whatever madman plan he's involved in. I guarantee he'll be more than happy to ruin Lachlan in the process if he knows his toy has moved on.

I try Lachlan on his cell phone again, and there's still no answer. It's only five p.m. I could get dressed for the gala, go inside, and warn Lachlan, then head back home before anyone else arrives.

Trying his cell phone once more, I get no answer.

"This is a good idea; I have to warn him," I say out loud.

Whether this is true or not, I have to get to Lachlan first. I have to try before something terrible happens.

When I get out of the shower, I pick up my phone to find a series of texts from Lachlan. His phone has bad service inside the event venue, and he's not sure if I've been trying to reach him. He'll be home by ten tonight.

At least I know that he must not be getting any of my calls.

I have a feeling the rest of the night won't be as easy to clear up.

CHAPTER 29

AVERY

Looking at myself in the mirror, I do a final check that everything is in the right place. Not bad for pulling this look together in thirty minutes.

In my signature blue color, I swish my gown around. It's adorned with small sequins on the bottom, giving it that extra something special I like to have on when I get dressed up for an event.

I change out my purse for one that matches my dress and make my way to leave.

I have to do this.

Now is the time to be confident, to be brave. I can't let Lachlan be blindsided by Kevin now that I have this final confirmation he's aware we are seeing one another.

I send Lachlan a text explaining everything. I'll be there soon enough.

My transportation is waiting for me downstairs. I hop in the waiting car and head to the venue to warn Lachlan.

I know I'll get there in time. I have to.

The venue we picked is gorgeous. It has an intimate feel to it but has the space to host the five hundred guests that will be here tonight. Everything looks exactly as we planned.

I look around to see roses spilling from everywhere. Candles are lit throughout the entrance and walkway to get to the main space. Glasses of champagne are ready for guests on arrival.

Reaching the check-in desk, I find Patricia.

"Hi, Patricia, great job," I beam.

I'm proud of what we've done.

"Oh dear, we have certainly missed you. Thank you, but this is all you. We just brought it to life," she warmly replies.

"That's not true; it was a team effort. Thank you for letting me be part of it," I answer.

"Nonsense," she says.

"Is Father Lachlan here?" I ask.

She smiles almost knowingly.

"Yes, dear. Straight through the doors, he should be speaking with the venue event coordinator. We've had a bit of a mishap already," she sighs.

"Thank you."

I find Lachlan exactly where Patricia told me he'd be. Lachlan and the venue coordinator are speaking rapidly, trying to solve the issue, so I wait outside the office door.

"That would be great," I hear Lachlan say, sounding pleased.

I wish I could have been here to help him earlier today.

The sound of men's dress shoes catches my attention.

Lachlan is looking down at his cell phone, not paying attention to his surroundings. His eyebrows are pinched together, jaw clenched, clearly annoyed that he still doesn't have any cell service here.

I have to take a step back before he walks into me.

"Oh, excuse me," he says apologetically, glancing up at me before returning his gaze to his phone.

Then he realizes it's me.

Lachlan's eyes widen in surprise before concern takes over.

"Avery, what are you doing here? Are you okay?"

Lachlan grips my outer arms gently and looks me over. He scans my body for any sign of harm from our run-in.

"Lachlan, I'm fine, you didn't hurt me. But I've been trying to reach you."

He looks around before he pulls me into an open, unused office across the hallway.

"My cell phone has no service in this place. Are you okay? What happened?"

Lachlan frantically searches my face for anything wrong. He's on guard now, looking around us and back to me.

"I'm good. I'm safe," I start. "But I got another package."

I recap the events from earlier today with him.

"Fuck," he mutters under his breath.

"I wish you wouldn't have come—it's not safe for you. But I understand why you did. If anything were to happen to you..." Lachlan trails off.

His eyes close momentarily. I rest a comforting hand on his chest.

"Lachlan, I feel the same way, which is why I'm here. It's definitely Kevin. Should you leave?"

"Fuck no, I'm not running away with my tail between my legs because of him. Let him come. That's barely proof of anything," he scoffs.

"Lachlan..."

"Avery, I love you. Fuck, I was so worried when I first saw you here. But I will be fine. It's you that I'm worried about. Let's get you home and safe."

I lean into his chest and inhale his woodsy scent. It's calming to be near him.

"Goldie girl, let's get you home," he repeats.

Wrapping me into his chest, he holds me tightly in his arms, almost as if he, too, needs the reassurance that everything is okay. I wrap my arms around him as well.

Slowly, his hands go up and down my back. "That feels nice," I whisper.

"I was so worried when I saw you," he whispers back.

"I just had to let you know."

"I know."

His hands continue to caress me.

Lachlan pauses before bringing one of his hands to the bottom of my chin. His thumb is tracing around my lips while his fingers keep my chin held up to him.

He tilts my chin up more so we're gazing at each other.

A small kiss comes to my lips.

Lachlan breaks away for a moment to look at me once again.

"I'm okay, really."

Lachlan lets out a sigh before regrouping. He brings his mouth to mine and kisses me.

Lightly biting my bottom lip, causing it to sting. He then licks the spot to soothe it. His tongue enters my mouth this time, and my body is pulled tightly against his.

The way his mouth consumes mine is intoxicating.

I pull away slightly.

"I didn't mean to scare you."

"I know. It's hard not to be worried with everything we have going on. I sure as fuck won't let Kevin hurt you anymore," he says evenly.

"Let me make it up to you," I whisper.

Lachlan's eyes go wide momentarily before collecting himself.

"I know I should say we really shouldn't, but we've done riskier things, haven't we, baby?"

I nod my head in agreement almost frantically. His warm lips crash to mine again, causing a moan to naturally break free.

Pulling away, I sink to my knees before him.

"Father Lachlan, can I please have your cock in my mouth?"

I bat my eyes up at him with a pout of my lips.

"Do you deserve to have my cock after what you just put me through, Avery?" he asks sternly.

"If you'd rather I suck another priest's cock, I can," I smirk.

Lachlan's eyes are smoldering with desire before letting a grin appear.

"I think I need to fill this smart mouth up to keep you from being disobedient, don't I?" he muses.

"Yes," I whimper.

"Let's see if my cock is big enough to keep you occupied."

I undo his zipper first and pull down his dress pants.

For a brief moment, Lachlan leans back and locks the door behind him.

"Lessons learned and all," he smirks.

"Right," I say, trying to stifle my laugh and get back into our scene.

I pull down his boxers next. Lachlan's beautiful cock springs free. It's already weeping with pre-cum.

I naturally lick my lips.

"Come on, Goldie, let me fill that mouth of yours with my cum." He grins.

I take his full length in my mouth and suck it back.

Bobbing my head back and forth, I worship his cock as quickly as I can. I use my hands to help encourage him to come as I continue to suck him from root to tip repeatedly.

When it hits the back of my throat, it's his undoing.

Lachlan begins fucking my mouth to try to come. He's in control now as he holds the outside of my head and thrusts again and again.

"Get ready to swallow. We can't leave any mess behind," he rasps.

Moments later, his cum is spurting into my mouth. I drink it all and lick his cock a final time to clean him up.

"You are utter perfection, Avery Parker," Lachlan says adorningly.

I wipe what's remaining around my mouth before standing up to meet him.

"You go first. I'll see you in the hallway. Knock if it's clear for me to join you," I whisper with a faint smile.

Lachlan pulls up his boxers and pants before attempting to fix his tuxedo so he doesn't look disheveled. I smooth out my dress before reapplying my lipstick in my compact. You can barely tell I just had his cock in my mouth.

A few moments later, Lachlan is out the door. Waiting for his signal, I stand with my hand on the doorknob.

Only a few moments go by when I hear Lachlan's knock, and I make my way out of the office and back into the hallway. Lachlan is a few paces ahead of me already. I reach Patricia's welcome desk and see Lachlan has paused there.

"Patricia, Ms. Parker won't be staying, but before she leaves, I wanted to thank you both for your help. I had no clue how to put a gala together, so thank you."

I didn't notice when he was speaking that there were two small bags in his hands. He gives Patricia hers first and then hands me mine. Lachlan must have picked these gifts up on his way to the gala earlier.

Patricia opens hers up to find a gold necklace with a cross pendant at the center.

"It's way too much, Father, but thank you." She blushes.

Lachlan has done the impossible—Patricia is finally a fan.

He waits patiently for me to open mine. Instead of a cross, it's a locket on a gold chain. I open it and find a picture of us inside, one of the few we've taken together. Quickly snapping it shut, I look up to thank him.

"It's beautiful. Thank you, Father Lachlan. Can you help put it on me?"

"Of course."

I turn around and hand him the small diamond-crusted locket. The details are so intricate you would have to stare at it to capture its full beauty.

The feel of Lachlan's fingertips skimming against my skin sends shivers down my body.

I turn back to face them both and try to get rid of the thoughts of how I really would like to be thanking him right now.

Patricia has a warm smile on her face as she eyes us both.

"Well, I just have to use the ladies' room, and then I'll be out of here. Thank you again," I say.

I appreciate that Patricia hasn't questioned why I'm not here. I have a feeling she knows something is going on between Lachlan and me.

I can feel Lachlan's eyes tracking my movements through the event as I head to the closest restroom I can locate.

I'm glad I came to warn him, but something feels off. Not between us, but this evening. Kevin will be here soon, and I just hope he doesn't ruin the night or try to confront Lachlan.

I really have no idea how Kevin will try to play this out with so many community members expected to be here as well.

Passing by the opulently decorated tables, I feel proud of this work. Champagne glasses are stacked on each other, forming towers filled to the brim with the finest of champagnes all around the room. A last-minute touch I added before saying goodbye to my planning efforts.

As I finish washing my hands in the restroom, I stare at my reflection in the mirror. The changes that have taken place, the woman I am turning into, it's all there looking back at me.

I like what I see in front of me. This version of me is one I've worked hard to become.

Deep breaths, it's time to get out of here.

While slipping out of the door I'm jerked back suddenly. I feel a hand go over my mouth and another around my waist. These hands grip me harshly, and I can barely breathe.

What is happening to me?

I begin to panic as my eyes race frantically around my surroundings.

My mind is going a million miles per hour, but my body has shut down. I'm unmoving as I let this person assault me. Frozen in place as horror takes over.

I try to speak but can't as my body finally starts to act. I begin trying to escape from this person's hold on me. I must not really be moving much because it's not working. My eyes begin to prick with tears.

The person slowly starts to drag me backward into the dark between the restrooms and an emergency exit sign flashing brightly.

Looking away from the sign, I see the door slightly ajar. This must be how this person got in here unnoticed. No one is manning the side doors.

And why would they be?

This is meant to be a special event for a Catholic church. A Christian function, not the place where a woman should be afraid of being assaulted.

My body knows it should be fighting back more than it is, but I can't move one way or the other as my brain shuts down. I shouldn't be letting this person take control.

Breathe, Avery, breathe.

"That's right, be my meek little sweetheart, *wife*," the voice grates.

My mind blocks out the surrounding noise.

It's him.

Kevin is my attacker.

Of course, the average woman wouldn't need to be afraid to be here. But I knew I did, and I let my guard down.

Kevin is here.

He's come for me.

Noah had tried to warn me not to leave my apartment under any circumstances because of all of the filings we were doing to nail Kevin down and clear my name. And here I am, now under Kevin's punishing grasp, fighting for my life.

He kicks what is holding the door slightly open and attempts to pull us both through the exit. That's when my instincts finally kick in, and I know I have to take my chance.

I am not helpless. I have to do something before I'm taken somewhere else where no one will know where I am or who I am.

I need to act. And I need to act now.

I bite down hard on his fingers covering my mouth. Blood is on my lips—I must have broken his skin.

"Fuck," he yells loudly.

I stomp one of my heels down onto one of his feet, causing him to partially let go of me and lurch over in pain. My arm slips from his hold. I rip his hand away from my mouth fully and scream.

Trying to break further away, I pull all of my weight to get out of his grasp. I'm almost there as I swing my elbow back as hard as I can into his stomach.

His hold is gone completely.

About to dart away, something hard and heavy hits the top of my head.

Everything goes dark around me.

CHAPTER 30

LACHLAN

Looking down at my watch, I realize it's been several minutes since Avery went to the restroom. I've been waiting to say goodbye to her before everyone arrives.

People will be here soon, and I don't want Avery around for a chance encounter with Kevin. I can handle whatever Kevin wants to throw my way, whatever scene he wants to make, but I can't let her get hurt.

Making my way to the restroom, I stop in my tracks. A blood-curdling scream rips through the venue.

Avery.

I shout for someone to call the police as I sprint to where the sound came from. If anything happens to Avery, I'll never be able to forgive myself. She is mine to keep safe.

What was I thinking, not walking with her to the restroom when we knew Kevin had been taunting us? We both knew we needed to be on high alert.

Even with the restraining order, there is no way that someone like Kevin would be taken down so easily. I should have known better. This will be my fault if anything happens to Avery tonight.

I dash into the women's restroom, not caring if someone is in here. I kick open each stall to make sure no one is hiding. Frantically, I run my hand through my hair to try to think of what to do next.

There is no sign of Avery in here. I have to keep searching the area.

Leaving the restroom, I'm about to head back toward the front to see if the police have arrived when I notice sequins on the ground.

Navy-blue sequins that look similar to the ones that were on Avery's gown. They are right between the two restrooms and another door.

Looking up, I see a low-flashing light appear through what looks like an emergency entrance.

Fuck.

I open the door to the stairwell and run down the two flights of stairs.

That's when I see Avery. And Kevin... and Frank? Fucking Frank. Kevin and Frank are carrying Avery's almost-lifeless body and heading for the exit door.

Panic fills me as I stare at her limp in their arms.

"Fucking stop," I shout at them.

Kevin and Frank's eyes shoot up to me as my chest hangs over the railing. I'm heaving uncontrollably witnessing this.

I dart down the flight of stairs as they freeze because of my presence. I hop over the last few stairs to be face-to-face with her kidnappers now. Frank is surprised by me finding them like this. He's sweating uncontrollably, looking at me like a deer in headlights. Meanwhile, I'm surprised Kevin hasn't forced him to keep going.

Instead, Kevin is sneering at me like a child who just found out he couldn't play with me on the playground.

I slowly take a step toward them both. Letting out a stabling, low sigh, I glance down to Avery before looking Kevin in the eye.

"You don't have to do this, Kevin; let her go," I demand.

He scoffs at me, shaking his head while rolling his eyes.

Kevin may have the upper hand right now, but he's still nervous. I can see his deep swallow and a vein protruding from his neck. Back to facing me directly, I can see nothing but venom in his eyes.

"Go fuck yourself, *Father*," he snarls.

I can't react to that, not when I have Avery to think about. Normally, I'd tell him to stop being a little bitch because she didn't want to be with him.

"Kevin. Let. Her. Go. Now," I say, enunciating each word slowly.

Let that sink in. I have to play this right. If I let them leave this stairwell, it'll only mean more harm will come to Avery.

Kevin turns his head slightly to glance through the square window box on the door. He's waiting for someone else. I just need to buy more time for the police to get here. It's not like Kevin or Frank know that they should be arriving any minute.

"Kevin, it's over. You shouldn't have gotten Avery mixed up in whatever the fuck business this is of yours. Leave her behind and run."

Kevin turns back to me.

"You don't have any fucking clue, do you?" Kevin screams.

It causes Frank and me both to flinch.

"I guess not, so here. Put Avery down, and why don't you tell me?"

I'm trying to remain as calm as possible, but it's becoming harder to do.

"You think I'm running this? That's fucking rich. Why don't you ask your precious Father Greg what all this is about first," Kevin responds.

There is panic and anger coursing through his body.

"I thought it was you leading him? I'll be honest here; I haven't worked that piece out," I say truthfully.

"That's because this whole operation is bigger than you, me, or even Frank here," Kevin snarls as he waves a gun I hadn't noticed before around mindlessly in the air above his head.

Where did that come from? Was it in his other hand this whole time?

"Okay, calm down, Kevin. You don't have to make things worse than they already are."

"Calm down? Right." He laughs maniacally.

Frank keeps darting his focus between Kevin and me. Unsure of what the fuck is going to happen next.

Suddenly, a cool breeze washes over me as someone opens the door that Kevin has been waiting at. Lo and behold, it's Greg.

"Now, now, boys. Let's not cause a bigger scene than needed," Greg calmly says.

Greg fixes his black trench coat collar before fidgeting with his black gloves. Kevin rolls his eyes before refocusing back on me.

"Lachlan, it's unfortunate Kevin here can't keep his mouth shut because now you'll be coming with us," Greg states matter-of-factly.

"I'm not going anywhere with you," I almost laugh.

Greg starts to laugh, too, as if I just told him a joke instead of saying I'm not letting them take me with them. Looking down, he sees Avery's still breathing but unconscious.

"Oh dear, what do we have here?"

Concern actually causes Greg's eyebrows to pinch together momentarily.

"You know what she did. I couldn't leave her behind when I saw her," Kevin sneers.

"Hmmm..." Greg muses.

His eyebrows unfurrow, and he gives a light shrug of his shoulders.

"Very well, but you still managed to get the final documents we need?"

Greg turns toward Kevin more directly now.

"In my jacket," Kevin replies.

"Let's go then," Greg nods.

Then he gestures for us all to walk out into the dimly lit alley while putting his hands inside his trench coat pockets.

"And for fucks sake, put that gun away, I have mine," he says to Kevin.

He pulls out a small gun from his pocket before shaking it in the air to signal for me to join them. I can't let Avery out of my sight. Of fucking course, I'm coming along now.

A blacked-out SUV is waiting in the alley.

I need a fucking miracle to happen. I know that I can't let us get in that SUV, but Avery is unconscious, and in order to protect her, I think we might have to.

Greg opens up the passenger door for Kevin and Frank to put Avery down. I look inside to see Missy is there waiting. I knew she was fully involved in this matter.

"Missy," I seethe.

She taps her red nails against the front seat chair and grimaces.

"In the flesh, Father," she smoothly replies.

"Of course you're involved," I say almost in disbelief.

Avery and I had suspected Missy's involvement, but I never thought she would be this aware of everything. I had assumed if anything it was just for stolen money. Now she's involved in kidnapping?

Missy laughs from her seat.

"Like my photos?"

She smiles wickedly at me.

The world is spinning on its axis as it all starts to come together.

"Everyone, stop. Just fucking leave us be," I shout.

Greg and Missy laugh loudly.

Kevin is still shooting glares at me while Frank continues to be panic-stricken.

"No chance in hell," Greg replies as he waves the gun in my face.

He thinks he's in control, but I know this is my time to act. With the gun in the air, I move quickly and punch him in the gut, causing him to fall over.

Kevin lets go of Avery's legs making them slam to the ground as Frank struggles to keep her up.

Kevin steps forward to me.

"Lachlan, you can't have her. What you don't seem to understand is that she's my property. She should have stayed in the dark like she was before. But no, it didn't work out that way, and now she has to die."

He stalks forward even more, but I hold my ground.

He's getting closer.

"Fuck you, Kevin," I swing and hit him clear across the jaw.

He steps back and laughs darkly before drawing his gun from his pocket. Fumbling to keep control of it, he drops it to the ground and lets out a frustrated sigh. In a matter of moments, he's lunging for me next instead of picking up the gun. In a desperate attempt, he tries to tackle me to the ground.

My build is bigger than his, and he can't manage to take me down on his own. We're in a scuffle I'm desperately trying to end when I hear sirens.

A woman's voice shouts in the distance, "Down here!"

Kevin quickly pulls himself off me and darts for the SUV door. I get up fast and head in the same direction.

"You can't fucking have her," he shouts to the sky like an enraged monster.

Greg is in the driver's seat with the engine running.

"Kevin, get the fuck in the car, and leave her. She's not part of the plan."

I pull Avery from Frank's arms and see fumes practically coming off Kevin. He has to decide now. Come to where Frank and I are, or hop into the SUV and have a chance of escaping.

"Fuck," he screams.

Frank has turned away from me and is running down the alley away from the building.

I can't let Kevin get away with this.

It feels like time has slowed down as I pull my cell phone out of my jacket pocket and throw it right at the back of Kevin's head as he attempts to get into the vehicle.

It strikes him directly, causing him to stumble backward. He loses his footing and begins falling to the ground. Kevin's head hits the asphalt hard, leaving him unconscious.

The police are screaming at us from a distance in the alley. Slowly, the voices get closer until they're right next to the three of us.

I sink to the ground with Avery in my arms, and she falls into my lap. My past that I'd been running from and my new reality are now overlapping.

I look down at Avery.

I'm back on the side of a road with a woman I care deeply for dying next to me. Avery can't have the same fate as Jenny. I won't fucking stand for that.

"I need an ambulance!" I scream to no one in particular.

Tears are welling up in my eyes as my surroundings continue to be a blur.

Greg attempts to take off in the vehicle with the backdoor open.

The police begin firing immediately. He speeds up, but the bullets flying at the car cause him to lose control of it.

A loud bang of metal crashing into metal rings out. He's crashed the SUV into a nearby dumpster. Glass goes flying into the air as airbags are deployed, and a crunch takes over the night.

Police are aiming guns at me, Kevin, and Avery.

Kevin has started to gain consciousness and sits up. I see when he realizes he has guns being pointed at him.

"I'm Father Lachlan; this woman has a restraining order against this man, her husband. He did this," I manage to get out.

Two medics come over to us and help me with Avery. They try to pull her from my arms, but I can't let go.

"Sir, we need to get her out of here," one of them says.

I nod, realizing it's true. The medic places her on a gurney.

An officer puts Kevin in handcuffs while this is happening.

"Fuck you," he shouts at me.

"You think I'm bad?" he's talking to no one in particular as he screams in frustration.

"That priest is fucking my wife," he scoffs.

"So fucking pure and godlike, my ass," Kevin continues.

We have a small crowd of gala guests gathered around us. Close enough to hear his statement.

The police have put up a small barrier trying to block the alley from where we are, but it doesn't prevent the truth from remaining a secret any longer.

"See? He's not even denying it! Fuck you, man, fuck you!" Kevin seethes as the officer finishes reading him his Miranda rights.

Kevin tries to launch for me, but the officer holds him back.

He's being escorted to the back of a waiting police car. In the distance, police have surrounded the SUV. Greg and Missy are both being put into handcuffs near the vehicle, while Frank is being escorted back toward me in handcuffs by a different police officer.

I hop into the ambulance with Avery.

"I'm her boyfriend," I inform them.

One of the medics appears shocked but quickly recomposes herself.

"I'm going too," I say just so they don't dare try to tell me I can't.

Avery is breathing with an oxygen mask. She's alive. My Goldie girl has survived so much, but she's still here with me.

Thank fucking Christ.

CHAPTER 31

LACHLAN

The length of time I had to wait in the hospital lobby to hear from Avery's doctors was excruciating. It was painful to know that she was lying there helpless, and there was nothing I could do to help.

I pace the lengths of the halls. Removing my bowtie first, then hours later my jacket, and finally here I am now, sitting with a stale cup of coffee, sleeves rolled up my forearms, praying for a final miracle.

I know God is probably done granting me miracles, but if there's the possibility for just one more, I want it for my Avery. She has been through so much in her short twenty-eight years. Avery deserves the world. I just hope I'll get the news I'm waiting for to give her just that.

After some time here, her doctor did find me to tell me she wasn't going to die. Of course, he had better bedside manners than that, but that's the fucking gist of it.

Letting my head fall forward, I say a silent prayer. One that allows me to hang onto a thread of hope that everything is going to be okay. It's almost two in the morning, and I haven't heard anything in hours.

After we arrived and Avery was taken back, I called her attorney Noah to update him on the situation. There is no doubt in my mind that one of the attorneys at his office is still hard at work for Avery right now. Dealing with police and Kevin's attorney.

Now, I'm grateful that Avery found someone who wasn't just a divorce attorney. Someone who knew that his practice should have legal experts in every area. For an attorney, you would think his practice handles mob cases or politicians. I don't fucking know, but he just has connections that even surprise me.

Getting up to stretch my legs, I see Grayson coming through the automatic doors.

"Hey, man, how are you holding up?" he asks, patting my shoulder.

"Still waiting, but a few hours ago, her doctor said they were taking her into surgery. I thought I would have heard back by now."

I have no concept of how long this will take but fuck, over five hours? It's insanity.

We walk back to the lobby seating area I was sitting in before.

"She'll pull through," he reassures me.

"I know, it's just taking too fucking long."

I sigh loudly and sweep my hand through my hair. We sit in a comfortable, reassuring silence for some time.

"You know this is all over the news, right?"

Fuck. I wondered.

"I assumed it would be, but I haven't seen any reporters through those windows yet..."

"I'm surprised by that too. I bet there will be in the morning. You better figure out a plan to leave."

"I'll call Avery's attorney in the morning again; he'll have a plan for us," I reply, trying to stay calm.

Noah will be able to get us out without being seen.

Avery's new shift doctor emerges from the corridor and greets me.

"Lachlan? Avery's fiancé, correct?"

When I got to the hospital, I had to change my tune to the doctors. They really wouldn't let me in as just a boyfriend, and I couldn't intimidate them into not questioning my role in her life.

I sure as fuck won't be wasting any time making her officially my fiancée once she gets out of here.

"Yes, that's me."

Grayson waits in his seat as I walk closer to the doctor.

"Well, I have great news. Ms. Matheson is awake. You can go to see her now," he informs me.

I want to wince at the reference to her old last name. Since she isn't officially divorced, it's still the one on her license. At least he didn't refer to her as Mrs. Matheson.

"Thank you, doctor," I reply before shaking his hand.

Grayson stands, clearly understanding that it's good news. He walks over to me and pulls me into a hug momentarily.

"I'm going to head out. I'll be back in the morning. Go get your girl."

He doesn't have to tell me twice. I head up to room 402, where Avery is waiting for me.

I open the door to her hospital room quietly in case she's fallen back asleep. Sitting up tall, watching the door, is Avery, my Goldie girl. She really is okay.

"Fuck," I breathe out.

My eyes close shut before I open them to find Avery staring at me.

"Lachlan," she answers in a daze.

I rush over to her side and pull her hands into mine.

"Fuck, Goldie. You had me worried there."

"You saved me," she whispers.

"You're alive," I whisper.

I'm sitting on an uncomfortable chair next to her bedside. I lean up and gently kiss her forehead.

"It's over, Avery. You're going to finally be okay. Kevin is going to jail," I tell her.

She's visibly relieved by my words. She locks eyes with me as we continue to hold each other's hands for comfort.

"Lachlan, you and me. Forever, right?"

"There isn't a lifetime where I'll ever be separated from you, Avery Parker. You are mine in every sense of the word possible. Forever. I love you."

"And I love you."

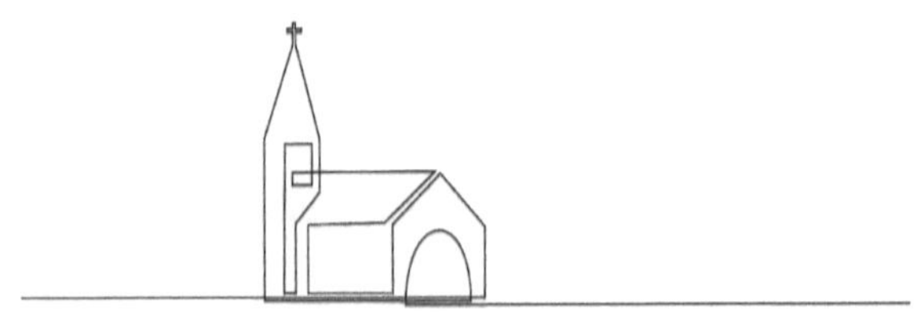

I slept in the uncomfortable chair most of the night and the following one too. I didn't leave her side.

Avery had offered for me to join her, but honestly, I was too nervous after the events that had transpired. I didn't want to have Avery move too much. We're waiting for news from her shift doctor that she can be discharged and taken home.

"Anxious?" she asks me.

"No, Goldie. Just ready to get you home again."

I squeeze her hand to reassure her before double-checking the hospital room once more. Since we both slept here the past two nights, I had Grayson grab a few new sets of clothes for us both. Packing up our bag is a good sign that after all the turmoil, we finally will have peace.

Today is meant to be the first day of my last week, but I called the last remaining priest of the parish, Nick, and told him I wouldn't be coming in. For a quiet older man, he was surprisingly kind without any ulterior motives. He told me he understood and that it was probably best I only return this week to clear out my office and home.

News spread quickly in Charleston about that night.

It's still so fresh in my mind that I know I won't be able to shake it for some time. I'll have to put on a brave front for Avery—she deserves that much from me after everything she's been through.

Surrounding parishes have volunteered for their priests to rotate in and out to help fill the schedule to give Nick time to add on new staff. He's the new leader, and I have a good feeling under him there will be real change at the parish.

"Father Nick was awfully understanding, don't you think?" Avery muses.

"I think the fact that Kevin tried to kidnap and kill you, Missy and Frank were part of a giant scheme to funnel money, Greg was the mastermind behind the whole thing, and oh, it was announced to the world that we're together... yeah he was totally understanding," I tease back.

"Well, when you put it like that..."

One of Avery's wide smiles takes over her face, and I can't help but reciprocate it.

"How do you feel about that last part?"

I'm anxious for her response.

"This weekend, next month, next year, everyone is going to find out we're together eventually. So be it that it's happening now."

My body was tense up until that moment, and I can feel the relief course through me.

"Good, I'm glad. I wasn't sure if you would be upset," I start.

Before I can continue, Avery sits upright in her bed and reaches out for me. I take a few steps forward to connect hands with her.

"How do you feel, Father Lachlan?"

I grin at the name.

"Play nice, Avery." I grin with a wink.

Avery giggles.

"It makes it easier to deal with the bishop, that's for sure," I say.

"What interesting timing, you meet with him tomorrow right?"

"That's the plan, but I can't help but assume this has already made it to him."

I lean down and give Avery a kiss on her lips. Pulling away, I notice she's distracted by someone entering the room. Turning around I find it's her shift doctor.

"Good morning; I have good news. You are all cleared," he begins.

"Oh, that's wonderful, thank you," Avery replies.

"Just a few last bits of paperwork, and you are free to go. Just stop by the reception desk on this level."

"Will do."

The doctor heads out the door, and now it's Avery who's visibly relieved.

"Finally."

"Let's go home," I answer.

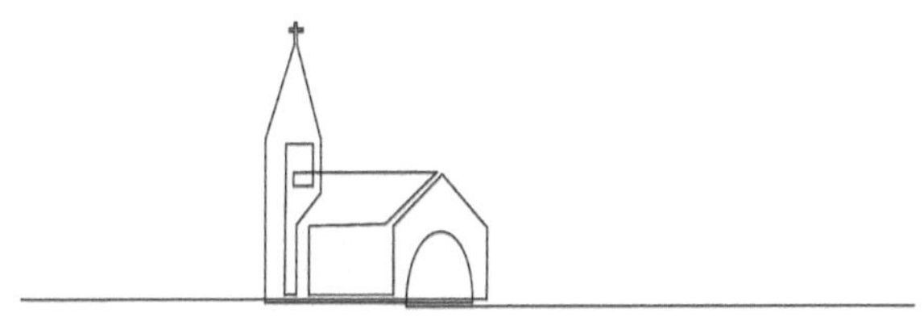

Being home in our space is the comfort we both need. It's the evening, with the stars shining through the uncovered windows. This moment feels like we are in a world of our own.

Avery is wrapped in a buffalo plaid blanket in my arms, light 1940s music is playing softly, and the fireplace is glowing. It's the perfect evening. One of the many I look forward to having with her every day for the rest of our lives.

Earlier, Avery spoke to Noah and found out exactly what had transpired. Her divorce will be finalized by the end of the month. Kevin is in jail, being held without bond, along with Missy, Frank, and Greg. Apparently, Missy is willing to talk in exchange for a lower sentence. I doubt she cares if her husband stays in jail for good.

While full details of their operations, plot, and scheming are still unfolding, what we have pieced together is primarily the truth.

Kevin started a shell corporation to funnel money from the company where he was the legitimate CEO. Greg found out about it through a contact of his and blackmailed him into joining his money scheme with Missy, who then got her husband Frank involved.

That's also why large lumps of real money had been disappearing from Avery and Kevin's joint bank account. He was being forced to spend his money and also funnel money from his shell corporation scheme to Greg's operation as well.

It's a tangled web of lies, deceit, and power games. With so many chess pieces on the board, it was bound to end up like this eventually. It's one game that I am glad Avery and I are no longer playing.

Avery may have to testify at his trial, but that won't be for a while. The police believe there is a lot more to unravel as time goes on. Eventually, the world will find out all of the details. Honestly, I won't think about it again unless one of them gets out and comes for Avery.

As fucking cheesy as this is, she's my heaven here on earth.

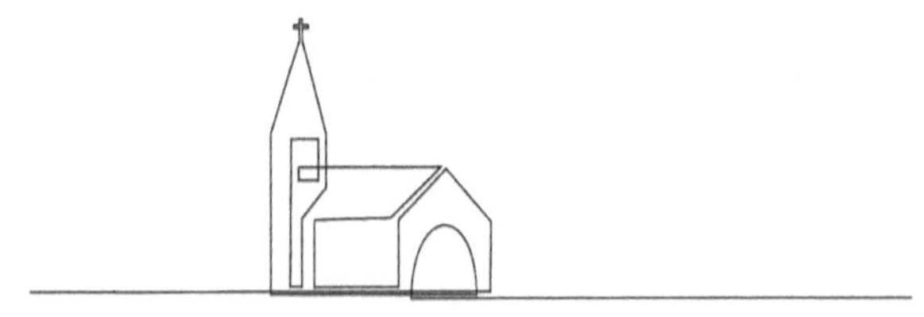

The following day, I met with the bishop. As expected, he did already know all about Avery and me. To make the scandal go away, he agreed that I could leave the Church. It is still a technicality since I took my vows, but I am officially no longer a priest.

After my meeting with him, I decide to head back to my house on the church grounds and finish packing my belongings.

I scheduled movers to come to get my boxes later today and bring them to my new home with Avery.

After this, I'm no longer connected with the church, and we can start our new beginning. Looking around the place I once called home feels like one of the last boxes I have to check off before I can move on. Moving forward is the only path I want.

Throughout the day, I notice that some people recognize me. Especially the few women I saw staring at me as I got out of my car and headed inside my former residence.

Members of the church were rocked by the scandals that unfolded. But honestly, I doubt many were all that surprised about the root of the issue.

Greed.

It's what I first noticed when I came here. Just because this scandal unfolded here doesn't mean something like this won't ever happen again in these affluent communities. Everything is for show; it's no wonder it reached this point. Everyone wants more.

For the time being, Avery and I will remain in Charleston. But I sure as fuck don't see how we can stay here forever. Who knows, I could be wrong. I'll follow Avery anywhere she wants to go as long as I get to be by her side.

I walk through the house one last time and turn off any remaining lights before heading for the front door. With a final glance, this is it.

I squint as the fall sun still bakes against my skin. It's getting cooler, but the sun still shines brightly in Charleston.

I make my way down the path to the parish office to pack up what little personal items I have. This will be a quick process to knock out and say a final goodbye to the few people I like.

I'm surprised Nick is even allowing me inside the parish.

News crews have been stationed outside for the past few days. A new story must be breaking because as I reach the glass doors,

I don't see anyone out here. A lucky break in my day. I know people want to hear Avery's story, but it's not theirs to know.

Stepping inside the parish offices, I notice it's quiet. I used to love these days here. Being one of the only souls inside the building. Patricia isn't at her desk to greet me, so I head straight for my office.

As I expected, gathering up my final items takes no time at all. *This is it*—my last goodbye and tie to being a priest.

Taking my one small box of goods in my hand, I head to leave for the last time. I won't be coming back here.

My faith has been restored, but my relationship with Catholicism needs a new type of foundation. I will forever believe that the Church saved me that fateful day, but it's time to build on something with my faith that isn't based on lies.

"Lachlan," someone calls out to me.

I look up to find Patricia waiting for me outside by her desk.

"You take care of that girl, or you'll have a sea of trouble," she says, pretending to be threatening.

"Wouldn't dream of anything else."

"Take care of yourself too."

"You too, Patricia. Thank you."

CHAPTER 32

AVERY

Blessed are the clean of heart, for they will see God.
Matthew 5:8

Life feels different now. It's been several weeks since the night of the gala. Charleston has mostly recovered after the scandal broke loose. Which one? I suppose I should say scandals.

Kevin is sitting in prison, awaiting his trial. A date has been set for the new year. Noah informed me I would need to testify. He's working out the details.

Part of me wonders how scared I should be for my safety, but Noah told me that, for now, I can live the life I have been fighting for. The life of someone who enjoys laughing and trying every recipe in a cookbook for fun instead of to one-up my peers.

The holiday season is a secret gem of Charleston. The lights downtown are magical. Wandering the streets and looking at all the twinkling lights feels more relaxing now.

Lachlan and I agreed that we both would take this season to just enjoy each other's company. Because of our savings, we are fortunate enough to be able to wait until the New Year to ramp up our new endeavors.

Outside of weekly check-ins from Noah, my past has almost completely disappeared. Since I was never close with anyone at the church, I don't see anyone who really knows about Lachlan and my beginning.

Some peers outside of the church knew, but things died down when the next major piece of gossip landed. I'm sure I will always get some second glances or long stares, but it doesn't bother me.

I did meet with Elaine's sister, Emily, one day after the gala. I needed to know as much as I could to determine who I could face, trust, or even believe.

I was initially so distrusting of everyone around me after what happened. I had known that Missy was a snake in disguise as a socialite, but I never would have dreamt up that she would condone my kidnapping and, most likely, death.

I couldn't shake it, knowing I would still possibly see her best friend and best friend's younger sister around, so I called her. Emily agreed to meet with me at Jackson's one late afternoon. That's when she explained how in the dark she even was about Elaine.

"So you really had no idea why she wanted you at the gala so early?" I recall asking her.

"No idea," she responded.

"What did you do early there?"

"Apparently, the whole thing was a ploy to make it not look so obvious that something bigger was happening behind the scenes. Missy demanded that Elaine's husband, Rob, and I be there early to greet a couple who was being seated with us."

I had encouraged her to continue.

"We arrived, and the couple seated next to us was the one who had supplied Kevin with the file he had to get that night. I have a feeling this couple is another set of victims of their schemes. We were barely there when everything unfolded."

I realized then that I couldn't expect answers from her, but I believed what she told me. Emily was always nice and considerate; by proxy, she was involved in this social circle, but she never liked it.

When we left that day, I asked her if we could see each other again as friends. I'm glad she agreed. Now Emily and I spend some time together, and it's the first real friend I've had in a long time.

I tried playing matchmaker between Emily and Grayson, but they weren't right for each other. Grayson isn't rushing to settle down, and Emily is a bit mysterious about what she's looking for in a partner.

At thirty-four, Grayson is driven by his business. At least he isn't a total heartbreaker like many of the other single men in Charleston are known to be.

Having a broken heart is a terrible experience. I'm grateful for getting to this place in my relationship with Lachlan, regardless of how rocky it was to get here. I trust Lachlan completely to not let my heart even crack.

I worked hard to get to this point with Lachlan and at the end of the day, isn't happiness what all of us want? Security, love, trust, and happiness. With those on hand, I would live a very full life.

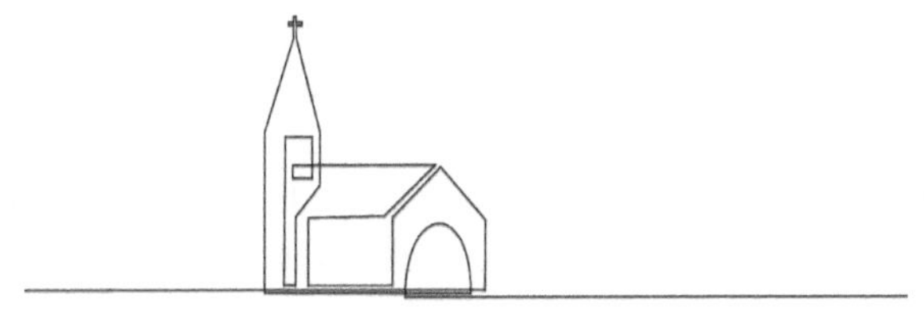

"Avery?" Lachlan walks through our apartment door with bags in his hands.

"A little shopping? Why didn't you tell me?" I pout.

Lachlan grins before coming up to me in the kitchen and placing the bags on the counter, wrapping his arms around me. I continue to stir the simmering pot of chili on the stove. One of the recipes I tested recently that Lachlan and I both love.

"Some presents for my Goldie girl," he whispers into my ear.

A faint smile touches my lips.

Lachlan nips at my ear, and I squeal in surprise. Before walking away, he slaps my butt playfully.

"That smells delicious, is it the chili?" he asks as he uncorks a bottle of wine and takes out two glasses.

"It is! I know you mentioned wanting to set up the perfect night in, so I figured this is more us than take out or a fancy restaurant."

"It is more us. I love it, but I would have cooked for you tonight."

He slides a glass of wine my way. Going into our adjacent living room, he turns on the gas fireplace and starts lighting a few surrounding candles for ambiance.

"You know I love cooking."

I move around the kitchen with an ease that I never had before. Cooking has become a new way to relax for me. I've been dying to do one of the cooking classes at some of the high-end boutique hotels and restaurants they have around here.

I let the chili simmer as I follow Lachlan into the living room and head for our record player.

"Our favorite Christmas classics record?" I ask Lachlan.

"Yeah, baby, let's see how the classic gentlemen are doing tonight?"

"Let's," I answer before putting the record onto the player.

Lachlan comes up beside me and entangles his hand in mine. Walking me over to the couch, he gestures for me to be seated and then takes a seat next to me.

Looking at Lachlan will never get old. The way he looks in this hunter-green sweater makes my skin flush, just thinking of what I want to be doing to him right now.

I see fire dancing in his eyes as they smolder.

"Avery, baby, let's save that for later?"

"Are you sure..." I start to tease my fingers along the outside of his jeans.

He stops my hand in place with a grin.

"Okay, fine." I pout. "I do have this chili on the stove; otherwise, you'd be mine, Lachlan," I laugh as I playfully swat his chest.

He winks in response.

"Every day with you is the best day of my life. You brought me back to life. A life I didn't know I could dream or hope for."

"You saved me too, Lachlan. That's why we're perfect together."

"We are, aren't we?"

Lachlan slowly rises before taking a knee in front of me. A black velvet box appears in his hand. He slowly opens it, revealing a two-carat, emerald-cut diamond.

"Lachlan." I gasp, bringing my hands to my cheeks. I can't contain my smile.

This ring is me. My dream ring. We had talked about getting married one day, but I never thought it would come this soon.

"Avery, I promise to love you every day in this lifetime and any that come after. I will always find you, love you, protect you, and cherish every moment I can get with you."

Tears begin to prick my eyes. I love this man with every fiber of my being.

"Will you make me the happiest man on the planet..."

"Yes!" I'm nodding yes uncontrollably.

Pushing myself closer to him, I wrap my arms around his waist. I place a kiss on his soft lips before resting my head against his shoulder. This is the happiest moment of my life. I can feel his grin spread wider against my cheek.

"Goldie girl, I've got to ask you first." He chuckles.

I pull back and wipe the tears away from my cheeks. Lachlan takes my hand in his and places a gentle kiss on my forehead before pulling back to face me again.

Letting go of my hands, he pulls out the ring from the velvet box and slowly slides it down my ring finger.

"Avery Jayne Parker, will you do me the honor of becoming my wife?"

EPILOGUE

LACHLAN

EPILOGUE
FIVE YEARS LATER

Those who sow in tears will reap with cries of joy.
Psalm 126:5

Boston weather during the holiday season is never favorable to the crisp weather of Charleston. But this year would be our last one coming to visit my ma for the holiday.

I look down at my adoring wife, Avery, who is nestled in tightly by my side, her hand caressing her belly. She's five months pregnant with our first child.

Avery and I decided to wait to try to conceive after we got married, to enjoy our time together as a couple. It was the right decision for us.

Now that we'll have our first child coming into the world, we want every holiday to be spent in our home in Charleston.

Ma isn't too old for it to be of concern. This visit is us trying to convince her that time is moving on. We are hoping she will come to live with us in our FROG, or free-standing room above the garage. It's essentially the Charleston equivalent of a mother-in-law suite.

A one-bedroom apartment that would allow her to have her own space but still be on our property.

After Avery became pregnant, we decided to leave the downtown life behind us. It is possible to still raise a family in Charleston—there are plenty of properties. But Avery didn't want to live close to her former life. We moved two bridges away onto Daniel Island. It worked for our future. I can't wait to bring new life into this world with Avery.

"What are we picking up?" I ask.

We are running behind schedule. We have to get to my hometown before it gets dark. I'm not taking any unnecessary risks with Avery.

Avery and I decided to hold off telling my ma about the baby. We wanted to tell her in person.

"The store is right there," she points across the street to a boutique she found online. The store does custom pieces. Avery had an ornament made and wanted to pick it up in person instead of shipping it to us to ensure it wouldn't be broken.

I guide her across the street to the storefront, where she excitedly enters. She's still the bright light to my darkness. I will always be grateful that she brought me back to life.

Ten years ago, did I imagine I would be wandering these same Boston streets holding my pregnant wife's hand and picking up a custom Christmas ornament for my ma? I would have bet on the other option every time.

"It's perfect isn't it, Lachlan?"

Avery holds up the ornament that reads "Officially a Granny" in sparkling white cursive.

Avery is positive my ma will insist on being called Granny over a different grandmother name. It's common among the Irish.

"Absolutely, Goldie." I smile back at her.

After wrapping up at the store, Avery and I make our drive to Ma's house. It's not long, but I'll be glad when we arrive. We'll be staying here for a few days before returning to Boston. I have a romantic night planned for Avery, and we have plans to see Patrick too.

Pulling up to my childhood home, I reflect on the years I had here. Wonderful years with my parents. I can't wait to be the kind of da I had growing up.

My ma hears our car pull up and is outside waiting in the cold.

"Ma, get back inside; it's freezing out here," I shout from the driveway.

I'll come back for our bags. I round the car and open the door for Avery.

Ma's eyes instantly go to her belly, and even in the distance, I can see the tears start to shine through. It's clearly a pregnancy belly on Avery's frame.

Avery is holding the ornament package in her hands as she reaches my mother.

"Open this, please." Avery smiles as she hands Ma the package.

Deliberately, she opens the package to see if the ornament confirms her thoughts.

"Thank you, Avery, a day I've dreamed of forever," Ma says before engulfing Avery in a hug.

Watching my two favorite women together makes my tears start to well up. This life isn't one I'll ever take for fucking granted.

THE END

Acknowledgments

First, thank you so much for reading Forgive Me For My Sins! I hope you loved Lachlan and Avery as much as I did.

Writing my debut novel was such an exciting roller coaster ride to be on. I couldn't have done it without my support system.

The first person I have to thank is the person who, without her support, Forgive Me For My Sins wouldn't have become a reality. To my sister Allie, who was there for me every step of the way. From being an alpha reader to just supporting this dream of mine and everything in between. Thank you. I appreciate you more than you'll ever know.

To my husband Brian, thank you for supporting me and telling me to just go for it. You believed in my writing during times I certainly did not. You brought reading back into my life, and that set me on this crazy journey. You encouraged me to read, to start a Bookstagram, and then publish my first book. It's been a wild ride, but I'm so glad you're on this journey with me. Love you so much, always.

To my sister Courtney, thank you for being there for me as I go through this experience. You're my number one hype woman always, and I wouldn't have it any other way. Thank you for always encouraging me to keep going.

To my son, who has no idea what I'm writing but has been the most supportive six-year-old out there. "Everyone is going to love your book, and I'll read it when I'm an adult too!" I have a feeling when you're eighteen, you won't want to, but I love your kind spirit.

Thank you to my family and friends for being supportive as I write a spicy romance book... even you, Dad!

Now, to the women who have been there on my book journey. Without you, I would not have been able to complete this process as a new author. A few names I have to mention...

Thank you to Kymmie for being the best friend I could have asked for as I wrote this book. You have been my sounding board for all things Forgive Me For My Sins, and I appreciate you so much. From alpha reading to me asking you questions like "Is this too much cum being painted?" and "What if I made Kevin nice?" daily and so much more.

Thank you to my beta readers, Angie, Brittany, Kim, and Peggy. Your opinions and feedback were so critical to my process. This book wouldn't be what it is if it wasn't for you. Thank you endlessly.

Thank you to Sandra, my brilliant designer, who worked with my endless questions as I went through this process for the first time. I love what you created for me and can't wait to continue to work together.

Thank you to the whole team at Kat's Literary Services for guiding me through the editing process. Kat, SJ, Steph, and Vanessa, thank you for your patience with my numerous emails and questions.

Thank you to Jen (and the team) at Grey's Promotions, I appreciate you going with my questions and guiding me as I navigated this part of the process!

To all of the creators on TikTok, Instagram, and beyond, thank you for everything. I promise I squeal every single time I get tagged in a post bringing these characters to life.

And to you, the readers, a heartfelt thank you for picking my book to read. It's such a wild concept to me, but thank you. Stay tuned because there is so much more to come now!

ANGEL ANDERS

ANGEL ANDERS HAS BEEN A PROFESSIONAL COPYWRITER FOR OVER 10 YEARS. HER LOVE OF ROMANCE BOOKS INSPIRED HER TO WRITE HER DEBUT NOVEL, FORGIVE ME FOR MY SINS. ANGEL LOVES THE RANGE OF CHARACTERS AND COMPLEXITIES OF STORIES THAT CAN NATURALLY UNFOLD WHEN A STORY COMES TO LIFE.

WHEN SHE S NOT WRITING, ANGEL ENJOYS SPENDING HER DAYS ALONG THE SOUTH CAROLINA COAST WITH HER HUSBAND, SON, AND DOG. SHE ENJOYS STRONG COFFEE, WHITE WINE, AND CURLING UP WITH A GOOD BOOK BY THE FIREPLACE.

WWW.ANGELANDERSBOOKS.COM

www.ingramcontent.com/pod-product-compliance
Lightning Source LLC
Chambersburg PA
CBHW031841310726
48972CB00005B/1360